Deciding he could ... **do his best to** ... **Marshall went in search of Evelyn.**

It took only a few minutes to find her.

"We seem to be forever walking out on one another."

Evelyn turned to find the marquis standing surprisingly close. She blamed herself for being engrossed in a bout of self-pity. Had she been thinking clearly, she would have heard his boots on the flat stones of the walkway. She looked at the black onyx pin in his cravat, rather than his face, and replied, "Perhaps it is because we are at cross purposes, my lord."

"A situation I am doing my best to rectify, if only you will stop seeing me as a seducer of innocents. My motives may not be those of a saint, but I do want to be your friend."

She met his gaze then, and for a brief second she could almost believe him. "It may be obdurate of me, my lord, but I cannot allow myself to entertain a friendship that will gain me nothing but the title of mistress."

Marshall had thought his anger under control, but it rose again, like a trout to a well-baited hook. "Then allow this, my lovely Miss Dennsworth."

Before she could think to stop him, Evelyn found herself in his arms. Instead of the gentle, arousing kisses he had given her in the past, his mouth was hard and hungry, punishing her in the most seductive way possible.

She trembled, both in response to his kiss and to the knowledge that she wasn't being nearly as stubborn as she should be.

BOOK YOUR PLACE ON OUR WEBSITE AND MAKE THE READING CONNECTION!

We've created a customized website just for our very special readers, where you can get the inside scoop on everything that's going on with Zebra, Pinnacle and Kensington books.

When you come online, you'll have the exciting opportunity to:

- View covers of upcoming books
- Read sample chapters
- Learn about our future publishing schedule (listed by publication month *and author*)
- Find out when your favorite authors will be visiting a city near you
- Search for and order backlist books from our online catalog
- Check out author bios and background information
- Send e-mail to your favorite authors
- Meet the Kensington staff online
- Join us in weekly chats with authors, readers and other guests
- Get writing guidelines
- AND MUCH MORE!

**Visit our website at
http://www.kensingtonbooks.com**

HE SAID YES

Patricia Waddell

ZEBRA BOOKS
KENSINGTON PUBLISHING CORP.
http://www.kensingtonbooks.com

ZEBRA BOOKS are published by

Kensington Publishing Corp.
850 Third Avenue
New York, NY 10022

All Kensington titles, imprints and distributed lines are available at special quantity discounts for bulk purchases for sales
promotion, premiums, fund-raising, educational or institutional
use.

Special book excerpts or customized printings can also be
created to fit specific needs. For details, write or phone the
office of the Kensington Special Sales Manager: Kensington
Publishing Corp., 850 Third Avenue, New York, NY 10022.
Attn. Special Sales Department. Phone: 1-800-221-2647.

Zebra and the Z logo Reg. U.S. Pat. & TM Off.

First Printing: September 2003
10 9 8 7 6 5 4 3 2 1

Printed in the United States of America

One

Marshall Hanley Bedford, Marquis of Waltham, looked down at his cards and decided the royal flush he'd just been dealt was the best thing that had happened to him in days. He'd come to Brook's on St. James Street as he did each week that Parliament was in session to play cards with a select group of friends. The club had become his sanctuary of late, the only place he could escape the responsibilities and constant chatter that came with having a younger sister taken up by the Season.

Normally his stepmother would be seeing to Winnifred's introduction into society, but Constance had taken to her bed several weeks ago, and Marshall now realized that she intended to stay there. She'd always been a frail woman. The death of her husband had added to the frailty, bringing on an extended period of mourning that Marshall feared was being taken to the extreme.

As a result, he had no choice but to sponsor Winnifred's activities. The endless circle of balls and soirees was an ordeal Marshall had hoped to avoid. Until recently, the mania that overtook English mothers during the Season had never failed to amuse him. However, being forced to actively chaperone Winnie had him seeing things in a different light. The sooner he found his sister a suitable husband, the better.

He looked around the table, thinking the solution might be close at hand. A survey of his friends, all current bachelors, ended quickly. As much as Marshall loved his sister, Winnie wasn't a match for any man in the room.

The Earl of Granby sat to his right. Norton Russell Foxhall was undoubtedly an eligible bachelor, but his reputation as a ladies' man, and Marshall's personal knowledge of just how worthy Granby was of that reputation, immediately removed the earl's name from the suitable-as-a-husband list.

William Fitch Minstead, the Earl of Ackerman, was a far more fitting candidate, but Marshall feared his friend had too much on his mind, having recently inherited a title he had never thought to gain. A second son, Fitch, as the group affectionately called him, had returned from the Crimean War with scars Marshall couldn't see but knew existed. Fitch didn't need the distraction of a wife right now. Duty and the necessity of an heir would force him to the altar soon enough. As it would them all.

Marshall's gaze moved around the table as the Viscount Rathbone stubbed out a smoking cheroot. Benjamin Edward Exeter was the last man Marshall would solicit for a brother-in-law. The youngest of the group, the handsome viscount possessed an alarming and scandalous enthusiasm for departure from the acceptable path. Although Marshall considered him a trusted friend, that trust didn't extend to his sister's happiness.

The last man at the table was the fourth Duke of Morland. Orton Leopold Haversham was the reason Marshall and his friends walked dutifully through the doors of Brook's each Wednesday night. Now in his late sixties, the duke had known and befriended each of their fathers. That friendship had been inherited by the younger men along with their titles. Stodgy on his best days, crotchety on his worst, the duke was a scholarly statesman who wasn't averse to meddling in their lives whenever the fancy struck him. Though they complained of it outside his presence, none of them had the discourtesy to refute the elderly lord.

"I suppose I'll be seeing you at Lord Trehearn's this weekend," the duke said as he reached for a glass of port. "I understand the eldest son has expressed some interest in Winnifred."

Lord Trehearn's heir wasn't on Marshall's suitable list, either. The young man was known to enjoy drinking far too much for the marquis to allow his pursuit of Winnie to progress to the point of a proposal. "The young man can express all the interest he wants," Marshall replied as he waited for the duke to place his bet. "He won't drain the Bedford coffers along with his father's."

Granby laughed. "Poor Winnifred. I fear no one will meet your sterling qualifications for a brother-in-law, old friend. Since the Season is upon us, you've developed the scruples of a monk. Look all you will, Waltham, you'll find few sheep among London's flock of wolves."

"Don't remind me," Marshall groaned as a white-gloved servant refilled his brandy glass. "No wonder my father's hair was silver before its time. Three females in a house is three too many. If it isn't Constance lying abed, complaining of one ailment or another, it's Winnie insisting that she needs a new gown. She can't possibly be seen in the same one twice. And Catherine . . . I swear all the girl knows how to do is giggle."

"What about Apsley?" Fitch's suggestion followed the show of Marshall's royal flush and the raking in of a sizeable pot by the marquis. "He's a decent enough chap. Winnie could do worse than a baronet with profitable estates and—"

"And a mother with apron strings longer than my arm," Marshall inserted.

"I would recommend Lansdowne," the duke said. "Comes from good stock with a sound head on his shoulders. Old enough to know what being a husband requires from a man."

"Lansdowne," Marshall said, rolling the possibility around in his head. The duke's advice usually proved worthy of consideration. Nathaniel Linton, Earl of Lansdowne, was a man of wealth and property with a cordial disposition. "He does seem to be around whenever Winnie needs to be partnered in a quadrille. He might do."

The debate over the town's best and worst bachelors continued as the deal fell to the Earl of Granby. By the time the evening drew to a close, Marshall was weary of discussing the pedigree of Britain's male aristocracy. He climbed into his carriage, ironically thinking that he could use another woman in his life; an amicable mistress came to mind. Unfortunately, there was no discreet address to which he could direct his driver. Although he was a lusty man, the last year and a half had been monopolized by his responsibilities to his family and title.

As the carriage clattered over the cobblestone streets on its way to Mayfair where he kept a comfortable London house, the marquis decided the lack of womanly comfort in his life was an oversight that needed to be addressed. A merry widow perhaps, London had them aplenty.

Selecting a mistress required the same painstaking attention as choosing a wife. Whoever he decided upon would have to be attractive, attentive, and amicable. There were other qualifications, as well. His preferences ran toward slender women with long legs and light-colored eyes. The size of a woman's breasts had never been a major concern for him. He also liked spirit. Of course, he would expect a mistress to conduct herself discreetly. Whatever wantonness she possessed would be reserved for his personal enjoyment alone.

When it came to bedding a woman, Marshall stripped off his social status along with his clothes. He enjoyed sex too much to let his title impede his actions. One of his past lovers had complimented him on his open-mindedness after confessing that her previous protector, a duke, had insisted on always being on top. Marshall wasn't snobbish about positions. If a woman wanted to ride him, he was more than willing to lie on his back and enjoy the experience.

A kindred spirit would be nice, too. Someone who could satisfy his needs in and out of bed. A woman he could talk to before and after making love. The image came close to that of a wife, but Marshall shied away from admitting that he might be ready to marry. Once Winnifred was respectfully wed, and his stepmother showed signs of resuming her life or had a grandchild to dote over, he might consider marriage. But not now. He was only thirty-two. There was plenty of time to find a wife and beget the heir his title required. Duty and obligation could wait for a few years. In the interim, he would concentrate on the finer things in life.

"There you are," Winnifred said, her tone a bit impatient. "Have you forgotten that I have an appointment with Madame La Roschelle?"

"Of course not," Marshall replied, leaning down so she could kiss his cheek. Winnifred was a brown-haired, younger version of her mother. "Druggs marked my schedule accordingly. The carriage is being readied as we speak."

Like other young women her age, his sister understood that she had been brought to London for the express purpose of finding a husband. It was an acceptable objective, one that came as naturally as breathing for the young ladies who were among the privileged of society. Knowing that goal, and having an eye for fashion, Winnie was anxious to have the most dazzling gown possible. The Trehearns' ball was at the end of the week, and Madame La Roschelle had promised a dress that would turn any young man's head. The style was

French, the money English, coughed up by her dutiful older brother.

"What will you be about while I'm being fitted?" Winnie asked.

"I have business that will hold my attention until Madame La Roschelle has finished with you," Marshall answered, thinking that an afternoon at Brook's might prove helpful in ferreting out a few eligible ladies. Rathbone always knew the latest gossip, having created most of it himself. His young friend would probably be able to produce a list of satisfactory names in less time than it took for Marshall to settle into an easy chair and light a cigar.

The carriage ride from the town house to Madame La Roschelle's shop didn't take long. Bond Street ran through the heart of Mayfair, from Oxford Street in the north to Piccadilly in the south. Aside from fashionable couturiers, such as the one they would be visiting, the district also provided jewelry, millinery, and specialty shops.

Marshall gazed out the window, seeing nothing that he hadn't seen a hundred times before, but finding himself elated at the prospect the new day had brought with it. Suddenly he had an overwhelming urge to find a woman, strip her naked, and spend the next three days in an orgy of exhausting sex, French wine, and sated sleep.

Reaching their destination, Marshall pushed his personal thoughts aside and handed Winnifred down from the carriage. They entered the shop where tables were artfully arranged, displaying an assortment of ribbons, fans, and other female accessories. Madame La Roschelle, a petite woman with flaming red hair, wearing a perfectly sewn blue silk dress, came rushing toward her newest customer. Marshall responded to the couturiere's greeting, but his gaze found something far more interesting.

She was undoubtedly one of Madame's assistants, tall

and slender with light brown hair fashioned into a severe knot at the nape of her neck. A seamstress's apron was tied around her waist, its pocket bulging with pins and fabric chalk. The apron covered a modest black skirt worn with a starched white blouse. There was no definable beauty to her features, but she caught his eye, nevertheless. Perhaps because she moved calmly amidst a chattering flock of females. Quiet where they were loud. Shy where they were bold. A head taller than any other woman in the shop, she moved with an easy grace. Her complexion glowed with health, giving Marshall the impression that she could be a country lass recent to the city. She looked in his direction for a fleeting second, and he saw that her eyes were blue.

A patron, whom the marquis recognized as Lady Monfrey, chose that moment to come charging out of one of the fitting rooms. The woman was a tedious gossip, but her husband's fortune and sizeable earldom placed her at the top of the social pedestal. She spoke briefly to Winnifred, then, apparently realizing that she was late for one appointment or other, turned so quickly she all but trampled the shop girl into the floor.

The bolt of fabric the young woman had been carrying went in one direction, the pins in her hand another. She managed not to fall, but only because she was as graceful as a ballerina. Lady Monfrey staggered precariously for a moment before Madame La Roschelle, always aware of everything that went on in her shop, rushed forward to catch the older woman by the arm and steady her. A stream of harshly spoken French followed, admonishing her employee for being so clumsy.

Before Madame could finish the scolding, Marshall was bending down to gather up tiny silver pins. Madame turned her attention to Lady Monfrey, apologizing profusely.

"Please, my lord," the young woman whispered to him. "I

know you mean well, but you'll only make matters worse. Madame will dismiss me for inconveniencing you as well as Lady Monfrey."

Her voice was soft. Her enunciation clear and precise. If she was a country lass, she'd received some formal education. He watched as she frantically reached out to collect the scattered sewing pins. Her fingers were long and elegant, her nails manicured and clean. So close their shoulders were almost touching, he inhaled the fresh scent of her. Unlike the heavy French perfume that followed Madame La Roschelle about the room, the girl smelled of soap and . . . He inhaled again. Spice. Something herbal and wild, as if she'd gathered up the morning sunshine and rubbed it over her body.

"Let me worry about Madame La Roschelle," he replied, picking up a piece of tailoring chalk and handing it to her. "The mishap wasn't your fault."

When the last of the pins had been collected and returned to the young woman's apron pocket, Marshall stood up. He was well over six feet tall. The girl came to his shoulder. His stepmother would call her unfashionably tall, but she seemed a perfect height to him.

"Thank you, my lord," she whispered, then turned and hurried toward the rear of the shop.

Marshall watched her go, his gaze focused on the graceful sway of her hips beneath the coarse black skirt. Her legs would be long. Very long. He took a deep breath and fantasized about them being wrapped around him. Her body would fit his perfectly. Unfortunately, she wasn't a widow. One look into those blue eyes had confirmed her innocence. Yet, he'd seen a fire burning in their depths, a thirst for life that only a man could recognize.

As the bell over the door tinkled, confirming Lady Monfrey's departure, Marshall found himself wondering what it would take to convince a Bond Street shop girl to expand her horizons. The life he could offer her, a comfortable home with someone to cook and clean, a fashionable wardrobe, an allowance for her personal use, would certainly be better than the life she had now. Neither London nor the girl's proficiency with needle and thread offered her any real security. The city gobbled up young women. She could spend her life working for Madame La Roschelle, never having more than the clothes on her back and a few shillings to her name. Worse, she could end up married to a man who drank up his wages, then staggered home to beat her because his supper had grown cold.

Marshall imagined the grim future she might face if she didn't become his mistress, knowing all the while that he was simply justifying his desire by telling himself that he'd be saving her rather than ruining her. Until that moment, he hadn't thought to take anyone but an experienced woman into his bed, but having looked into those blue eyes, having heard the soft whisper of her voice, he knew he had inadvertently found the woman he wanted.

Desire, after all, was the motive for taking a mistress.

"My apologies," Madame said, joining Marshall and his sister. "Evelyn is not usually so awkward."

"She wasn't awkward now," Marshall said, coming to the girl's defense. It was the gentlemanly thing to do. "A mishap, nothing more," he added. "Think nothing of it."

Winnifred was busy selecting a length of ribbon to go with her new gown. She'd seemingly dismissed the accident the moment after Lady Monfrey had left the shop. Marshall glanced at his sister, then back to Madame La Roschelle. "I will return in two hours. Is that adequate time?"

Agreeing that it was, the petite Frenchwoman snapped her fingers, bringing another girl out from behind the curtains that draped the doorway leading to the fitting rooms. "Assist Lady Winnifred. We will need to finish the hem this afternoon."

The girl nodded and pushed back the curtain, holding it

in place as if Winnifred was about to make a grand entry onto an imaginary stage.

"I'll return with the carriage in two hours," Marshall told his sister. He kissed her on the cheek, then glanced toward the rear of the shop where Evelyn had disappeared. He would like to know more about the girl, but this wasn't the time for inquiries.

Leaving Winnifred in the couturiere's capable hands, Marshall instructed his driver to take him to his club. Feeling confident that he'd unexpectedly found the woman he wanted, he now had to contemplate the best way to approach her. Her position as a shop girl prohibited a chance meeting at a party or ball. Their paths would not cross again unless Winnie required a second fitting. He supposed he could arrange to be in the neighborhood when the shop closed, but the idea of following her home didn't sit well with him. Gentlemen didn't stalk young ladies, at least not openly. Marshall decided something would come to mind. In the meanwhile, he'd entrust Druggs, his secretary, with the task of finding an appropriate residence.

Unaware of the impact she'd had on the marquis, Evelyn stood in the empty fitting room preparing herself for another dose of Madame's temper. The excitable Frenchwoman valued her customers above anyone else. Evelyn prayed she wouldn't be dismissed from her job, but beneath that worry another emotion had her feeling slightly off course.

Lord Waltham had smiled at her.

It had been more than a faint smile, one bestowed by a gentleman who had been taught from his youngest years to treat females with courtesy and respect. There had been something special in the smile. Something that had shook Evelyn to her very core.

She began to sort through the pins and chalk in her apron

pockets, needing a task for her trembling hands. She knew she wasn't trembling out of fear of losing her job. The marquis was the cause of her anxiety. Though he hadn't touched her in the slightest way, she had felt the warmth of his breath, smelled the clean, crisp scent of his expensive cologne, and sensed the heat of his body. His gaze had been dark and mysterious, an unspoken promise of things to come.

She was being foolish.

The Marquis of Waltham was a man beyond her common reach, a titled gentleman who had done nothing but help her pick up a few pins, and yet the sound of his voice when he'd told her not to worry about Madame, as if a mere word from him would settle the issue, had been disquieting. It had also been a pleasing voice, strong and confident. But then, why wouldn't it be. He was a man of property and power, a man accustomed to having others bend to do his bidding.

Evelyn knew about such men. She saw them every day, escorting their wives, daughters, mothers, and even their mistresses into the shop. The marquis wasn't the first gentleman to smile at her, but he had been the first to make her react to the expression. Devastatingly handsome with dark brown hair and even darker eyes, his appearance alone was enough to turn a lady's head. But Evelyn was no lady, at least not a titled one.

Gentlemen like the Marquis of Waltham didn't waste their smiles upon common-born young women unless they wanted something, and Evelyn knew what that something was. She didn't come from a sophisticated background, but she was twenty and six. She had witnessed the effect handsome young men of the aristocracy could have on women. One of the girls in her village had been forced to leave, disgraced by a pregnancy that had produced nothing but a bastard child and shame.

Evelyn had come to realize that the peerage with all its

manner and wealth was a show, a disguise used to separate them from the common people. The women who came into the shop were far more conceited than the men. They rarely bothered with a simple courtesy once they were in the fitting room, beyond the sight and sound of their own kind. Even Madame's best customers didn't speak to her by name, although she'd worked for the couturiere for almost two years and they knew her well. She knelt on the floor at their feet, pinning hems and lace while they prattled on about the ball they would be attending and how the dress had to be just right. Never once had she had one of them thank her for her painstaking handiwork. The compliments were rained upon Madame La Roschelle instead.

Evelyn accepted the way of things, although it left a bitter taste in her mouth. She had no choice but to support herself the only way she knew how, and she enjoyed creating beautiful clothes. Although Madame would never admit it, the dress Lady Winnifred Bedford was being fitted for today was more of Evelyn's design than the Frenchwoman's. Evelyn had an uncanny gift for detail and color, an innate knowledge of what would complement a woman's appearance, and Madame didn't hesitate to use that ability to the shop's advantage.

Evelyn had inherited a small sum of money after her father's death. Nothing extravagant, but enough, if she minded her expenses and saved every possible coin. One day Evelyn hoped to open her own shop. Not in London. The rent would be far too expensive, and she had no real desire to remain in the city. No, she'd open a modest shop in one of the more prospering villages.

But before she could see her dream come true, Evelyn knew she needed the experience only a shop like Madame La Roschelle's could offer. That was why she bit her tongue numb instead of snapping back at the flamboyant proprietor, why she studied design and fabrics, why she watched and observed and learned the ways of business. When the day came, when she had enough money to set out on her own, she'd gladly give Madame notice and wave goodbye to London with its smelly sewers and smoky air.

"Evelyn!"

She returned to the main room expecting a lecture from her employer. Instead, she was told to assist in the fitting of Lady Winnifred's gown.

"Lenore needs help pinning the hem," Madame instructed her, waving an elegantly jeweled hand toward the largest fitting room. "See that it's done properly."

Nodding wordlessly, Evelyn hurried to join her coworker and the marquis's sister. As she pulled back the curtain, she couldn't help but hope that the young lady would say a word or two about her brother. Surely no damage would be done if she learned the gentleman's given name.

TWO

Marshall was frowning as he walked into Brook's. The brief carriage ride from Bond Street to St. James had him brooding over the best way to approach Evelyn . . . He had to learn her full name. Who was she, did she have family in the city, but more importantly did she have any suitors? The best way, he concluded, as he handed his hat and gloves over to one of the club's footmen, was to assign Druggs or a Bow Street runner to look into the matter. A few discreet inquiries, and he'd know all he needed to know. Then, if things proved satisfactory, he'd find a way to speak with her. Madame La Roschelle's shop would offer them no privacy. A walk in one of the lesser parks or a modest meal in a local eatery would better present the opportunity he needed.

He'd never had this particular problem before, and he'd had lots of women. More than enough to make him an expert on getting one into bed. But then, he'd never set his sights on a common woman before. Not that there was anything common about Evelyn. The graceful way she carried herself, the gentleness of her blue eyes, the sound of her voice, made her vastly different from the tavern girls he'd enjoyed in his randy youth.

Cambridge had never seen a more lusty band of young lads than the illustrious men he now played cards with each Wednesday night. He and the Earl of Granby had spent a vast amount of time carousing the countryside, drinking and wenching, gambling, and having a wonderful time being young and irresponsible.

Unfortunately, his days of running wild were over now. They had been since his father had taken ill, and he'd been called home. When his father had died, the title had fallen upon Marshall's shoulders, a task he had been well trained to accept, but one that nevertheless restricted some of his former enthusiasm for life. He was obliged to be in London when Parliament was sitting, but he preferred the country. The ocean-swept shores of Ipswich called to him, and he longed for the quiet times when he rode along the coastline unhindered by anything but a brisk wind. He didn't consider himself an ambitious man, but rather one who had an ability to see life as it was rather than the way it should be. A gentleman of means, he had always opened his eyes to the future and its possibilities more readily than his peers. That foresight made him successful in business and politics alike.

Marshall sat down in a comfortable chair next to a mahogany reading table. Every newspaper the city had to offer was stacked neatly on its glossy top. Accepting a glass of sherry from one of the club's footmen, he settled back and stared out the window, too preoccupied by his personal thoughts to care about the London news.

"Weaving cobwebs?" the Earl of Granby asked when he joined him a short time later.

Marshall looked up. As always, his best friend was immaculately garbed in a coat of fine wool with a perfectly tied cravat at his throat. His steely blue eyes were gleaming, as if he had somehow guessed what had Marshall brooding.

"Who is she?"

"What makes you think that I'm thinking about a woman?"

Granby laughed as he made himself comfortable in a matching chair at the opposite end of the table. "Females are the only thing that can bring that sort of look to a man's face."

"What look?" Marshall muttered with chilly disdain.

"A frustrated one," the earl chuckled. "What you need is a little excitement, my friend. And I'm not referring to the kind dished out at a society ball. You're letting your title get in the way of things." Granby paused as he stretched out his legs. "It so happens, I've the perfect solution to your problem. Last night I met a charming female. Since I was already sporting her friend on my arm, I had no choice but to promise her the pleasure of my company another time. However, I'm more than willing to make the introduction."

Marshall shook his head. "I can find my own amusement."

"Then, find it," Granby demanded as only a close friend could. "You've been brooding about since Parliament called its first session. All duty and no play will make an old man of you before your time."

Marshall knew Granby's idea of play all too well. Their friendship was founded on their childhood years and common background, but it had been forever sealed during their days at Cambridge. The earl had a way with women that made him the foremost authority on sex to be found in all of England. He also had an abundance of common sense. The combination made him an ally.

"I've found a woman," Marshall confessed, "or should I say, I think I've found a woman."

"Either you have or you haven't," the earl said, then frowned. "She isn't married, is she? God forbid that you follow Rathbone down the path to lunacy. Married women are more trouble than virgins."

Marshall met the earl's gaze with a bland smile. "No. At least, I don't think she's married. I didn't see a wedding ring. But then, her husband might not have the coin to buy one."

The earl gave him a quizzical look. "Not enough coin? Don't tell me the girl is someone's serving maid. That wouldn't be well done of you, Waltham. Consorting with servants is the act of a desperate man."

"A shop girl at Madame La Roschelle's," Marshall told him because he could trust his friend to keep the information confidential.

"A shop girl."

"I find her appealing," Marshall defended his selection. "Besides taking a widow from the aristocracy for a mistress has its own set of complications."

"A mistress," Granby mused with interest. "I didn't know you were looking for a permanent means of amusement."

Both men knew a mistress wasn't permanent, but putting a woman up in a house so she could be at one's sexual beck and call was vastly different than seeking occasional pleasure in a widow's bed. The man was required to maintain the comforts of a mistress as much as she was expected to see that the bed they shared never became boring.

Marshall didn't see himself becoming bored with Evelyn. The few moments he'd spent in her company had his blood tingling. He'd left the shop half aroused and aching for the moment when he could do more than look at her.

"You're brooding again," Granby pointed out as he reached for the latest issue of the *Observer* and scanned the headlines. "If you want the girl, and she isn't married, I don't see the difficulty. From what I know of Bond Street wages, she'd be better off with you for a benefactor."

"And how do you propose I go about becoming her benefactor? Should I ask Madame La Roschelle for a formal introduction, or perhaps Winnie would do the honors?" Marshall asked, clearly annoyed by obstacles he hadn't encountered before.

Granby looked up from his paper, his eyes sparkling with amusement. "I'm beginning to see the problem."

"Exactly," Marshall mumbled under his breath. Withdrawing his timepiece from his vest pocket, he checked the hour.

"Maybe I should have a look at the lady in question," Granby suggested, folding his paper and returning it to the table. "Having no female relatives to clothe in fashionable silks, Madame La Roschelle's shop is one I've had little reason to frequent."

"I don't need your approval," Marshall scoffed. "I need to find a way to introduce myself to the young woman. I need to—"

"Present an irresistible petition," Granby supplied. "One the lady can't refuse."

Marshall didn't respond, because he had no certainty that Evelyn wouldn't refuse him, especially if she was engaged or already had a husband. God forbid that she might actually be married to a man who couldn't afford to put a ring on her finger. No matter how tempting she was, Granby was right. Married women were more trouble than virgins.

Strange, but the prospect of Evelyn being a virgin didn't disturb Marshall half as much as it should. The thought of teaching her how to please a man kept his mind occupied for several minutes. Passion was a delicate emotion, but once aroused it could turn the most restrained woman into a willing wanton.

"Now you're smiling," Granby announced. "I confess I'm growing more curious by the moment. You aren't by chance returning to Bond Street any time soon, are you?"

"In less than an hour," Marshall said. "Winnie's being fitted for a new gown."

"A note, perhaps," Granby suggested. "An invitation for

the young woman to meet you someplace discreet. If she's interested, and I've never known you to have trouble holding a woman's interest, she'll keep the appointment."

Marshall considered the suggestion. He declined it for the time being, preferring to know more about Evelyn before he confronted her again. Deciding he'd put Druggs on the scent as soon as he returned home, he turned the conversation to politics and the upcoming race at Epsom Downs.

Shortly thereafter, Marshall bid his friend an enjoyable afternoon and left the club. His carriage pulled up short of the intended shop on Bond Street, forced to the curb by the presence of a jail wagon.

The wagon was actually a metal cage riveted to a wooden base. One constable was sitting on the high seat, holding the reins, while the other was busy dragging a young woman toward the gapping door of the cage.

Marshall jumped down from his carriage, then hurried along the street. It wouldn't do to have his future mistress hauled off to jail before he'd learned her last name.

"What's going on here?" he demanded as the constable encouraged Evelyn toward the wagon with a firm warning that she'd be better off to stop causing trouble.

"I didn't steal anything," she insisted, doing her best to jerk away from the burly man. Her actions only caused him to tighten his grip.

Marshall stepped between the constable and the wagon. "I said, what is going on?"

"Excuse me, yer lordship," the constable said, not recognizing Marshall personally but recognizing the cut of a gentleman's clothes. "I've a job to do."

"And what job would that be, my good man? Manhandling a lady?"

Marshall didn't look at Evelyn. The thought of her being shoved unceremoniously into a wagon that reeked of human vomit was enough to make his temper boil. Whatever had happened, no woman deserved that kind of treatment. He'd never had the misfortune of seeing the inside of a jail, but he'd heard enough about them to know what was in store for Evelyn once the constable got her there. She'd be searched, forced to shed her clothing while the guards watched. What could, and most probably would, happen next wasn't something Marshall allowed himself to think about. The legal system gave little justice to those who couldn't afford the bribery that flourished within it.

He glanced toward the shop. Winnifred was inside, staring out the window, enthralled by the scandalous scene taking place. Madame La Roschelle was standing in the doorway, watching as her employee struggled to free herself.

"I didn't steal anything," Evelyn pleaded, her voice shaking with fear and outrage.

"What exactly is the young woman accused of?" Marshall asked with a stern authority that captured the constable's immediate attention.

"Thievery. Lady Monfrey presented the charges. Miss Dennsworth is accused of stealing a family heirloom. A diamond and ruby brooch. She can plead her case to the magistrate in the morning."

Well, at least he knew her name. *Evelyn Dennsworth.* Marshall stiffened his shoulders as his gaze moved from the constable's ruddy face to the young woman he felt an overwhelming need to protect. Her face was streaked with tears, her expression that of a frightened, cornered animal. She looked alone and vulnerable. Marshall wanted to pull her into his arms, to promise her that nothing would do her harm.

"You will wait a moment," he said, his tone offering the constable no room for argument. His dark gaze moved from the law officer's face to the thick fingers wrapped around Evelyn's slender wrist. "If the lady promises not to bolt, will you unhand her?"

Evelyn couldn't believe the marquis was coming to her rescue a second time. Frantically praying that he was successful, she promised the constable she wouldn't try to run away. What good would it do her? She had no place to run, and the man would surely catch up with her if she tried.

She clutched her bruised wrist to her chest the moment it was freed, then looked at the marquis. He gave her a quick, reassuring smile before moving toward the shop where he began to exchange words with Madame. Evelyn's heart was pounding so hard her chest hurt. Her eyes stung from crying. She closed them, too ashamed to look around and meet the gawking eyes of the people who were quickly forming an inquisitive crowd around the shop. She'd never be allowed to work on Bond Street again, no matter the outcome of this vile misunderstanding. And it was a misunderstanding. She had admired Lady Monfrey's brooch, more for courtesy's sake than because the gaudy piece of jewelry appealed to her.

Hoping against hope that the marquis might be able to find some solution, Evelyn kept her eyes on him instead of the jail wagon.

"Would you care to explain this?" Marshall asked, after telling Winnifred to stay inside.

Madame La Roschelle waved a fan frantically in front of her face, appearing to need the air before she fainted dead away. "Lady Monfrey's brooch. She was wearing it when she came for her fitting. Upon returning home, her ladyship found it missing. She insists, or so the constable informs me, that Evelyn had been admiring it. So much so, that she's accused her of stealing it."

"Have you searched the shop?"

"But, of course," Madame assured him. "Top to bottom. We found nothing. What will my customers think? I'll be ruined if word gets out that my help is unreliable."

Marshall didn't pause to ask if Madame La Roschelle assumed the worst of Evelyn. It was easy to see that she was more concerned about her shop's fashionable reputation than a young woman's innocence or guilt. The street was full of shoppers, most of them staring curiously at the shop girl who was about to be carted off to jail. The marquis wasn't a stranger to the people who frequented the elite Bond Street, but he didn't see anyone he recognized.

"Marshall," Winnie's voice came from inside. "I want to go home now, if you please."

"A few moments longer," Marshall said, using a reassuring tone. "I want a word with the constable first."

"Whatever for?" his sister insisted as she moved to stand behind Madame La Roschelle.

"Common courtesy and compassion," Marshall replied. "You may wait in the carriage if it makes you feel more at ease. Please excuse us, Madame."

The Frenchwoman stepped aside, upset by the possibility of losing both Lady Monfrey and Lady Winnifred as customers.

Glancing over his shoulder to make sure the constable hadn't herded Evelyn inside the jail wagon behind his back, Marshall escorted his sister to their waiting carriage. He settled her inside, insisting that she keep the door closed and the curtains drawn. "I'll only be a moment," he told her. "Then right home, I promise."

He marched back to where the constable was growing impatient and Evelyn was growing pale. She didn't say a word, just stared at him with dazed eyes that told him all he needed to know. She hadn't stolen anything. There was no guilt in her gaze, only the shocked horror of a young woman being accused of a crime she hadn't committed. Marshall sensed her fear and knew he was temporarily incapable of abolishing it. His rank offered some influence, but not enough to instantaneously overturn a magistrate's warrant.

He stared into Evelyn's eyes for a long moment, willing

her to see what he couldn't say out loud, that he would help
her. Her hair was in disarray, making her look younger. Sometime during the last two hours she'd removed her apron,
probably so the constable or Madame La Roschelle could
search the pockets. Her black skirt was streaked with dirt as
if she'd been crawling around on the floor, looking for the
brooch, hoping to prove that the charge against her was in-
valid.

"Are you all right?" he asked, taking a step toward her. It
was a ridiculous question, but he needed to express his concern in some way.

"No," she whispered, her voice so faint he had to strain to
hear it. "I . . . I'm innocent."

"Trust me," he said, keeping his back to the constable and
his voice pitched low so only she could hear it. "Do as they
ask until I can come to you."

She blinked, then stared at him unbelievingly.

"I promise you that I will see the matter dealt with, but I
can't do anything at this very moment. Do you understand?
You will have to tolerate the next few hours the best you
can." He hated having to say it. Damn the circumstances. If
he didn't have Winnifred waiting in the carriage, he might be
able to convince the constable to let him escort Evelyn to the
detention house. "It won't be more than a few hours. Can
you bear it that long?"

Evelyn nodded, too numb to do anything else. All she
could think about was being hauled away like some rogue
animal.

"What magistrate will hear her plea?" Marshall turned to
question the constable.

"Rivenhall. 'E sits his bench promptly every morning,"
the officer informed him. "As fair as any, I wager."

The magistrate's fairness didn't reassure Marshall. Lord
Monfrey was a powerful man. If his wife persisted in accusing Evelyn of theft, the nobleman could put that power to

use, and Evelyn's fate would be sealed. He had to reach the magistrate first.

"I 'ave to take her in, milord," the constable said. "Unless you can prove she didn't pilfer the brooch."

Sadly, Marshall shook his head. The only thing he could prove was his growing concern about Evelyn's safety until he could find Rivenhall and convince the man to release her into his custody. He didn't stop to consider the consequences of what he was about to do; if money could free her, then he'd gladly grease the magistrate's palm with silver.

He looked at the wagon. The wooden floor had been washed by dumping buckets of water onto it, but without the use of a scrub brush and broom, the washing had done nothing more than turn what had been dried sewage into a pasty mass of God knew what. The stench was unbearable. How could he ask any woman to willingly climb inside it?

Damnation! How in the hell had the day turned into such a bloody mess?

Helpless to do anything but watch as the constable reached for Evelyn, Marshall clenched his fists against the impulse to knock the man aside and swish her away to safety.

She began to cry, dragging her feet and struggling to get away from the law officer, the foul-smelling wagon, and its obvious destination.

It was too much for Marshall to take. He reached out, clasping his hand over the constable's upper arm. "I'll get her to go peacefully."

Marshall reached inside his jacket. His back was to the crowd, so only the constable and Evelyn could see what he was doing.

The stout officer released his prisoner and reached for the money the finely dressed gent was offering him.

"This is to make sure the *lady* is treated with courtesy and respect," Marshall said firmly. "Do I make myself clear?"

"Aye, milord. She'll come to no harm during my watch."

"She'll come to no harm at all," Marshall said with a threatening voice. "I am the Marquis of Waltham, and I assure you that I will see any recompense for Miss Dennsworth's suffering delivered directly upon your balding head. Now, where precisely are you taking her?"

"Clerkenwell Close," the constable said, keeping his voice low and respectful.

Marshall knew where the prison was located. The conditions were appalling, the prisoners often kept in solitary confinement for the pettiest of crimes. He swallowed the bile that rose in his throat at the thought of his sweet Evelyn being exposed to the hellish conditions for even a few short hours.

When she had become *his* Evelyn, Marshall wasn't precisely certain. What he was certain of was his resolve to see her cleared of the charge of theft and set free. He looked at her, his hands aching to comfort her, his body tight with anger that he could do nothing more than he'd already done.

Her eyes had turned into blue pools, glistening with tears. Like most men, he found it hard to deal with womanly emotions, but this time he understood them all too well. She was afraid of the same thing he was, that once she entered the jail wagon, it would be years before she gained her freedom.

"Evelyn."

The sound of her name being spoken so tenderly by the marquis was Evelyn's undoing. Shivers of fear raked her body, making it tremble uncontrollably. She slumped, her legs unable to support her any longer. The maddening events of the last hour began to swirl around in her head as the shop windows fronting Bond Street blurred into a black haze.

Marshall caught her around the waist before she fell to the street. She lay limp against his side. He loathed the thought of having to release her. The warm rush of her breath as he swept her into his arms steeled his resolve to see her placed under his custody as quickly as possible. He used

the brief moment to study her features more closely. Her
lashes were thick and dark, several shades darker than her
hair. Her skin was clear and understandably pale, her breathing slow and easy now that her mind had blocked out the
fear of the future. Her mouth was parted, her lips a tempting
shade of pink.

He longed to kiss her, to taste but a sampling of her sweet
mouth, but he didn't dare. People were watching, and he had
no excuse for the chivalry he had already displayed. Society
demanded he be a gentleman, but it was a rarity for a man of
his rank to become entangled in a commoner's fate.

"I'll take her," the constable said. "She'll be no trouble
now."

Hating it, but having no recourse, Marshall allowed the
burly officer to take charge. He cringed with unexplainable
guilt as the man carried Evelyn toward the wagon, then
placed her inside on the grimy floor. The cage door closed
with a menacing creak of rusty hinges.

Adding to his guilt, Evelyn began to stir, her senses
brought to life by the unbearable stench that surrounded her.
She raised her head, crying out as the constable turned the
key in the lock. Climbing to her knees, she stared out from
behind the bars, her blue eyes pleading with Marshall, with
the world, to set her free.

Unaware of his clenched fists, Marshall watched as the
wagon rolled away from the curb. Never in his life had he
felt so helpless. So angry. He was seething inside, an emotion he had to swallow hard to control as he turned and
walked toward his waiting carriage.

"Home, and be quick about it," Marshall told the driver.
He no more than closed the door when the carriage lurched
forward.

"Are you all right?" his sister asked as he sat stiffly across
from her.

"I'm fine," he lied, unable to explain why a woman he had

simply wanted to bed a few hours earlier had turned into someone much more important. "Do you think she stole the brooch?"

"I have no way of knowing. Madame La Roschelle argued with the constable in Miss Dennsworth's favor, but the man was insistent that he had no choice but to take her into custody."

Blessedly they arrived at the town house without any delays. Marshall handed his sister down from the carriage, then instructed the driver to return to the carriage house but to keep the horses harnessed and ready. He walked into the foyer, handing off his hat to the butler. "Find Druggs," he instructed the servant. "Immediately."

Saying nothing more, Marshall entered his library and shut the door. After pouring himself a stiff drink, he tried to erase the image of Evelyn's fear-stricken face from his memory. It was impossible. No matter how much two sisters and a grieving stepmother complicated his life, he couldn't turn his back on the young woman whom he had just promised to help. Nor, did he wish to. He was a man who kept his word, but more than that, his decision to take Evelyn Dennsworth as his mistress had somehow entrusted her into his care.

It didn't make any sense, but then, nothing about the situation was sane or reasonable.

The clock in the foyer chimed four in the afternoon as Marshall walked to his desk. He sat down and unlocked the drawer where he kept the household strongbox. Once he'd returned the key to his vest pocket, he lifted the lid and counted out enough money to bribe someone at the legal ministry if the information he needed wasn't readily supplied to the footman he meant to dispatch. He needed to find Rivenhall. There was no way in hell he was going to leave Evelyn in Clerkenwell overnight.

He was lighting a cigar when Druggs knocked on the door.

"Come in," Marshall called out.

Druggs was an unimpressive man in his late forties with thinning hair, spectacles, and a keen mind. He had worked for Marshall's father, and the new marquis had found no reason to replace him.

It took less than five minutes for Marshall to tell Druggs exactly what he needed done.

"I'll make the necessary inquiries, my lord. Discreetly, of course."

"Of course," Marshall echoed. "Just make them quickly. I want Miss Dennsworth freed as soon as possible."

Druggs nodded, then exited the library.

Marshall stared at the cigar smoke swirling lazily toward the ceiling, a vaulted plasterwork affair with painted roundels. He looked toward the closed library doors, thankful they would keep his family at bay for a while. He was also thankful that Winnifred had accepted no invitation for the evening. That meant he had nothing ahead of him but several long, nerve-wrenching hours in which he could get drunk or address the correspondence on his desk, which he'd pushed aside that morning.

The first appealed to him far more than the last, but drinking himself into a stupor wasn't the answer to Evelyn's current state of affairs.

Just what the answer was, Marshall couldn't be sure until he gathered a few facts. First, would Rivenhall welcome his petition to transfer Evelyn into his hands? If not, he'd open the strongbox again and buy her freedom, although he suspected it would cost him a hefty sum. Then there was the problem of what he'd do with her once he had her. He'd given Druggs the task of finding suitable lodgings, but the item had been the last of a long list. Could she return to her home after the fiasco this afternoon? He certainly couldn't bring her back to Mayfair with him. As much as he'd like nothing better than to keep her within sight, and within reach, the option wasn't open to him. His stepmother and sisters were in the house, and Winnifred had witnessed Evelyn's arrest.

The questions piled up as Marshall sipped on his brandy.

The biggest question was why in the world had he stepped onto such a risky limb for the mere pleasure of getting a woman into his bed?

The answer was as simple as it was selfish.

He'd come to Miss Dennsworth's aid because he wanted to bed her.

It was a good two hours, and a second brandy later, before Druggs knocked on the door of the library. Marshall all but pulled the man into the room, firing questions at him before the secretary had time to wipe the rain from his spectacles.

"Did you find Rivenhall?"

"Yes, milord. He's currently enjoying an evening ale at an establishment called the Strangled Goose, a tavern not far from Westminster Bridge. I addressed the gentleman, persuading him to linger over his refreshment until you could engage him in conversation."

"Well done," Marshall said, reaching for his coat. "Tell Carlow to have the carriage brought round."

Half an hour later, Marshall walked into the alehouse. The building was divided into two parts. The bar, where the less lofty of the city consumed beer and gin, and the parlor, reserved for the more prominent customers. Druggs had described the magistrate to Marshall, so he had no problem picking the man out of the crowd that was gathering now that the day's work had ended. Rivenhall was a thin man with an overabundance of wavy brown hair and ill-fitting clothes.

"Rivenhall."

"Lord Waltham," Rivenhall replied.

"I assume my secretary told you the preliminaries,"

Marshall began. He waved off the potboy carrying a jug of warm beer in one hand and a pitcher of cheap gin in the other.

"Enough to know what you're thinking to do," Rivenhall said, before biting into the meat pie he'd ordered to go with his ale. He chewed, then swallowed the greasy fare, washing it down with a generous swig of dark beer. "Tell me, milord, what do you hope to gain by taking the lady under your wing, except the obvious, of course?"

Marshall didn't deny his intentions, nor did he defend them. "Why did you issue the warrant without an investigation? You could end up eating crow with your ale if the brooch turns up in Lady Monfrey's laundry."

"Lord Monfrey penned the request himself, asking that a constable be dispatched forthwith." Rivenhall shrugged his thin shoulders. "The lady's husband is well known to the legal ministry. What else could I do?"

Marshall didn't comment. The evening was upon them and with it the possibility of a long and dangerous night for Evelyn.

"I understand your eldest son has an inspiration to read the law," Marshall remarked. "Would a contribution to his education persuade you to consider my petition?"

"Ahhh, that it might. The Inner Temple has its price," Rivenhall said, not at all embarrassed by the transaction. "I suppose you'll be wantin' Miss Dennsworth out of Clerkenwell this evening."

"Within the hour," Marshall said impatiently. "Shall we go?"

The magistrate hesitated a moment before speaking. "You will guarantee the lady's presence when the time comes, of course. She'll be required to stand. Can't brush something like this under the rug, not with Lord Monfrey being who he is."

"Miss Dennsworth will stand," Marshall said, then added, "with council."

Both men knew it was unlikely that Evelyn's case would come before the bench anytime in the immediate future. Most people charged with theft could expect to spend six months in prison before being called in front of a magistrate. Marshall hoped the time would be to Evelyn's advantage once he had her released. If Lady Monfrey had misplaced the brooch, then the possibility of it being found was in their favor. If it was truly lost or stolen, then the time could be put to good use in the preparation of a defense.

"Very well, milord," Rivenhall relented with a deep sigh.

The police magistrate looked none too happy about having to leave his meat pie and ale, but he stood, nevertheless, waiting for the marquis to place the necessary coins on the stained table to pay for the meal. Once that had been done, the two men, one tall and impressively dressed, the other thin as a lamppost, exited the tavern.

Nothing more was said until the driver halted the carriage in front of the Clerkenwell Detention House. The sky had turned dark with rain and the late hour. It was approaching eight o'clock. Marshall followed the magistrate inside. He was shown into a small anteroom and told to wait.

Pacing the square room, Marshall inhaled a deep breath of relief and almost gagged on the stench that came with it. He stopped pacing and stared out the barred window instead. Beyond the small front courtyard, the quiet lamplit street glowed with rain. His breath formed faint wisps of vapor in the cold evening air.

Reviewing his thoughts, Marshall felt more than a profound sympathy for Evelyn Dennsworth, not only because she'd been hastily accused of a crime, but because she appeared to be alone in the world. She had no relatives in the city, no one upon whom she could call for aid, or so she had told the bailiff who had checked her into Clerkenwell. Who had in turn passed the information along to Druggs when he'd told him where the police magistrate could be found.

But she had him now.

Marshall had no idea how he was going to persuade Evelyn into his arms. He certainly didn't want her surrendering to him out of gratitude, although he knew most men would use the circumstances to bring about just that thing. Regardless of his motive, his pride wouldn't let him take advantage of the situation. When the time came, and he intended to make sure it did, Evelyn would come to him of her own free will.

Three

Evelyn tried to view her surroundings with cold detachment, as if she were looking at a stranger locked inside a damp stone cage no bigger than a pantry. Beneath her soiled clothing, her skin was cold from the clammy sweat of fear that had her chilled to the bone. She was tired and hungry, but she refused to sit down on the lice-infested straw mattress. Refusing to panic, she paced back and forth, hoping against hope that the marquis hadn't lied to her, that he would find some way to free her before she lost the strength to fight the unbelievable events that had her behind bars.

In her mind, Evelyn knew if she surrendered to the fear, it would defeat her.

The last few hours had been terrifying, the day the most dreadful of her life. When the constable had arrived at the dress shop with the warrant, she'd stared speechlessly at him, unable to believe that anyone could accuse her of theft without the slightest shred of evidence. She'd stood numbly by while he'd searched the shop with Madame La Roschelle's help. Willingly handing over her apron, she'd again watched as he'd dumped its contents onto one of the tables and sorted through the pins and chalk. Nothing had been found, of course. She wasn't a thief, nor had she coveted Lady Monfrey's brooch.

Evelyn had suffered having Lady Winnifred Bedford watching the entire time, feeling a private shame because she was the sister of the marquis. Knowing his sister would surely tell Lord Waltham the sordid details of the afternoon, Evelyn had borne the humiliation in resigned silence until the constable had informed her that she was under arrest.

Evelyn clamped her eyes shut at the memory of the terrible ride through the streets, caged for all to see as the wagon rolled awkwardly through the city. The afternoon sun had been warm on her face, but her heart had felt lifeless. The only thing that had kept her from losing her sanity altogether was the marquis. He had paid the constable to see that she wasn't mistreated, and he'd promised her that he would come to her aid.

Dear God, make it soon, Evelyn prayed. The walls seemed to be pressing in on her, suffocating the hope from her heart. The marquis's face was a memory. The prison was reality. Cold and threatening and fearful.

The scraping sound of a metal key being turned in a rusty lock startled Evelyn out of her self-pity. She turned toward the door, not knowing what to expect.

"Yer'll be steppin' out, miss," the guard said.

Evelyn froze in place. What did the man want with her? His gaze was as cold as the night air coming through the barred window.

"Yer've a visitor," he clarified impatiently.

A visitor! Her heart began to pound. It had to be the marquis. No one else would bother coming to see her, not even Madame La Roschelle. Whatever the future held, Evelyn knew she'd find no sympathy among the few people she knew in the city.

Evelyn walked out of the cell and into the dim corridor of the jail. Heavy doors, like the one on her own cell, lined the cold hallway. They were all closed and locked, their occupants unable to see anything but their own misery.

"This way," the guard said, closing the door but not locking it this time.

Evelyn followed him, her legs so weak she all but staggered down the hall. She could hear muffled voices, men talking and laughing crudely, but she saw no one until they reached the room where the constable had transferred her into the prison's custody. She stepped inside to find a reed-thin man dressed in coarse brown wool. He looked at her for a long moment before introducing himself as Henry Rivenhall, the police magistrate.

"Am I to be offered an opportunity to defend myself?" she asked shakily.

"In due time, Miss Dennsworth," he replied dryly. "Until then, I've been persuaded to give you over to Lord Waltham. He'll be seeing to your comforts, until you're called to stand before the bench."

"I'm not sure I understand," Evelyn said, her mind racing right along with her heart.

The magistrate gave her a strange smile, then shook his head. "Lord Waltham will be responsible for you until such time as you're summoned to answer the charges against you," the magistrate told her. His gaze became more pointed as he continued. "If you try to run away, his lordship will be held accountable. He's a powerful man. And a generous one to be taking on the burden of seeing to your welfare. I'd be appreciative if I were you."

There was an insinuation in his words that Evelyn heard but was too stunned to decipher at the moment. The marquis had kept his promise. He'd come for her.

"The guard will take you to Lord Waltham," Rivenhall informed her.

She turned to find another guard standing in the doorway. His deep-set eyes evaluated her as if she'd just been put on the auction block. The gaze made her feel dirty, but Evelyn refused to lower her head and leave the room as though she were ashamed.

"This way," the guard said.

Evelyn followed him, acutely aware that she was walking toward freedom. There were no cells in this section of the prison, although she could make out several offices, closed for the night, and what appeared to be an infirmary. The door was ajar, and she could see several people lying on narrow cots. Their gaunt bodies were draped in thin wool blankets that desperately needed washing. One poor man was shivering so violently she could see the cot moving as the chills raked his body.

Suddenly the guard stopped and turned around to face her. "In there," he said, nodding in the direction of yet another closed door.

Her hand was shaking so badly, Evelyn could barely turn the doorknob. When she finally managed to open it, she stepped into another cold, bare room. But this time she found a friendly face. The marquis was standing in front of the window. The moment his dark eyes settled on her, Evelyn felt the heat of his gaze. Such an intangible thing, yet it warmed her both inside and out.

"Miss Dennsworth," he said, moving away from the drafty window and toward her.

Her face and hands were streaked with dirt, her eyes glistening with unshed tears, but still she stood as regally as a queen, her shoulders straight, her body as gracefully proportioned as Marshall had remembered it. He wanted to scoop her into his arms and carry her away to safety, to tell her that she had no more fears, but he didn't. She was teetering on the brink of exhaustion. He needed to get her somewhere clean and warm as quickly as possible.

"My lord," she managed, knowing that if she dipped into a curtsey, she'd fall flat on her face. Her body couldn't fight the shock any longer. She felt herself beginning to tremble. "Thank you."

The words were whispered, but Marshall heard them and smiled. The brief expression was quickly replaced with one of concern. "You're shivering," he said. "Come, let's be rid of this place. I have a carriage waiting."

Evelyn tried to speak, to thank him more eloquently, but she ended up biting her lower lip to lessen its trembling. There was so much she wanted to say, but nervous fatigue convinced her to accept his generosity for the moment. There would be time to thank him later.

The night was chilly, but it was a clean chill, one brought on by a brisk wind instead of fear and uncertainty. The rain had stopped, the sky pitch black, the moon covered by clouds that promised more wet weather. The milky haze of the street-lamps outlined the carriage waiting just beyond the iron gates. Another guard, this one almost as thin as the magistrate, stuck a large key into the last of the locks and passed them through.

"Hurry, inside with you," Marshall said, motioning for his driver to stay atop the carriage as he opened the door and ushered Evelyn inside.

Once she was seated, he lifted the lid of a small compartment and pulled out a lap robe. He draped it over her shoulders, being careful not to touch her any more than necessary. Although the desire he had felt the first time he'd looked at her was still burning brightly, it was overshadowed by a deeper concern for her physical well-being. "Try to rest," he encouraged her before closing the door.

"Where to, milord?" his driver asked as the marquis took a step back from the carriage.

Marshall racked his brain for a moment, then remembering a lodging house in Southwark that had once been a ren-dezvous for a more youthful liaison, he gave the driver the address. The inn was on the south side of the city. It was clean and well managed, and the owner was a discreet woman in her fifties. Marshall corrected himself as he opened the carriage door and climbed inside. The proprietor, a widow by the name of Reardon, would be closer to sixty now, if she was still alive. He hadn't frequented the lodgings for many years. Regardless, the time it would take to reach the establishment would offer him the opportunity to sort things out.

The moment Marshall was seated, the carriage began to move. The streetlamp offered just enough light to see the apprehension on Evelyn's face. Once he closed the door, they were separated by darkness and a silence that lingered for several minutes as the carriage rattled over the cobblestone streets on its way across the Thames.

There was a flask of brandy in the compartment where the lap robe had been stored, and for a moment Marshall considered offering Evelyn a drink. He decided against it after realizing that she probably hadn't eaten for hours. Whiskey on an empty stomach was the last thing she needed. He wished he could say the same thing for himself. At the moment, a stout drink would be just the thing. There was no reason for him to be nervous, yet he was. His insides were trembling almost as badly as Evelyn's shoulders before he'd draped the blanket around her.

"Where are you taking me?" she asked as the carriage weaved through the evening traffic of hansom cabs and private carriages, carrying people to the theater or one of the private parties that filled the London schedule this time of year.

"Is there someplace you can go?" he countered, ready to give the driver new directions if she preferred to return to her own home.

Evelyn shook her head, then realized he might not be able to see the movement. The curtains were drawn over the windows, and it was very dark inside the carriage. Dark but peaceful. "No. At least, I don't think so. My wages include a room above Madame's shop. I . . . I'm not sure she would want me to return."

"Just as well," he replied. "I would think Bond Street would be the last place you'd want to be tonight."

Silence reigned for another few minutes. Evelyn was feeling somewhat warmer now. The lap robe was of heavy wool, and it smelled clean, not like the rag that had been tossed over the straw mattress in the cell. Thinking about the detention house sent another chill through her, and she drew the corners of the small blanket close. "Then, where?" she asked, afraid to think of more than this night. Tomorrow would be soon enough to confront the uncertainty of her future.

"An inn," the marquis told her. "A comfortable place where you can have a good meal and rest for a while."

"I . . . I can't . . . I mean—"

"Don't worry," Marshall said, realizing she was about to mention the cost of a night's shelter and a meal. "I want you to forget what happened today. Wipe it from your mind. You'll not be returning to Clerkenwell, or any place like it."

Hearing the surety in his voice, the confidence that allowed him to decree the future, brought tears to her eyes. They spilled down her face. She cried silently for a moment, then smiled, hoping he could see the small amount of gratitude she was able express. Although she was feeling much warmer, her wits were still numb.

Marshall didn't see Evelyn smile, but he could feel her presence. The hem of her skirt brushed against his trouser leg as the carriage swung around the corner and approached Blackfriar's Bridge. He reached for the cloth grip to steady himself as the carriage moved on at a brisk pace. The curtains swayed, letting in the light from the triple-globed lampposts at the end of the bridge. He saw the tears streaming down her face and grasped the cloth handle more fiercely.

The urge to pull her into his arms was so strong he silently cursed the fact that they still had several miles to travel before he could offer her more than a woolen blanket.

"I understand you have no family in the city," Marshall said. "Where are you from?"

"Sussex," she told him.

When she offered no other information, Marshall relented to the unpleasantness of the situation and allowed her to ride in silence. There would be time to talk later. The worst was over. She was in his custody, and he'd see that she never regretted it.

Evelyn could feel his gaze in the darkness. He was sitting opposite her, assessing her, probably mentally weighing the dreadful mess she'd gotten herself into because she had endeavored to be polite to a customer.

"Why?" Evelyn asked before she could think better of it.

"We will talk after you've rested." A carriage in the middle of a busy London street wasn't the place to discuss his plans. Nor was this the best of times. He wanted Evelyn relaxed and comfortable before he approached her on a more intimate level. As things stood now, he'd be lucky to get her inside the inn before she collapsed.

Evelyn gave in to the exhaustion and leaned back against the seat, letting the swaying rhythm of the carriage lull her into a dreamy state where her thoughts strayed to the man sitting across from her. The marquis was exactly what a well-bred gentleman should be. Educated, wealthy, influential, dressed by the best tailors on Savile Row, and well aware that no one would expect him to be doing what he was doing.

Being in the dark with him, with nothing more than a sliver of light creeping into the carriage whenever they passed a lamppost, seemed strangely intimate. The carriage smelled of old leather and expensive cologne, of cigar smoke and wool dampened by the recent rain. Evelyn hoped the scent of the prison wasn't clinging to her clothes in the same way. Her skirt was smeared with whatever had been caked on the wagon bed. The blouse she'd ironed with crisp perfection that very morning was soiled and unsalvageable. Fortunately, the only thing she could smell about her own person was the blanket now draped snugly around her shoulders. It wasn't an unpleasant odor, so she relaxed.

Fog curled around the carriage wheels when it finally came to a stop. Marshall pulled back the curtain and looked outside. The inn was just as he'd remembered it, a large stone and shingled structure with a soot-blackened chimney. Smoke curled lazily upward, its misty grayness blending into the night. "Stay here until I've arranged for a room," he said.

Evelyn nodded as the carriage swayed under the driver's shifting weight. An instant later the door was opened, and the marquis stepped down.

Marshall smiled as he opened the front door of the inn. Nothing had changed. The front room was large and comfortable, a fire blazing on the hearth, the aroma of baked bread and warm beer thick in the air. The floor was streaked with mud from the patrons who had come inside to get away from the weather, but the rest was as clean as any traveling lodge he'd ever seen and cleaner than most. A gangly young lad who had outgrown his jacket was wiping down the empty tables while two locals, sitting near the fire, relaxed with an evening ale. A woman whom he recognized as the Widow Reardon came through the baize door that led to the kitchen.

"What can I do fer your lordship?" she asked.

Marshall wasn't sure if the widow remembered him or the number of times he'd rented a room from her in his randy youth, but he suspected she did. There was a gleam of recognition in her eyes, though she said nothing to acknowledge him directly.

"I would like accommodations," he told her. "For two, perhaps three days."

"I 'ave a nice set of rooms upstairs, milord."

She quoted him a price that included meals, then asked if he'd be needing anything from the kitchen at this late hour.

"Yes. Something nourishing, but not too heavy," he told her. "And water for a hot bath."

"Aye, milord, I 'ave me boy set the water to boilin'."

"Very good," Marshall said, adding a fresh pot of tea to his list of immediate needs.

He returned to the carriage for Evelyn. One look at her told him all he needed to know about her current condition. Instead of handing her down from the carriage, he reached inside and scooped her into his arms.

Evelyn gasped with surprise at finding herself being carried like a child. "I can walk," she insisted.

"Nonsense," Marshall said as he strode toward the inn. Since he'd been aching to touch her for the last hour, he was more than content to have her cradled against his chest. Halfway between the carriage and the inn, she relented with a soft sigh and rested her head in the curve of his shoulder.

"Is the lady feelin' poorly?" the widow asked when Marshall entered the inn with Evelyn in his arms.

"Just tired." He headed for the staircase. "Which door?" he asked over his shoulder.

"The last one on yer right, milord. I'll be up with tea as soon as the kettle's hot."

Evelyn kept her eyes closed as the marquis marched up the stairs. She really should protest, but it felt so good, so utterly wonderful, to have his strength supporting her. The clink of his boot heels on the wooden floor matched her heartbeat as he strode down the corridor, not stopping until he reached the appropriate door. Then, with only the slightest shifting of her weight in his arms, he reached out, opened the door, and stepped inside.

"You can open your eyes now," Marshall said softy.

Evelyn did and caught a quick glimpse of the bed before he set her down in the middle of it. She glanced up at him, unsure what to say, and found herself spellbound by his reassuring smile. He turned up the gas lamp sitting on the table. The room went from almost dark to pleasantly dim. Knowing she wasn't alone had her feeling stronger already.

Marshall stared down at her for a brief moment. Her hands were knotted in the carriage blanket, her eyes swollen from crying, her face pale. But none of those things kept him from seeing the beauty beneath the distress, the elegant cheekbones and small, straight nose, the sweet swell of her bottom lip.

"I'll start a fire," he said, needing something to do before he sank down on the bed beside her. The fire grate had been swept and cleaned, the rack newly blackened, and a neat stack of dried wood waited to be lit.

Evelyn sat in the middle of the bed and watched him build a fire. Even with his back to her, he was an impressive man. The longer she was with him, the more she wanted to ask him why he was being so kind, but she sensed he didn't want to talk.

Afraid that she'd be caught staring, Evelyn looked around the room. It was larger than she had expected, with a tall chest of drawers, a chair, and a vanity table. An interior door led to another room. Evelyn leaned to the side and stretched her neck just enough to see around the corner. A brass tub! Oh, how she wanted a bath. With lots of hot water to wash the memory of the jail wagon and Clerkenwell from her body.

Once the fire was blazing to Marshall's satisfaction, he turned around to find Evelyn exactly as he'd left her. There were circles under her eyes where the skin was the most delicate. She'd been in jail for only a few hours, but the time and fear had left its mark. She looked like a blue-eyed angel who had accidentally misplaced her wings.

A knock disrupted his thoughts. Marshall opened the door to reveal the inn's proprietor. The widow handed him a tray with a teapot, an enameled sugar caddie, and two cups. "It'd be a while yet 'fore the bathwater is boiling," she told him.

Marshall thanked her, then waited until she had closed the door before carrying the tray to the table beside the bed. He poured the tea, passing the cup into Evelyn's waiting hands.

Evelyn looked at him, wondering what he was thinking. She'd been nothing but trouble to him since she'd spilled sewing pins all over the floor. His gaze intensified, and for a moment she wasn't sure if she should stay or run. She held her breath when he sat down beside her, stretching one arm over her lap and resting it palm down on the faded coverlet. The glow from the gas lamp lit his strong features: the angle of his nose and jaw, the firm mouth and piercing eyes. It was a handsome face, one that showed both intelligence and strength.

He smiled then, and Evelyn felt her heart swell inside her chest.

"A cup of tea should settle your nerves," he said. "Then——"

"A bath," she blurted out. She wanted one so badly.

"A bath, then." He laughed. "Then something to eat, then a good night's sleep."

"You're being so kind," she whispered. "I . . ." Her voice broke.

Marshall took the teacup before her shaky hands upended it. He wasn't sure what had started her to crying again. Setting the cup aside, he pulled her into his arms and held her against his chest, rocking her as he would a child. The silent tears gradually turned into broken sobs that shook her whole body. Every protective instinct he possessed came into play as he held her close, pleased that she'd turned to him instead of away.

She cried and cried, as if once started she couldn't cease until every drop of moisture had been wrenched from her body. Marshall began to fear that the tears would never stop.

When the sobs finally subsided, he wiped her face with his handkerchief, then hooking a knuckle underneath her chin, tilted her face up. She was pretty, her features delicately boned. Feminine yet strong. There was no shadow of deception, no guilt, in the teary depth of her eyes, only a reflection of exhaustion and an innocence that touched his heart. His hand slid around her neck as he lowered his head to claim the kiss he'd wanted all day.

Evelyn let her eyes close as his lips came to rest ever so gently upon her own. His breath felt warm, his arms even warmer. She hadn't expected him to kiss her, but she knew it was what she wanted, had wanted ever since he'd smiled at her in the dress shop. When his lips pressed more firmly against hers, she yielded to the unnamed desire. When his hand pressed against the small of her back, she melted against him.

Marshall held her in place as he drank at her mouth, tasting salty tears and soft, gentle woman. His mouth pressed harder, and hers opened, letting him explore. And explore he did, keeping the kiss gentle but thorough. He licked at her lips, then probed between them, entering slowly then retreating, building the excitement of the intimacy.

Evelyn sighed with pleasure. The marquis felt wonderful, smelled wonderful, tasted wonderful. His kiss was everything a kiss should be, warm and passionate, gentle but dominating. It drained the last ounce of willpower from her body. She leaned against him, shyly returning the kiss, unsure of what she was doing but willing to let her instincts guide her. Her heart began to pound as a sweet euphoria filled her body.

When she found herself pressed back against the pillows, his body half covering hers, all she could do was cling to his shoulders. His arm moved underneath her, lifting her, arching her upper body into his, holding her safe and secure, chasing the fear and uncertainty away until there was nothing but warm, tingling sensations.

Keeping himself in check, Marshall slowly deepened the kiss, teaching her what he liked. She was weakened by the day's events, but she wasn't a frail female. She was a woman full grown with more passion than she realized. His fingers found a wayward strand of hair and played with it at the same time his mouth played with her senses. God, she felt good. Just how he had imagined she would feel, all soft and pliable, warm and womanly.

Finally he had to stop kissing her for fear that he'd soon go beyond the limits of what she could tolerate in her current condition. For now, he'd have to be satisfied with knowing that he could arouse her.

Evelyn's eyes opened as he lifted his mouth. She had no idea what to say, especially when he smiled down at her as if she'd just given him a gift.

"I'll leave you to your tea and bath," he said, leaning down to brush the lightest of kisses across her forehead.

Then, with her senses whirling, he left her lying on the bed.

Evelyn stared at the closed door for the longest time, her mind grappling with the fact that she'd just been kissed by a marquis.

Four

Evelyn awoke to see the pink flush of dawn staining the sky and the marquis silhouetted against it. He stood at the window, his back to the bed where she'd lain sleeping for hours. She blinked away the drowsiness and stared at the marquis, doing her best to see the man and not the aristocrat, but they were too intricately woven together, too inseparable for her to see anything except a peer of the realm.

She pulled the coverlet up to her neck. After she'd bathed last night, she'd used what was left of the hot water to wash out her things. Then, thinking the marquis had returned to his home, she'd climbed into bed and fallen into an exhausted sleep.

Marshall heard the slight creaking of the bed and turned around. He smiled at the provocative image Evelyn made with her hair cascading about her bare shoulders and the coverlet clutched to her bosom like a shield of armor.

He had retired to the main parlor of the lodge after kissing her, leaving her to the privacy she required for a bath and a hot meal of soup and bread that had seemed to satisfy her appetite. When he'd returned to the room, close to midnight, she'd been sleeping. A quick inspection of the small premises had alerted him to the fact that she was naked under the sheets. Her clothing was draped over the edge of the brass tub, left to dry after being scrubbed.

"Good morning," he said, thankful that she hadn't slept the day away. There was much to be done, but he'd stayed, wanting to reassure himself that she had recovered from her ordeal before leaving to meet with Druggs.

"Good morning, my lord," she replied shyly.

Marshall wondered how deeply she'd blush if she knew that he'd seen quite a bit of her lovely body during the last few hours. She'd slept, but restlessly. He had dozed in the chair where he'd positioned himself after returning to the room. Twice during the night he had walked to the bed to tuck the covers neatly around her. Although she hadn't tossed and turned enough to completely throw off the linens, he had seen her bare shoulders and pale back, the graceful length of her arms and a slender foot. He'd even brushed a tendril of hair away from her face, letting his fingertips savor the softness of her skin at the same time. Once, the last time he'd seen to her comfort, he'd allowed himself the pleasure of kissing her again. A soft touch of his mouth to her lips, nothing more, but enough to arouse him again.

Just before dawn, he had left the chair and moved to the window where he had watched the sun rise. Sometime during those silent moments, he had stopped questioning his intentions to take a shop girl, charged with theft, as his mistress. Once the decision had been made, it didn't disturb him in the least, regardless of the unorthodox manner in which he'd reached it.

"I shall inform the Widow Reardon that you are awake and in need of a cup of tea," he said, moving toward the fireplace.

The room had taken on a chill, so he stacked more wood

on the grate and prodded the embers until the fire was blazing once again. Satisfied that Evelyn would be comfortable when she left the bed to retrieve her clothing, Marshall turned to face her. "Are you hungry? Perhaps some jam and bread to go with the tea?"

"That is very kind of you," Evelyn said. Had the marquis spent the night in the room with her? His clothing was wrinkled, and his face, although still uncommonly handsome, displayed a certain fatigue.

She grew increasingly uncomfortable as he continued to look at her. "Jam and bread will do nicely," she finally said.

"Then I shall leave you for a while."

Evelyn breathed a shaky sigh of relief when she was alone. She climbed out of bed, shivering as the air touched every bare inch of her. Hurrying into the small room that served as both bathing and dressing area, she gathered up her clothes. Her skirt was still damp, but her undergarments were dry, along with the white blouse that wasn't suited for anything but a cleaning rag now.

She got dressed, then walked to the window and shoved the shutters open, letting the bright rays of the morning sun flood into the room. The sky was filled with translucent pink and gold streaks, the air cool and exquisitely clear. She had no idea where she was, other than an establishment owned by a widow who had been pleasant to her the previous evening. She hadn't asked the proprietor any questions, fearing that she might trigger unpleasant inquiries in return.

From what Evelyn could see from the window, the lodging house had a side courtyard where carriages and coaches could be tended while their occupants ate or lingered over a drink before either going about their business or renting a room for the night. Beyond a thin cluster of trees, she could make out the rooftops of other buildings, but not enough to see if they were businesses or residences. She hadn't had enough presence of mind the previous evening to determine if the carriage had moved north or south. The only thing that had mattered was that the driver had quickly put Clerkenwell behind them.

Evelyn stared out the window, her smile fading as the ramifications of the previous day's events began to unfurl within her mind. She had to face the facts, the unpleasantness of her current situation. Although she was innocent of the charges Lady Monfrey had so hurriedly placed against her, she had no way of proving it other than the simple fact that the brooch hadn't been discovered upon her person or in the shop. Madame La Roschelle had somewhat supported her cause by arguing with the constable, but she was too earnest of a businesswoman to take the side of a shop girl over that of an influential lady of London. The ladies of society weren't likely to patronize a shop if one of the employees was thought to be a thief.

She had some money saved, but that would be quickly exhausted if she was forced to find lodgings with no guarantee of obtaining another position. Another shop on Bond Street was out of the question. Everyone on the avenue had seen her being hauled away in the jail wagon. It wasn't a sight they'd soon forget.

That left the marquis.

He did seem earnest in his desire to help her, but was the gesture based on gentlemanly chivalry or true compassion? Or something else?

Evelyn couldn't forget the way he had kissed her, or the way she'd felt afterward. He had still been there this morning watching over her. She was almost certain that he had spent the night in the room. But why? He could afford another, or he could have returned to his home or his club. Yet he hadn't. He'd stayed with her.

She felt a rush of excitement over his obvious concern. He'd behaved like a footman this morning, stirring the fire, going downstairs to fetch her breakfast, and yet one had only to look at him to know he was a man of quality. He wore his birthright with an aura of solid British respectability. His posture, his clothing, his faultless manners, all attested to his highborn status. There was nothing frivolous or bohemian about him. He was distinguished, but not ostentatious.

He was, Evelyn concluded with a heavy sigh, very nearly perfect.

She turned away from the window, but left it open. The more light she shed on her surroundings, the more likely she was to remember that the marquis could desert her at any time.

Without the aid of a comb or brush, she managed to get her hair pulled back and secured in a bun at the base of her neck. It would have to do until she could think of some way to retrieve her belongings from the dress shop. She dreaded the upcoming confrontation with Madame La Roschelle.

Evelyn allowed herself a brief smile of recognition when the marquis returned to the room. She had already tidied up the bed, thinking the whole time that he could have easily stretched out beside her.

Seeing two cups, she immediately went about filling both of them with strong, hot tea. The aroma lifted her spirits. He thanked her, then carried his cup to the window where he had been standing when she'd awakened earlier. The sound of his voice made her smile again. He glanced at her, and she felt herself blush.

"Don't be shy," he coaxed her. "Please, eat your bread and jam. Enjoy your tea."

A confusing and contradictory thought flashed through Evelyn's mind as she spooned sugar into her cup. Why should she trust the marquis? She'd seen enough of noblemen and their high-handed ways to know the man must have more than a compassionate constitution fueling his concern. The unwelcomed thought linked with another. What if the marquis thought her a thief? What if he had offered her his protection, provided her sanctuary, only because he wanted her to be obligated to him? Did he think to use that obligation to make her his servant, a woman who would do his bidding because she had no choice?

A small internal voice warned Evelyn to proceed with caution.

Marshall saw the change in her expression and knew the morning had brought a whole set of new thoughts with it. His lovely ward was no doubt putting two and two together.

"You are not to worry," he said, after taking a sip of tea. "Although there are some things we must manage before the day is out, I want you to rest and trust me to see after matters."

"Why?" she asked. "I am grateful, my lord, as I shall always be for your generosity and understanding, but regardless . . . I mean to say, it doesn't make much sense to me. One doesn't require a Cambridge education to know that gentlemen of your rank do not go about London rescuing shop girls from prison."

He smiled at her candor. "Make sense of it all, you ask. I fear I cannot. As to the why of things, the only answer I can give you at the moment is to say that I find you charming and in need of a friend."

Evelyn studied him with open curiosity. She wanted to believe that he was what he appeared to be, a man of conscience who realized that she had been falsely accused and was offering his help, but she knew she would be foolish if she discounted the possibility of there being more to the marquis's charity. He had called her charming, but she'd gotten a good look at herself in the mirror and knew she looked more like a waif who had slept in her clothes than the sort of lady he was accustomed to greeting on a late spring morning.

"I can't stay here," she told him.

"It won't be for long," Marshall said, glancing about the room. "A day or two, no more. By then I will have made other arrangements. I don't think returning to Bond Street is the right thing for you. Not yet."

"Other arrangements, my lord?" Evelyn's instincts stirred in warning. "May I again ask why?"

"My lovely Miss Dennsworth, you may ask me anything you like. And please don't 'my lord' me to death. I think we have progressed enough for you to call me by my first name. It is Marshall, after a great uncle my father held in high regard. And I shall call you Evelyn, in private, of course."

"In private? Then, you expect us to be spending a great deal of time together."

"Yes, I do," he replied honestly.

"You must forgive me, my lord, but I can't help but think that your kindness stems from more than a generous disposition."

Marshall laughed. "Amply put and rightfully questioned, Miss Dennsworth." He regarded her for a moment, unsure of how honestly he should answer her. Deciding a lie would serve no purpose, he tempered his reply with a smile. "I find no gratification in exploiting innocent women. I also admit to finding you attractive. But then, I'm sure you have already reached that conclusion. I am not in the habit of kissing women who do not appeal to me."

"And you think to kiss me again," she said as calmly as possible.

"If you allow me the pleasure, I would be hard-pressed to refuse it." His eyes were gleaming now, all traces of fatigue washed away by the topic they were discussing.

"And if I refuse?"

"Then I shall endeavor to persuade you otherwise."

Evelyn considered his reply for a long moment, realizing that she could very well be cutting off her nose to spite her face. Since the marquis was being forthright enough to admit that he hoped to seduce her, the least she could do was to let him know she had no intentions of making the seduction an easy one.

"We encountered one another on Bond Street, not Whitechapel Road."

"And I thought I had met a soft-spoken shop girl," Marshall replied, thoroughly enjoying the conversation. "I see now that your tongue can have a sharp edge."

"Only when necessary, my lord. I am not guilty of stealing anything, nor am I intimidated enough to become a willing victim of another aristocrat's ego." She straightened her shoulders and met his gaze. "I am indebted to you, but not to the extent that I will become your fool."

"I suppose you have no reason to trust any of us," he conceded. "However, I assure you that I will ask nothing more than you are willing to give."

"And if I decline to give you anything, my lord, what should I expect in return? To be returned to the place where you found me?"

His gaze lingered on the stubborn angle of her chin. "No matter what transpires between us, I will never take you back to Clerkenwell. You have my word."

Evelyn believed him, believed the conviction in his voice and the honesty in his eyes. She nodded. The conversation wasn't what one would expect to have over tea in the early hours of the morning, but it was a necessary one. She realized that what she was agreeing to was near insanity, but until she had time to reason things out, and hopefully find an alternative course of action, there was little she could do but accept the man's generosity and hope for the best.

"Very well, my lord. I will accept your word if you will accept mine. I am duly appreciative of your kindness, but do not expect it to be repaid with anything more than Christian gratitude."

Marshall focused on her face as a cool smile curled his mouth. "You can begin expressing your gratitude by doing as I asked. My name is Marshall."

Addressing the marquis by his first name seemed more intimate than the kiss they had shared last night. Evelyn knew the kiss, not his benevolent actions, was the reason he had used the term "progressed" and the telling phrase "in private."

Needing a few minutes to sort out what her response would be, Evelyn nibbled on a slice of toasted bread, then finished her tea. She refilled her cup before seeking the marquis's attention a second time. "You believe me innocent, then?"

"I believe you innocent," he replied, his gaze unwavering. "I also believe that Lady Monfrey encouraged her husband to dispatch the constable far too quickly. No doubt her maid will find the brooch when she does the weekly laundry, or the lady herself will happen upon it. The charges will be dropped, and the future will once again look bright."

Marshall didn't say that he intended to make sure Evelyn's future was brightened by his presence. He realized that his words were deceptive, but he'd deal with his conscience later. For now, he was pleased that she looked rested and some of what he suspected was a dry and biting wit had returned to her speech.

He moved away from the window and sat down, stretching his long legs out in front of him. The hour required him to be on his way, but he found himself wanting to linger. Although he had spent the night in a chair, he had rented a room for his driver. The man was now seeing to the horses.

Marshall allowed himself to relax. It seemed unusually pleasant to simply sit in the same room with Evelyn Dennsworth while they both took tea. The silence between them was pleasant rather than strained. The morning sunshine brightened the room, making him think of his childhood and all the days he had hurried to watch the morning tide wash over the beach near their Ipswich estate. He'd often taken his breakfast on the cliffs overlooking the English Channel, biscuits and fried meat pilfered from the sideboard as he made a mad dash through the house.

It had been a long time since he'd thought of those days. His father had been alive then and as full of life as any man could be. The summers spent in the country had been wonderful. They both enjoyed sailing and had spent as much time as they could on the Channel, returning to the seaside manor late in the afternoon, dripping wet, but content in each other's company.

Marshall stared into the fire for a long moment before turning up the cup and finishing off its contents. It returned to his saucer with a soft but audible clang that drew Evelyn's attention.

It was awkward not knowing what to say. Deciding it was best to keep the conversation focused on the problems at hand, Evelyn said, "The magistrate, I've forgotten his name—"

"Rivenhall," Marshall supplied. "A fair enough man, or so I've been told."

"Yes, well, I certainly hope so," she mumbled, then continued in a more audible voice. "The magistrate informed me that I was being placed in your custody. I assure you, my lord, I will do nothing to dishonor your faith in me."

"I don't expect you to. I will arrange for whatever belongings you have at Madame La Roschelle's to be retreived and brought to you as soon as possible. In the meanwhile, will you be content here? I'm sure the Widow

Reardon can find a book to occupy your time until I return this evening."

"You will be coming back?"

Marshall noted the hint of excitement in her voice. If he played his cards right, and he was a very good gambler, their current estranged friendship could satisfy both of their needs. Of course, he'd have to play his hand with delicate skill. It could prove uncomfortable for both of them if he tried to be her friend on one hand and the seducer of her innocence on the other. Still, things could work out. She trusted him, somewhat at least. Time and patience would remove any other obstacles.

He pulled his timepiece out of his vest pocket, noting the hour. "I must leave you now," he said. "Do not hesitate to ask for anything you need."

"Thank you," Evelyn said, coming to her feet. She'd been sitting on the side of the bed for lack of another chair. She took a quick breath, then said what was on her mind. "I will repay your generosity as soon as I am able," she told him. "I have a little money."

"Keep it," Marshall said, walking to where she was standing by the bed.

"I realize you are not concerned about the coin you have spent, my lord, but I am," she replied, holding on to what self-respect the previous day's events hadn't already shredded. "I was not raised to accept charity easily."

"Then accept my friendship," Marshall replied softly.

For the life of her, Evelyn couldn't think of a thing to say. The marquis was standing so close she could see the stains on the front of his shirt where she'd cried her eyes out while he'd held her securely in his arms.

Marshall looked at Evelyn with the same unconfined interest. He stared into her bright blue eyes and felt a disturbing emotion, one that had nothing to do with lust. It was a soothing feeling, indefinable, but strangely comforting. Then she licked her lips, and he had to clench his hands to keep from reaching for her.

She'd taste like tea and plum jam, he thought, then smiled.

Evelyn smiled back. "I accept your friendship, my lord, and offer mine in return. Although why a man such as yourself would want it, I haven't a clue. There is nothing extraordinary about me."

"On the contrary, I find you extremely extraordinary," he said softly. "And my name is Marshall, not my lord. I would very much like to hear you say it."

Evelyn looked away, staring at the enameled sugar caddie on the tray instead of the man.

When she didn't respond, Marshall stepped closer. "Friends often refer to each other by their given names. It isn't a punishable offense, Evelyn."

The sound of her own name being spoken so gently brought her head around, but she still couldn't make herself say his name. It came too close to admitting that she longed for more than his friendship.

"We know nothing of each other," she said instead.

"It takes time for people to become acquainted."

The sun was fully risen. A single shaft of golden light spilled through the open window, making Evelyn's hair shine. Cautiously, Marshall reached out to touch a curly wisp of it, gently pushing it back behind her ear. "Can you not accept what has passed between us without question for the time being?"

Once again Evelyn was reminded of the kiss. A full minute ticked away, each second counted by the small pendulum clock on the dresser, before she spoke. "I will do my best."

"Good. Then relax, sleep the day away if you wish," Marshall said. "I will return this evening, and we shall begin our acquaintance."

She stared at him, feeling more helpless than she had in jail. There was something about this man, something beyond his surprising kindness, that made her feel as if her life was no longer her own. At any moment she expected him to turn into what she'd heard most gentlemen of his class thrived on being, selfish and extravagant in their ways, mindless to anything but their own pleasure. And yet, he was smiling at her, and looking for all the world as if he simply enjoyed her company.

Evelyn knew she was being foolish. She had nothing in common with the Marquis of Waltham. Nothing upon which to base a friendship, or anything else.

Uncomfortably aware of her thoughts, she searched for the words that would bring their goodbye to a close. Thinking of nothing more than what anyone would say to someone who was about to leave, she smiled cordially and said, "Good day, my lord."

"Ahhh, so easily you forget," he laughed lightly. "I will not budge an inch until you have spoken my name," he insisted. He hadn't had more than an hour's uncomfortable sleep in a lumpy chair, but he felt unusually light of spirit. It was as if by taking on this woman's burden he had somehow lightened his own.

Evelyn held her breath for several heartbeats before releasing it to say, "Good day, Marshall."

"That's better," he replied softly.

A silent duel began between them, each knowing it was time for him to leave, each dreading it for their own private reasons.

Finally, Marshall did what Evelyn had unknowingly been waiting for him to do. He lowered his head and kissed her. While his hands remained at his sides, the kiss was beyond the boundaries of a normal friendship. The experience of being kissed was still so new and enchanting, it was impossible for Evelyn not to feel as if all her dreams had suddenly come true.

She returned the kiss, not as brazenly as Marshall was giving it, but with enough enthusiasm for him to know that he could arouse a spark within her. His eyes opened and glanced toward the bed. For an instant he imagined himself picking her up and putting her in the middle of it, then coming down on top of her. He imagined her response, shock then protest, followed by a sweet surrender.

He closed his eyes again, deepening the kiss as much as he could with only their mouths touching. Then he pulled back, slowly.

"Until this evening," he said, stepping back, then turning toward the door. He paused short of putting his hand on the knob and looked back at her. "Enjoy your day. And remember, you are not to worry."

She almost bobbed a curtsey and said, "Yes, milord." Instead she nodded, unable to do anything else until the door closed behind the marquis. Then she sank onto the bed.

Not worry!

How could she do anything but worry? Besides facing the possibility of being labeled a thief in a court of law and being hauled off to prison or a workhouse for God only knew how long, she now had to worry about her heart. For having it broken would be the end result if she allowed herself to become enthralled of the Marquis of Waltham.

And the man was most definitely enthralling. She'd never met anyone like him. Aside from the fact that he had managed to free her from Clerkenwell, he believed her innocent of any crime. That in itself was more blessing than Evelyn could imagine. She couldn't bear the thought of having people believe her a thief.

Why had she allowed him to kiss her a second time?

Already knowing the answer, Evelyn looked about the room. What would she do for an entire day? Unaccustomed to being idle, she collected the teacup from the windowsill where the marquis had left it and carried it to the tray. Then she nibbled on a slice of toasted bread and finished off the tea. Once that was done, she simply sat down in the chair and stared out the window, hoping some order would come to her thoughts before the marquis returned that evening.

Five

Marshall arrived at his Mayfair town house and immediately summoned Druggs to join him in the library. The secretary appeared in a freshly starched shirt and dark suit.

"Clear my calendar as much as possible for the remainder of the week," he was told as his employer removed his jacket and tossed it onto the chair in front of the fireplace. "Do you have my sister's calendar available? I dread the thought of how many balls will be forced upon me this week."

Druggs sat down in his customary chair. Having an excellent memory, he rarely had to refer to his notes. "Lady Winnifred will be attending the opera this evening. Afterward, you will be expected to dine with Lord and Lady Clarendon. Tomorrow night is the Granmer ball, a small affair compared to most. Nothing the following evening that I have been informed of as yet. The end of the week will bring the Trehearn ball, an event I am told your sister awaits with high anticipation."

"Bloody hell!" Marshall said. He poured himself a drink. It was too early for spirits, but since his intention was to have a bath then a few hours sleep, the brandy served a useful purpose. "I suppose there's no way out of it," he relented with a frustrated sigh. "Very well, do what you can to give me a few hours of peace and quiet."

"Yes, your lordship. Will there be anything else?"

Marshall sat down behind his desk. "I installed Miss Dennsworth in Southwark. The accommodations are less than desirable. How soon can you find a suitable residence?"

Druggs addressed this question with the same ease in which he had answered the first. "I looked into the matter late yesterday, after realizing the haste at which you wanted things done. I believe I have already achieved the goal. There is a small, but suitable, house in Lambeth. The rent is reasonable and the neighborhood well kept. The former resident, a gentleman in his late sixties with a fondness for gardening, has put it up for lease. Failing health forced him to the country and into the care of a relative, or so the agent informed me. I viewed the house early this morning."

"And?" Marshall prompted impatiently.

"It is a well-maintained residence, my lord. The size is somewhat smaller than you are accustomed to, of course, but I think it will meet the lady's needs. The footman is willing to stay on, and he assured me that his wife would be agreeable to assuming the role of cook and housekeeper, if the position were to become available."

"Excellent," Marshall said. "As always, Druggs, your efficiency is impressive."

"Thank you, my lord. As to the other items on your list, I am seeing to their satisfaction as quickly as possible."

"Clothes."

"Clothes, my lord?"

"Miss Dennsworth's wardrobe," Marshall said. "She lived above the shop. Send someone, a very discreet someone, to collect her things. I want the house readied today. I shall collect the new resident and escort her there myself, before I'm forced to endure the opera and Lord Clarendon's dinner conversation. The man talks more than a magpie."

Druggs didn't seem the least bit flustered by the challenge before him. He stood up, nodding respectfully before saying, "Very well, my lord."

After the secretary departed, Marshall allowed himself the pleasure of a few minutes alone. Druggs had the matter of a suitable house under control. Once he had Evelyn living comfortably within its walls, he would begin the task of changing his role from friend to lover. The attraction already existed, and if the way she responded to him was any indication, it wouldn't take long. The lovely Miss Dennsworth wouldn't surrender easily, he was sure of it, and in many ways that made the chase more appealing. Like most men, he enjoyed a challenge, especially if the reward was worth having.

Several hours later, freshly shaven and rested, Marshall returned to the library. He was sorting through the correspondence on his desk when a light knock on the door interrupted him. He wasn't surprised when it opened to reveal a pretty young girl of ten with bouncing blond curls and vibrant blue eyes.

"May I come in?"

"Of course," he said. "And to what do I owe the pleasure of your company, Lady Catherine?"

The youngest of his two sisters walked undauntedly around the desk and placed a kiss on his cheek. "Nothing in particular," she confessed, shrugging her shoulders. "Miss Perry is taking a nap. I'm supposed to be doing the same, but I came down the back stairs so she wouldn't know I'd left my room." She smiled, as if sneaking away from her governess was worthy of a reward. "I just wanted to see you. You're always going about with Winnie."

"Your time will come," Marshall assured her, disliking the idea of Catherine growing up too fast. She was a nymph of a child, always poking her adorable nose into things that didn't concern her. He'd never been able to resist the way she grinned up at him, knowing full well that if any female in the household had the ability to twist him about her little finger, it was she. She also had a knack for saying the most outrageous things in such a youthful manner that she often caught him off guard. Today was no exception.

"I won't be easy to please when it comes to a husband," she announced precociously, then climbed onto the edge of his desk. She crossed her legs at the ankles and folded her hands in her small lap. "When I'm old enough to fall in love, I shall find a nice young farmer, smile at him in just the right way, and have the whole thing over with before my eighteenth birthday. You will have to marry one day, and Winnifred has her eye on at least an earl, so my husband can be whomever I wish him to be. Papa said so."

"God help me," Marshall groaned mockingly. "Prince, farmer, or fisherman, I pity the poor man who falls under your thumb."

Catherine raised her hands, inspecting them thoroughly before she replied. "But they are both very nice thumbs. Don't you agree, my lord?"

He laughed, then snatched up her hand and kissed one of the aforementioned digits before shooing her off the corner of his desk. "Young ladies do not perch. They sit."

"You sound like Mama."

"How is she?" Marshall asked, grateful there was nothing on his desk that required his immediate attention. When Catherine settled in for a talk, she rambled on in a guileless fashion, always startling him with her blunt presentation.

"Brooding, as usual," she announced with blank honesty.

"Should I have Dr. Bradshaw attend her?"

"She isn't sick, Marshall, she's brooding. An elixir won't bring back her spirits."

Catherine's insight never ceased to amaze him. "I'll talk to her again."

"She needs to laugh," his sister stated. "Papa always made her laugh."

"She loved him very much."

"I know that," Catherine replied somewhat stiffly. Since Marshall couldn't disagree, he simply listened. "She's upset with me, you know."

He eyed her pensively for a moment, then asked, "Why?"

"Because I told her she should marry Uncle Robert."

Robert Hants, the Earl of Kniveton, had been a close friend of their father's. He had never married. If he thought to take a wife to add to the comfort of his later years, Marshall wouldn't gainsay him. He and Constance would make a good match. As usual, leave it up to Catherine to see the possibility long before anyone else.

"We have to be patient, sweetheart. Your mother will put her mourning aside one day, and when that day comes, she'll laugh again." Marshall hoped he wasn't being overly optimistic.

"Well, I hope it's soon," Catherine said with a maturity that outweighed her tender years. "Winnifred is taking this coming-out business much too seriously; you're off to Parliament or your club whenever you aren't escorting her about town; mother stays in her room, dressed in black and swooning whenever she doesn't want to talk about something. It's all becoming too much, I tell you."

Marshall masked a laugh by clearing his throat. "Parliament will be adjourning soon. Then it's off to the country for clean air and sunshine and walks on the beach. Can you manage a few more weeks?"

"I'll try." She climbed down from the desk, giving him a mischievous smile before pressing her advantage. "Will you let me sail with you in the regatta?"

"Absolutely not," Marshall said. "The club would have my colors if I smuggled a blond pixie on board."

"I'll bring you luck."

"You'll make me old before my time," he vowed. "Now, off with you. I have letters to answer and an opera to attend."

"But you hate the opera," Catherine reminded him before skipping out of the room.

Evelyn opened the door to find the marquis, looking exceptionally handsome.

"May I come in?"

"Of course," she said, uncertain if she was happy or sad to see the gentleman again. No amount of window staring or bed napping had been able to erase the marquis from her thoughts. In fact, one kiss had permanently planted him in her mind. Fate was having fun with her, teasing her senses with a man who was beyond her reach.

"I trust you had a pleasant day," Marshall said, thinking she looked much better than she had the previous evening. Her eyes were bright, her hair glowing as if she'd just brushed it. He preferred it tied back from her face, flowing down her back and teasing the curve of her hips when she moved. The color was a rich golden brown that would shine like burnished gold in the sunlight.

"Pleasant enough," Evelyn replied, wishing she hadn't spent most of it thinking about the marquis. She'd be much better off if he didn't possess a gentleman's charm. It would be her undoing, if Lady Monfrey's charges didn't ruin her life first.

"Since you do not have a wrap, I will not ask you to fetch it. Fortunately, it is a pleasant evening."

"For what purpose is it pleasant, my lord?"

Marshall frowned. She was back to my lording him. "For a ride in my carriage. It is waiting."

As much as she wanted to get out of the room, Evelyn

was hesitant to let the marquis know it. The man already had far too much power over her.

"Come," he said, opening the door. "If you have anything to take, gather it now. We will not be returning."

It would be a waste of breath to remind him that all she had were the clothes on her back. He was being polite, nothing more. Good manners were the inbred teaching of the aristocracy.

Evelyn allowed herself to be escorted downstairs. She'd had her eyes closed when the marquis, she refused to think of him as Marshall, had carried her inside, so she hadn't seen more than the rented room. Looking around her now, she could see that the inn would be considered one of the best in the city. The widow, who had carried her lunch upstairs and served up a few minutes of idle conversation along with the food, was nowhere in sight. Since the dinner hour was not yet upon them, the main parlor was empty of customers. Evelyn knew the evening coaches would have it filled soon enough

When they stepped outside, she blinked her eyes against the vivid light. The day had been breezy, with alternating bouts of cloudiness and sunshine. The approaching sunset was an ethereal display of deep purples, subtle golds, and crimson red. She paused for a moment to enjoy it. After her experience in Clerkenwell, she vowed never to take such beauty for granted again.

It had been a pleasant day that was turning into an even more impressive evening. The air was sharp, the fading sunlight falling clean and bright upon the paving stones of the courtyard. There was the slightest tingle of a chill in the air, but it wasn't uncomfortable. In fact, she found it refreshing. She looked toward the waiting carriage. It appeared to have been freshly washed and polished, its harnesses jingling musically as the matched bays snorted, impatient to be on their way. Somewhere in the distance, a dog barked, and the voice of a street vendor could be heard marketing his wares. A normal day for most, but not for Evelyn. She was walking beside a marquis, her hand resting lightly on his arm, as if she was the grandest of ladies instead of an accused criminal in a wrinkled skirt.

As the marquis handed her into the carriage, Evelyn was aware of what a contrast they made. Fortunately, there was no one in the courtyard to take note of their departure.

"Where are we going?" she asked as he seated himself.

"It's a surprise."

"I'm not sure I like surprises," she told him. "The last two days have had more than their share."

"This is a pleasant surprise," Marshall assured her.

Instead of thinking about the handsome man seated across from her, Evelyn turned her thoughts to the previous morning and Madame La Roschelle's shop. She mentally retraced her steps, the time spent in the fitting room with Lady Monfrey, and each minute thereafter, trying to pinpoint when the brooch might have become insecure and fallen from the lady's lapel. Had it come loose when Lady Monfrey had bumped into her, and if so, then where could it have ended up, under the table skirt of a display table, or perhaps tangled in the fringe of the fitting room curtains? What if the brooch wasn't found? What if it had, indeed, been stolen? There was little hope the real thief would surrender it to the authorities. Where would that leave her?

"I specifically asked you not to worry."

Evelyn stirred from her thoughts and found herself staring into a pair of dark eyes. "That would be like asking me not to breathe, my lord. I am charged with a crime I did not commit with no means to prove my innocence. What would you have me do?"

"Trust me," he replied. "I have promised that you will not be returned to Clerkenwell, nor any place like it. I may not have Lord Monfrey's political influence, but I am not without means. A defense will be prepared and presented. The charges will be dropped."

"You make it all sound so easy. I suppose I shouldn't be surprised. Your class is a world apart from mine, is it not? Tell me, is the upcoming surprise part of my seduction?"

Marshall bristled, but he didn't deny the accusation. It was, after all, the truth. "Somehow I think it will take more than a modest house in a pleasant neighborhood to bring about your seduction, Miss Dennsworth."

"A house!"

"I see the idea excites you."

Evelyn didn't know what to say. The idea of having a house, no matter how modest, was indeed exciting. She had lived in cramped quarters for so long it would be heaven having more than one room to call her own. Her excitement faded as she realized that the house wouldn't really be hers. It would belong to the marquis, the same way he wanted her to belong to him. A possession to be enjoyed at his leisure.

She considered saying as much, then decided against it. If Lord Waltham was set upon seduction, he'd learn soon enough that she was not some country lass schooled in the kitchen. Her circumstances were desperate, but her self-worth was fully intact.

Marshall refused to let her sink back into silence. Instead, he began to talk about Parliament and Palmerston's latest speech, one that had raised several shouts of protest from the more liberal members of the legislature.

When the carriage finally came to a stop, after following a path from New Kent Road to St. George's, then onto Lambeth Road, Evelyn had to keep herself from pushing back the curtains. It wouldn't do to show her enthusiasm.

"I hope you like it," Marshall said, opening the door. He stepped down first, then offered his hand.

Evelyn stared at the house. It was red brick, two stories

high, with white columns fronting the doorway. A waist-
high, wrought-iron fence separated it from the street. She
glanced up and down the avenue, seeing a neat row of similar houses. It was a nice neighborhood where the residents
were given to keeping their shrubbery trimmed and the
streets swept clean of horse droppings. Trees lined the paved
walkway in front of the houses, their shade more shadow
now that the sun had set.

"Inside with you," Marshall said, offering his arm.

They were greeted at the door by a stout man with a wide
nose and a spark of candor in his eyes. "Milord," he said, accepting the hat and gloves Marshall passed his way. "Miss
Dennsworth," he added, greeting her in turn.

"This is Grunne," Marshall told her. Druggs had supplied
the names of the servants along with other information re-
garding the house. "He and his wife will be seeing to your
comfort."

Servants! The only servant her father had been able to afford was a complaining washwoman who had never used
enough starch to keep his vicar's collar stiff.

Since the house was small, Marshall had no problem finding the parlor. He thought the room a disaster. The furnishings
were too dark, the windows too small, but the expression on
Evelyn's face was priceless. She looked very much like she
had the first time he had kissed her. Surprised and pleasantly
pleased. He found himself wondering what kind of home she
had left behind in Sussex.

Evelyn forgot her prior decision to show indifference to
the residence. She turned slowly around, taking in each corner of the room. There was an echo of masculinity about it.
The air held the slight odor of old cigar smoke, but a thorough airing would soon have it smelling fresh. The room had
possibilities, a vase of flowers on the corner table, lace pan-
els beneath the heavy drapes. If the dark green chair in the
corner were to be redone in a bold stripe . . . Her eye for

color and texture took over, and she saw the room the way it could be, cozy and pleasant.

Her gaze moved to a set of glass-paned doors that led outside. She could see a small garden. It looked to be neglected, but a few roses were still stubbornly blooming among the greedy weeds. She hadn't worked in a garden since leaving Sussex. Suddenly her hands itched to be knuckle deep in the dirt, nourishing the flowers back to life.

"Forgive me for rushing you into the house before Mrs. Grunne could see to a proper cleaning," Marshall said apologetically.

"There's nothing to forgive," Evelyn said, turning to look at her benefactor. How did one thank a man for an entire house? Especially when that man had every intention of seducing her into sharing one of the bedrooms?

Before Marshall could suggest a tour, a matronly female, wearing a maid's apron, appeared in the doorway. Her hair was braided and pinned around the crown of her head, making her face seem overly round. A sagging chin danced as she moved, brushing against the collar of her dress, but she was smiling bright enough to make one forget those details.

"Henry told me yer had arrived, milord," she said, dipping into an awkward curtsey. "I'm sorry things ain't as they should be. There was no time, what with Mr. Druggs renting the place right away and the kitchen bein' such a fright. Will the lady be wanting tea?"

"The lady's name is Evelyn," she said, introducing herself. "And a cup of tea would be earnestly appreciated. Thank you, Mrs. Grunne."

The maid excused herself and hurried toward the kitchen.

"I wonder what she expected," Evelyn said in a chilly tone that bordered on blatant rudeness. "An actress with a painted face, no doubt."

Marshall was too accustomed to females and their ways to be baited by the remark. "What servants expect or don't expect isn't the issue. They are being paid to work, not pass judgment."

"How convenient," Evelyn retorted, knowing full well what Mrs. Grunne and her husband had to be thinking. "What of the neighbors, my lord? Am I to present myself as a spinster or a grieving widow?"

"You may tell them anything you like."

His tone was as sarcastic as hers had been. Evelyn sought a way to rephrase her words, to make them more acceptable, but there was none. The marquis had set her up in a house. There was only one reason that a man of his rank would do such a thing. The moment she had walked through the door, she had become his mistress by name if not by deed.

"I should apologize, my lord," she replied, realizing she had spoken too harshly, even though her remarks fitted the occasion. "I suppose you find it overly rude of me to be biting the only hand in London that cares to see me fed."

Suddenly she began to laugh. Marshall's astonishment was just as great as her own. He waited for her to collect herself, wondering if she was having a bout of delayed hysteria. When she finally spoke, her eyes were damp with tears.

"You are a puzzlement to me," she admitted, sitting down on the sofa. "I would have to be a simpleton not to recognize your motives. Yet, your kindness overwhelms me."

"Perhaps our meeting was fortuitous," he said, smiling down at her.

"Perhaps, but I doubt that Godly providence had anything to do with it. My father would call it the devil's own luck."

"Your father? Does he still live in Sussex?"

Evelyn shook her head. "Both my parents are gone. My mother when I was very young, my father several years past. He was a scholarly man. A theorist, if you will."

That explained her educated ways. Marshall longed to stay and talk to her, to learn more about her, but he was pressed for time. Damn the opera, he almost said, then stopped himself. He knelt by her side, then reached out and brushed a wayward tear from her face with the pad of his thumb.

"What kind of man are you?" she asked in a whisper.

"One that finds you very desirable," he replied candidly.

"I made use of the mirror before we left the lodge. There is nothing about my appearance that provokes such a compliment."

"The mirror doesn't see the same thing I do."

At a loss for words, Evelyn simply looked into his eyes. The question she had posed was a valid one. Who was this man who had suddenly stepped into her life and turned it upside down? She had reminded herself a hundred times during the long day that they had nothing in common, nothing upon which to base a friendship, but for some strange reason, she found herself wanting to be his friend, sensing that he needed one as desperately as she did.

"I am forced to leave you again," he said, sounding regretful. "Obligations." He shrugged his well-tailored shoulders. "The opera."

Evelyn tried not to frown. Few of the aristocracy attended the opera for love of music. It was a social event. Would the marquis be escorting his sister or one of the fashionable young ladies of society, a potential bride perhaps? The question was irrelative. Of course he mingled with the most beautiful women in London. He was a marquis, a man of wealth and power, who would one day select a wife from the elite of the realm. Just as his sister would pick a husband from among his peers. On the other hand, her station as an ordinary woman delegated that she seek a husband from among the tradesmen and farmers who shared her common heritage. For the first time in her life, Evelyn felt inadequate.

"Then, by all means, don't let me be the cause of your tardiness," she said, keeping her voice neutral. "I'm sure I can settle in well enough with Mrs. Grunne's help."

"I dislike leaving you so quickly."

Evelyn forced a cordial smile to her face. "You have already done more than I can ever thank you for, my lord. Please do not be distressed over such a minor thing. I'm sure your obligations are far more important than my discovering my way about the house."

He was being dismissed. It was almost amusing how graciously she was going about it. Marshall wasn't sure if he should laugh or remind her that he was the one renting the house she was tactfully asking him to leave.

"I will call upon you tomorrow," he informed her, doing his best to push aside the conflicting emotions she evoked. "Until then, do as I ask. Put your worries aside."

"I will try, my lord." She didn't come to her feet. If she did, Evelyn was sure he would pull her into his arms and kiss her again.

Unfortunately, the marquis was a resourceful man.

He raised her hand, turned it palm up, and placed a kiss against the sensitive flesh of her inner wrist. As his mouth pressed against her skin, Evelyn couldn't help but feel the supple glide of his tongue across her pulse point. She'd never been more aware of him than at that very moment. She could feel his breath. The fading sunlight, coming through the French doors, caught in his thick hair, causing it to gleam. The hand holding hers was strong and warm.

"My lord," she said, her voice shaky. She closed her eyes, hoping the feelings would subside, but it only served to make them more intense.

The kiss was like a brush of hot air over her nerve endings. Sensual and slow, provoking yet tender. A quiver of pure pleasure raced up her arm, then went deeper, entering the most private parts of her body.

Instead of releasing her, Marshall turned the caress into a dance. His used the tip of his tongue, moving it in a lazy circle over her skin, forcing her to feel everything he could make her feel. His nostrils flared slightly as he inhaled the scent of her. Soap and warm woman, clean, vibrant, and so alive it was all he could do not to drag her down on the floor and bury himself in her until everything else faded into oblivion.

When he did release her hand, Evelyn felt light-headed. Uneasiness swept through her as she realized just how vulnerable she was to a man of his charms. She was too honest with herself not to realize that if she allowed him to continue trying to seduce her, she would probably find herself surrendering. But even as she told herself to be wary of the marquis, she couldn't help but be aware of him as only a woman could be aware of a man. It was a staggering realization, one that made her breath catch in her throat.

Marshall looked at her, knowing she had experienced the same primal emotion that was rippling through his own body. He could see it in the dilation of her eyes and the slight trembling of her body. He wanted her more at that moment than he'd ever wanted another woman. He wanted her laughter and her stinging wit, her tears and the warmth of her body, the quiet hours just before dawn and the passionate ones that came in the darkest hours of the night. It was difficult to gather his thoughts. All he could think about was the sweet passion that would erupt the moment he joined their bodies.

He smiled to himself. It was only a matter of time before the attraction between them erupted into an explosion neither one would be able to control. The knowledge helped him to keep his patience. "Until tomorrow, Miss Dennsworth," he said, turning her name into another caress before leaving her to her own thoughts.

Six

Marshall left as soon as the House rose, leaving the parliamentary hall, passing the statue of Richard the Lionhearted, and hurrying toward his carriage. After giving the driver instructions, he settled back against the well-cushioned seat as the carriage clattered past St. Stephen's Tower where Big Ben was striking the hour. Within minutes the driver was making his way across Westminster Bridge.

Marshall used the time it would take to reach the small house near the junction of Lambeth and St. George's Road to consider his good fortune. It wasn't the best way to think of poor Winnie's ailment, brought on by what he suspected was too much goose liver the previous evening, but at least he didn't have to suffer the Granmers' ball. His sister had sent her regrets to the lord and lady, which meant his schedule was clear to spend the evening with Evelyn.

He had thought about her most of the day, finding the distraction both pleasing and frustrating. On more than one occasion his conscience had started prickling. Although she was a woman full grown, she was still an innocent. Seduction was something he hadn't counted on when making the decision to seek a mistress. Had he picked a willing widow, seduction wouldn't be necessary at all, no more than the short masquerade such a woman would require for vanity's sake.

But having chosen Miss Evelyn Dennsworth, Marshall was looking forward to the challenge. Hers would be a gentle wooing, one that would soon have the lady admitting that she desired him as much as he desired her. It would be a mutual decision, when the time came, for he was still determined to have her walk willingly into his arms.

As the carriage slowed in front of the house on Lambeth Road, Marshall found himself wondering how Evelyn had passed the day. It hadn't been well done of him to deposit her so abruptly then rush to the opera. Stepping down from the carriage, he thought of several ways he could make it up to her. Each one of them began with a kiss.

Grunne met him at the door. The servant informed him that Miss Dennsworth could be found in the garden, then asked if his lordship would be taking dinner with the lady.

"Yes," Marshall informed him, before strolling into the parlor and out the doors that led to the small private garden at the rear of the house. He saw Evelyn almost immediately.

She was wearing a dove gray skirt and blue blouse. Her thick fall of golden brown hair was held back with a ribbon. He watched as she plucked a rose from one of the bushes. Holding it gently between her fingers, she twirled it one way then another, watching the fading light play upon its pink petals. Hearing his footsteps, she turned to face him.

Marshall smiled, his first true smile of the day. He watched the rise and fall of her breasts, saw the tremor of awareness that went through her as he approached, and hoped that she had missed him one-tenth as much as he had found himself missing her.

The moment she saw the marquis, Evelyn felt the air grow suddenly warm, as though the sun were rising instead of setting. Her heart began to pound wildly as he came closer and closer, his features outlined in the last of the day's light.

She had awakened that morning more determined than ever to end the charade he insisted on playing. No good would come from allowing him to believe that she would compromise herself and become his mistress. The most she could hope for was a ruined life and a broken heart if she allowed herself to be seduced into his bed. He had come into her life so quickly, so abruptly, and considering the charges against her, he could disappear just as easily. It wouldn't do to become overly dependent upon him. Reminding herself to keep her wits about her, she greeted him with a cordial smile. "Hello, your lordship."

"Hello," he said, thinking she looked more beautiful each time he saw her. "You look rested. May I presume that you find the house to your liking?"

"It is very comfortable," she replied. "Mrs. Grunne and her husband have endeavored to make me feel at home."

"As they should. I want you to think of it as your home."

Evelyn's smile faded. Still holding the rose, she walked to a nearby bench, one of three in the small stone-walled garden that separated the house from the neighboring residences. She had taken his advice and had not offered any explanation to either Mrs. Grunne or her husband as to why she had taken up residence. Nor had she made any mention of the unfortunate circumstances that had brought her and the Marquis of Waltham together. Time would prove that she was not the lord's mistress.

Knowing she had to say what was on her mind, Evelyn framed her thoughts, then chose her words carefully. Now was not the time for euphemisms. "My lord, I cannot thank you enough for all that you have done for me. Words are inadequate to express what I fear I can never repay, but in all honesty, and I must be honest, this house can never be my home."

"Let us get one thing clear, Miss Dennsworth," Marshall said. "I do not want to spend our time together replying 'you are welcome' to your endless stream of 'thank you, my lord.' Please let the gratitude you have expressed up to this point be sufficient. In addition, I will once again request that you forego formality when addressing me in private. My name is Marshall."

Evelyn had inherited her father's strong will and his flare for speaking the truth no matter how inappropriate. Needing both at the moment, she did not hesitate to use them. "Very well, my lord." She used the address with a deliberate tone. "I have spent the majority of the day thinking about my current circumstances and your part in them. It seems I have no recourse but to speak bluntly."

Marshall's smile was pure devilry. "By all means," he said, sitting down at the opposite end of the bench so they could converse at eye level.

It was apparent that Evelyn was preparing to give him a verbal dressing down for his sinful intentions. She was a stubborn bit of baggage, he thought, as she folded her hands in her lap and straightened her shoulders. God, how he wanted to kiss her, to put an end to all this prim and proper behavior. The fire in her blood could be put to much better use.

"I will not be your mistress," she said firmly, holding up her hand when he would have interrupted her. "The more I contemplate the *friendship* you request from me, the more apparent it becomes that your definition of the term differs greatly from mine. I cannot in all good conscience surrender so easily the principles my parents instilled in me." Evelyn glanced around the garden. It was easier to keep her thoughts flowing when she wasn't distracted by the marquis's handsome face. "Therefore, I will make arrangements to find other lodging. As I mentioned, I have some funds. Granted, they are small compared to the fortune associated with the Bedford name, but hopefully adequate enough to sustain me until I can find other employment. I will, of course, inform Magistrate Rivenhall of my whereabouts."

"How old are you?"

The unexpected question brought her head around.

"I'm aware that it's an inappropriate question to ask a lady, but I'm curious," Marshall clarified the request. "Indulge me."

"Twenty and six."

"And your birthday?"

Evelyn shook her head. "The twelfth day of September. My lord, if one did not know better, one would think you suffer from a hearing impairment. Have you not heard what I have been saying?"

"Every word, my lovely Evelyn," he responded with a smile that sent a peculiar rush of emotion through her body. "Do you have any brothers or sisters?"

"Don't think to change my mind," she said impatiently. "I will not stand idly by while you seduce me with a charming smile and gentlemanly ways. Be assured that pretending to ignore my decision will not change it."

"I am endeavoring to become acquainted," Marshall told her. He wasn't ignoring her words, but he was determined to change her mind. "This is how people become acquainted. They exchange bits of information about themselves. You will admit that this is the first opportunity we've had to converse freely. Therefore, you tell me about your family, and I will do my best not to bore you with details of my own."

Evelyn laughed in spite of herself. "You are not a gentleman. You are a rascal of the worst sort."

Marshall threw back his head and laughed so loudly a small wren, nesting in one of the garden bushes, flapped it wings. Chirping indignantly, it sought refuge in a tree at the far end of the garden. "You are a delight," he said. Suddenly he found himself wanting the moment never to end. He enjoyed debating with the woman who was slowly revealing herself to be a charming adversary. "You must have brothers. I have found from my own experience that my sisters use me to sharpen their tongues."

"There are no brothers. Nor sisters," she informed him, deciding she would have to reconsider her forthright approach. It was apparent the marquis was having none of it. "If my tongue is sharp, it is because my father insisted upon the truth no matter how disquieting. Once instilled, it is a habit hard to break."

His interest peaked. "And what was the dreadful truth? Don't tell me that the lovely young woman who sits before me today was once a childish hellion, climbing trees and stealing sweets from the kitchen."

"It was an apple," Evelyn told him.

"Ahhh, the forbidden fruit."

There was a subtle change in his tone, and Evelyn would have had to be a complete fool not to notice it. Deciding she might be able to best the marquis at his own game, she continued, saying, "I stole an apple from a church basket. I was only five at the time, not yet old enough to understand that the food had been collected for a higher cause than my own immediate hunger. Father saw me. Needless to say, he did not hesitate to enlighten me as to my Christian duty."

Marshall found himself laughing again. Knowing fathers, he could well imagine how Evelyn's had enlightened her. He could also imagine her as a little girl with a tangle of golden brown curls hanging down her back and an impish nose that found its way into everything.

"As restitution for eating the apple, I had to scrub the rectory steps."

"An enlightening experience if ever I've heard one," Marshall conceded.

"There were twenty-two of them, inside and out," Evelyn informed him. "A formidable task for a five-year-old, but one that taught me a lesson I have never forgotten. It is wrong to take that which was never intended for your possession."

Her arrow hit home with unmistakable accuracy. Not only was Evelyn reaffirming her innocence about Lady Monfrey's brooch, but she was telling Marshall that her virginity was intended for the man she would one day marry and none other. As a dressing down, it was one of the best he'd ever received.

Looking at her, Marshall got the uneasy feeling that his next question was not going to bring about an answer that would please him. "You mentioned that your father was a scholar of sorts. What exactly was his vocation?"

"He was vicar of a small parish north of Sussex," she replied.

"You might have told me," Marshall groaned, giving Evelyn her rightful due. Her ingenuous face was luminous with delight, an expression that increased his desire rather than diminishing it.

A virgin, and a vicar's daughter!

Persuading a woman of twenty-six years out of her innocence was one thing; seducing the daughter of a man of the cloth was something altogether different.

"As you pointed out, we have had little time to converse," Evelyn said, knowing she had caught him totally off guard.

"Most certainly a delight," he said, surprising her even more.

The casual affair he'd been seeking was taking on a far more complex design. Marshall knew he should retreat, having been given the opportunity, but he couldn't. Which meant that he'd lost either his mind or his morals.

Standing up, he offered her his hand. "The garden is small enough for me to see in one setting, but I've yet to have a tour of the house. Would you accompany me?"

Evelyn frowned, but she didn't refrain from accepting his

hand. The sun had set behind the trees, casting the garden into golden shadows that would soon take on the softer, muted shades of twilight. The air had taken on a slight chill, and she didn't have a shawl at hand.

He had removed his gloves upon entering the house, and she felt the unsettling touch of his skin next to hers. A frisson of awareness overtook her as he casually placed her hand, palm down, on his folded arm. They stood for the length of a heartbeat, his eyes searching her face, her mind unable to think of anything to say that would break the silence.

Then, as if he realized the moment was becoming awkward for her, he turned slightly to the side, breaking the intense contact of their gazes, and began to walk toward the house. Evelyn fell into step beside him, thinking she would have to stay on her toes around the man. He was becoming more alluring by the moment.

They walked through the parlor, with its too dark, over-furnished appearance, and into the foyer. Neither Mr. Grunne nor his wife were anywhere to be seen. Thinking the library, across the hall, might be the safest place to start, Evelyn disengaged herself from the marquis's gentle hold. The doors gave way with a slight creaking of hinges that she would ask Grunne to oil first thing in the morning.

As expected, the library was as much of a disaster as the parlor. The desk was large and cumbersome. A small desk globe sat at a precocious angle, displaying the lower hemisphere rather than the stately Isles of Britain. The remaining furniture was done in a profusion of dark woods that gave the room a morbid influence. Curtains that had once been a deep crimson red now hung dully over the windows, their vibrant color faded to a muddy brownish red, reminding Marshall of dried blood.

"It's an insult to the eye," he said harshly. "I apologize."

"New drapes would make a vast improvement," Evelyn

said, sensing he was embarrassed. She looked at him instead of the atrocious boar's head hanging over the fireplace. "I sometimes think the aristocracy oversensitive, my lord. No apology is needed unless you furnished the room yourself." Her remark gained her a slight smile, so she continued. "The carpet is too dark and the furniture crowded too tightly together, but the room is of ample proportion. With a little attention it could be righted."

"You are an optimist, Miss Dennsworth. The only way to right this room would be to burn the house down."

In that moment, Evelyn longed to prove him wrong. How she would love to take charge of this fine little house, to turn it into the home she longed for, to toss the heavy draperies into the fire and replace them with lighter ones that would let sunlight and warmth flood the rooms. The furnishings were old and heavy, but with the right patterns and positioning, she knew she could create a male haven where Marshall could relax. She could picture him now, sitting behind the massive desk in casual repose, his jacket cast aside, a brandy at his fingertips.

Realizing the direction of her thoughts, Evelyn immediately reminded herself that she would not be staying in the house. She had voiced her decision to leave, and she had every intention of vacating the premises as soon as she could get up the nerve to ask Mr. Grunne for the loan of the hansom fare she would need to travel to the bank.

Marshall strolled about the room, wiggling his nose in disgust at the drab colors and tight quarters created by a sofa large enough to seat three elephants sitting abreast. When his gaze wandered higher, he shook his head. The molting boar's head over the mantel was missing one tusk, greatly lessening the animal's original ferocity.

He turned to find Evelyn inspecting the room. Her expression said she was seeing it from a different point of view. An idea came to mind, and he immediately acted upon it. She had told him that the house could never be her home, but if she had a hand in its transformation, her mind might be changed. "I shall arrange for the household allowance to be increased. I care not what you do with this room, but please make it habitable as quickly as possible. I do enjoy a quiet brandy when I'm reading the *Evening Mail*. If Grunne requires an additional man to help with the furniture, then hire one."

Since he was looking directly at her as he spoke, she was unable to disguise the instant pleasure that overtook her features. Marshall knew he had baited the proper hook to catch his lovely little fish when she immediately tried to look anything but happy over his request.

"I'm sure you can find—"

"You have said that you wish to repay me in some small way," he interrupted her. "After viewing this room, I am now willing to let you. I beseech you, make this house livable, if not for yourself, then for me."

"But you reside in Mayfair, my lord."

"You are going to be difficult no matter what, aren't you?" He moved toward her, his lithe stride not unlike that of a stalking cat.

Fortunately, Mr. Grunne chose that moment to announce that dinner was served. Evelyn looked from the footman to the marquis. It seemed that her benefactor would not be dashing out the door this evening.

The thought of them sharing a meal as though they were residing in a normal household was disquieting. She could handle the dinner hour well enough. Grunne would be there as footman, his presence at the serving board all the defense she required. It was the interlude following dinner that had Evelyn worried. Whether she liked it or not, the marquis meant to linger.

"Come," Marshall said, placing her hand on his arm.

"Shall we see if we can find the dining room. I suddenly find myself very hungry."

The innuendo was unmistakable, but he was holding her hand much too tightly for Evelyn to think she could free herself. He escorted her into the foyer, then turned in the direction of voices, the house being small enough for them to hear Mrs. Grunne's flustered remark that this would be the first meal they would be serving the marquis, thus it had to be perfect.

Once they were seated in the dining room, Marshall immediately pointed out the room's shortcomings. "You should have plenty to keep yourself occupied," he remarked as they began the meal with a thick asparagus soup. "Every room in the house seems to need attention."

Evelyn refrained from replying. Grunne was standing behind her, posed to serve the next course. Deciding silence would serve her better than trite words, she concentrated on her food.

Marshall sensed what she was about. He instructed Grunne to set the dishes on the table, then dismissed him, insinuating that he and the lady preferred to dine without an audience.

Evelyn remained silent until the footman quit the room, then turned to look at the man sitting at the head of the table. "You are, without a doubt, the most irritating man I have ever met. Is there no way I can convince you that your intentions, while flattering, are wasted."

"No," he replied candidly. "Nor can you convince me that you aren't itching to redecorate this dreadful house." When she set her mouth in a hard line, he laughed. "Where is the admirable honesty you were speaking of earlier, Miss Dennsworth?"

She relented with a frustrated sigh. "Very well, my lord. I would dearly love to take this neglected house under my wing. It is a project that would keep me occupied for months. But need I remind you again that I have no intention of remaining under this roof."

"Need I remind you that you are under my authority," he said, his expression suddenly stern. "I gave the magistrate my word that I would see to your comfort."

"You bribed him into giving me over," she retorted, recalling Rivenhall's choice of words. "That is not the same thing, and well you know it."

"The end result remains the same."

"Then I am a prisoner here, as I was at Clerkenwell."

Marshall tossed his napkin to the table. "Damnation, woman! Must you twist every word I say."

"You requested honesty of me," she reminded him.

"Then be honest with yourself," he said more harshly than he intended. "You are without funds, accused of theft, and soon to stand before the bench. You are under my care, whether it pleases you or not. Why make a difficult situation worse by fighting me at every turn?"

"Because if I don't fight you, I'll—" Evelyn stopped herself before blurting out the words. It was not her manner to rant and rave. She had been raised with quiet dignity, and she refused to relinquish it. Removing her napkin from her lap, she laid it beside her plate and swept out of the room before the marquis could stop her. "If you'll excuse me, my lord. I find my appetite lacking."

Marshall watched her go, angry with himself for losing his temper.

Evelyn stopped in the middle of the foyer. She wanted to go upstairs and shut herself away in the bedroom, but she wasn't certain Lord Waltham wouldn't come looking for her. Deciding on fresh air instead, she took a shawl from the closet in the foyer and returned to the garden.

The roses she had been tending before the marquis's arrival were now dressed in moonlight. Evelyn drew the shawl more closely about her shoulders and looked up at the waning moon. She had always had faith that her destiny would be found in a dress shop, among bolts of silk and satin. Beyond that dream, she had sometimes thought of a husband and a family, but never in specific terms. And never had she imagined her life becoming so intricately entwined with a man like the Marquis of Waltham.

Marshall finished his dinner, taking time to compliment Mrs. Grunne on the broiled turbot she had served. The matronly servant blushed; then being too well versed in her role to inquire about Evelyn's unfinished meal, she began clearing the table.

Marshall retired to the library, unpleasant as it was, to smoke a cigar and think. Relaxing in a somewhat lumpy wingback chair, he considered the challenge he had undertaken. His lot in life was not an unhappy one. He loved his family, enjoyed the estates he had inherited, and the time he spent sailing. The only thing he lacked was a woman who could satisfy his physical needs without the complications of marriage.

What he had found was an unexpected virgin, a vicar's daughter. It was almost laughable that he, a man of experienced means, was now sitting in an ill-furbished library suffering from sexual frustration. If he had any sense, he'd leave Miss Evelyn Dennsworth to her high-and-mighty morals and find another female.

If he had any sense?

He frowned. The question was becoming redundant. A riddle without an obvious answer, a puzzle as perplexing as it was challenging.

Deciding he could either retreat to his club or do his best to resurrect the evening, Marshall snubbed out the thin cheroot in a small brass ashtray and went in search of Evelyn.

It took only a few minutes to find her.

"We seem to be forever walking out on one another."

Evelyn turned to find the marquis standing surprisingly close. She blamed herself for being engrossed in a bout of self-pity. Had she been thinking clearly, she would have heard his boots on the flat stones of the walkway. She looked at the black onyx pin in his cravat, rather than his face, and replied, "Perhaps it is because we are at cross purposes, my lord."

"A situation I am doing my best to rectify, if only you will stop seeing me as a seducer of innocents. My motives may not be those of a saint, but I do want to be your friend."

She met his gaze then, and for a brief second she could almost believe him. "It may be obdurate of me, my lord, but I cannot allow myself to entertain a friendship that will gain me nothing but the title of mistress."

Marshall had thought his anger under control, but it rose again, like trout to a well-baited hook. "Then allow this, my lovely Miss Dennsworth."

Before she could think to stop him, Evelyn found herself in his arms. Instead of the gentle, arousing kisses he had given her in the past, his mouth was hard and hungry, punishing her in the most seductive way possible.

She trembled, both in response to his kiss and to the knowledge that she wasn't being nearly as stubborn as she should be. There was no way she could prevent herself from reacting to the marquis's touch. Especially when he softened the kiss, running his tongue along the seam of her lips, enticing them to open. When they did, he took her mouth with a carnality that made her legs go weak. Warm pleasure began to radiate from the very depths of her, and Evelyn knew she had lost another battle in the ongoing war.

Slowly Marshall lifted his mouth. It was all he could do not to drag her into the shadows and take what he wanted. He took a deep breath of cool air, forcing his body to relax.

Restraint had never been a problem before. Why did this woman make it seem an impossible task? He tipped her chin up, waiting until she met his gaze.

"I have promised that I will not use force or circumstance against you," he said. "I will keep my word."

Still dazed by his kiss, Evelyn stared up at him.

"You will learn to trust me," he said. "And I will trust you when you tell me that you will not run away. You will remain here and let me aid in your defense."

When she didn't reply immediately, he kissed her again. A quick, hard kiss that made her blink with surprise.

"Promise me that you will remain under this roof until you are freed of the charges. Give me your word. And know that whatever happens between us will happen because *we* both want it."

Hoping she could continue to resist what the marquis assumed was inevitable, and realizing that if she had really wanted to leave she could have marched out the door any hour of the day, Evelyn was forced to admit that she was already too deeply involved with the marquis to sneak out in the middle of the night.

"I won't leave," she said, seeing the triumph in his eyes the moment the words were spoken.

"Good, then we can get back to becoming acquainted."

He tugged her inside, picked up his wineglass and sat down on the sofa.

Once Evelyn was seated in a nearby chair, he began to regale her with tales of his childhood and the first time his father had taken him sailing in the Channel. She told him about her dream to own her own dress shop, of the pleasure she gained by creating something beautiful from a bolt of cloth. They talked for several hours, discussing whatever came to mind. Before she knew it, the clock was chiming midnight.

Marshall, acting as casually as possible, stood and

stretched. "The hour is late," he said, knowing full well she wasn't going to invite him to stay the night. He could insist, but then the last few hours would have been in vain. He smiled to himself. Wooing a stubborn young woman was more work than he had expected.

Unsure what to do, Evelyn remained seated. Their conversation had taken her mind off the real reason the marquis had come calling. A momentary panic rose within her when he moved to where she was sitting beside the fireplace. The night was warm, so there had been no reason to light the logs Mr. Grunne had stacked on the grate.

"I will call again as soon as time allows," he told her.

Evelyn wasn't sure if she should be relieved or insulted. One moment the man was acting as if having her was his sole purpose in life, the next he was bidding her good night as though she was an old and dear friend.

"I shall show you to the door," she replied, knowing how ridiculous the remark must sound to him.

"There is no need. I can find my way out."

Accepting that and the fact that the evening had turned out to be an enjoyable one after all, she gave him a cordial smile. "Good night, my lord."

"Marshall," he said. "I shall not leave until you have said it."

"Good night, Marshall."

"Excellent. We are making progress." He leaned down and kissed her then, not the intoxicating way he had kissed her in the garden, but a gentle, lingering kiss that made her body feel so light she grasped the arms of the chair for fear that she might actually float into his embrace.

She sat in the parlor for a long time after he left, thinking about the chain of events that Lady Monfrey's false accusation had started. The marquis was everything the men of her previous acquaintance had not been. He had come to her rescue when she had needed a knight in shining armor. He was

titled, handsome, generous to a fault, highly intelligent, irre-
sistibly charming, and definitely stubborn. But she was strong
enough to resist him.

The problem was, Evelyn wasn't entirely sure she wanted
to resist him.

The nuances of society that made their relationship such
an unorthodox one had to be considered, of course. A
woman's social acceptance was a matter of birth. No matter
how well-mannered or educated she was, her recognition
was dependent upon either her father or her husband. While
highly respected for his devoted lifestyle, her father had still
been a commoner. As for a husband, Evelyn knew she was
spinning dreams around the marquis, but she couldn't help
herself. If he was this kind, this solicitous of a woman he
only wanted to bed, what would he be like with a woman he
truly loved?

Seven

"You have a caller, Miss Dennsworth."

"A caller?" Evelyn turned away from the painting she had been studying, an atrocious battle scene that added to the bleak atmosphere of the library.

"Mr. Druggs," Grunne informed her. "He is employed by Lord Waltham."

"Oh," she said, more than slightly surprised. "Then, I shall see him, of course." She paused midway of the room. "Please ask Mrs. Grunne to serve some refreshments."

Evelyn wondered what Mr. Druggs could possibly want of her. Reminding herself that regardless of what anyone thought she had nothing to be ashamed of, she strolled into the parlor with her chin high.

"Mr. Druggs," she said, smiling at the slenderly built man. He was clean shaven with a long nose, upon which a pair of spectacles were perched. His features expressed a certain seriousness, but his gaze seemed friendly and his manner reassured, as if he thought nothing of the circumstances that had catapulted her into his employer's life.

"Miss Dennsworth," he greeted her in a pleasant but formal tone. "I hope I am not intruding."

"Of course not," she replied, waving him back into the chair. "I must admit some surprise. Lord Waltham did not mention that anyone would be calling."

"I met with his lordship this morning, as is my custom," Druggs explained. "He has delegated certain matters into my hands."

"And those matters concern me?"

"Most assuredly. The first one is of course a household allowance. The marquis mentioned that you have decided to do some refurbishing of the interior. I am to make funds available, including enough to pay for additional servants. However, Lord Waltham was at a loss as to how many you would require. If you will enlighten me, I shall arrange for their temporary employment."

Evelyn looked at him in amazement. "Just like that? I suggest that a carpet or two needs replacing and the marquis sends you to call."

"His lordship wishes for you to be comfortable."

That wasn't all his lordship wished, but Evelyn refrained from commenting on the marquis's personal agenda. "I really don't see the necessity of hiring anyone," she said, determined to get her point across even if she had to do it through a third party. "My tenure here is only temporary. There is no need for Lord Waltham to expend any more funds than he is doing already. I can manage very well with the house in its present state."

Druggs cleared his throat with the ease of a practiced politician. "Lord Waltham made it quite clear that he found the house in need. Will three servants—two footmen and a maid of all work—be sufficient? I can have them here promptly at nine tomorrow morning."

"Are you by any chance related to Lord Waltham?" Evelyn remarked evenly. "I noticed the same hearing impairment in his lordship, or is it an innate stubbornness?"

Druggs's smile was sudden but genuine. "Lord Waltham is a man of strong temperament. I have known him for a good number of years, ever since his father employed my services. Whatever the reason for his actions, I would not presume to interfere, nor would I take it upon myself to do anything but that which he has commissioned me to do."

"Yes, of course," she agreed, keeping the balance of her opinion to herself. "Very well, Mr. Druggs, I do not want you blamed for my lack of enthusiasm. Send the servants if you must."

The secretary quickly moved on to the second item on his list. Evelyn's mouth gaped open. She knew the marquis was a wealthy man, but the amount Mr. Druggs had just mentioned was more than she could earn in a year working for Madame La Roschelle, and he was calling it a *monthly* allowance.

"Miss Dennsworth," he urged after several minutes. "Is there anything else you require?"

Evelyn blinked, then blurted out, "I can't accept it."

"Beg your pardon."

"I can't accept the money," she said adamantly. "I assume that Lord Waltham has informed you of the charges against me." When the secretary nodded, she continued. "He has already been more than generous in providing food and shelter; I cannot allow my debt to him to be increased a hundred fold."

"I do not believe his lordship considers it a debt."

"I do," she told him. "One I intend to repay if at all possible. Please understand that I cannot in good conscience allow the marquis to spend money unnecessarily on my behalf. I have agreed to remain here until such time as I am called to stand before the magistrate. Having given Lord Waltham my word, I will accept whatever allowance is necessary to see myself fed and to provide anything his lordship may require when he calls. Men do like their brandy and cigars."

"Yes, they do," Druggs agreed wholeheartedly.

"As for anything else, I have no immediate needs. Please see that the allowance is reduced accordingly."

"Lord Waltham will not be pleased."

"Then he will not be pleased," she replied levelly.

The smallest flicker of doubt rose in her thoughts, but Evelyn quickly mastered it. She had debated over her feelings most of the night. If she accepted more than was absolutely necessary, purchased a new wardrobe or spent lavishly on the house, then the marquis was sure to think that she was softening to his seduction. There was also the possibility that she could be found guilty of theft. In that case, both a wardrobe and new furnishings would be a waste of time and money.

"Shall we move on to the matter of your legal representation," Druggs said, his diplomatic tone implying that the funds would be deposited into the household account. Whether or not Evelyn used them was a matter to be settled between herself and the marquis. "I have, with Lord Waltham's approval, of course, retained a lawyer for your upcoming defense. His name is James Portsman. He has experience in matters such as yours and an excellent accounting before the bench. I have given him the rudimentary details of the case, but he will need to speak directly with you. Would two weeks from today be convenient?"

"Yes," she agreed. Another necessary debt. If she tried to defend herself, it would turn into nothing more than a plea of innocence that may or may not be believed. Knowing Lady Monfrey's sense of drama, she was going to need someone with oratorical skills.

Mrs. Grunne knocked on the door, then entered, pushing a tea trolley. Evelyn passed a plate of pastries to Mr. Druggs while she poured tea. He studied them carefully, chose one, then smiled before biting into the flaky crust.

They sat silently for a time, Evelyn unsure how to broach the subject of the marquis. Finally, she decided directness had always served her best. "You mentioned that you worked for the late Lord Waltham."

"Yes," Druggs said. "A gentleman of the highest reputation. Always kept his affairs in excellent order." Then, sensing the true cause of her interest, he continued. "The current lord is very much like his father. I must say, I've been very impressed with him since he acquired the title. It wasn't easy for him. He and his father were extremely close, but he rose to the occasion, accepting his responsibilities without hesitation. As I said, he is a man of strong temperament. But he has proven to be fair in his judgment and in the handling of family matters."

A dozen questions came to mind, but Evelyn thought better of asking them. It went without saying that if the marquis trusted Mr. Druggs to be discreet in the handling of her situation, he would display the same attribute when speaking of his employer. Containing her curiosity, she spoke of casual things until Mr. Druggs finished his tea and bid her a good day.

Marshall arrived at the house on Lambeth street late in the afternoon. He anticipated spending a few hours with Evelyn before going on to Brook's for his weekly card game with the Duke of Morland. Grunne greeted him at the door. Knowing precisely whom he'd come to see, the footman promptly informed him that Miss Dennsworth was in the attic.

"The attic! What the blazes is she doing up there?"

"I believe she said something about a treasure hunt, milord," Grunne replied with the utmost dignity.

Peeling off his gloves, Marshall tossed them into his hat, which he then handed off to Grunne before marching up the main staircase. It took only a few moments to find the door to the attic. The amber glow of a gas lantern told him some-one was in residence at the top of the narrow steps that took a sharp turn to the right before disappearing into the loft above the second floor.

A lantern sat in the middle of the attic, barely illuminating the dusty corners. He saw Evelyn on the far side of the cav-ernous room, near the chimney that broke through the floor and climbed upward through the rafters like a great stone tree. The attic was cluttered with boxes and trunks, stacks of unwanted bric-a-brac. It smelled of dust and cloth that needed to be aired. An empty wicker birdcage hung listlessly from one of the rafters. Evelyn was on her knees, rummaging through an old trunk with her backside high in the air. Marshall watched her for some time, smiling all the while.

She pulled an unidentifiable bundle from the trunk, dis-covering him when she turned around to place it on the floor. The lamp cast her face in golden shadows. There was a smudge of dirt on her nose and down her cheek, but he couldn't help thinking she grew more lovely each time he saw her.

"My lord," she said, coming to her feet and hastily brush-ing the dust from her skirt. "I didn't expect to see you this early in the day. I hope nothing is amiss."

"Nothing that a kiss won't cure," he said teasingly, ad-vancing toward her.

Evelyn stepped backward, but the movement put her against the trunk. Another step would have her sitting in it. The first sight of him had brought a disconcerting heat to her body that she was forced to acknowledge as anticipation. The impulse to flee touched her briefly, but his smile van-quished it.

For a long moment, he simply stood and stared at her, as

if he was feeling the same emotional upheaval. If only she could determine what he did feel. If his own heart was at risk, she wouldn't be so reluctant to place hers in jeopardy.

"I missed you today," he said. The clarity of her blue eyes made him think of open skies and windswept seas; things he missed here in the city. What was it about this woman that enticed him so? She was a puzzling combination of strength and vulnerability, determination and dependence, innocence and maturity.

A flush of heated pleasure swept through Evelyn. She had missed him, too, had done nothing but think of him since she'd awakened that morning. Mr. Druggs's visit had escalated the thoughts, bringing the marquis to the forefront of her mind and keeping him there. She'd come to the attic seeking work for her idle hands, hoping to find another focus for her mind. Now he was here, his dark gaze searching her face, his scent, a pleasing hint of expensive cologne and man, tempting her senses.

He reached out and touched her cheek, the very corner of her mouth.

Evelyn knew she should say something, do something, yet she didn't. Her body felt unsettled. His mere presence was triggering things deep within her, things her mind warned her to resist.

But there was no resistance when he slid his fingers around to the back of her neck, gently caressing her skin. He met her gaze, still smiling. "Have you by chance missed me?"

Evelyn tried to return his gaze with indifference, but it was impossible.

Marshall smiled, accepting the lack of a response as confirmation that she had, indeed, missed him, but was too honest to lie about it. He had called thinking to bait the trap a little at a time, to slowly entice her into his arms, but now—

having her so close—the strategy was forgotten. He lowered his head and kissed her.

She stiffened for a moment, then relented, allowing his mouth to leisurely search hers, gently at first, then more heatedly, more demanding.

Marshall felt the sensations begin to build, swirling unhurriedly one moment, the next churning with the intensity of a storm blowing across the Channel. The tenuous control he'd been maintaining for the last few days failed him. He moved his hand from her neck to her waist, pulling her forcibly against him, letting her feel the hardness of his body, the heat of his embrace, the need that was quickly making him forget his well-laid plans.

The kiss was long and achingly sweet as he took his time, tasting her. She tasted different than other women, Marshall decided, then wondered what in blazes had brought the thought to mind. He held himself in check, his experience telling him to go slowly, to entice not tease.

Her response told him that he'd made the right choice. She yielded her mouth, parting her lips, allowing his tongue inside. Her tongue responded, hesitantly at first, then with growing curiosity, wanting to taste him in return.

Evelyn's knees went weak. She leaned into him, her mind darkened by turmoil, her body singing with entrancing sensation. She felt trapped, but it was a sweet prison this time, one she loathed to leave. Each time the marquis touched her, she felt herself weakening, her resolve slowly melting under his expertise. But no matter how many times her mind and morals told her it was wrong, her body and heart argued that it felt too right, too perfect.

Very slowly, Marshall raised his head and looked down at her. Her eyes were closed, dark lashes resting against her skin. He allowed his eyes to drink in the sight of her, the telltale rise and fall of her breasts beneath the misty blue fabric of her blouse. Some of his control returned, the need to tread gently where this particular woman was concerned. Her innocence wasn't that of youth, but of conviction. When she gave herself, it would be with a womanly willingness that he knew would be far more satisfying than any he'd ever felt before.

He glanced around the attic, looking for a resting place where he could hold her more comfortably. An old Grecian bed stood against the eastern wall. Once colorful with gilt inlaid in the curved headrest and draped canopy, its faded grandeur was all the disorderly attic had to offer.

"I want to hold you," he whispered, not giving her time to protest as he swept her into his arms and carried her to where the long, narrow bed waited.

Evelyn eyed the bed with disapproval. "My lord—"

"Shhh," he silenced her. Then he was sitting on the bed, the long cushion sinking under their weight as he sat her on his lap as if she were a child to whom he was about to read a bedtime story.

He took her mouth again, possessing her senses gently, awakening all the dreams she had fought all day to extinguish. The images that began to spin inside her head were upsetting: a future that held love and laughter, contentment and security. Evelyn knew she shouldn't dare think of them, but the marquis aroused her imagination as easily as he aroused her body.

The glide of his hands as they moved up and down her arms, then around to her back, stimulated the dream. His touch was firm. Possessive, but gentle. The heat was incredible.

Evelyn could feel it flaming deep within her own body. The warmth of his arms added fuel to the rising fire as his hands moved from her back to her waist, then higher. Suddenly his fingertips were moving, teasing the undersides of her breasts.

She wasn't wearing a corset or a crinoline, nor did she, unless her clothing demanded it. The soft, purrlike sound the marquis made alerted Evelyn to the fact that he'd just discovered that her undergarments consisted of a chemise and one petticoat worn under her last serviceable black skirt. She opened her eyes and looked at him, thinking to explain that she had dressed for a day alone, but the amused grin on his face stopped her.

"You are a delight," he said. "A pure delight."

Then he was kissing her again with an almost savage tenderness, devouring her with his mouth, driving resistance from her mind.

Evelyn felt his hands moving, gently kneading her breasts, making them swell under the muslin of her chemise. The dream was back: the marquis holding her, kissing her, making her feel special. The warm mating of their mouths and the heat of his hands fired the unsettling anticipation that always came with his kisses. But more so now that he was touching her so intimately. His fingers brushed over her aroused nipples, teasing them, making her arch unconsciously.

Marshall felt the firmness under his hands, the growing heat of her breasts as he forced himself to tease instead of satisfy. Slowly, with the tactical skill of a general on the battlefield, he reached for the buttons at the collar of her blouse. He shifted her in his lap, holding back a groan as her weight settled against his arousal. Then his fingers were touching the soft flesh under the starched fabric, sliding gently forward and back. His mouth lifted from her lips, damp from his kisses, and moved leisurely down her throat. He inhaled the scent of her, reined his control in tighter, and moved on, nibbling and kissing the skin he exposed as button after button came loose of its moorings.

Evelyn felt a moment of panic when his breath heated the valley between her breasts, but it felt so wonderful, so amazingly glorious, that all she could do was lean back in his arms and let him enjoy it as well. He traced the swell of each breast, his fingertips heating her skin until she felt as if she were on fire. She'd never imagined a man's gentleness, not in this way.

Marshall drew a ragged breath, intent now on making her forget all the reasons why they shouldn't become lovers. He kissed her tenderly, slowly building the desire that he knew would rage out of control once she surrendered to the need he was creating within her. He used all his expertise to keep her on the edge, to maintain the sensual trust she'd unexpectedly gifted upon him.

He could make the fire blaze; she was close to that point, but instead of fanning the fire, Marshall began to bank it. When he finally had her, it wouldn't be on a dusty Grecian bed in the corner of an attic. He didn't want her going downstairs afterward, feeling ashamed or embarrassed if she encountered one of the servants in the hallway.

Evelyn's breath shuddered, an audible sign of the shimmering shivers that were threading through her body. She couldn't think, couldn't reason her way out of Marshall's arms. She knew it was because there was no place she'd rather be. No man she'd rather having touching her.

His breath was still warm upon her skin, his kisses as light as a feather. Somehow, her mind found its way out of the sensual haze. The marquis was looking at her as he buttoned her blouse. Stopping just short of the last button, he smiled. There was a radiance to his gaze, a reverent quality that made her feel cherished rather than betrayed.

For a moment, they didn't speak, neither wanting to shatter the delicate moment that had happened between them. The realization of what she had allowed him to do should have her running down the stairs, humiliated by her actions, but all Evelyn could manage was an answering smile. She hadn't been prepared for his arrival or this turn of events.

There was an element of emotion about him this day, an un-predictability that didn't suit a man bent on seduction. It was as disconcerting as his kisses.

"Would you like to take a walk in the park before dinner?" Marshall asked, still cradling her in his arms. "It's a lovely day. The evening air should be pleasant."

"The park?"

He laughed lightly as he set her on her feet. "There's a nice little square not far from here. I'm sure Mrs. Grunne has some bread scraps about. We can feed the birds."

A short time later, they were strolling under the wide branches of the sprawling birch trees that shaded the park. The area was devoid of people this time of day, the only busy chatter that of squirrels with their tails curled high over their backs as they scampered from tree limb to tree limb. The sun was low on the horizon, most people inside attending to the end of the day, preparing for dinner, then a quiet evening in the parlor. There was no one about to see the well-dressed gentleman in a coat of charcoal gray and pin-striped trousers, calmly escorting a lady on his arm.

Evelyn knew the impression they would give anyone who saw them would be an illusion, but she couldn't help but enjoy the alternating shadows and sunshine that added to the natural quietness of the small wooded area. The breeze was refreshing as it blew across the Thames and the greens near Lambeth Palace, only a mile or so to the southwest.

"Mr. Druggs told me that you were somewhat concerned about the allowance I offered," Marshall said as they stopped so she could toss a handful of dried bread to a gathering of small brown wrens. He watched as the tiny birds quickly scoffed up the offering, then flew away. "Is that what you were doing in the attic? Looking for things, so my pockets wouldn't be strained to purchase them."

"To some degree," she confessed. "I was looking for a

painting or a tapestry, anything to replace that hideous painting in the library. If all battles were so uninspiring, men would soon cease thinking war glamorous and stop trotting off to prove themselves worthy of honor and medals."

"Are you trying to distract me from the matter at hand by insulting men and their admirable pursuit of a battle well waged," Marshall said laughingly. "If so, then think again, Miss Dennsworth, for I will not allow you to scavenge about the attic like a squirrel hunting nuts for winter. I can well afford the few furnishings you seek."

"The extent of your wealth isn't in question, my lord," she said, allowing him to seat her on a wrought-iron bench circling the trunk of a sturdy elm. "I already owe you far more than I can ever repay."

He frowned at her, his displeasure apparent. "We have had this conversation before. We will not have it again. You owe me nothing," he said firmly

"And I am just as stolidly convinced that I do," she retorted. While she might melt in his arms whenever he kissed her, Evelyn was determined not to yield on this issue. The moment she did, she was likely to find herself in far greater danger than the dusty attic had presented an hour earlier.

"Then we have reached an impasse," he said, sitting down beside her. "For I'm as stubborn as a northern gale, or so my sisters keep telling me."

"My father noted my stubbornness on more than one occasion," Evelyn countered. "In fact, he once commented that—"

"I'm more stubborn," he insisted, breaking into her words. "You are free to test the fact if you wish, but I warn you that my patience doesn't have the same stamina. I may be forced to use more persuasive means." His tone was far from braggish. Instead, it was low and slightly amused, as if he'd like nothing better than to have her keep arguing with him.

Evelyn knew he was thinking of the way he had kissed her in the attic, of the liberties she'd allowed him to take.

"Is that so, my lord?" she challenged, refusing to concede to his charms twice in one day.

Marshall opened his hand, spreading a banquet of dried, grainy bread over the emerald grass. A flock of birds immediately appeared to pluck the delicacy up and carry it away. He didn't respond to her challenge. Instead, he reached into the bag a second time. She watched as more birds, wings flapping and bills pecking, danced in front of them. After several minutes, she accepted the lack of conversation, enjoying the simple act of feeding pigeons and wrens with a marquis who was proving to be somewhat of a puzzlement.

They returned to the house, speaking only of common things, the speeches in Parliament and the recent speculation that the queen would spend the summer in Balmoral, mourning her lost consort for another full season.

"I fear my stepmother has taken up the black even more seriously than our monarch," Marshall remarked as they entered the parlor. "It's been almost two years since I buried my father, but Constance shows no sign of giving up her paramatta and crepe."

"Many widows never wear color again," Evelyn reminded him.

"It isn't her wardrobe that concerns me; it's her attitude. She's growing increasingly dejected. Our family physician called upon her yesterday. After giving his assurance that her health is better than that of most ladies her age, he left, prescribing nothing but patience for the family and laudanum if she needed help in sleeping."

At the mention of his family, Evelyn grew quiet. The wind had stirred his hair, making him look younger, but the serious tone he had used when talking of his stepmother re-

minded her that he was a man full grown with heavy responsibilities upon his shoulder, including a shop girl whose
freedom he had willingly purchased. Not knowing his stepmother, but sensing that she was grieving in all sincerity,
Evelyn sought to comfort him.

"When my mother died, my father sulked about the house
for five years before he realized he was harming the parish
by not getting on with his life. I'm sure Lady Waltham will
soon realize that no matter how deeply she feels the loss of
your father, she has a family who needs her."

"Hopefully," Marshall sighed, wishing it could be soon.
"Winnifred and Catherine need their mother back in their
lives."

"Will you be staying for dinner?" Evelyn asked, not wanting to loose his company.

"I'm afraid not," he replied, sounding equally disappointed. "A previous engagement," he said, then explained
the weekly card game that came and went with the regularity
of Big Ben's chimes. "The duke scolds us like schoolboys if
we're late."

Evelyn couldn't imagine anyone scolding the Marquis of
Waltham. Her gaze fixed on his tall frame, the immaculate
cut of his clothes, the gold stickpin in his cravat, all the
things that clearly stated he was a gentleman. This was no
merchant's son, or country farmer, but a titled member of the
nobility. A man beyond her reach.

The following days increased Evelyn's feelings for the
marquis. The time they spent together was rarely scheduled.
He called unannounced, to spend time with her in the garden
or strolling the park, feeding pigeons and a flock of wrens
that appeared almost the moment they climbed down from
the carriage. Mrs. Grunne had taken to keeping a bowl of

bread in the kitchen, never knowing when his lordship and Miss Dennsworth would feel the need for some fresh air.

Evelyn had supervised the additional servants sent by Mr. Druggs. Furniture was moved from room to room in an attempt to find a more comfortable match. Some items she delegated to the attic for storage; others she set about recovering, slowly ridding the house of its drab greens and adding bolder, brighter colors that brought the rented house to life. The library's transformation took several days. The carpet was removed and the floors waxed before a large oval rug was placed in the center of the room, giving it the illusion of being larger than it actually was. The drapes had been cast out and new ones put in their place. The boar's head had been graciously delegated to the attic along with the painting of the battle fought near Quatre Bras.

Evenings were spent in the parlor, "becoming acquainted," as Marshall insisted on phrasing it. Sometimes he would bring a paper and read while she sat in a nearby chair, sewing. Often they talked of their childhoods and the things that still made them smile years later.

Evelyn thought it quite strange that they fell into the peaceful routine practiced by couples who had been married for years. The only time it wasn't peaceful was when the marquis pulled her into his arms and kissed her senseless.

She never knew when it was going to happen; thus she was never prepared for the debilitating effects that remained long after he took his leave. Each kiss was a promise, a reminder that while he might act passively, his intentions were still very active. The evocative encounters always left her breathless, wanting, sensually confused. The temptation was becoming more potent by the day. Marshall's kisses more addicting. He was administering just such a kiss, one that had her clinging to his shoulders, when Grunne discreetly cleared his throat and announced that they had a visitor.

"Who is it?" Marshall asked, keeping his arm around Evelyn's waist.

"A Mr. James Portsman, my lord."

The sensual haven that always accompanied Marshall's kisses was shattered as Evelyn recognized the name of the lawyer who had been retained to keep her out of prison.

Eight

James Portsman was of average height and far younger than Marshall had expected for a seasoned man of the law. His hair was fair, his eyes an attention-getting green. Clothes of costly material showed good tailoring and a superior cut that fit him well. He was a man who would be considered handsome by the ladies.

"Lord Waltham," Portsman greeted him. "How advantageous that you are here."

"Mr. Portsman," Marshall replied, turning his attention to Evelyn. She gave him an anxious look. Her hands were clasped so tightly in front of her the knuckles were white. "May I introduce Miss Dennsworth. Your client."

Portsman greeted her with a sincere smile, followed by a suggestion that she might want to take a seat. He had several questions to put to her.

"I'm impressed by your promptness, Mr. Portsman," Marshall said. "However, it seems a trifle too prompt. Is there a problem?"

"I fear so, my lord. Lord Monfrey's second son is soon to wed a young lady on the Continent. The earl had petitioned the bench for expediency, wishing the matter dealt with before the family travels abroad for the wedding. I was given notice this morning. We stand before the bench at week's end."

"So soon," Evelyn said, unable to hide her distress.

"It is certainly more quickly than a normal case would be heard," Portsman agreed. "I have cases that have been pending for almost a year." He turned his head slightly, once again addressing Marshall. "As soon as the court summons was served, I took the liberty of calling. Mr. Druggs assured me that Miss Dennsworth could receive me without notice."

Marshall drew a deep breath, then looked at Evelyn. Her distress was building; he could see it in the stiff pose of her shoulders and the way her hands were folded in her lap. He felt no hesitation about reaching for one of those hands, cradling it warmly in his own. Portsman had been informed of the entire situation. There was no reason for Marshall not to comfort Evelyn when she needed comforting the most.

"If you prefer," he said, giving her cold hand a quick squeeze, "I can speak with Mr. Portsman."

"I need to speak for myself," she said. "But, I'm glad you're here."

"So am I," he replied. "Don't worry. I'm not going to let anything happen to you."

Grunne entered carrying a tray. Once Evelyn had a cup of hot tea to ease her nerves, Marshall waited for the lawyer to start the conversation.

"In order for me to properly represent Miss Dennsworth, I will need to know everything that transpired the day she was arrested." The lawyer looked directly at her. "I know this is upsetting for you, Miss Dennsworth. If it wasn't necessary, I wouldn't ask. But it is imperative that I understand why Lady Monfrey would make such a charge."

"I understand," Evelyn replied. Despite Mr. Portsman's calm, professional voice, she was truly glad that Marshall hadn't left. Just having him close, his arm resting casually on the back of the sofa, helped to ease her nervousness. She refused to think of where she'd be if he hadn't championed her.

Knowing her future freedom depended upon the defense Mr. Portsman was preparing, Evelyn took a calming breath, then focused on the unpleasantness of that day and told him everything she could remember.

"I see," Portsman said, once she'd finished the recitation. "Then, you had two encounters with Lady Monfrey. One in the fitting room of Madame La Roschelle's shop, when you complimented her ladyship's brooch, and the other a short time later when you bumped into her."

"It was Lady Monfrey who did the bumping," Marshall said. "She came flying out of the fitting room like an over-stuffed hen fleeing the oven."

"I have seen the lady about town," Portsman replied with the neutrality only a lawyer possessed. "She is rather—"

"Fat," Marshall said, not bothering to disguise his dislike.

Portsman tried to hide his amusement behind his teacup, but Evelyn saw the smile on his face. When he spoke again, it was to direct a list of questions to her. She answered each and every one.

"Excellent," he complimented her. "That is exactly how you should reply to any questions put to you by myself or the magistrate. When you stand before the bench, do not hesitate to look Rivenhall in the eye. He may be somewhat intimidating, sitting above you dressed in a black robe, but I assure you he will know the truth when he hears it."

"What about Lady Monfrey?" Evelyn asked.

"I will question her," Portsman replied. "After reading the charges and the constable's report that a thorough search of Madame La Roschelle's establishment produced nothing, I do not think it will be too difficult to get Lady Monfrey to admit that she suspects you simply because you passed a compliment her way. You have no wrongdoing in your background, nor is there anything about your person or appearance to reflect badly upon your creditability."

"What if the magistrate doesn't believe me?"

"He will believe the facts, Miss Dennsworth. There are no witnesses against you. Without finding the brooch on your person or amongst your belongings, there is no case, only assumption."

"I will be there," Marshall said.

Portsman gave him a pensive look, then spoke, his voice taking on the quality of a lawyer addressing a jury. "I would ask that you reconsider making an appearance, my lord. Of course, you may sit in the gallery. It will be an open courtroom."

Evelyn looked from the lawyer to the marquis, then back again. "I understand, but I'm not sure Lord Waltham does."

"What don't I understand?" Marshall replied somewhat stiffly. He had no intention of abandoning Evelyn to suffer the trauma of a trial alone.

Portsman addressed the issue. "You and Lady Monfrey are socially acquainted, are you not, my lord?"

"Most of the peerage is socially acquainted," Marshall retorted. "Explain yourself."

"I do not wish to offend Miss Dennsworth, but you have retained me to speak to her best interest. That interest demands that I be candid with you. Lady Monfrey would be sure to recognize you, no matter where you are seated in the courtroom. The level of this case, although of extreme import to my client, is not the type of trial that would draw the attention of a marquis. Lady Monfrey could assume a connection between yourself and Miss Dennsworth, especially since you were in the shop that day. Her condemnation at seeing one of her class being supportive of one she considers socially inferior could create . . . shall we say, a certain unpredictability in her testimony." He paused to let his words sink in. "There is also the possibility that seeing you in the courtroom could cause the magistrate some discomfort. You did *persuade* him to release Miss Dennsworth into your custody."

Marshall couldn't argue with either point. Lady Monfrey was one of those dislikeable women who flaunted her superior status at every opportunity. Having met Rivenhall, Marshall wasn't overly concerned that the man would feel uncomfortable, but he didn't comment on the magistrate's willingness to accept the money that had been offered that night in the tavern. Instead, he was forced to agree with Portsman. "In other words, my presence could do more harm than good."

"I believe it would, my lord," Portsman replied. "I assure you, Miss Dennsworth will be shown every courtesy in the courtroom. I will not allow anyone to slander her good name."

The lawyer's assurance didn't appease the need for Marshall to be close to Evelyn on the day she would need him the most, but it did confirm that he'd hired the right man to defend her. Portsman might be young, but he was intelligent. It would be interesting to see how he managed Lady Monfrey once she was in the witness booth.

"Very well," he said reluctantly, "I will not attend the hearing."

"I think it's best," Evelyn said for her own reasons. If she was found guilty, she didn't want Marshall seeing her being led from the courtroom by more constables.

"I will call again the day before the trial," Portsman said. "At that time, I will go over the specific questions I'll be presenting in the courtroom. Try not to worry," he said. "I'm confident that we shall see this matter to a just resolution."

Marshall showed the man to the door personally, wanting a few words with him in private. "I will not allow her to be sent to prison," he told Portsman. "Do whatever you have to do to make sure it doesn't happen."

The attorney nodded. "Your affection for the lady is apparent, my lord. Rest assured, all will be well. If I can discern the truth, so will Rivenhall. Miss Dennsworth's character will shine through her nervousness, and she will be believed."

Marshall prayed that the young lawyer was right. He didn't want Evelyn subjected to days or weeks in a workhouse until he could ferret out the people he would need to bribe to obtain her freedom. If such a thing was possible, and he highly suspected it was.

After asking the lawyer to inform him before calling again, Marshall bid Mr. Portsman a good day and returned to the parlor. Evelyn was sitting where he had left her, her gaze unfocused, her thoughts obviously inward.

"I think something stronger than tea is in order," he said, shutting the parlor door behind him. "A sherry to soothe your nerves."

Evelyn didn't dispute that her nerves needed soothing. The last few days had instilled an artificial calm in her life that Mr. Portsman's visit had disrupted. She didn't want to think about the upcoming trial, but she had little choice. So much depended upon it.

Marshall sat down beside her, determined to rid the room of the ghosts Portsman had left behind. Waiting until she'd finished the sherry, he took the glass from her hand and set it aside.

"You've been told not to worry."

"How can I not," she said, close to tears.

"No," he said, pulling her into his arms. "I will not let this day be ruined by Lady Monfrey and her ridiculous charges."

He sensed the momentary doubt in her, felt her stiffen ever so slightly as he threaded his fingers through her hair, tilting her head back so he could kiss her. His gaze dropped to her bodice and the starched front of her white blouse, tucked neatly into the waistband of a dark blue skirt. Her wardrobe was sadly lacking. He wanted to clothe her in satins and lace, but she continued to refuse anything more than food and shelter.

"Don't push me away," Marshall said as he saw that certain expression on her face, the one she always wore when she was concentrating on the social differences between them.

"I don't want to," she confessed. She reached out her hand and caressed his cheek.

He saw the teary sheen of her eyes, felt the slight tremor of her body. He kissed her, his lips clinging to the taste of hers, sweetened by sherry and the confession that he hadn't been wrong. She wanted this as much as he wanted it. Each time he kissed her, he could feel the bond between them growing stronger. It was what he had hoped for, what he had planned on these last few days.

He tightened his hold on her, allowing one hand to move up and down her back, gradually, skillfully pressing her closer. He used every ounce of experience he'd gleaned over the years, the knowledge that a woman burned more slowly than a man, that she needed to be coaxed not rushed. Now that the moment was at hand, Marshall wanted it to last.

Another kiss and his hands were around her waist, his thumbs brushing provocatively against the swell of her breasts. There was no corset to hinder his actions, thank God. He shifted his weight, using the length of the sofa to his advantage. Her head rested against the fringed pillows as she watched him.

Slowly, he raised his hands and reached for the buttons on her blouse. He undid them one by one. When there were no more buttons, he opened the blouse to reveal the soft muslin of a lace-trimmed chemise. Beneath the sheer fabric he could see the dark outline of her peaked nipples. He looked from her swelled breasts to her mouth, then into her eyes. "You are lovely," he whispered.

The husky sound of his voice was a caress. Evelyn felt it, just as she had felt his kiss, his hands, gentle but urgent. Everything about him beckoned, enticed, and tempted her to forget herself at the same time it begged her to remember each time he had touched her before, kissed her before. The right and wrong of it faded under the piercing heat of his gaze.

She watched as he stood up and took off his jacket and waistcoat. His shirt followed, falling soundlessly onto the floor. He was a well-made man, and she gloried in the knowledge that he could have any woman, yet wanted her.

Marshall wanted to strip both their clothes away and toss them to the far corners of the room, but he maintained his control. Evelyn would be his soon enough, and he vowed to make their first joining as pleasurable as it could be for both of them.

He sat down beside her. Her lips parted as if to speak, but he sealed them with his own. It was a long, lingering kiss. His tongue teased the corner of her mouth. Hers hesitatingly did the same. The sensual duel continued for several more kisses, each one teasing, each one teaching, each one more satisfying than the last until her hands were laced behind his neck and she was holding on to him.

His hands splayed low at her back, Marshall kept her arched, her body pressed tightly against his own. Finally, he lifted his mouth, took a breath, and began kissing new territory. The curve of her throat, the swell of her breasts just above the top of her chemise. When he reached the valley between her breasts, he inhaled the scent of her.

Evelyn felt the heat of his breath. It was hotter than any summer wind. She shivered in his arms, felt his hands at the base of her spine keeping her body arched like a bow while he began to kiss her again. His tongue glided hotly over her skin. Another shiver, more pleasure than surprise this time.

He lifted his head and looked at her. There was tenderness in his gaze. Tenderness and something else, something wild and deep and unnamed. She felt it, just as wildly and just as deeply. Sinking back into the pillows, she smiled at him. No words. Just a smile that said all there was to say. She was his—for now.

How often these last few days had she dreamed of this, of his touch, of his tender ways and captivating smile. Was it so wrong to let him be her knight in shining armor again, to think of him as hers and hers alone? It was an illusion, yes, but if fate turned against her again, it could well be the only illusion, the only splendid memory she would have for a long time. She was old enough to know what she was doing, old enough to experience the ultimate act of womanhood. And she wanted it to be with this man. She wanted his touch to banish the demons, his kiss to melt away the fear.

There would be regrets, consequences, but she'd face them tomorrow. Today she would be what he wanted her to be—a lover.

Slowly, Marshall reached for the ribbons of her chemise. A gentle tug and they were loose. He held her gaze as he unlaced them, freeing her breasts to his gaze. She was even more perfect than he had imagined. Her skin was white, her nipples a dusky rose, pearled and waiting for his mouth. He lowered his head and kissed each ruby crown. She gasped with pleasure, and he kissed them again, this time raking his teeth ever so gently over each aroused peak. Her response was a soft moan. Then he drew her deeply into his mouth and began to suck.

Waves of sensation swept through Evelyn's body, ripples of pleasure that began where Marshall's mouth was feasting on her, ending deep inside the very core of her. Her head fell back, her eyes drifting closed as she let the enjoyment rule.

Marshall felt her nails digging into his shoulders, then sliding down his back. Tiny claws raked at his skin. Then her hands were rubbing, soothing away the minuscule pain, kneading the muscles of his back and shoulders the same way he was kneading the heavy weight of her breasts in his hands. He closed his mouth over one budded nipple and sucked hard. She began to twist beneath him, her body demanding what his had waited days to give.

One hand smoothed her skirt as it traveled downward, lifting it on the upward journey. Her calves were slender and firm, covered by cotton stockings that stopped just above her knees. There was nothing softer than a woman's thighs, except her . . . He shuddered at the thought, at the open wantonness of her response as his hand began to randomly caress a new patch of skin.

Now that she had decided there was no hesitation in her. Her hands roamed just as freely as his, touching him, curling in the hair on his chest and pulling. He flinched, then smiled.

"You are a delight," he chuckled. His own exploration advanced, until he was untying the string at the top of her drawers and easing them slowly down her thighs. "I want you so much it hurts."

She smiled then, a beguiling smile, a woman's smile. "I want you, too."

The acknowledgement was all he needed to hear. He reached for the buttons that held her skirt, then the tie of her petticoat. Within seconds, she was lying naked before him, her slender body glowing in the sunlight. He drew in a breath, reminding himself that although she had finally decided to become his lover, she was still new to the game of love.

He traced the curves of her body, molding his hands to the valley of her waist and the flare of her hips, to the length of her graceful legs, then back up again, savoring her response, the way she curled into his hands like a contented cat. When he kissed her belly, he felt her muscles clench, then relax. His hands were gentle, but insistent, learning all her secrets save the sweetest one.

Evelyn gloried in the discovery as much as he did. She could feel her body blooming under his expert touch, coming alive. She returned his caresses when she could, letting her fingertips enjoy the crisp hair on his chest, the bulge of muscles in his upper arms, the leanness of his stomach and back.

She cried out his name when he finally touched the center of her. She was hot and slick, her body now begging for the ultimate fulfillment. Marshall looked from her flushed face to where her legs had spread wider, offering him the access he needed. He played in the soft curls that covered her mound, drawing out the pleasure, stroking and probing with tender care, feeling her response dampen his fingers.

She was more than ready for him. He stood and quickly shed the rest of his clothes. He'd taken the precaution of locking the parlor door. There would be no intrusion, only the sunlight streaming through the windows and the faint chatter of birds in the outer garden.

There was no shock on her face when he turned to stare down at her, no show of regret or disgust, only a faint smile that said she found the sight of him pleasing. He covered her then, letting her feel the full impact of their bodies touching shoulder to shoulder, belly to belly, thigh to thigh. His fingers softly massaged her bare shoulders, her neck, then moved slowly downward to her breasts. He pinched the aching tips, then soothed them with his mouth.

Evelyn sucked in her breath at the scandalizing pleasure of it. His weight felt delicious, his body hot and hard above hers, his eyes still tender as he studied her face. They kissed, long and deep, each savoring the intimacy of the moment.

He pushed into her slowly, stopping when her body began to resist.

"Look at me," he whispered. "Look at us."

Evelyn did as he asked, letting her gaze move from his face to the expanse of his chest, then lower, to where crisp, dark hair circled his navel. His muscles were tight, his strength controlled. Then she saw where they were almost joined, the rigid length of his manhood posed at the gate of her femininity, ready to take possession.

"I've wanted you from the first moment I saw you," he said in a husky whisper.

He withdrew, then thrust his hips forward, breaking through her barrier with as little pain as he could. She tightened for a brief moment, and he almost lost his control. She was even hotter than he'd imagined, sleek and wet and tight. "Relax," he whispered. "Let me love you."

He kissed her then, tenderly, his lips warm and coaxing. The touch of his hands was reassuring as he waited for the discomfort to pass, the surprise to pass. When it did, Evelyn took a deep breath and did as he asked, relaxing the tense muscles of her legs, her clenched stomach. He slid deeper, filling her more fully, stretching her to accommodate him.

Her body was finally his, and he used it to bring them both pleasure, withdrawing then pushing slowly forward, deeper, until all she could feel was him. He sank into her again and again, building the pleasure, making it spiral, until she was writhing beneath him, arching up, clasping his hips with her naked thighs to hold him to her.

Their bodies met, slid together, separated but not entirely. The need became shattering, a blaze so strong it demanded satisfaction. Marshall moved more forcefully, feeling the small ripples of pleasure deep inside her, feeding them, building the hunger until there was nothing but a frenzied need to find that moment, that one instant when all that existed was a deep, throbbing satisfaction.

Evelyn followed him into the storm. Breathing heavily, she clung to his sweat-dampened shoulders, arched her hips to meet his, used her inner muscles to hold him as tightly as she could, and let the sensations take over.

He looked at her, and she found the strength to smile.

Then he withdrew, almost leaving her. She shuddered with the need to have him return, whispered his name in an urgent plea. He answered, holding her hips, then plunging hard and deep.

Evelyn felt as if the world was exploding. Sensual, breath-stealing convulsions swept through her body. It was incredible. Unbelievable. She felt his body swell in response, stretching her, filling her, then bathing her in a hot, wet heat.

Marshall held her for a long while, their breathing relaxed, their bodies lethargic with satisfaction. Reluctantly he slid free of her embracing arms and reached for his trousers, pulling them up and over his hips, then sitting down beside her. If they were upstairs in her bed, he'd willingly lie with her all day. Taking her again at his leisure, holding her while they slept.

Evelyn went into his arms with a deep sigh of contentment. Reality was back, but not yet full force. She wanted to enjoy what they had shared for a few more minutes.

Marshall rested her head on his shoulder and stared at the ceiling. "I didn't plan on making love to you in the parlor."

She laughed lightly. "Some things shouldn't be planned, my lord."

"Marshall," he corrected her, reaching his hand down to squeeze the soft globe of her bottom. "After what just happened, formality is the farthest thing from my mind."

Slowly, Evelyn untangled herself, loathing to give up the warmth of his embrace. She retrieved her clothing from the floor and began to dress.

Marshall did the same. "I'll return this evening," he said, reaching out to pull her into his arms, then planting a kiss on the tip of her nose. "We can dine together."

"I'd rather you didn't, my lord."

He looked down at her, unsure if he'd heard her correctly. "What?"

"I'd rather you didn't return this evening," Evelyn said.

"What we did doesn't change anything. I won't be your mistress."

He stared at her as if she'd lost her mind along with her virginity.

"This can't happen again," she stated, knowing it shouldn't have happened the first time but unable to regret it. "I wanted to." She paused to chose the right words. "Being your lover for the morning suited me. Being your mistress doesn't."

Marshall released her and walked to the table in the corner. He poured himself a drink, not looking at her again until the glass was drained dry. "I'm not sure I understand," he said, doing his best to keep his voice even. "You just let me make love to you on a sofa. I took your virginity. Now you say that it changes nothing. I disagree. It changes everything. Look at me and tell me that you didn't enjoy what we did." He marched to where she was standing and pulled her roughly into his arms. "Tell me that you don't want me to touch you again."

"I can't," she whispered.

"Then, what's all this about? We are lovers now. If you think for one moment that I'm going to take you, then forget you, I will not. I cannot," he confessed, wishing he could explain how he felt. But he couldn't. Making love with her had been different. Vastly different than it would have been with the kind of woman he'd originally meant to install in a house for his personal pleasure. But telling her that would make him too vulnerable, admitting that more than his body had been engaged in the act wasn't something he could do easily. Everything about their relationship was unorthodox. He cared about her, held a deep affection for her, but that was all he was willing to admit.

Evelyn shook her head. "I can't be your mistress. I want more than the comfort of a house and a lavish allowance that will buy things I can well live without. I want a man to care for me, to enjoy more than my body. I have no guarantee what my future will hold. But one day I want children. Children who can proudly claim their father's name. Can you give me those things, my lord? Your heart? Your name?"

Marshall frowned. God, how could things get worse. He continued to hold her, but she didn't yield in the slightest.

"I will leave," she said. "I have enough money to provide lodgings for myself until I stand before Magistrate Rivenhall."

"This is ridiculous!" He released her and stepped back. If he had any sense, he'd carry her upstairs and keep her there until she admitted . . . what? That she needed him, wanted him, loved him? How could he ask those things of her without giving them in return. Marriage wasn't something he was willing to consider with any woman, regardless of her social station. But he had taken a virgin, seduced an innocent, no matter how willing she had been.

He studied her face. It was still flushed with pleasure, her eyes still bright with satisfaction. There was a glimmer of tears, but he knew she wasn't going to release them. She was just as proud as he was, and just as determined to choose her own path in life. He could see there was no winning the argument; she didn't want what he had to offer.

Marshall got hold of himself, containing his temper, forcing logic to overrule emotion, putting aside his bruised pride. "I assumed responsibility for you. I am not willing to relinquish it. Having said that, I shall be the one to leave. I will not call again until you meet with Mr. Portsman. Whether you like it or not, I have a vested interest in the court's decision."

Nothing more was said as he scooped up his jacket and strolled from the room.

Evelyn watched, knowing she had won the battle, but lost the war.

Nine

The butler who opened the door of the Belgrave Square town house recognized Marshall immediately. "Lord Granby is in the library, your lordship. Shall I announce you?"

"Don't bother. I'll announce myself."

The room the marquis entered was a well-furnished man's domain. The drapes were closed, blocking out the sights and sounds of the stylish neighborhood. Granby was sitting at his desk, writing a letter. Marshall nodded to his best friend, then marched unceremoniously to the liquor cabinet and poured himself a drink.

"Mind telling me what you're celebrating?"

"Nothing," Marshall retorted dryly. "I'm about to get swaggering, staggering drunk. Care to join me?"

"Normally one gets swaggering, staggering drunk in one's own home. Much easier to swagger or stagger one's way into bed afterward," Granby replied casually.

"Can't," Marshall grunted. He carried the glass to the nearest chair and sat down. "Too many women in my house to get properly drunk. That's why I'm here."

"By all means," Granby said, spreading his hands in a show of hospitality. "I haven't been completely foxed since our Cambridge days. Have I forgotten a momentous anniversary?"

Marshall raised the glass to his mouth, then frowned. Evelyn's scent was still on his hands. Grimacing, he finished off the port, then stared at the empty glass. "Do you have any whiskey?"

Granby pulled the service cord. A moment later a footman appeared in the doorway. "Bring us two bottles of whiskey," he informed the servant. "Then see that we're not disturbed."

Marshall waited until the footman had come and gone. Once the door was shut, sealing off his misery, he opened a bottle and passed it to Granby. "We're celebrating the stupidity of man," he announced, raising the second bottle high. "Drink up."

"Mankind's stupidity in general or one man's stupidity in particular?"

Marshall upended his bottle. The hot rush of aged whiskey burned his throat.

"I see," Granby remarked. "Very well, in that case, you could at least do me the courtesy of expounding upon your particular stupidity before we're both too drunk to give a damn."

Marshall slumped back in the chair, put his feet on a nearby table, and looked at his best friend. "We're celebrating a lesson hard learned. A mistake I won't make twice."

Granby shed his jacket, sat down, added another pair of boots to the table, and smiled. "This mistake wouldn't have anything to do with a woman, would it?"

"Blasted nuisances is what they are," Marshall grumbled, taking another drink. "Blasted, bloody nuisances."

He knew he shouldn't be angry with Evelyn. In fact, he wasn't. He was furious with himself for getting caught in his own trap. Two weeks of watching his words, planning her seduction, allowing himself no more than a few kisses, playing the role of a perfect gentleman—well, almost perfect—and what had it gotten him? An invitation *not* to call again!

It wasn't that he couldn't understand her point of view. It was natural for a woman to want what she wanted, the security of a husband's name before she had children.

He could have given her a child this morning.

The thought provoked another drink.

"This woman wouldn't be the one formerly employed on Bond Street?" Granby asked. "Or is that the problem? She's still on Bond Street."

"She isn't on Bond Street," Marshall informed him. "She's living in a house that I rented on Lambeth Road. A house which I have graciously been asked not to visit."

"She threw you out of a house that *you're* renting," the earl chuckled. "I'll drink to that."

Over the course of the next several hours, Marshall related the story of his bizarre involvement with a vicar's daughter, slurring the last episode, but conveying the basic idea that he had finally had the woman he wanted only to be told that he couldn't have her again.

"Bloody hell, no wonder you want to get drunk . . . are drunk," Granby concurred midway of the afternoon, slurring right along with his friend. "Damned if you do, damned if you don't, sort of thing."

"It's enough to make a man swear off women."

"I wouldn't go so far as to say that," Granby replied. He poured the last of the whiskey into a glass, sloshing half of it onto the carpet. "Damn fine thing, women. If you keep them in their place."

Marshall stood up, swaying from side to side for a moment before flopping back down in the chair. "What place would that be?"

"On their backs," Granby replied, so drunk his smile was as crooked as his once well-tied cravat. "Only place for them."

Marshall shook his head. "Doesn't make any difference," he stammered. "The little darlings still manage to get their claws into you."

He looked toward the liquor cabinet, thinking a bottle of port might be just the thing to top off the whiskey. That was the problem. He could still think. Still remember how wonderful it had been to hold Evelyn in his arms, how hot she'd been inside and out, how her body had accepted his, held it, fulfilled it. Damn her pretty hide.

Granby tipped up his glass and finished off the last of his personal bottle. He studied the clock sitting on the marble mantel, then groaned. "Bloody hell, we're in for it now."

"In for what?"

Granby came to his feet and strolled as gracefully as his inebriated state would allow toward the service cord. It took several tries before he had it clutched in his right hand. "Morland," he groaned. "He'll be expecting us at the club."

Marshall's reply was something between a curse and a prayer. "Send a footman."

Granby pulled the cord. "And have the old man show up on the doorstep. Not bloody likely."

The butler arrived just in time to keep his employer from sinking to the floor like a sack of potatoes. "My lord!" He grabbed Granby under the arms, holding him upright.

"Ahhh, Briggs, my good man. Lord Waltham insisted that I get staggering, swaggering drunk. Or was that, swaggering, staggering?" He smiled drunkenly at the butler. "Think you can get us sober in time to keep His Grace, the dreaded Duke of Morland, from seeing our shameful plight?"

"Ahhh, milord. I'll have Cook brew up something to clear your heads. No, milord. Don't sit down. You and his lordship need a bit of walking about."

"Can't walk," Marshall said laughingly from across the room. "I'm as drunk as a wheelbarrow."

A short time later, three footmen, two drunken lords, and

one butler climbed the stairs to the second floor of the town house.

"Can you stagger a bit to the left, your lordship? Can't have you falling over the railing," Briggs said. "No, milord, to the left! Aye, that's the way of it. One foot up, then the other. We'll have a go at a cold bath, then Cook's elixir. You'll be right as rain in no time."

It took the better part of two days before Marshall was feeling anywhere near "right." He could barely remember what had happened after Briggs had poured half a pot of Cook's elixir down his throat. What he did remember was giving him fits. *Evelyn.* The beguiling way she had of look-ing at him, the way she'd responded to his every touch. The range of her reactions had been like nothing he'd ever expe-rienced—innocently hesitant at first, then wantonly eager. But each heartfelt, each a commitment to their lovemaking.

The only consolation he had was knowing that if anyone had been seduced, it was he. Evelyn had decided for what-ever reason to become his lover, if only for one bright sun-drenched morning. Why? Was her fear of prison so strong that she had wanted to experience all a woman could experi-ence before being locked away? Didn't she know that he'd do everything within his power to make sure that didn't hap-pen?

Or had he awakened more than desire in her?

The question evoked both pleasure and concern. Marshall rose from behind his desk to stare out the window. He was making assumptions, he decided. He wasn't dealing with a merry widow content to play at a lover's game. Nor was Evelyn a naïve innocent who expected commitment. She was mature enough to understand that he wasn't seeking marriage, and equally mature in knowing what she wanted for herself—a husband and children.

The thought of her eventually finding those things with another man didn't sit well.

"The Earl of Granby is here, milord."

Marshall swung around to find the butler standing in the doorway.

"Show him in," he told Carlow, wondering if Granby had stopped by to turn the screws. He'd be a long time living down the drunken fiasco he'd engaged in two days ago.

"Ah. It's a sober and serious friend who greets me this morning," the earl said, strolling into the library. "Pity. I had thought to find you brooding over a bottle of whiskey again." He glanced toward the desk. "Instead I find you brooding over your ledgers. I warned you not to bet too zealously the other evening. Did you loose the family knickers?"

"The family knickers are intact," Marshall replied stiffly.

"Excellent," Granby said, sinking into one of the two leather chairs that fronted the desk. "It wouldn't do to add another worry to your already overburdened shoulders."

Marshall resumed his seat, frowning. "There is nothing wrong with my shoulders."

The earl took a moment to study his friend. "Granted, they appear strong enough." He steepled his fingers under his chin, grinning all the while. "Should I concern myself with your heart?"

Marshall stiffened. "What the hell is that supposed to mean?"

The earl's only answer was a knowing smile. After a few moments, he inquired, "Very well, if all your parts are intact, then how are you going to handle the situation? I assume the lovely Miss Dennsworth is still in residence."

"She is," Marshall replied, having had Druggs confirm the fact earlier that morning. Grunne had been told to notify the secretary if Evelyn attempted to vacate the house.

Marshall had considered calling upon her himself, but his

pride wouldn't let him tuck his tail between his legs and go begging. If the lady didn't want his company, then so be it.

"And . . . ," the earl urged.

"And, nothing," Marshall snapped. "Do you want some tea? I've still got a headache, haven't even been able to handle so much as a glass of brandy."

"That doesn't surprise me. I haven't seen you that drunk since we were fresh milk at Cambridge."

Neither man said anything for a long while. Once Carlow had provided the requested tea, Marshall poured two cups, passing one across the desk to the earl. "I'll keep my promise to see her through the charges," he said, knowing full well Granby knew to whom he was referring.

"Wouldn't expect you to do anything less," his friend replied. "From what I can remember of our intoxicated conversation, you expect things to go in her favor. Then what?"

"I'm not sure," Marshall admitted. A smile curved his lips. "She wants to open a dress shop."

"An admirable goal," the earl agreed. "Here in London?"

Marshall shook his head. "She doesn't care for the city or its aristocratic patrons. Can't say that I blame her. We've certainly given her no reason to trust us."

"So that's what has you brooding?"

Marshall didn't comment.

"Need I point out that you rescued the lady."

"And then I . . . What difference does it make. As I said, I'll see her through the charges. After that, I'll bid her a good future and find a real mistress."

As he said the words, Marshall knew they were a lie. The last two days had been hell, struggling with a horde of emotions: anger, remorse, desire, admiration. He'd suffered from a caged restlessness, an indefinable unease that hadn't left him since he'd stormed out of the house on Lambeth Road. He also realized just how much the quiet times he'd spent with Evelyn meant to him. The way she had given herself to him that last morning was a memory no amount of whiskey could wash away.

He still wanted her. She wasn't the mistress he had planned on acquiring, and he knew he was insane to get entangled with a woman who had candidly told him she wanted far more than he was willing to offer. She was honest, sincere, and maddeningly stubborn. Still, something uniquely wonderful had happened between them. For the first time in his life the physical act of making love had taken on an emotional dimension. No. He wasn't ready to let Evelyn waltz out of his life as easily as she'd stumbled into it. At least not yet.

Evelyn strolled through the garden. The house was quiet, too quiet, so she'd come outside to listen to the sounds of the neighborhood. The chatter of squirrels, birds calling to their mates, the distant sound of a door opening and closing, carriages rolling along Lambeth Road on their way into the heart of the city. Each noise reaffirming that beyond the garden walls and the sanctuary of the small house, life went on. Just as she would have to go on. On to survive either incarceration or a future that had been mapped out until a few short weeks ago.

Her work at Madame La Roschelle's had filled up her day and many of her nights, if a lady needed her gown finished quickly. The work had kept her hands busy while she'd filled her head with thoughts of her own shop, always looking at the future, rarely allowing herself to evaluate the present.

Now, with nothing to keep her busy but the new covers she was sewing for a chair in the library, she had little recourse but to think of the present, of how everything in her life had changed, was still changing. The biggest change was the marquis. His appearance, his voice, his smile, everything about him had suddenly become the focal point upon which her mind revolved. Then, of course, there was the trial, her day of justice.

Mr. Portsman's clerk, a young, strapping man with an overabundance of wavy blond hair, had delivered a note, informing her that the lawyer planned to call at three that afternoon. Evelyn wasn't looking forward to what she assumed would be a partial enactment of the drama scheduled to unfold in the Old Bailey. But it wasn't the trial that had her seeking the solace of the private garden where the roses were quickly coming to life since she'd pruned away the smothering weeds.

The marquis was sure to make an appearance either just before or just after James Portsman's arrival. It had been four long days since she had watched him depart the house, stiff-shouldered and highly insulted by her request.

Still believing that she'd done the right thing, Evelyn struggled with the memory of that morning. She had allowed him to make love to her, had enjoyed it, wanted to enjoy it again. Thus the crux of the problem. If she allowed her feelings, and they ran deeper with each passing moment, to get in the way of her conscience, she'd be right where she didn't want to be. A mistress to a high-and-mighty lord, with nothing to look forward to but his next clandestine visit.

She didn't give a whit about being a marchioness. She had no ambition to climb the ladder of peerage society. Everyone within its rank would condemn her insolence in marrying a man who was her social superior. The assumption of their reaction was apparent in every condescending word Evelyn had heard spoken by Madame La Roschelle's patrons. She was being foolish, of course. There would be no marriage between herself and Lord Waltham. He had made his intentions clear from the very beginning. He wanted a mistress, not a wife.

Constrained by his intentions, Evelyn had given herself

with only one purpose in mind. Men always had a high-sounding excuse for taking their pleasure as they found it, perhaps some women had the same, but for her making love with Marshall—she could now use his first name without hesitation, having shared such an intimate exchange—had been more than an impulsive reaction to the morning's events. It had been a selfish fulfillment of the dream that had woven itself into her thoughts and heart ever since meeting him.

When they parted, either by the decision of the court or by her freedom to finally bid London ado, she wanted something to take with her. A memory that would burn bright throughout the years.

Of course, she wasn't oblivious to the far-reaching consequences of her actions. She had given her virginity, risked the possibility of a child, and far more dangerous, had chanced that she might never be able to love again. For Evelyn strongly suspected that her feelings, which she did her best to suppress, but which nevertheless came bubbling to the surface regardless of her common sense, warned her that she was very close to giving her heart completely to the marquis. A heart he didn't want.

The gift was doomed to be a disastrous one if she couldn't find a way to lessen their relationship, weaning herself away from him, until she could resume her life.

The ramifications of giving her virginity weren't nearly as involved as she had assumed. Granted, a future husband might question her lack of innocence, but when she left London, it could be under the guise of a widow, a necessity that would be demanded if she found herself with child. The very idea of giving birth to Marshall's baby was enough to send Evelyn back into the house to find some mundane task to occupy her idle hands. Another trip to the attic, this one without interruption, had gleaned several items that added a touch of charm to the parlor. Her favorite was a large floral vase decorating a half-moon table near the window. She stopped to reposition the white and yellow chrysanthemums she had placed in the vase earlier that morning. When she finished the task and turned around, it was to find the marquis standing in the doorway.

Evelyn froze. She had thought herself well prepared to see him again, but she was wrong. As her eyes fixed on him, the image of a well-dressed, titled gentleman vanished, replaced by the steamier vision of the man who had made love to her, his hair hanging over his brow, his face tight with passionate tension, his body buried deeply inside hers.

Marshall was having an equally difficult time. Seeing her again had taken the wind out of his sails. She looked picturesque, standing in the sunlight, dressed in a dark blue frock that accented the color of her eyes. A rush of desire went through him, and he wanted nothing more than for her to run into his arms. He stopped short of opening them wide, fearful she would reject the invitation. "Hello," he said rather formally. "Druggs told me that Mr. Portsman is expected by three."

"Yes," Evelyn said. She did not move, standing near the garden doors, facing him, her body unable to move, numbed by the feelings he evoked.

Marshall stepped into the room. He couldn't keep his gaze from traveling to the sofa. "I trust you've been well," he said, then added the words, "You look fully recovered from our last encounter. Tell me, do you think to offer me tea and cake while we converse about the weather?"

Evelyn flinched inwardly. She had sorely dented his pride. Knowing that, she allowed him his due. "I hadn't thought to do anything of the sort," she said in a normal voice. "If you like, we can argue."

He laughed, not surprised by her forthright attitude. It was one of the things he liked best about her. For a moment he drank in the sight of her looking lovely and as stubborn as ever. "If arguing will clear the air between us, then by all means, start flinging insults."

Evelyn bowed her head for a moment. When she looked up, she smiled. "I have no insults, my lord. Only a pleasant hello, if you will let us begin anew."

"By all means," he said with fierce honesty. "I wasn't sure what type of reception I would receive, considering the way we last parted. Am I bold in assuming that you have missed me?"

"Not overly bold," she confessed. "I have missed our conversations."

"Is that all?" he asked, closing the distance between them. He grasped her hands in his own, refusing to let her escape when she resisted with a gentle tug. "Have you missed my kisses, Miss Dennsworth? If I were to kiss you now, would you slap my face or bolt upstairs, locking the door against me?"

"I think it best if we base our friendship on words," she replied, meeting his gaze. "Your kisses are wonderful, but—"

He sealed her mouth with one of those wonderful kisses, forcing Evelyn to admit that she'd made a mistake by describing them so accurately.

Marshall freed her hands only to capture her more snugly within his arms. He used one hand to hold her head in place, while he gently ravished her mouth, not stopping until she was clinging to him. When he finally released her, she stepped away, lowering her head as if she could hide the effect he had on her.

"There is no going back," he said. "Neither of us can undo what has been done."

"I have no wish to undo it," Evelyn replied, promising herself there would be no lies between them. "You didn't coerce me into your arms."

"I'm glad you aren't expecting an apology from me," he

replied. "Although a true gentleman should regret what I did, I cannot find any repentance. I enjoyed making love to you."

Evelyn forced herself to look into his eyes. "As you pointed out, the past cannot be undone. Nor is the present ours to determine. I am under the control of the courts. Once that is finished, then we both must face the future. One way or the other." She looked out the window at the garden, seeing the roses but feeling the loss of the man. "It is the future that concerns me the most," she said, speaking over the lump in her throat. "We want different things. It serves no purpose to pretend otherwise."

"I may have given you a child," he said, speaking his mind as frankly as she seemed determined to speak hers. "What of that, Miss Dennsworth?"

"If I am with child, then you need not worry that I will become a burden. I have the means to support myself, unless . . ." She took a fortifying breath. "If I must go to—"

"Don't even speak of it," Marshall demanded. "As for a child, it would not be a burden." He reached out and touched her cheek. "I will not turn my back on you or a child."

"I believe you," she said. "You're too compassionate, too honorable, to cast me aside. You would do your duty, I'm sure. A comfortable cottage in the country, an allowance, perhaps you'd even find time to visit the child once you grow bored with me and retain a younger, more attentive woman to satisfy your needs. Forgive me if I sound vicious or ungrateful, but the truth is often unpleasant. Nevertheless, it serves us best, don't you agree?"

Marshall stifled a curse, holding on to his temper by a thread. "I hold a certain affection for you, Miss Dennsworth, but at this moment nothing would please me more than to shake you until your teeth rattle."

Before the argument could escalate to colossal proportions, Grunne announced that Mr. Portsman had arrived. Knowing it could be several hours before he'd have the maddening Evelyn to himself again, Marshall reined in his anger, his expression letting her know that the subject was far from closed.

Over the course of the next hour, Marshall found himself gritting his teeth. If James Portsman became any more solicitous of Evelyn's feelings and worries, he was going to show the handsome lawyer to the door without Grunne's assistance. Still, the lawyer's questions were worthwhile, preparing Evelyn for what she would face on the morrow. But damn it, he should be the one assuring her that all would be well; instead, he was delegated to the role of listener. Worse, he had agreed not to be present in the Bailey during the trial.

Marshall sipped a brandy as Portsman explained that he would allow Lady Monfrey to make her statement, then present his case, questioning Evelyn only when it was absolutely necessary. Portsman reviewed his questions and Evelyn's answers, then brought his visit to an end.

None too soon for Marshall. He could see that the lawyer was attracted to Evelyn, knew that if Portsman didn't assume she was his mistress, he'd willingly pursue her. If the circumstances were different, if Evelyn wasn't under his protection, she would be free to accept Portsman's attention. He was of her class, a man without social barriers or titled obligations, the kind of man who could give her the home and children she wanted. Marshall bristled at the idea of anyone taking his place.

"Mr. Druggs will call for you in the morning. He will escort you to my office. It is within walking distance of the Bailey. I fear it must be early," the lawyer said. "We will be the second case to stand before Rivenhall."

"Druggs?" Marshall asked, arching a brow. "Nothing was said to me of Mr. Druggs escorting Miss Dennsworth."

"My apologies, my lord. I had thought the matter agreed upon when we last spoke," Portsman replied. "Have you changed your mind about being in the courtroom?"

"No. I will not attend the actual trial, agreeing that my presence could cause repercussions. I will, however, call for Miss Dennsworth in the morning and see that she is properly delivered to your office." He gave the lawyer a hard look. "My carriage will be waiting when she leaves the courtroom, as well."

There was no doubt from his tone that Marshall expected a verdict of not guilty.

Portsman came to his feet. "Then, I shall see both of you in the morning. Good day, Miss Dennsworth."

Evelyn waited until the rattle of a hansom's harness signaled Portsman's complete departure before meeting Marshall's gaze. She could tell that he hadn't forgotten their previous conversation and was more than willing to pick up where they had left off. Her mood wasn't an argumentative one, despite what had passed between them before Mr. Portsman's arrival.

If only she could make him understand, explain that she yearned for his embrace, longed to have him hold her. Just hold her. Perhaps then she could sleep. But she knew him well enough to know that if she flung herself into his arms for a good cry, he would misunderstand, and they'd be right back where they had started. She couldn't allow that to happen. Her pride was as badly dented as his. Tomorrow she would be forced to stand before a public audience, strangers greedily waiting to see if she'd be found guilty.

"Do you want me to stay?" Marshall asked, seeing the apprehension in her eyes. He was still angry enough to thrash her, but she looked tired.

"I had thought to retire early," Evelyn said, knowing she was taking the coward's way out.

It wasn't like her, but then, she hadn't been herself of late. The anger at being labeled a thief, the anxiety of awaiting a trial, and the avalanche of emotions that had started with the marquis's first kiss were all taking their toll. The last decent night's sleep she had had was when she'd been at the lodge in Southwark. Marshall had been there with her then, sitting in the chair, watching over her. Since moving into the house, she would retire, only to lie awake, staring at the ceiling, pondering the peculiarity of their relationship.

"If you prefer being alone, I will take my leave."

"Please, don't be angry," she said, standing as well. "It isn't that I want to be alone. You've been so kind, so generous. It's only—"

"Only what?" he demanded. My God, the woman could make him lose his temper faster than anyone he'd ever known. "I warn you, Evelyn, my patience is wearing thin. I have tried to understand, taken your feelings into consideration, but that doesn't change the fact that you want the same thing I want. I can feel it every time I touch you."

Evelyn kept her expression neutral. She had said all there was to say.

"So we are back to that, are we? Very well, if you insist on being stubborn. I have no desire to remain where I am obviously not wanted," Marshall said. He'd made an ass of himself once, getting drunk and crying on Granby's shoulders like some besotted fool. Not again. "Good night," he said. "I will call for you in the morning. Sleep well, Miss Dennsworth."

Hands clenched in the folds of her dress, Evelyn forced herself to watch him leave, forced herself to admit the truth that one day he would walk out of her life never to return. She opened her mouth to call him back, then shut it again. It was better this way.

Ten

The next morning arrived with the gray bleakness of drizzling rain and thick clouds that mixed with the fog to create a wet, soggy blanket over the city. Evelyn had been awake for hours, unable to sleep, wishing for the morning to be quickly over while at the same time she dreaded each minute that passed, fearing the day might be the last one she spent beyond prison walls for a very long time.

She bathed, then dressed in her best clothes, a dark brown suit. The short-waisted jacket was worn with an ivory-colored blouse. She wouldn't be as ostentatiously dressed as Lady Monfrey, but neither would she embarrass herself. Choosing to wear her hair up, she added pearl earrings that had once been her mother's, then looked in the mirror and pronounced herself as ready to meet fate as any woman could possibly be.

She was having tea in the parlor, too nervous to eat even a bite of the toast and jam Mrs. Grunne had added to the tray, when the marquis arrived. The sound of his voice as he bid the footman a good morning filled Evelyn with a longing so deep and painful she had to fight against tears. She had spent a good portion of the night wishing she hadn't dismissed him so quickly last evening. With her pride intact, she had lain awake thinking of him instead of sleeping in his arms, which was what she truthfully preferred. Near dawn she had rebuked herself for being so prideful, but there was nothing she could do to reverse her actions.

"Good morning," Marshall said upon entering the room.

Suddenly, Evelyn had a sharp recollection of how he had smiled at her that first day in Madame La Roschelle's shop. Instinctively, she got up and walked to him—right into his arms.

Marshall didn't question what had prompted the action; he held her close, savoring the feel of her, praying the day's rain had the power to wash all their problems away. "Everything will be all right. Mr. Portsman will bring both authority and discernment to the courtroom, setting this dreadful business aside, once and for all. You must trust in that."

Evelyn lifted her face and met his gaze.

"No doubts," Marshall said firmly. "And no downcast looks. Where is the woman who sent me packing without so much as the blink of an eye? Face Lady Monfrey with half as much tenacity and all will be well."

"I will try, my lord."

"Then we had best be on our way. Do you have a cloak?"

"Yes," she said, reluctant to leave his embrace.

He wrapped an arm around her waist, walking with her into the foyer where Grunne was waiting with the cloak. Marshall draped it over her shoulders, pulling up the hood to keep her dry before they stepped outside. Rain was still falling, and the early morning sky gave no sign that it would stop anytime soon.

Once they were in the carriage, Evelyn stared out the window, unsure what to say for fear that words would break the fragile truce between them. She clasped her hands tightly in her lap, refusing to give in to the dread, the uncertainty she still had to face.

Marshall remained quiet as well. He had left Evelyn last night and returned home to find even more problems awaiting him. His stepmother's depression was becoming impossible to ignore; even Winnifred and Catherine were becoming worried. Another visit from the physician had gleaned no more assurance than the previous visit had brought. Lady Waltham was mourning her husband as if she wanted to join him in the graveyard. Marshall had tried speaking with her, but she had simply stared at him, her ears and heart closed to any semblance of logic.

He had escaped to the library where after several hours of jumbled concentration—his mind being filled with thoughts of Evelyn, as well as his family—he had reached what he hoped would be a redeemable solution for all of them. Of course, the basis of his plan depended upon the magistrate abolishing the charges against Evelyn. Once that was done, he would set things in motion.

They arrived at Mr. Portsman's office on schedule. The rooms were quiet, dulled by the lack of sunlight, but nevertheless comfortable. Once they were seated, the young lawyer wasted no time in reaffirming what he expected. "You are to answer only what I ask of you, Miss Dennsworth. Do not elaborate, and please disdain from using overly emotional terms. Do not fidget, or wrench your hands. Look at the bench when you are answering a question posed by the magistrate, and meet my gaze when replying to my inquiries. Simply answer the questions as honestly as possible, and leave the rest to me."

"I'll try," she said.

"Excellent," he replied, giving her a charming smile, before turning his attention to the marquis. "I will escort Miss Dennsworth from here to the Bailey."

Marshall's reluctance was obvious. "Surely no one will notice if she leaves my carriage. There is no crest on the door, and I doubt we will encounter any of my parliamentary friends this early in the morning."

"I will be fine," Evelyn said, forcing a smile to her face.

"I shall wait in the outer office," Portsman announced as he closed the thin leather pouch that contained the legal documents he would need for the day.

Once they were alone, Evelyn stood up. "You know he's right."

"I know," Marshall replied, sounding for all the world like a disgruntled child.

It was then that Evelyn knew why he was being so hesitant about leaving her. He wanted to kiss her goodbye and regardless of his usual confidence wasn't entirely sure how to go about it. She solved the problem for him.

"Would you kiss me?" she asked, moving to stand before him. "A long kiss, if you please. One that will last through the trial."

Marshall smiled. For some unknown reason, this woman seemed to have the ability to feel his thoughts as vividly as he felt them himself. He pulled her into his arms.

The kiss was just as she asked, long and lingering, deep and arousing. It was all Evelyn could do not to cling to him, to let go of the tears she had fought all morning. When the kiss finally ended, she took a shaky breath and smiled up at him.

"Promise me you will not come into the Bailey."

"Damnation woman, but you ask a lot of me," Marshall gritted out. "I would not have you face this alone."

"I am not alone," she replied. "Mr. Portsman is with me. He will escort me back here, and we shall return to Lambeth Road to resume the argument that is not yet finished between us."

Marshall shook his head. "You will be the end of me, Miss Dennsworth."

"I doubt that," Evelyn said, regaining some of her former flippancy. Then because time allowed nothing more, she kissed him on the cheek. "Thank you," she whispered, then moved away before he could stop her.

Marshall fisted his hands at his sides and watched her leave. After half an hour of pacing Portsman's office, he'd had enough. He walked outside, grateful to discover that the rain had stopped. A brisk east wind was blowing off the Thames, shaking belated raindrops off the leaves. Jerking off his greatcoat, he commanded his driver, a man by the name of Emerson, to do the same.

"Milord?"

"Your coat, Emerson, and be quick about it."

Having served the family for a good many years, enough to know that the marquis was an indomitable man in his own right, Emerson took off his coat and handed it to his employer.

"If memory serves, there's a coffeehouse around the corner," Marshall said, slipping his arms into the coat. The two men were close in height, but Emerson's shoulders weren't nearly as wide. It would have to do, just the same. He reached into the pocket of his trousers and pulled out several coins. "Buy yourself a pint of hot cider. I shan't be gone long."

Marshall turned and walked briskly toward the Central Court of the Old Bailey.

The chamber was large, with high ceilings and darkly paneled walls. The gallery was crowded with people, pressed together like fish in a vendor's wagon. Marshall could smell them, their clothing dampened by the morning's rain. He tugged the driver's coat closed, concealing the fine broadcloth of his jacket and the embroidered silk of his vest. Pulling up the collar to cover as much of his identity as possible, he stood in the back of the balcony that overlooked the courtroom.

Portsman was already there, looking perfectly at ease in

his black robe and white wig. Rivenhall sat behind the bench, wearing the same attire, his thin face appearing almost gaunt with the judicial wig flapping about his ears. The magistrate would forfeit his seat after the morning adjournment, giving way to a higher judge who would hear more serious matters, those that could easily result in a death sentence.

Lady Monfrey sat near the bench, at a mahogany table. Lord Monfrey was nowhere in sight, but Marshall recognized the young man sitting next to the plaintiff. He was the couple's youngest son, a vain young man who expected his father's wealth and reputation to carry him through life.

Marshall's gaze was torn away from the overweight social matron when the doors at the far end of the court opened to reveal Evelyn, escorted by a bailiff. She stared straight ahead, walking gracefully toward the dock where she would be required to stand until Rivenhall rendered his decision. A jury would hear the case, but it was the magistrate who would determine the sentence.

The man in front of Marshall jostled for position, as did most of the men in the courtroom, each wanting a closer look at the lovely young woman accused of theft.

Marshall watched and listened as Rivenhall read the charges. For a man who looked more like a black-robed scarecrow than an administrator of the law, his voice was extremely loud, carrying to every corner of the room. Upon finishing, he looked toward Evelyn.

"Are you prepared to accept the charges against you, Miss Dennsworth?"

"I am not, my lord," she replied. "I am innocent of the crime."

The barrister seated to the right of Lady Monfrey stood, and the trial began. He was an elderly man with a broad forehead and small, deep-set eyes. After a lengthy speech that depicted Lady Monfrey as so distressed over the loss of her beloved brooch, she was unable to speak without bursting into tears, he addressed the jury, reaffirming the charges and accusing Evelyn of stealing the brooch, citing the low wages of a shop girl as sufficient cause.

After finishing, the barrister retired to his seat, not bothering to call a single witness. His arrogance didn't go unnoticed by the man standing next to Marshall. "Bloody puffed-up peacock," the man said in a raspy voice.

Marshall silently echoed the opinion.

The next hour convinced him that if he should ever have to stand before the law, he wanted James Portsman at his side. The young man skillfully cut through the pomp and circumstance, summoning Lady Monfrey to the witness box. Dressed in a bright yellow dress that was better suited for entertaining in the parlor than testifying in a courtroom, the plump lady looked more like a fat parakeet than a victim.

Once Portsman had finished questioning Lady Monfrey, getting the facts from her so dexterously that she didn't realize she was admitting to nothing less than snobbish speculation, he dismissed her from the witness box. Her own barrister having no questions, the court moved on.

The next person questioned was the constable who had taken Evelyn into custody after searching Madame La Roschelle's shop.

"Are you saying that you thoroughly searched both the dress shop and Miss Dennsworth's personal apartment and found nothing?" Portsman asked.

"That's right," Constable Wilverton told the court. "Went back the next day and had a second look, just to make sure. There weren't no brooch. Nothing more than what you'd expect to find in a young woman's room, clothes and a few trinkets."

"What of her person?" Portsman asked. "Did you search Miss Dennsworth before taking her into custody?"

"Aye," the constable said. "I went through her apron and

the pockets of her skirt. Madame La Roschelle saw to the rest, behind one of the fitting curtains."

"Thank you, Constable."

Portsman then turned to question the accused, addressing Evelyn with the same respect he had shown for Lady Monfrey. She recited the day's events with precision and clarity, making Marshall's heart swell with pride. He knew she was terrified inside, knew she felt humiliated and hurt by being forced to defend herself, and yet not a hint of it showed. She appeared as well composed as a saint, sure of herself and her innocence.

When it came time for Evelyn to be questioned by her ladyship's barrister, she stood with the same unwavering confidence, not giving in to the man's baited remarks. Not once did she measure her words or hesitate to reply in a clear, firm voice. She spoke the truth, and everyone heard it. When she finished, Marshall half expected to hear a cheer go up from the crowd; she had won the heart of everyone in the courtroom.

Lady Monfrey sat at the plaintiff's table, red faced and clearly upset that the supposed thief was, in fact, an eloquently spoken young woman whose father had maintained a respected parish for thirty of his sixty-two years, a common woman who carried herself with the regal grace of a queen, and who hadn't once hesitated to look her accuser straight in the eye.

The jury took less than ten minutes to reach a verdict of not guilty.

The sound of Rivenhall's gavel coming down in dismissal was drowned out by a noisy protest from Lady Monfrey, who was quickly quieted by her barrister. The lady looked ready to split her corset as the barrister and her son hauled her from the room, while Portsman graciously thanked the court for its wisdom.

Marshall watched as the lawyer helped Evelyn down

from the dock platform, speaking to her for a brief second before handing her over to the bailiff who escorted her out of the chamber. Wanting to be by her side as quickly as possible, Marshall pushed through the crowd. He found her at the bottom of the colonnade, near the curb, looking lost.

"Marshall!" she said, using his given name because he caught her completely off guard. Her eyes were shining with unshed tears.

"Come along," he said, not caring if all of London saw him take her arm and escort her down the street. "It's going to rain again. I don't want you catching a chill."

A coatless Emerson was waiting by the carriage. Marshall gladly surrendered the driver's missing garment, then quickly ushered Evelyn into the carriage. "I will leave word with Portsman's clerk that I once again have you in custody," he said. "Wait here."

Evelyn sat in the carriage, listless now that the trial was finally over. It had been horrible, standing in the dock, having everyone studying her, waiting to see if she would slip up and say something the barrister could use against her. Even Rivenhall had stared at her as though he had never seen her before, though of course he had. Portsman hadn't varied from their chosen path, asking exactly what he had told her he would ask, waiting for her to answer, then moving on to the next question. Lady Monfrey had stared at her the entire time, her hawkish gaze growing more uncomfortable, more accusing, as the proceedings came to a close.

Evelyn leaned her head back and rested it against the cushioned seat. She closed her eyes. She was free now. Free to leave the house on Lambeth Road, free to make her way back to Sussex or another village. Try as she might, she couldn't help but think of Marshall, of saying goodbye to him. The mere thought of never seeing him again was enough to start the tears flowing.

"None of that," he said, climbing into the carriage. "It's a day to celebrate."

She offered him a weak smile. The next thing she knew she was being scooped up and onto his lap. He wrapped his arms around her, holding tight when she tried to wiggle free.

"No. I will hold you and you will cry, and then there will be no more tears. Is that understood?"

"You just told me not to cry."

"I have recently discovered that telling you to do one thing results in you doing just the opposite," Marshall said with a long sigh. "Besides, having you cry on my shoulder suits my purposes perfectly at the moment, so please indulge yourself."

It was all the encouragement she needed. The tears were silent, flowing down her face as she rested it against his chest. She cried because her body demanded it, letting go of the anxiety she had held in check for hours, letting the emotions out. The anger, the pain, the fear that came from feeling her heart begin to break, all flowed from her, leaving her so exhausted it was all she could do not to fall asleep in the marquis's arms.

Marshall held her close the entire time, saying nothing, letting the warmth of his body and the comfort of his arms speak for themselves. Anticipation pooled inside him.

Evelyn was finally free of the worries that had stood between them since the day of her arrest. Despite the good news delivered by the jury, Marshall knew the path ahead would not be without its stumbling blocks. He had made love to her once, given her a glimpse of the pleasures they could share together, but she was still hesitant to embrace them. The second part of his plan would have to be executed with the utmost skill or she would run from him.

When they reached Lambeth Road, Marshall again ignored her protests and carried her inside. "Tell Mrs. Grunne that something warm and nourishing is required," he said, stepping past the startled footman. "She is to bring it upstairs as quickly as possible."

"Please, I can manage on my own," Evelyn said, despite the enjoyment of being cradled in the arms of her favorite marquis.

"For once, you will do as you are told," Marshall told her. He marched directly up the steps, stopping once he'd reached the second floor. "Where to from here?"

"The first door on the right," Evelyn replied, knowing she had no choice in the matter.

Marshall couldn't help but note the irony of the situation. He had installed this woman in this house, thinking to make her his mistress, and yet he had to ask directions to find the room in which she slept. He carried her to the bed, depositing her in the center of it, then reached for the buttons on her jacket.

"What are you doing?"

"Getting you into bed," he said matter-of-factly. "You can't rest all trussed up like a Christmas goose."

"No," Evelyn said, slapping at his hands.

"Yes," he responded just as fiercely. The remark was followed by a vigorous attack upon her clothing. Buttons, hooks and eyes, and laces were dispensed with in a hurried fashion. "You are exhausted. You gave the court a grand show." He sent her shoes flying to the far corner of the room, then began expertly stripping her down to nothing but her chemise and stockings. "And a grand show, it was," he added, tossing the last of her petticoats onto the chair, "but I can see the exhaustion in your eyes. Having already confessed to not sleeping well, there is no point in denying the charge. You will rest, or I'll tie you to this bed and make sure of it."

Smiling as if to say she wasn't at all surprised that his

lordship had finally found his way upstairs, Mrs. Grunne came into the room, carrying a tray laden with hot tea, soup, and fresh-baked bread.

"You may put the tray on the table, Mrs. Grunne," Marshall said. "I will see that Miss Dennsworth is fed."

"Is the lady all right, milord?"

"She's fine," Evelyn replied, frowning at them both. She pulled the sheet up to her chin. "Just a bit tired is all."

"More than a bit," Marshall contradicted her. "She will not be downstairs for some time. Please see that her evening meal is brought up on a tray."

"Yes, milord," Mrs. Grunne said. "Will you be needing anything more?"

"Brandy," he replied, daring Evelyn with a heated glance to countermand his order.

Once the door was closed, she sat up. "I can feed myself."

Marshall didn't waste his time replying. He took off his jacket, shedding his vest and cravat with the same haste he had used to strip her almost bare. He immediately came to the bed and sat down beside her. He tucked the blankets in around her, and smiled. "The soup is for you; the brandy is for me," he said gruffly. "I will have some solace for being forced into the public gallery. God, I wanted to strangle that strutting peacock of a barrister. How dare he treat you with such contempt."

"You weren't supposed to be there. Your reaction is exactly why Mr. Portsman specifically requested that you stay away."

"As if I could," Marshall grunted. "But it is all behind us now."

Evelyn closed her eyes for a moment, wishing it were true. Unfortunately, the worst was yet to come. She had to find a way to leave the kindhearted man who was even now testing her soup to make sure it didn't burn her tongue.

Knowing he would spoon-feed her like a child if she didn't

eat, Evelyn took the bowl from his hands. Once she had finished, the bowl was replaced with a cup of tea. In the interim, Grunne had brought up a bottle of brandy. Marshall poured himself a drink, sipping it while she did the same with the tea. When both cup and glass were empty, he set them aside and stood up.

To Evelyn's amazement, he stripped out of his clothes, flipped back the blanket, and joined her in the bed. Before she could make her way out from beneath the covers, Marshall's arms hooked around her waist, pulling her back against his bare chest. He pulled her down beside him. "I'll hold you until you fall asleep."

A small dream come true, Evelyn thought as she found the chill of a rainy day smothered by the incredible warmth of Marshall's body. Her hands couldn't refuse the sensual temptation his naked chest presented. He felt so alive, so strong and vital. She let her fingertips settle into the crisp, curly hair on his chest and began to relax, then wiggled closer, letting her body fit against his as naturally as it had that morning on the sofa.

If only the peace she felt at this moment could last forever. If only . . . Evelyn quenched her thoughts. She'd be crying again if she didn't, and she refused to shed any more tears over fate and its unpredictable turns. The morning had come and gone. She'd survived the courtroom. She would survive the following morning, as well. But for now, she would cherish the present, the lullaby of the rain, the restful quiet that permeated the house, the warmth of Marshall's embrace. He seemed content to hold her, not pushing comfort into passion, which they both knew he could easily do. All it would take was one kiss, and she'd be lost again, pulled into a feverish dream.

"This is nice," Marshall murmured. He smiled as he watched Evelyn's eyes drifting closed. A few moments later, he joined her to sleep the afternoon away.

* * *

It was nearing dark when Marshall woke. He stretched, smiling as he felt Evelyn move against him. How long had it been since he'd actually slept with a woman? So long he couldn't recall the last time he'd enjoyed waking up beside one. He rolled to his side, bringing her even closer. She turned her head slightly, mumbling something against his skin. Her breath felt warm. It was just the aphrodisiac his body needed to come fully awake.

Her hair had come undone, tumbling over the pillow in a cloud of golden brown curls. He reached for a wayward strand, curling it around his finger. What was he going to do with her? What his body wanted was easy enough to determine. He was hard and ready to pull her beneath him, to satisfy himself in her silky depths. It was tempting. Oh, so tempting.

Knowing he'd have a sleepy, scratching she-cat on his hands if he tried to seduce her a second time, Marshall forced himself from the bed. Once he was wearing his trousers and a loosely buttoned shirt, he walked to the window.

Even with his back to the room, he couldn't distance himself from Evelyn. He could hear her breathing, see in his mind the delicate rise and fall of her breasts beneath her chemise. His body ached to be reunited with hers, to feel the hot, satiny warmth of her channel accepting him, to hear the soft sounds she made when he loved her.

Evelyn opened her eyes to the dim light of a shadow-filled room. She blinked lazily, adjusting to the encroaching darkness, then smiled. The bed felt so cozy and warm, making her snuggle deeper into the feather mattress. Sighing, she turned on her side to find Marshall standing by the window, watching her. The memories came rushing back: the ordeal of the trial, crying in the carriage, being carried upstairs and fed her lunch like a sick child, then his body coming to rest beside hers, his warmth surrounding her.

"Good, you're awake," he said, coming to sit on the side of the bed.

"My lord," she said, knowing she should be ashamed of having shared a bed with him, even if all he had done was hold her.

"My lord," he mimicked, frowning. "Will I ever convince you to call me Marshall on a regular basis?"

"I fear not," she said, sitting up as she came fully awake. Keeping the coverlet high about her shoulders, she frowned at him in return. "It seems I am forever saying thank you."

"And I am forever telling you it isn't necessary."

Nothing more was said for a long moment, each wanting to speak, but both unable to think of the appropriate words. For Evelyn it was the new experience of sleeping beside a man. Making love with the marquis on the sofa in the parlor had been erotic and wonderful. Lying beside him for several hours, lost in sleep, seemed vastly more intimate.

For Marshall it was knowing that he couldn't allow her to slip from his grasp, and he knew that was exactly what she planned to do. Deciding to nip the idea in the bud before it rooted itself any deeper in her mind, he said, "I want to ask you something. A favor, if you are willing to give it."

"A favor?"

"Parliament is soon to adjourn for the summer. As its members move to the country, so shall the dreaded Season that has my sister in its grip. There will be lawn parties, more balls, country weekends entertaining people I'd rather not see," he said, clearly dreading the idea of society following him to his beloved Ipswich.

"What has that to do with me?" Evelyn asked, wishing he would button his shirt. It was gapping open over his chest, and the sight of him was making her thoughts begin to wander.

"I have spoken of my stepmother," he said. "She refuses to leave her room of late, and I am becoming increasingly concerned about her health. The physician insists that she is simply grieving in her own way, but I will not accept that explanation. She is far too young to spend the rest of her life behind closed doors, shutting out the real world. The girls need her guidance, her social expertise. Catherine is only ten. Her governess sees to her studies, but she needs her mother."

"Then, the country air should do Lady Waltham good."

"I think it will take more than fresh air and a change of scenery," Marshall replied. He stood up and began to pace the room, his movements demonstrating his frustration at not being able to understand the female mind.

"What favor are you asking of me?" Evelyn finally asked.

"Constance needs someone, a companion who can ease her despair. The girls love her, of course, and they join in her grief over our father's death, but they are too young to understand. They are getting on with their lives: Winnifred stepping into society, Catherine bubbling about each new sunrise. It's the contradiction of personalities I face each and every day."

"You want me to be your stepmother's companion!"

"Yes." Marshall smiled at her. "I know Constance would warm to you, especially after seeing you in the courtroom this morning. You have a way about you, Miss Dennsworth, a way of reaching out to people, to total strangers, making them want to reach back in return."

"But—"

He stopped her protest with a touch of his fingertips to her mouth. "No, don't recite all the reasons you cannot accept the position. I told you I wanted no repayment for what had passed between us, and I meant it. I am not demanding that you come to Ipswich with me. I am asking nothing except that you take the position as companion to Lady

Waltham. You will be paid a fair salary for the job, funds you will need if you still plan on opening your own shop."

Evelyn was taken back by the offer, both the outrageousness of the marquis thinking he could install her in the family's lap and the knowledge that the money he would pay her would go a long way in making the dream of her own dress shop come true. "Would you have me live in the house?"

He shrugged his shoulders, making his shirt gap open even more. "I hadn't thought about it, but then, most companions do, don't they?"

"I would not be most companions, and well you know it," Evelyn replied. Her curious gaze turned into an accusing glare. "If you think to install me in the country for your pleasure, the answer is definitely no."

Marshall laughed. "I see your principles are back in full force, not that you've ever strayed too far from them."

"I . . . It would make for an impossible situation," she told him. On the inside, Evelyn was shocked by the proposal of employment. She did need a job, but she'd prepared herself to return to her needle and thread, to make her way without any assistance from anyone. Living in the country, at the marquis's estate, would be suicidal to her heart.

"There is a cottage on the grounds," Marshall said. "Between the house and the beach. It hasn't been used for quite some time and would require a thorough cleaning. Would that suit you better?"

Her own cottage, and near the beach.

"I'm told it's drafty when a storm moves in," he said.

"Living in a drafty cottage is no bar to my comfort."

"You'll come!"

He smiled that rakishly handsome smile that she found impossible to resist. How could she refuse him or the smile? He had done so much for her, and she could tell that his concern for Lady Waltham was sincere. If she lived apart from the family, there would be less chance of them meeting in what she was sure was a massive manor house. As far as her principles were concerned, they were hers to uphold, not Marshall's. If she surrendered to the temptation he presented, it was her weakness, not his.

"Yes, but only for the summer," she answered. A thought flashed through her mind. "What about your sister? Lady Winnifred is sure to recognize me. How are going to explain that a shop girl accused of theft is now companion to her mother?"

"I am master in my own house," Marshall said confidently. "Leave Winnifred to me."

Evelyn started to shake her head, but his mouth came swooping down before she could elaborate on her doubts. He stole any words of protest with the hungry kiss, teasing her lips until they parted, allowing him inside.

Streamers of sensation began to flutter inside Evelyn. Her head fell back against the pillows, and he followed, deepening the kiss until she had no other choice but to abandon herself into his tender care. And he was tender—tenderly passionate.

Marshall raked his hands through her hair, holding her head in place while he gently ravished her mouth. His fingers stroked the sides of her throat, then lower, stopping at the lace of her chemise.

Evelyn accepted his touch with a sigh that signaled she was as passionate as she was wary. She kissed him with an honesty that was just as passionate, just as arousing as it had been that day in the parlor. Her body swelled to meet his gentle demands. She arched under his hands, unable to stop the instinctive movement that stated she wanted more of his touch not less.

"My lovely lady," he whispered against her lips. Her took her mouth again, more demandingly this time, his hands moving restlessly over her breasts.

Then his mouth joined his hands. It closed over the tip of one breast, his tongue hot and rough as it licked and teased, circled and tormented. Evelyn felt the heat all the way to the soles of her feet. He gave her other breast the same unerring attention, not stopping until her chemise was wet and clinging to her aching nipples.

Marshall raised his head and admired his handiwork. When he lightly pinched one damp, muslin-covered tip, she gasped.

"You are the most distracting woman I have ever known," he said huskily. "I want to strip off my clothes again and come back to bed with you."

Evelyn's conscience surfaced at his words. How could she give herself a second time, especially now that she had agreed to travel to Ipswich with him, and not become his mistress? She looked up at him, torn between helping him out of his clothes and the consequences if she did. She bit down on her lower lip, holding the words back, holding her feelings in check.

Marshall saw the battle Evelyn was waging with herself. It was in her eyes and the sudden tautness of her body. She was nearly as aroused as he was, but still aware enough to know that if he returned to bed, it would be the last sensual battle between them. Deciding that it might serve him well to let the beguiling, irritating woman stew in her own juices, he kissed her again, quick and hard, then stood up. "The next time we make love, my dear Miss Dennsworth, you will do the seducing. Until then, know that I shall look forward to it."

Eleven

Bedford Hall was a red brick Tudor mansion rising up from the center of a vast, well-manicured lawn. A graveled drive formed a perfect semicircle in front of the country estate. Evelyn stared out the coach window, duly impressed by the grandeur of Marshall's family home. The house was constructed in an open courtyard fashion with both an east and west wing that flanked the main section of the house. Two symmetrical bell towers rose above the flat roof and bricked chimneys.

"I hope you will be happy here," Mr. Druggs said, smiling as he, too, glanced out the window. "It's a grand old house."

The secretary had traveled with her from London, at the express orders of the marquis, to see that she was settled into the cottage before the family arrived at week's end. The journey had been a pleasant one, the weather being fair, the lanes shaded by thick-leaved trees.

Mr. Druggs, who had turned out to be an amicable traveling companion, had told her that Harwich lay to the south of them, along the coast. The marquis was a member of the Royal Harwich Yacht Club, founded in 1843 when a group of yacht owners, the previous marquis among them, had decided to form an east coast club that could contend with the Royal Thames Yacht Club. The result was a lively competition of sailing craft that raced from Harwich south to the Thames estuary in an annual event. Shortly after its formation, the club had been accorded royal patronage by the dowager Queen Adelaide, the widow of William IV, known as "Sailor Bill." The current marquis proudly flew the blue ensign, emblazoned with a lion rampart, each time he took his thirty-foot sloop into the Channel.

Evelyn recalled the times Marshall had talked about sailing with his father. She knew the sport was close to his heart. Whenever he spoke of sailing, his eyes took on a warm glow, as though he could feel the wind brushing against his face and the sting of salt water as it wiped over the bow of the ship. Evelyn had never been on the water, never sailed, yet she had shared his excitement when he'd told her of racing in his first regatta.

As the carriage moved down the main drive, passing Bedford Hall, Evelyn could see that the estate was a working farm, complete with a dovecote and landscaped park. The cottage sat near the dovecote, on a small knoll above the beach.

Mr. Druggs helped her down, then smiled as she stared longingly toward the small stone house with its freshly painted green door and matching shutters. There was a small flower bed beneath the front window and a row of shrubbery bordering the path that lead to the front door.

"Lord Waltham hopes it will be to your liking," the secretary announced. "Go ahead, take a look inside."

Evelyn, feeling as giddy as a schoolgirl, hurried along the flat stone path toward the most lovely little cottage she had ever seen. Its steepled roof was outlined by blue sky, while the cottage itself sat on a high windy bluff, overlooking the Channel. The parklands ran parallel to the sandy beach, broken only by the occasional outcropping of ribbed limestone.

Beyond the beach lay the vista of the English Channel, miles and miles of uninterrupted water. Wind whipped over the liquid surface, churning up small white-capped waves, causing them to fold over themselves before sending them rippling onto the sandy shore.

The sound was just as enthralling, a melody of earth, wind, and water. The thought of hearing the song each night as she lay in her bed sent a shiver of expectation through Evelyn's body. The vision of being held in Marshall's arms, while the ocean lulled them to sleep, was enough to make her emotions churn. Emotions that were beginning to be viewed in a different light now that she knew she did, in fact, love the marquis. She'd finally admitted the inevitable somewhere between London and Ipswich, calling her feelings by their true name, labeling them boldly within her mind. It was somewhat of a relief, she supposed. There'd be no more wondering, no more doubts about her actions or reactions. Love could be blamed for all.

"I will leave you to your unpacking and settling in," Mr. Druggs said, coming to stand beside her. "If you need anything, my quarters are in the back of the house, near the entrance to the east wing. Any of the servants can direct you to me. Dinner is normally served at eight. I will introduce you to the staff at that time. Most of them have been with the family as long, if not longer, than I. You will find them a friendly lot."

"Thank you," Evelyn said, looking past him to where the footman, who had ridden on the perch next to the driver, was carrying her valise to the front door. "I shall see you at dinner then."

"It will be dark," Druggs said. "I will send a footman to escort you."

Having concluded over the course of their journey that the secretary could be just as obstinate as his employer, Evelyn didn't argue. Instead, she thanked him again, then waved as the coach turned around and headed back toward the main house.

She stood outside a few minutes longer, silently appreciating the scenery. The water, wind, and sea combined to create a savage beauty. The fantastic coloring of the beach, muted shades of brown and white, clumps of tall, wispy green grass that bent gracefully under the wind, the wet tide line thick with seaweed, this was where the marquis had played as a child, running barefoot with a kite fluttering overhead. Smiling to herself, Evelyn could easily imagine him racing the wind.

Still smiling, she turned to investigate the cottage. Stepping over the threshold seemed a ceremonious affair since it represented a significant change in her life. London was behind her; ahead lay a summer of uncertainty, yet one she found herself eager to begin.

As expected the cottage had been thoroughly cleaned. The main room was spacious with a high ceiling and a stone fireplace large enough to roast an entire boar. The furnishings were remnants of the lavish lifestyle of a manor house, each piece sturdy and smelling of beeswax from a recent polishing. Chintz curtains in a light floral pattern covered the windows.

The bedroom was small but extremely comfortable, with a four-poster bed covered by a blue canopy and matching coverlet. Evelyn opened the shutters to the wind and the scent of the sea while she unpacked.

It had been a week since she'd last seen the marquis. He had called on her, confirming the date she was to leave London with Mr. Druggs as her traveling companion. Since she had agreed to come to Ipswich, Marshall had relaxed his efforts to entice her into bed a second time. They had resumed their walks in the park, having dinner together when his schedule permitted, talking late into the evenings. He never left without kissing her goodbye.

It was the memory of those kisses that had set Evelyn to thinking during the trip from London to the coastal estate of Bedford Hall.

She knew the marquis expected her to fall into his trap again. His thinking process was ironic, since she had not fallen into it the first time but had given herself of her own free will for her own reasons. Still, Evelyn knew the months ahead would have their difficulties. She had to face the upcoming disappointment of saying goodbye at the end of the summer, for she had no plans of returning to London and the house on Lambeth Road.

She could fight her feelings all she wanted, deny them all she wanted, but they weren't going to go away. There was no mistaking her affection for Marshall, no disguising it. It was love, at least on her part. The marquis had been a haven, an invincible knight who had charged to her rescue when she had needed one the most. In return, he was asking nothing more than she was willing to give.

Therein lay the question. How much was she willing to give?

More importantly, how much was she willing to risk?

By finally admitting that she was in love with the marquis, Evelyn knew she was risking not only her heart, but her future happiness. A lifetime of happiness that might never be gained if the marquis couldn't bring himself to love her.

"I do not understand why you have employed a companion," Lady Waltham said, staring at her stepson, who was seated opposite her in the family's traveling coach. Her blue eyes, once warm and full of life, were now dulled by grief. "Bedford Hall has an abundance of servants, and I have two daughters."

Marshall, accustomed to arguing with females, especially since assuming the role of head of the family, smiled slightly before replying. "Your daughters, although devoted to you, shouldn't be shackled to your side. As for the servants, they are just that. Servants."

"I am not shackled to Mama," Catherine said, quickly jumping into the conversation. "Nor is Winnie."

"Your mother understands the remark," Marshall replied, his tone letting both his sisters know that the conversation was not one they were invited to join.

"Who is she?" Lady Waltham asked noncommittally.

"Her name is Evelyn Dennsworth, a young woman who has recently found herself unemployed due to circumstances beyond her control. Her references are excellent, I assure you."

He cut a glance at Winnie, but his sister showed no sign of connecting Evelyn's name with the events that had taken place on Bond Street several weeks past. Of course, she was sure to recognize Evelyn, but he'd address that problem when he had the opportunity to speak with his sister alone. For now, his only intention was to make his family aware that an additional employee had been added to the staff.

"What will she do that I cannot do for myself?" Lady Waltham inquired, folding her hands in her lap. She was clothed in unrelieved black, her shimmering satin skirts spotless. The veil of her hat had been lifted to reveal a profusion of jet beads and stiff black lace.

"Anything you wish her to do," Marshall replied. "Don't forget the regatta party. As I recall, the event always consumed a good deal of time."

"I had not thought about it," Lady Waltham replied stiffly.

"Then you should," Marshall told her. "Forsaking the event last summer was understandable and acceptable. However, it has always been held at Bedford Hall. We will resume the tradition this year. What better opportunity will we have to present an invitation to Lord Lansdowne?"

"Lord Lansdowne?" His stepmother arched a pale brow. "I did not realize he was a member of the yacht club."

"He isn't," Marshall replied with a sheepish grin. "He is, however, the man who seems to be paying more than a passing interest in your oldest daughter. I think it is time you met him."

His stepmother looked at Winnifred. "Would extending an invitation to Lord Lansdowne please you, Winnie?"

"Yes, Mama," she said, doing her best not to blush and failing miserably.

"Then the matter of the party is settled," Marshall announced. "Miss Dennsworth is an accomplished seamstress. I'm sure she can help."

His youngest sister immediately picked up the conversation, filling the coach with endless chatter and questions about the beau Winnie had failed to mention.

Marshall listened, but his thoughts were elsewhere. Each turn of the coach's wheels brought him closer to a reunion with Evelyn. Her image haunted him, an image that brought with it a confusion of reactions. No woman had ever created such questions for him while at the same time bringing him a sense of well-being. His motives for wanting her at Bedford Hall were clear enough, but beyond that he knew lay the possibility of the very thing he had wished to avoid in taking a mistress and assuming a benign relationship that would give him pleasure without complications. There was certainly nothing benign about his relationship with Evelyn. In truth, he was certain that having her on the estate would only serve to complicate an already complex set of circumstances. Still, he was not ready to dismiss her from his life, nor, did he believe, was Evelyn all that eager to go her separate way.

* * *

Marshall stood atop the bluff watching her, marveling at how young and carefree she looked with her hair hanging down her back. She was wading, her feet bare, her skirt hiked up to her knees as she played catch-me-if-you-can with the incoming waves. He walked down the bluff, his riding boots digging into the soft sand, leaving a trail behind him as he strolled onto the sun-laden beach. He called out her name, and she turned.

"Druggs told me not to expect you until tomorrow," Evelyn said, unable to take her eyes off him. He was dressed for riding in snug-fitting pants and a lawn shirt that was only partially buttoned. His expression was relaxed, making him look very much like a man glad to be home.

"It's easy to see that you've settled in. Tell me, how do you like Bedford Hall?"

"As Druggs would say, 'It's a grand old house,' " Evelyn replied. She stepped free of the water, loving the feel of the warm, damp sand under her feet as she shook out her skirts. "I've only seen a small part of it, of course."

"Been busy playing with the tide?" Marshall mused, taking a step closer.

"There's been little else to do. The staff refuses to let me assume a single duty." She spread her hands wide. "So I have plenty of time to walk the beach. It's lovely."

"Yes, it is," Marshall replied, taking another step forward. His gaze roamed over her features, the glow of her skin that hadn't been there in London, the sparkle in her eyes that made him suspect she was glad to see him, the sensual curve of her mouth as it lifted into a smile.

They stared into each other's eyes. For Evelyn the world began here and now, the soft whisper of the wind through the beach grass, the heat of the afternoon sun, and the scalding intensity of Marshall's gaze as he took one more step forward. He would kiss her, she knew.

Her body was incapable of moving away from him. She

couldn't avert her gaze, couldn't stop thinking of how wonderful his mouth would feel when he finally pressed it to hers, couldn't breathe for wanting him to hurry and get on with it.

She wet her lips.

"Sweet God," he said sharply, then pulled her hard against his chest.

Evelyn gasped, then grabbed his shoulders to keep from stumbling in the soft sand. A second later she knew the reaction had been unnecessary. Marshall held her in an inescapable embrace. His feet were braced apart, his arms firmly about her as he lifted her high and tight against his body. She could feel the proof of his desire, hard and warm as it pressed against her belly. Unable to prevent it, she felt her body yielding, softening in reply.

The kiss went on and on, hot and deep, insistent. She kissed him back just as insistently, delighting in the sensual pleasure of man and wind and water. There was no holding back this time, no hesitation, no doubts. Within seconds, her body was humming, her blood running hot and wild through her veins. Under her clothing, her breasts swelled and her skin grew warm. This was what she had missed, this feeling of being alive, wildly alive and utterly feminine. The social differences between them faded into nothingness at moments like this. The marquis became a man, just a man, and she became his woman.

Marshall ended the kiss out of necessity. He held Evelyn close, taking deep, calming breaths to still the wildness of his blood. A man had only so much control, and his was being tested to the limit. Having had her, knowing the sweet pleasure of her body, was pure torment at times like these. He wanted nothing more than to strip her down to her lovely skin and appease the sexual hunger that was growing more urgent with each passing day. He had spent the last week thinking about her. His original preoccupation with her and her challenging ways had turned into an obsession. He would have her again—one way or the other.

Evelyn rested her cheek against his chest and listened to his heartbeat blend with the magical sound of the sea. Her feelings for the marquis continued to dismay her. In the seven years since her father's death, she had grown accustomed to having some control over her life.

But that control had been snatched away from her. First by Lady Monfrey's false accusation, then by the constable, and finally by the marquis, himself. Her life had turned topsy-turvy. In a matter of weeks, she'd gone from a small room above a dress shop on Bond Street to a rented house on Lambeth Road to a country estate that continuously reminded her of the vast differences between herself and the man who was currently holding her in his arms. The entire situation, her feelings included, defied logic. But then, no one had ever accused love of being logical.

"Let's walk," Marshall said, taking her hand.

Neither of them said anything. Instead, they strolled hand in hand, listening to the chatter of quarreling seagulls and the endless lapping of waves onto the shore.

Marshall realized that he had truly missed times like these. Moments spent in quiet reflection, unhindered by needless conversation. Evelyn's presence precipitated a sense of peace within him that he was unable to explain. It also triggered a passion unlike any he'd ever felt before. If she persisted in being stubborn about things, his tolerance was going to be put to the test. One kiss and he was ready to drag her off behind some isolated dune and have her right there on the beach with the afternoon sun gleaming down on their naked bodies and the tide nipping at their heels.

"I assume you've told Lady Waltham that she now has a companion," Evelyn finally spoke.

"Yes."

"And . . . ," she prompted, anxious as to how Marshall's family would react to her.

"She doesn't think she needs one," Marshall replied. "But then, I warned you to expect as much."

"And your sisters? What do they think?"

"It doesn't matter what they think," he told her, stopping at the edge of a small tide pool. In front of them, a crab scurried sideways across the sand. "You are here, and here you will stay."

"I'll stay until the end of the summer," she said, searching for a way to tell him of the decision she had reached.

Thinking she was going to use any and every excuse she could to keep them apart, Marshall prepared himself for another argument. "I refuse to talk about your leaving when you've only just arrived."

Having debated, argued, and analyzed her feelings thoroughly since leaving London, Evelyn wondered what the marquis would say when she told him that she'd decided to accept his offer.

It hadn't been an easy decision. She'd fought her conscience at first, a formidable foe to say the least. But having already surrendered her virginity to him, it served little purpose to consider herself a fallen woman. Her heart told her that love was too precious, too rare, to ignore. And she knew that she did, indeed, love the marquis. The exact moment the possibility had turned into a reality, Evelyn couldn't say. What she could say, what she knew with absolute certainty, was that this man made her feel special.

Having reached the most monumental decision of her life, Evelyn amazed herself by feeling little or no regret over it. She was, after all, a woman of twenty-six years, mature in her thinking, and accountable to no one but herself. Why should she rebuke the only man who had ever come close to making her feel loved? Why should she refuse a passionate liaison, deny herself the one thing she wanted? Having been his lover once, it was impossible to pretend that she didn't want to repeat the experience. She could love the marquis from afar, or she could seize the moment and love him for real. The possibility that her love wouldn't be returned was something she had to accept. There was also the possibility that by loving, she could be loved. Either way, it was a gamble, a risk not unlike so many other risks in life. Regardless, Evelyn knew a summer spent in Marshall's arms would be the most wonderful season of her life.

A season to be remembered.

"I've been thinking," Evelyn began, unsure what words to use now that it was time to say them. How did one negotiate an affair?

"If you've decided to refuse the position as companion to my stepmother, think again," he said firmly. He searched her face, not caring for the serious expression that had overtaken it. "You agreed to give me the summer."

"That's what I've been thinking about," she said softly. "The summer."

For several long minutes the only sound was the rush of wind over water. Marshall looked at her face, washed by the fading sunlight. Her expression was still serious, her chin tilted in the stubborn angle he knew so well.

"And . . . ," he urged, lifting a brow.

"I've decided to accept your offer," Evelyn said, looking him directly in the eye. "I will be your lover. But only for the summer. When you return to London, I will not be going with you. If those terms are agreeable, then I will share my bed with you."

If she had slapped him, Marshall couldn't have been more surprised. He had come to the country with a tactical seduction in mind, days, perhaps weeks, spent in carefully maneuvering the elusive Evelyn back into his arms. Her decision caught him completely off guard.

Surprised or not, he wasn't going to waste a moment of her cooperation. He looked around, the bluff hid them from the view of anyone coming from the main house, but it didn't guarantee them the privacy he wanted. Reaching for her hand, he tugged her forward, then started walking down the beach, toward the cottage.

"Dare I ask what brought about this change in attitude?" he asked, striding briskly toward the cottage and the bed she had mentioned.

"The reasons are my own," Evelyn told him, knowing exactly where he was taking her. "So are the rules."

Marshall stopped to stare at her. "Rules."

Evelyn drew a deep breath before divulging the second half of her decision. "I will be your lover, my lord. But I will not be your mistress."

Marshall gave her an inquiring look. "Are they not one and the same?"

"No," she told him. "As your mistress I would be at your disposal, day or night. I have no inclination to be a puppet on the end of any man's string. As your lover, I will have some control over our relationship. I will share my bed willingly, not because I am employed as a companion to Lady Waltham, not because I am dependent upon you for food and shelter, not because I owe you a debt of gratitude. I will share my bed, my body, myself, because it is what I wish to do." She took another quick breath, wishing with all her heart that the next words weren't necessary. "I will be your lover until the summer ends. When you are called back to London, to Parliament and the obligations of your title, I shall resume my own path, my own life."

Marshall's eyes met and held hers. Evelyn had just given him exactly what he wanted. She would share her bed voluntarily, welcome him into her body, and yet he felt as if the goal he had worked so patiently to obtain was a minor triumph. She was giving him the summer, a few months, nothing more. His pride, somewhat appeased at having her confess that she wished to be his lover, took another blow at being told he was wanted only temporarily. The irony of the situation didn't go unnoticed. For a man, taking a mistress was a provisional arrangement, a relationship he could end or extend as he saw fit. Evelyn had just taken that choice away from him. She would be his lover only for as long as *she* wanted. Her decision, one he could accept or reject, effectively turned the tables on him and his well-orchestrated plans.

Twelve

"Does this mean that you agree to my terms?" Evelyn asked, holding on to his hand because to do anything else meant she'd go tumbling back down the hill.

He glared at her over his shoulder. "It means I'm taking you to bed."

Evelyn glared right back at him, but it did little good. He was hell bent on reaching the cottage as quickly as possible, his eyes focused on the dark green door, not on her. She supposed she could have been slightly more diplomatic in her recital, but she'd spoken plainly for fear that he'd find someway around her resolve.

Once they reached the flat stones that formed a path from the edge of the bluff to the front door of the cottage, Marshall turned and scooped her up into his arms. When she started to protest, he stopped her with another fierce glare. Once they were inside, he instructed her to latch the door.

"I will have you for my lover, Miss Dennsworth," he said. "Are there any more rules you'd like to list before we spend the rest of the day in bed?"

"Ah . . . not that I can think of," she replied, realizing she'd just unleashed a very male animal from an invisible cage. She had the frightening thought that he actually meant what he'd said. But men didn't keep women in bed for hours, or did they?

He set her on the edge of the bed with a firm order that she wasn't to move.

Evelyn watched as he walked to the chest of drawers against the far wall. He poured water from a ceramic pitcher into a matching floral bowl. With basin in hand he returned to the bed.

"You have sand on your feet." Having said that, he placed the basin on the floor.

Evelyn sucked in a gasp of surprise as he flipped her dress and single petticoat up to her knees, exposing her bare feet and lower legs. A slow smile came to her face as he gingerly lifted one foot and soothingly bathed it with water, washing away the sand. The other foot was treated to the same tender care. When all traces of the beach had been removed, he slowly traced the instep of her right foot. The sensual glide of his index finger sent a shiver of anticipation through her entire body.

Her feet were still damp, but instead of drying them with a towel, Marshall used his hands, which were also damp. The friction of damp skin against damp skin was an unexpected pleasure Evelyn couldn't help but enjoy. He rubbed her feet, massaging them as if they'd just carried her the entire length of England. She was helpless to do anything but watch and feel and wonder what else he had in store for her. Her decision, once confessed, had freed them both to enjoy each other without the barriers of guilt or regret.

Marshall pushed the basin under the bed before moving closer. As he moved, his hands slid upward to cup her calves. "Do you know how many times I've thought of having you again?"

Supporting her weight on the palms of her hands, Evelyn leaned back and smiled the smile of a woman who was enjoying herself. "Not as many times as I've thought of it," she responded as his hands gently squeezed and kneaded her legs. "Are you surprised?"

"Nothing about you surprises me. Not anymore." He raised up, his hands moving over her knees to disappear under her tossed-up clothing. "But I've got a few surprises for you."

With that his hands moved again, spreading her legs wide as he came to kneel between them. Agilely he found the drawstrings that held her petticoat and drawers in place.

"Raise your hips."

She did, and the garments were swept away. He brushed the inside of her thighs with his fingertips, lightly tracing a path that stopped just short of where she was beginning to ache with a sweet need. The touch of his hands freed the last of her restraints as the pleasure built, running through her body and her blood, through every limb. She had never considered her feet or legs being anything more than necessary parts to get her from one place to another, but now Evelyn knew they were just as sensitive as her breasts or her lips.

"Lie back." His voice came to her. It was low and husky, like the sound of the ocean. And like the wildness of the currents that swept both the shores of England and France, it called forth her own wildness, her own need.

Evelyn did as he asked, slowly reclining until all she could see was the beamed ceiling and the play of sunlight and shadows on the upper walls. The windows were open. The wind blowing inland from the Channel filled the room with the scents and sounds of nature. Her eyes drifted closed as Marshall continued to caress her thighs, slowly tracing random patterns over her skin with his fingertips. Her body was humming with need, the song growing stronger as his hands moved freely, exploring her at his leisure.

The dance of fingertips over sensitive skin went on and on. First her thighs, then her hips, then the softness of her belly, coming closer and closer but never touching that special place where she was aching the most. Evelyn tried to relax, to concentrate on the sheer pleasure of being touched, but Marshall was slowly driving her insane. The breeze moved over the bed, cooling her flushed face. She reached out, wanting to touch him in return, but he wouldn't allow it.

"Not yet," he whispered, then stood up, ending the erotic play that had her body aching to feel so much more.

She opened her eyes and watched him as he tugged his shirt from the waistband of his breeches, then shrugged it off his shoulders and dropped it to the floor. She stared at the crisp, curling hair on his chest, the flat, firm planes of his stomach. He watched her, watching him, as he flicked open the buttons on his trousers. Unable to avert her gaze, wanting to see every inch of him painted in sunlight, caressed by wind, Evelyn looked her fill, admiring his naked body. The power of his masculinity was almost frightening. So was the desire building inside her.

He held out his hand.

Evelyn reached for it and found herself being raised to a sitting position. Then his hands were on her, his fingers nimbly undoing buttons and more laces, pushing her chemise away from her shoulders, exposing the swell of her breasts. He wrapped one arm around her and lifted her off the bed. She could feel the heat of his body burn into her own skin, rekindling the fire that had been smoldering for weeks.

"I want to watch you take off your clothes," he said. He moved away from her then, giving her room to finish what he'd so expertly begun.

She hesitated for a moment, knowing he was testing her, testing her decision to come to him of her own free will, on her own terms.

Slowly her hands came up to push her blouse the rest of the way off her shoulders, then down her arms. It dangled from her hand for a moment, then soundlessly joined his shirt on the floor. Her hands were shaking as they reached for the buttons on her skirt. He watched her the entire time, his gaze heated by desire and the knowledge that he could command and she would willingly obey. The skirt, once undone, slid easily over her hips, then down the length of her legs. She stepped out of it, standing in front of him in nothing but a cream-colored chemise of sheer muslin.

"All of them," he said. "I want to watch you walk naked into my arms."

The request was a husky reminder of the first time they had made love. The sun had been shining that morning, its inherent heat warming her skin the same way his gaze was warming her now. Bunching the fabric in her hands, Evelyn slowly worked it up, hesitating only a brief second as the muslin rose to the junction of her thighs. Then, eager to be in his arms again, she pulled it up and over her head.

Marshall watched her, smiling as the nest of tawny curls was entloingly revealed. Then she was standing before him, dressed in nothing but soft sunlight. Her hair had come undone to hang about her shoulders. It glowed, thick and golden, in the light.

She came to him then, and he cradled her face in his hands.

For a moment, Evelyn couldn't breathe, couldn't think. Then he kissed her, and all she wanted to do was feel. He was right. Naked was better.

Caution briefly called to Marshall. As much as his body wanted satisfaction, he wanted to pleasure her first. Her announcement that she would leave him at the end of the summer was still pricking at his ego, but he wanted her too much, had waited for her too long, to let it interfere with his present course of action. The summer was still ahead of them. There would be plenty of time to change her mind.

He held her close, letting her feel the ultimate intimacy of their nakedness. "I have lain awake at night remembering how it was between us." His mouth traced the line of her jaw, the soft indentation of her throat. "I want you now more than I did the first time."

Her hands moved slowly up his arms, coming to rest on his shoulders. "Then take me," she whispered. "Love me."

His hands slid around her, caressing her back, then lower, until he was cupping her bottom, lifting her high and tight against him.

Evelyn moaned softly as he kissed her again, harder this time. Deeper. He tasted like cigar smoke and brandy, sunlight and salt air. She kissed him back, needing to give of herself as unselfishly as he had given to her. She loved him. There was no shame attached to her feelings. She had given herself freely once, and she would do it again, every day of the summer if he wanted her. Whatever the future held, she would have this, the memory of his touch, of his whispered words, the dream of belonging to him if only for a few months.

They stood in the center of the room, totally naked, totally enthralled by the taste and feel of each other, oblivious to anything but the moment, the sensations, the power of a passion held in check for too long. Marshall's fingers dug into the soft flesh at the back of her thighs. She moaned as he took her mouth again, his tongue dipping and teasing, tormenting her until her legs grew weak and she leaned against him for support.

Then he was sitting down on the bed, pulling her forward until she was standing between his legs, her hands on his shoulders. He splayed his hand wide over her lower back, urging her even closer. "You have a mole," he whispered, then kissed the tiny imperfection on her hip.

His mouth branded her, his hands becoming rougher as they grasped her hips, holding her still for a long and enticing trail of kisses that moved slowly upward until he was licking the hard tips of her breasts. She arched backward, supported by his hands, as he feasted on her body, sucking her deeper into his mouth, tormenting her nipples with his tongue and teeth until she was literally shaking with a desire that demanded satisfaction.

She drew in a deep breath when he moved her again, lifting her onto the bed, then coming down beside her. He continued kissing her, taking his time, making the fire she already thought out of control burn even brighter.

"Please," she said, unable to hold her feelings inside. Her hands moved over his warm flesh, the muscles in his arms and shoulders, then down the center of his chest. When his mouth returned to her breasts, she fisted her hands in the bed linens and arched upward, offering herself, willing to give anything he wanted.

Knowing she'd burn even brighter, soar even higher, Marshall took his time. With a wild, controlled hunger he moved slowly down her body, kissing the flat of her stomach, nibbling at her hips, then lower still, until his breath warmed the very center of her.

"Spread your legs for me, sweetheart," he said. "Give yourself to me."

Still gripping the linens, Evelyn obeyed him again, thinking he was finally going to join their bodies. When she felt his breath on the most sensitive part of her, she gasped in sensual shock. She clutched at his shoulders, thinking to stop him, but his tongue was already dipping, tasting the very essence of her. Her fingers fisted in his hair as her hips instinctively rose off the bed, following the outrageous pleasure.

His tongue slid inside her, hot and wet. Again and again, he caressed her. Each gentle stab of his tongue sent her soaring higher and higher, splintering the last of her control. She writhed and twisted, mindless to anything now but the hot

sensations coursing through her body. Slowly, in rhythm
with his exploring mouth, another kind of sensation began to
build, deep inside her. Her fingers clenched and unclenched.

Suddenly the sunlight exploded, shattering behind the
lids of her closed eyes, bursting into a thousand tiny pin-
points of light, golden stars that danced wildly, then gradually gave way to a rich, soft darkness as her body convulsed,
then surrendered in a blissful moment of pure sensation.

Marshall laughed lightly, then moved up and over her. He
kissed her, long and deep. "That's one surprise," he whispered. "You'll have to wait until later for the other. I need to
be inside you now."

He entered her at that moment, one long, smooth stroke
that embedded him deeply inside her. Holding himself there,
totally accepted by her body, washed in the warmth of her
release, he felt the remnants of the pleasure he'd just given
her. Soft, female muscles clenched around him. Marshall
gritted his teeth. His blood was pounding in his veins, pool-
ing fiercely in his groin. He pushed harder, burrowing
deeper into the hot, moist channel of her body.

With every slow stroke, Evelyn felt Marshall claiming
more of her. Each kiss, each caressing touch of his hands,
stole more of her heart, of her very soul. Never had she
imagined a joining so sweet, so achingly gentle, yet so totally possessive, so absolute it forced her to admit that she
could never, would never, give herself so completely to another man.

She moved helplessly against him, rocking her pelvis.
Each movement brought them closer together, feeding the
fire, making it burn deep within her, deep within him. The
pleasure was extraordinary. He whispered her name. She
moaned softly, unable to form a coherent word. Her body
ached with need, her heart swelled with emotion, and still he
moved, pushing forward, then retreating until she was begging him to end the sweet torment.

Wanting fulfillment as much as Evelyn, Marshall came to his knees, forcing her legs wide and high. "Look at me," he demanded roughly.

Evelyn opened her eyes. His body was gleaming with sweat, his hair tousled and damp from the exertion of pleasuring her. She reached for him. Their hands touched, fingers entwining, palm to palm. Need vibrated through her body. She wrapped her legs around his waist and lifted her hips. The movement shattered the last of Marshall's control.

He moved fast and deep, his hips pumping repeatedly, straining to claim as much of her as he could, to give her as much pleasure as he could, to take as much in return.

A breeze, scented by the sea, swept over the bed as they reached for satisfaction, bodies gleaming with sweat, muscles taut with need, words whispered with an earthy urgency. Desperate to please both Evelyn and himself, Marshall rode her hard and fast. The first ripples of ecstasy started deep inside her, growing stronger with each forceful thrust of his hips. She stiffened and cried out his name.

He looked into her eyes. They were clear blue pools, and he longed to dive into them, to be swallowed up, to drown. He ducked his head in fierce homage to her beauty, kissing her breasts as he pushed deep inside her. He found oblivion between her thighs, felt himself drawn into her. He continued riding her until their skin was hot and gleaming with sweat, until their bodies began to melt and merge like fire and candlewax.

"Yes," Marshall groaned. "Don't fight it, sweetheart, let it happen."

Guided by his words, Evelyn closed her eyes and surrendered to a feeling so intense, so powerful, so indescribably beautiful, she wept. The world around her fell away, and she existed only in the essence of the moment. Then she felt Marshall plunge deep one last time, felt him swell and throb inside her, bathing her with liquid fire.

Gradually, contentment took the place of passion. Marshall eased his weight off Evelyn, then drew her into his arms. He held her close, smiling when she snuggled even closer. For the first time in weeks, he felt completely at ease with himself, at ease with the woman in his arms. Perhaps there was something to be said about acquiring a woman's friendship along with her body.

The following morning, Marshall rose from his desk in the library to greet his sister.

"Carlow said you wished to see me," Winnifred said, closing the door behind her.

"Yes," he replied, giving her a quick kiss on the cheek once she had crossed the room. "I would like to speak to you about a number of things."

She seated herself, looking very pretty in a royal blue frock with light blue trim. Her hair, the same dark brown as his and their father's, was arranged in a mass of ringlets that started at the crown of her head and fell onto her shoulders. "What things?"

"First, did I speak out of turn yesterday when I suggested inviting Lord Lansdowne to the regatta party? I would not want to force a suitor on you who is not welcome."

"You like him, don't you?" Winnie asked hesitantly.

"That isn't the question," Marshall replied, knowing young ladies were often more impressed with a man's appearance than his character. "What I wish to know is if you enjoy his company."

"Yes, but . . ."

"But what? Has he done something to offend you? Pressed his suit too forcefully perhaps?" Although he'd had little to do with his sisters' upbringing, Marshall knew Winnifred was far more vulnerable than she realized. She had been raised to be an acceptable young lady, gracious in her speech and manners. Such young ladies weren't always prepared to meet the more aggressive side of a man's nature.

"No," she insisted. "His lordship has always been a perfect gentleman while in my company."

"If he proposes marriage, will you accept?" Marshall asked, thinking it a good match but wanting to make sure that there was real affection between the couple before he formally endorsed the courtship.

"I'm not sure," Winnie replied. She left her chair to walk to the tall, latticed windows that overlooked the western lawn.

Marshall joined her. "Your flock of peacocks are giving the gardeners fits as usual," he said, watching as one of the men tending the lawn shooed several of the birds away from a patch of newly seeded grass. The male, splaying a colorful array of feathers, indignantly danced across the lawn, only to return the minute the gardener turned his back.

Winnie laughed. "Do you remember when Father brought the first ones home? I was so excited I was dancing on air."

"You were eight years old," he reminded her. "You'd been sulking for days because he'd scolded you for going into the stables and almost getting trampled by one of the horses."

"I remember," Winnie said forlornly. "I remember so much about him, Marshall. I can understand why Mama doesn't want to give up her mourning. She doesn't want to forget him."

"None of us will ever forget him." He pulled her close, knowing there was little he could say to comfort her. He had been away at Eton, then at Cambridge, during most of Winnie's childhood. His relationship with their father had been of a different sort. Instead of being protected and sheltered, he'd been raised to assume the duties and responsibilities of an only son.

"What of Lansdowne, or would you rather not discuss him?"

"He is very nice," Winnie admitted, looking out the window instead of meeting his gaze. "And handsome. And comfortably wealthy, or so I've heard."

"Then what is it?"

"His estates are near Newcastle," she finally told him. "That's so far away. If we married, I would see you and Mama and Catherine only when we are in London."

Marshall smiled, then drew her into his arm for a fraternal embrace. "Newcastle isn't the end of the world, Winnie. And there's more reason than just Parliament for a lord to travel. There will be holidays and hunts and all the other things that bring a family together."

She looked up at him with tears in her eyes, and Marshall wondered if perhaps another Season wouldn't serve her interests best. There was no commandment that she had to marry this year. "You don't have to marry anyone, Winnie. There's plenty of time. The right man will come along, if Lansdowne isn't he."

"I'm not sure," she confessed shyly. "He did kiss me, and it was very pleasant."

Pleasant!

Marshall thought of Evelyn, of the hours he'd spent kissing her yesterday. He certainly hoped she found it more than pleasant. It had been well after dark before he had left her to join the family for a late dinner. She'd been sleeping by then, exhausted from their lovemaking. He stopped himself from drawing any more comparisons. Evelyn certainly wasn't his sister, nor was he responsible for seeing that she made a suitable marriage.

"Then, shall we extend the invitation to Lord Lansdowne, as well as several other gentlemen, and see what the future brings?"

She nodded, then returned to her seat. "Catherine and I missed you at breakfast," she said, turning the conversation away from possible suitors.

"I rode out early to look over the fields, then met with the steward. Did your mother join you for breakfast?"

"No," Evelyn said sadly.

Marshall frowned. "Hopefully that will cease to be the case. I suspect Miss Dennsworth will have a strong impact on your mother's actions."

"How so? Mother may be taking her mourning too seriously, but I fail to see how a servant can alter her actions."

"Miss Dennsworth is not a servant," Marshall corrected her.

Winnifred shrugged her shoulders. "Then a member of the staff. I see little difference."

"The difference is that Miss Dennsworth has not been employed to polish the silver; she is here to try and help your mother."

"She misses Father," Winnie said defensively.

"We all do," Marshall replied. "That is not the issue. The point is that we must all get on with our lives." He hesitated, unsure how his sister would react to his next comment. "When I introduce Miss Dennsworth later this morning, I'm certain you will recognize her."

"Recognize her?" Winnie took on an inquisitive expression. "I don't recognize the name."

Marshall folded his hands behind his back. "You do recall the incident at Madame La Roschelle's shop. Lady Monfrey accused one of her employees of stealing a brooch."

"Oh, of course. It was very upsetting, seeing the poor woman hauled away in a jail cart."

"That poor woman was Miss Dennsworth."

"You can't mean . . . But what about Lady Monfrey? She will be beside herself should she discover that you have employed someone who—"

"Miss Dennsworth was found innocent of the charge," Marshall said sharply. "There was no proof that she had taken the brooch. The accusation was nothing more than an overenthusiastic assumption by Lady Monfrey. The magistrate dismissed the charges. Miss Dennsworth is not a thief."

"Of course," Evelyn said, looking doubtful. "But how is she to help? Does she have some kind of special talent?"

Marshall searched for a way to explain why he thought Evelyn could be the friend Constance seemed to need so desperately, but he couldn't think of anything to say that wouldn't reveal their personal relationship.

"Time will tell," he answered, avoiding any direct comment. "In the meantime, I would appreciate it, as will Miss Dennsworth, if you keep your brief but previous acquaintance to yourself."

"Are you saying that I shouldn't tell Mother that Miss Dennsworth was arrested?" His sister looked shocked.

"That's precisely what I'm saying. It will serve no purpose other than to embarrass Miss Dennsworth and make everyone in the household uncomfortable. Life isn't always fair, Winnie, and sometimes people deserve the chance to start anew. Miss Dennsworth has been employed for the summer. That being the case, I am confident that you will not abandon your manners and cause either her or the family any unnecessary distress."

Marshall waited, giving her a few moments to digest what he was saying. She was looking down at her lap, fidgeting with the lace on the cuff of her sleeve.

"You look worried," he said, resuming his seat behind his desk. "Don't you trust my judgment."

"Of course, I do," she said, looking up at him. "How did you come to hire her? I wouldn't think that she would know anyone of our acquaintance, yet you told Mama that she has excellent references. She's a seamstress, not a lady's companion."

"The details of how she came to be hired aren't important. The issue is that she is here, and I would not be pleased if she were to be insulted by either your remarks or gossip from the servants."

"It's just that . . . Well, it's a bit unusual, is all."

"I dare say, it is that," Marshall replied, thinking of the strange events that had brought Evelyn from a dress shop on Bond Street to his family's estate here in Ipswich. "But I also think it's necessary. I want this to be an enjoyable summer for the entire family. That means getting your mother out of her room and back into the thick of things. Don't you want to see her smiling again?"

"I'd like nothing better," his sister replied, although she still looked ill at ease about something. A wan smile lit her face for an instant, then vanished. "Very well. I do not understand, but I will do as you ask."

"Thank you," he said, holding out a hand to her.

She came around the desk for another hug, then left him to his morning paper.

Marshall watched her leave, hoping that her confusion over his request wouldn't prompt her to say anything out of turn to Evelyn. He was certain that his actions would be misinterpreted should either his stepmother or his sisters learn of his personal relationship with the young woman living in the cottage. A man did not bring his mistress—his lover—into such close proximity to his home while family members were in residence.

The chime of the mantel clock, a family heirloom passed down from his father's maternal grandmother, marked the half hour. Marshall smiled as he unfolded his paper and began to read. Evelyn would be arriving in a few minutes. She was to be formally introduced to Lady Waltham at eleven o'clock.

He wondered as he scanned the headlines if she'd awakened that morning the same way she'd fallen asleep last night—smiling.

Thirteen

Evelyn dressed with the utmost care, wanting to make a good impression on Lady Waltham and Marshall's two sisters, whom she was sure to meet as well. Already knowing Winnifred, but in a different capacity, Evelyn prayed that the assurances Marshall had given her last night hadn't been exaggerated. Just because he had asked his sister to give their new employee the benefit of doubt, didn't mean Winnifred would actually behave as if she knew nothing about her mother's new companion. Nor did it guarantee that Evelyn's assimilation into the household would be a smooth one.

She walked to the main house, having become familiar with the path and the majority of the eighty some servants employed by the large estate. She entered the house through the east entrance, then followed a maze of corridors until she reached the morning room, where the mistress of the house normally attended to affairs of the day: approving the menu, answering correspondences and addressing invitations, discussing matters with the housekeeper and butler. It was a pleasant room, decorated in shades of deep green and pale yellow with high latticed windows that overlooked the estate's green lawns.

She stood just outside the closed door, waiting for Marshall to join her. Evelyn smoothed her hands over the skirt of her plum-colored dress, hoping it was suitable for the occasion. She knew so little of the etiquette upon which society functioned, at least when it came to trivial things such as what dress was to be worn in the morning versus the afternoon. Her lifestyle up until now had never depended upon such things, but rather her ability to work ten hours a day without complaining.

She had, however, purchased some fabric before leaving London and used the time between her arrival and that of the family to refurbish her wardrobe.

A preoccupation with her thoughts and what she would say once she was presented to Lady Waltham kept Evelyn from hearing Marshall's approach. He appeared at her side, smiling as his eyes scanned the length of her, taking in her new attire. "You look lovely," he said in a low voice. "If my stepmother wasn't waiting on the other side of this door, I'd haul you off to some deserted corner of the house and—"

"Stop," Evelyn hissed at him. "I'm nervous enough as it is."

Marshall laughed lightly. "There is nothing to be nervous about. My stepmother is a pleasant lady. I'm sure the two of you will get along."

"I certainly hope so," Evelyn said, letting out a deep sigh. "It will make for an unpleasant summer if we don't."

Choosing not to comment, he tapped on the door, then pushed it open.

Evelyn stepped inside to find both Lady Waltham and her two daughters. The youngest, Catherine, a pretty little thing with radiant blue eyes, was sitting near the window on a bergere seat with curved arms. Winnifred was seated close to her mother in a straight-backed chair. Her posture exuded an upper-class English arrogance, a surety that she was a *lady*, and as such, would be treated accordingly. Evelyn gave them a brief glance, accompanied by a smile, then focused her attention on the mistress of the house.

As expected, Lady Waltham was garbed in severe black with a mourning brooch pinned to the bodice of her dress. Her hair was a deep blond, her eyes the same dark blue as her daughters'. But there was a stillness in her gaze, and a slack line to her mouth, as if she'd forgotten how to smile. The effect of her pale skin and the darkness of her clothing made her seem pitifully frail.

Evelyn could see the grief etched into her features. Her eyes were almost lifeless, reflecting the terrible loneliness of losing someone you loved, the emotional isolation of being forever separated from them.

Marshall stepped forward to make the introductions. Evelyn waited until Lady Waltham's eyes came to rest on her before she dipped into a graceful curtsey. "I am pleased to make your acquaintance, my lady."

"The marquis employed you, against my wishes, I might add," Lady Waltham responded, "but I will not hold that against you, Miss Dennsworth."

"How very gracious of you," Marshall said teasingly. He looked at his sisters. "I think we should find another room in which to occupy ourselves. Your mother and Miss Dennsworth should have some privacy in which to become acquainted."

Catherine made a pretty pout, then complied, stopping in front of Evelyn long enough to smile up at her. Winnifred rose, walked to her mother, placing a kiss upon her cheek, then exited the room without giving Evelyn so much as a cursory glance, cutting her most efficiently.

Evelyn looked at Marshall. His smile was reassuring as he, too, kissed his stepmother on the cheek, whispering something to her in private, before leaving the two women alone.

"Well, you might as well sit down," Lady Waltham said once the door was shut. "I'm not sure how to begin our conversation. As I said, I see no reason for your employment. Please, don't take that as an insult. It's simply—"

"It's just that you prefer to be alone with your misery," Evelyn said, sitting down in the chair Winnifred had just vacated. "I understand."

"Do you?" Lady Waltham replied, clearly taken back by Evelyn's bold manner.

"You loved your husband very much."

"Yes, I did," she replied, unable to erase the heartbreak from her voice. For a moment her eyes turned gentle, as if she were seeing some past happiness. "He was . . ." Her words faded into nothingness.

"Tell me about him."

Lady Waltham's head went up a notch. "I would rather not discuss my husband. My memories are my own."

"I didn't mean to be rude," Evelyn said. "When my mother died, my father locked himself in his study for days on end. It took me a long time to understand that life had become a burden for him. My mother's death left him feeling abandoned and alone."

"You are very perceptive, Miss Dennsworth. Extremely so for a woman your age," Marshall's stepmother remarked somewhat stiffly.

"Grief has no age requirement, Lady Waltham. Children lose their parents every day. I was young, but I grieved for my mother just as deeply as my father, in my own way. I can still hear her laughter, see her smile. My memories no longer bring me pain, but a quiet happiness that lightens my heart whenever I think of her."

For a moment, Evelyn feared she had gone beyond the boundaries of what a companion should say to her employer. Tears gleamed in Lady Waltham's eyes. She turned her face toward the window in an effort to hide them.

"I apologize. I've been rude," Evelyn said.

Lady Waltham did not reply for several minutes. Finally, having regained her composure, she pointed toward a small Queen Anne desk in the corner of the room. "The marquis wishes to have a party for the annual regatta. You may begin with the invitations. There will be at least two hundred people attending the lawn party. Pray that it doesn't rain."

Realizing that she had been accepted, Evelyn gladly walked to the desk and sat down. Lady Waltham began listing the names of the people to whom invitations would be issued. It was well over an hour before Evelyn exited the morning room to find a footman waiting in the hallway. The servant informed her that the marquis would like a word with her. She was shown to the study on the second floor of the house.

It was a man's room, void of the antimacassar coverlets that decorated the backs of most chairs in the house. The furniture was sturdy, the cushions of rich, dark leather. There was a small collection of family pictures on one table instead of the huge gallery that decorated the other rooms. The library walls were hung with paintings, landscapes and seascapes that seemed to take their life from the surrounding countryside. Evelyn decided the masculinity of the room echoed Marshall's own personality, well-ordered but not severe.

He greeted her formally, then as soon as the door was shut, an impudent, knowing grin brightened his face. "I see you survived. How did you leave Lady Waltham?"

"Wondering if she likes me or not," Evelyn replied frankly. "I'm not sure what a companion should do, but after meeting Lady Waltham, I know what I must do if I am to help her."

"And what is that?"

"Force her to talk about your father."

Marshall took a moment to think about what she had just said. "You are right; she rarely mentions his name."

He rose from his desk, holding out his hand to her. Evelyn accepted it, needing his touch as naturally as she needed air. His gaze softened with an intimate, tender look; then he lowered his head and captured her mouth. His kiss, longed for all morning, melted away the anxiety of the last few hours, leaving Evelyn content within his embrace.

With her cheek resting against his chest and his arms holding her snugly against him, Evelyn let out a deep sigh. "It is not going to be easy to pull her back to the real world," she said. "As long as she is allowed to hide away, to keep her memories locked deep inside herself, she will continue to grieve."

He pulled back so he could see her face. "You never cease to amaze me," he said. "Of course, you are right. But how do we bring her back to the real world?"

"I have a few ideas, but she will demand my dismissal should I employ them."

"What ideas?"

"Seeing her made me think of Mr. Hexworth. The man was big and gruff, but he attended church on a regular basis. Forced by his wife, or so my father always said. I had a hard time imagining such a thing because Mrs. Hexworth was a tiny woman who always spoke in whispers. After she died, Mr. Hexworth turned even more sour, shutting himself away, threatening people if they so much as looked his way." She paused to take a breath. "My father intentionally provoked him one day. They met in the village, and as usual Mr. Hexworth was shouting and cussing about something. I couldn't believe it when my father walked up to him and started shouting right back. Before anyone could stop them, they were wrestling around on the ground, all fists and feet."

"Who won?" Marshall asked.

"My father," Evelyn announced with a beaming smile. "Oh, Mr. Hexworth got more punches in, of course, but my father won back his soul. He said he'd started the fight because Mr. Hexworth's anger had been simmering for too long, that he had truly loved his wife. Had loved her with all his heart, so much so, that when she died he blamed God."

"And since he couldn't hit God, your father decided he'd be the next best target," Marshall said, thinking Evelyn had inherited her father's insight.

Evelyn nodded. "It worked. The next Sunday Mr. Hexworth was back in church."

Marshall laughed. "Short of engaging in fisticuffs, do what you can and let me take care of the repercussions."

He kissed her again. Evelyn returned the kiss, then diplomatically untangled herself from his embrace. "You have things to do, my lord, and I must make sure that Lady Waltham does not retreat to her bedroom for the balance of the day."

"I'd rather find a way for us to retreat to the cottage."

"I shall see you this evening, if time permits," she told him.

"I'll make sure it does," Marshall replied, giving her bottom an affectionate pat as she turned to leave.

She glared at him over her shoulder. "I thought you a gentleman."

"Which would you rather have, a gentleman or a lover?" he asked wickedly.

"A gentleman during the day and a lover at night," she replied openly. "Remember that, and mind your manners."

She had not stepped beyond his reach, so it was easy for Marshall to pull her back into his arms. "If memory serves me right, both times that I've had you the sun has been shining."

Evelyn couldn't deny it, but neither could she let him get away with being so smug. "True, my lord. It does makes me wonder how well you will perform in the moonlight."

"I accept the challenge," Marshall replied, kissing her breathless before he released her a second time.

She was halfway to the door when his voice stopped her.

"Make sure you take an afternoon nap, Miss Dennsworth. You'll get very little sleep tonight."

Evelyn left the library, knowing she'd just baited a delicious trap in which she'd be caught later that evening. Their lovemaking the previous day had changed their relationship. Whatever formality existed between them was strictly for appearance's sake.

Knowing that thoughts of the marquis would only serve to distract her, Evelyn forced them aside and returned to the morning room. As expected, she found it empty. She was on her way upstairs to find the lady's maid when she met Winnifred in the large, tiled foyer of the house.

"Lady Winnifred," she said respectfully, then deciding she might as well get the worst over with, added, "Perhaps we could have a private word."

Winnifred received her request with some surprise, then replied civilly. "We can speak in here."

She turned to enter the withdrawing room, a small salon with rich stucco and plasterwork on the principal walls and ceiling. Blue curtains with festooned pelmets covered the windows. The furniture, predominately of mahogany, with several silk damask chairs to add a touch of color, was tastefully arranged on a floral carpet of Brussels weave.

Evelyn followed Marshall's sister inside, then closed the door.

Winnifred stood silently, waiting for Evelyn to say whatever was on her mind. It was an awkward moment, one filled with embarrassment for both of them.

"I realize that you must be suspicious of my presence," Evelyn said, getting right to the point. "Whatever you might think of me, I remind you that I have met and conquered the accusation that Lady Monfrey placed against me. I hope I shall not have to defend myself again."

Winnifred wasn't accustomed to being spoken to so frankly. Her expression reflected the impertinence of what she assumed was a member of the staff thinking herself an equal. Evelyn regretfully realized that she had taken the wrong approach. Marshall's sister apparently lacked his fondness for forthrightness.

"My brother's decision to bring you here is one I admittedly do not understand, Miss Dennsworth, but knowing him as I do, he is not likely to change his mind. Therefore, my thoughts and opinions aren't important."

"On the contrary," Evelyn said, hoping to salvage the conversation. "You are your mother's daughter. As such, I will need your assistance, your understanding of the family, to help her return to its fold. I ask that and nothing more. The opportunity to help her realize that she is needed in the present as much as she was needed in the past."

Winnifred's expression took on a show of interest, but there was still a tilt to her chin, an underlying arrogance that said she didn't see how a common shop girl, once accused of theft, could possibly aid a lady of her mother's standing. "I'm not sure I understand what you are asking."

"My father was a vicar," Evelyn said. "Although it was not my place to attend the members of his parish, I frequently went with him when he called. I have seen people like your mother, men and women whose grief seemed impenetrable. Sometimes, it takes a shock, an event equal to the death of the one they loved, to make them realize that God left them alive for a purpose."

Winnifred's expression went from interested to doubtful. "My mother is not that possessed by grief. She has always been frail of health."

"Nothing I say or do will endanger her health," Evelyn

assured her. "But it may cause her some distress at first. All I ask is that you give me whatever cooperation you can."

"By cooperation you mean that I should keep my knowledge of your . . . situation to myself. My brother has already given me those instructions."

Evelyn felt her heart sink. Winnifred had already formed her opinion; nothing she could do at the moment was going to change it. Wishing she could bridge the gap between them, but knowing of no immediate way, Evelyn thanked Lady Winnifred for her time, then went up to the third floor, where Lady Waltham's suite was located.

The door was closed, but she could hear the slight sound of conversation. Tapping lightly on the door, she waited for the lady's maid to open it. She knew the suite, having purposely visited it before Lady Waltham's arrival. There was a sitting room in addition to the spacious bedroom which had a balcony overlooking the wooded parklands. The suite connected to the one previously occupied by the former marquis.

When Evelyn had inspected the rooms last week, she'd been struck by the number of husbandly mementos to be found. It was not going to be easy to get Lady Waltham to relinquish her hold on the things that kept her connected to her late husband.

The door was opened by the youngest of Marshall's two sisters. Catherine looked up at Evelyn, then smiling, opened the door wide.

"Mother said she was tired, so she came upstairs. I'm going to read to her."

"That's an excellent idea," Evelyn said, liking Catherine because it was impossible not to. She had the wide-eyed radiance of a child tempered by the manners of a young lady.

Evelyn entered the bedroom to find Lady Waltham reclined on a divan, eyes closed, hands folded over her middle as if she were posing for the undertaker. Not a good sign, she

thought, then looked toward young Catherine. The girl
shrugged her delicate shoulders, then returned to the chair
where she had been reading from gaslight because the curtains were drawn.

Not hesitating, Evelyn strolled to the windows and
twitched back the heavy draperies, letting sunlight flow into
the room. Lady Waltham opened her eyes with a start, then
blinked at the bright light.

"Please close the drapes, then retire downstairs. I have no
wish for anyone's company other than Catherine's."

Evelyn paid her no heed. She moved to the French doors.
Drawing back the drapes, she opened the doors wide, letting
in the brisk breeze in hopes that it might wash some of the
grief from the room. When she finally turned to face
Marshall's stepmother, the woman looked as if she'd like
nothing better than to push Evelyn over the balcony railing.

"It's a lovely day," Evelyn remarked, glancing toward
Catherine, who looked ready to burst into giggles. "After
you've rested, we can take a stroll in the garden."

"I am not strolling anywhere," Lady Waltham replied ob-
stinately. "Now, if you would be so kind as to honor my
wishes, I would rest for a while."

Again Evelyn ignored the request. Looking about the
room, she spied an amber bottle of laudanum sitting on the
bedside table next to a framed portrait of the lady's late husband. Realizing by Catherine's smile that she had an ally in
the house after all, Evelyn picked up the bottle. "Lady
Catherine, if you would be so kind as to take this to Carlow
and ask that it be locked away. I will sit with your mother."

"My physician prescribed laudanum to help me sleep,"
Lady Waltham said, clearly irritated. She sat up. "You have
no right to dismiss my daughter as if she were a maid."

Catherine put down her book and took possession of the
bottle. "I'll take it straightaway," she said. Then holding the bot-

tle behind her back as if it were a treasured secret, she placed a kiss upon her mother's flushed cheek and left the room.

"Your impertinence is beyond decency, Miss Dennsworth. How dare you—"

"It does you no good to lie in a dark room, my lady. Fresh air and sunshine will be more beneficial than laudanum, and sleep will come after an active day."

Evelyn retired to a nearby chair, picking up the book young Catherine had laid aside. "Would you like me to read, or shall we talk?"

"Whatever I have to say will be said to the marquis. Your behavior is inexcusable." The frailty of her expression had taken on a glint of anger.

"I have already spoken to the marquis, warning his lordship in advance that you would be demanding my dismissal by day's end."

"You think I have no right to grieve. No right to mourn my husband, a man I loved with all my heart." Her voice was high and tight, strained to the point of tears.

"I think you have every right to mourn, every right to grieve, but not in this fashion. If you loved Lord Waltham, then do his memory justice."

"*If* I loved him!" She stood up, her eyes blazing. "Get out this minute. Get out and leave me in peace."

Evelyn smiled to herself as she left the room. Anger was a far more active emotion than self-pity. It was a good start.

She met Catherine on the staircase.

"Thank you for helping me," Evelyn said. "I'm going to need a friend. Lady Waltham is going to ask the marquis that I be dismissed immediately."

Catherine shook her head, setting her blond curls to bouncing. "I won't let him," she decreed. "I don't like Mother's room dark, and I don't like reading to her by a gas lamp when we could be outside in the garden or walking along the beach. I shall tell Marshall so, and make him promise not to send you packing."

"And I shall inform Lord Waltham that I have a coconspirator," Evelyn said. She held out her hand. "Shall we seal the bargain with a shake of hands?"

"Oh, yes!" Catherine chimed, accepting Evelyn's hand. "We are going to be the best of friends. I just know it."

"What in the world did you do to Constance?" Marshall asked as he stepped into the cottage shortly after midnight. "She marched into my library this afternoon, demanding that I dispatch you from Bedford Hall posthaste."

"I made her angry."

"That wasn't difficult to surmise," he replied, thinking Evelyn looked lovely with her bare toes peeking out from beneath the hem of her nightgown. "She was seething."

"Good."

"Good?"

"Yes. When was the last time you saw her angry? It's a much more productive emotion than sitting around all day staring out the window, don't you agree?"

"You are a minx, Miss Dennsworth. I thought to retire to the country for a peaceful summer. I see now that I've stepped onto a battlefield."

"Let us hope it's a victorious one," she replied. "Did Winnifred seek my dismissal, as well?"

"She accompanied Constance to the library, but she didn't say anything. I got the impression she was there for moral support."

He pulled her close, then smiled. "Catherine, however, thinks you're smashing. She came to your defense the second her mother was out of sight."

"I can use a friend."

"You have me," Marshall said, ending the discussion with a kiss that curled her toes. When he lifted his mouth away, his smile was pure wickedness. "As I recall, I was challenged earlier today. Something about moonlight, wasn't it?"

It was Evelyn's turn to laugh. "Aye, my lord."

He opened the door and pulled her outside.

"Whatever are you doing?" She tried to free her hand, but it was trapped.

"Showing you the moonlight," Marshall replied matter-of-factly. He scooped her up, not into his arms, but over his shoulder, hauling her down to the beach as if she were a sack of supplies about to be tossed into a waiting skiff.

When he deposited her back on her feet, Evelyn found herself standing on a blanket. It was spread out over the sand. A basket sat nearby. The moonlight, beaming down full and bright on the water, glistened like lamplight on black velvet. The wind was a whisper over the dark landscape.

A moonlight picnic, she thought, then smiled.

Marshall smiled back, then looked from her to the water. He liked to watch the ocean at night, to listen to the sound of water and earth coming together. He'd always felt at peace in this place. Like the warm, willing body of a woman, the sea moved and moaned and whispered. It called to his senses, enticing him, beckoning him in a way no woman ever had done—until Evelyn.

"When I was a boy," he said, "I used to watch the Channel from my nursery window. It always seemed magical to me."

"It is," Evelyn said, reaching out to take his hand. "I like watching it, too. The sea has no boundaries. It moves constantly, touching England one day, France the next. Currents in the Atlantic have even more freedom. They move up and down the world with the simple brush of God's hand."

"You have a poetic heart," Marshall said, pulling her into his arms. He held her close, feeling the magic of the place the way he'd felt it during his childhood.

Being held in his embrace, Evelyn savored the quiet intensity of the moment. She could feel the physical pull of the man the same way the beach was feeling the tug of the tide. She raised her face and looked up at him. Nothing was said, but then, they didn't need words to describe the pleasure they drew from each other's company.

It made her feel sad and happy at the same time, knowing they shared a deep kinship that went beyond their physical attraction. It wasn't love, not for the marquis, but for Evelyn the emotional satisfaction she received when he spoke to her, shared his thoughts, was just as satisfying as his embrace. He was a very private man. A man who held his true feelings close to his heart, but who didn't hesitate to show them when it came to his family and friends. There had been no vacillation in his actions that day on Bond Street. He'd marched directly into the situation, holding nothing in reserve, demanding that the constable treat her respectfully, then giving him money to make sure she was handled just as fairly once they reached Clerkenwell Close. The extent of his generosity was far more than anyone else would have shown her.

"You're looking extremely serious," he said, wrapping his arms more snugly about her. "Why?"

"No reason in particular," she said, not wanting to reveal her thoughts because they came too close to revealing how much she loved him.

He lowered his head and kissed her, a soft, gentle kiss that was barely more than a touching of lips, an exchange of breath. "I can't get enough of you."

He kissed her for real then, and Evelyn felt herself being swept out to sea. Her arms curled around his neck as she pressed her body against his, surrendering to his touch, the compelling magic of the moonlight and the night.

When the kiss ended, Evelyn eased herself free of Marshall's strong arms and sat down on the blanket, pulling her knees up and tugging her nightgown down. It was a warm night with just the right amount of briskness to the air. The wind caught at the water, stirring it into foamy white-caps before spilling it onto the beach. The moonlight revealed the line of breakers farther out and the dim lights of a packet ship crossing the Channel. Overhead the moon hung full in the sky; stars danced with twinkling sparks of light. It was a magical night, a night meant for lovers.

She looked at her lover as he joined her on the blanket, at the moonlight that caught in his dark hair, at the silent message his smile sent her way. Even now she could feel the invisible draw of him, the taste of his kiss on her tongue. She loved him so much it was a little like dying to know that he didn't love her in return.

No! Stop thinking about what you can't have and start enjoying what you do have—the man and the night. Cherish him for the summer, then love him for a lifetime.

"Hungry?" Marshall asked, reaching for the basket. He began withdrawing delicacies: a wedge of cheese, a loaf of crusty bread, sliced apples, a cluster of grapes, then a bottle of wine. Once they were spread out on the blanket between them, he smiled. "I raided the pantry."

They ate by moonlight, feeding each other, laughing joyfully when the bottle of wine overturned and spilled onto the sand. Marshall scooped it up, wiping the sand off before offering it to Evelyn. She felt wicked drinking directly from the bottle, but she did it anyway, because it pleased him.

When she put the bottle down, he reached out and traced her lips, moist from the wine. "You look like a moon nymph," he said. "The sailors tell stories of women like you. Mermaids who tempt a man beyond reason."

"You're the one doing the tempting. I can't even swim," Evelyn said, as she gently bit down on the fingertip that was moving across her parted lips.

Marshall felt the small love bite like a gut punch. He wanted to lay her down on the blanket and love her until there was nothing left but the sound of the sea and the wind, nothing to feel but the caress of her body holding his deep inside it. Instead, he returned the favor, drawing out the anticipation that was half the pleasure. Pressing her open palm to his mouth, he nibbled at the very center of it, then gently ran his tongue over the tiny lines.

The sensual touch of Marshall's tongue sent a shiver through Evelyn. She laced her fingers through his and held on as tightly as she could, as if simply holding his hand could make time stand still. "What do they call male mermaids?"

"There's no such thing," Marshall told her. He drew her down onto the blanket, stretching out beside her, then touched her with hands that trembled. He claimed her mouth with a gentle ferocity that matched the unyielding currents of the sea.

Evelyn closed her eyes and tried not to cry out her love for him. The taste of him swept through her like the wind sweeping over the water, pure and clean. She made a small sound at the back of her throat as she felt herself being eased back until she was lying on the blanket. She bit at his lips just before his tongue thrust slowly into her mouth.

The pleasure of it mingled with the pain of knowing that she was desired, but not loved. Yet Marshall's touch was so loving, so gentle, that it was easy to imagine that he did care for her in a very special way. She was almost certain that he'd never shared a moonlight picnic with any other woman.

The marquis might not love her; but when their bodies were joined, the passion was almost more than Evelyn could bear, and she couldn't help but hope that love might find its way into his heart before the summer turned cold.

They made love in the moonlight.

Marshall stared up at the woman straddling his hips, her movements as gentle, as caressing, as the wind moving over the sea. His eyes drifted closed as he savored their joining. He pulled her down to him, his tongue licking over the crowns of her naked breasts. He groaned a deep sound of defeat as she moved her hips, provocatively chastising him for disrupting her ride.

"Move faster, sweetheart," he groaned roughly.

Evelyn pressed her knees against his hips as his fingers stroked the tiny gem between her legs, making her whole body tingle with pleasure. She started to protest, but all that came out was a soft, wild moan as his talented, teasing fingers stroked her more intimately.

Marshall watched her pleasure, letting it feed his own. "You have a beautiful body," he said almost reverently. "I like it dressed in moonlight."

The words became a benediction as Marshall took over, his hips moving reflexively, his hard length stroking deep inside her body while his fingers did the same on the outside. He smiled at her expression, at the ecstasy that shone in her eyes, at the way her body greedily accepted his, milking him, testing the limits of his control. He felt the delicate shivers, the tiny convulsions that told him she was close to the edge.

He pulled back and thrust deep one last time. The pleasure inside Evelyn shimmered for a breath-stealing moment, then exploded. His muscles went taut with release as hers became liquid, her senses drifting, her breathing coming in short gasps as she collapsed against his chest.

It was a long time before either one of them stirred.

Marshall ran his hand appreciatively over her bottom, then down the outside of her thighs before gently lifting her, turning them onto their sides without separating their bodies. Evelyn rested her cheek against his chest and curled her fingers into the crisp hair. He tightened his arms around her, silently telling her of his contentment.

Just as silently, Evelyn whispered the words, *I love you.*

Fourteen

"Miss Dennsworth, you have a jot of insanity if you believe I will receive you with any cordiality," Lady Waltham announced from her bed. "Please leave and close the door behind you."

Evelyn closed the door, but contrary to her ladyship's wishes, she was firmly inside the room. "It's a lovely morning," she announced. "Your daughters are taking breakfast on the east terrace. Would you care to join them?"

"Miss Dennsworth—"

"My name is Evelyn, your ladyship, and I would very much like to be your friend."

"You have a strange way of showing it," Lady Waltham said, drawing her bed jacket more snugly about her shoulders. "The marquis insists that whatever you do, it is for my own good. I disagree, of course, but he is very much like his father. Unwilling to abandon a decision once he has made it." She drew her shoulders back, her eyes bright with subdued anger. "Since I cannot discharge you, I am forced to tolerate you. But only to a point. Do I make myself clear?"

"Yes, your ladyship," Evelyn said, knowing she had ignited more than Lady Waltham's anger the previous day. The curtains were open this morning, the room flooded with natural light for the first time since her husband's death. It was a small sign, but one Evelyn quietly registered as progress.

The maid entered the room, delivering Lady's Waltham breakfast tray. The woman was broad about the hips with a ruddy complexion and a stiff smile that brightened upon seeing Evelyn. They had become acquainted since Evelyn's arrival. It was Jemima March who had supplied the most information about the household, tidbits of knowledge that had provided an insight into the family and the mistress who had once reigned happily at her husband's side.

"You may await me downstairs," Lady Waltham said. "The invitation list for the regatta party is far from finished."

"As you wish," Evelyn replied respectfully. She hoped she could reach the woman who had once filled Bedford Hall with love and laughter. Owing the marquis so much, it would be small recompense for all that he had done for her.

The following days took on a similar pattern. Evelyn would meet Lady Waltham in the morning room shortly after breakfast. Letters would be dictated and invitations issued. By the end of the first week, the guest list for the regatta festivities had been completed and the invitations posted.

All the acceptable families of the district would be attending the regatta celebration, plus another hundred guests traveling to Ipswich from as far away as Bristol and Coventry. The annual event demanded a flurry of parties: buffet luncheons served after morning rounds of croquet, afternoon teas filled with idle chatter, formal dinners followed by dancing in the grand ballroom which Evelyn had peeked into with envy, then tried to forget because she wasn't on the guest list. There would be no dancing in Marshall's arms, no magical waltz to add to her memories. Being a member of the staff, she would be expected to remember her place, becoming inconspicuously invisible for the duration of the festivities.

It wasn't that she craved parties or idle chatter or croquet lessons. Evelyn had never had those things in her life, and she didn't consider them important enough to brood over now. What she did covet was the heart of a marquis. Would it be so wrong to show him that she could fit into his life? His real life, not the one that began at midnight and ended before sunrise. Was it so wrong to dream that he might see her as more than a lover?

Futilely she wished that they had met under different circumstances. That they might have been presented to one another at a country gathering, but the reality of the situation shattered the daydream. Reality was a titled gentleman and a shop girl from Bond Street. Reality was two different worlds that rarely blended. Titled gentlemen didn't marry unless the arrangements were suitable, the proposed partner acceptable to society and their families. Although Marshall's closest friend might find her acceptable, his family, if her encounter with the courts were to be revealed, would most certainly not. If she had any doubts, all she need do was look at Winnifred. Marshall's sister would never accept her, never forget the scene she witnessed on Bond Street or Lady Monfrey's accusation. The past lay between, and there was no undoing it.

By the end of the week, Evelyn knew the name of everyone who would be attending the grand week-long celebration that would herald in the Harwick Regatta, but she'd come no closer to making a dent in Lady Waltham's grief than finding the curtains open more frequently than before. As she took her morning tea in the small garden just beyond the withdrawing room, Evelyn was beginning to wonder if she'd made a mistake by coming to Bedford Hall.

Catherine had received her well enough, but Winnifred

was still treating her like a complete stranger, speaking only when necessity and good manners demanded it. Lady Waltham was doing just as she had said, tolerating Evelyn's presence with no outward signs of mellowing toward her forced companion.

Marshall had advised her to be patient, that undoing things would take time, and that even if Evelyn feared she wasn't making progress, he could see a change in his stepmother. She had taken supper with the family the last three nights, a sizable improvement over her routine in London.

But Evelyn knew the roots of Lady Waltham's grief went much deeper than anyone suspected. Each time she looked into the older woman's eyes she could see the intolerable loneliness that had taken over her life. Feel it herself, because the time she spent with Marshall was like a world apart, time that would be forever locked in her memory. Evelyn knew that was how Lady Waltham was feeling. Perhaps if she could reach her, help her unlock the pain, she would be better prepared to handle her own grief if the marquis didn't open his heart to the love she was offering him. And nothing short of love could keep her for more than the summer.

"I thought I'd find you here."

Evelyn turned to see Marshall walking toward her. As soon as she saw him standing against a backdrop of golden sunlight, she knew the grief she would face at leaving him would be more than her heart could bear. He had such a strikingly handsome face. It was not so much that he was attractive, that he possessed a grace and vitality that commanded her attention, it was knowing that she'd always remember the way he smiled when they faced each other in the light of day, that secret look that said he was remembering what had transpired between them the previous night.

She couldn't help but notice that he was dressed for traveling. A sense of loss came over her, but she contained it, knowing she couldn't demand all his attention.

Keeping a respectable distance, Marshall smiled at her. "I'll be away for a few days," he said. "I have business in Norwich."

"I understand," Evelyn replied. "Mr. Druggs told me that you have several estates."

Marshall had hoped she'd take the news a little less casually; but then, they were just outside the main house, and servants were flittering about like butterflies. He'd been extremely careful in his comings and goings, making sure no one suspected that he'd been visiting the cottage on a regular basis. The last thing he wanted was to shine an unfavorable light on Evelyn's current position.

"The business is important enough to require my personal attention," he told her. "If not, I'd dispatch Druggs."

"Please, you don't have to explain," Evelyn replied. "You are a man with obligations. It would be selfish of me to ask you to put them aside."

He took a step, bringing them as close as propriety allowed. "I want to kiss you goodbye."

Evelyn tried not to blush, a feat she should have been able to manage quite well considering the things that had passed between them up to this point, but she failed. There was no embarrassment on Marshall's face. He stood looking at her, his expression as innocent as that of a choir boy, unless one looked into his eyes. They were gleaming with mischief.

The garden was small, a patch of roses and waist-high shrubbery that provided little privacy unless one was sitting down. His gaze turned to the house. "Meet me in the second-floor library."

Evelyn finished her tea, knowing she shouldn't follow him inside, but wanting the kiss as much as he did. After a few minutes, long enough for him to reach the designated room, she rose and entered the house, making her way to the second floor with a forced casualness that belied the excitement flowing through her veins.

The door to the library was unlocked, the handle and hinges well oiled so it opened soundlessly. She had seen the room before, having borrowed several books for her own pleasure as well as Lady Waltham's. The library faced south and was full of light this late in the morning. The parquet floor gleamed from a recent polishing, the draperies a rich golden brown that framed tall windows overlooking the main yard. Evelyn hesitated just inside the closed door.

Marshall, however, didn't share her patience. He wanted her in his arms as quickly as possible. He pulled her close, inhaling the light fragrance she wore, the scent that always reminded him of an herbal garden drenched in sunshine.

Evelyn saw the sensual curve of Marshall's smile as he lowered his head to claim her mouth. She felt a tiny shudder of pleasure as her lips parted for him. His taste swept through her, filling her senses as it always did, chasing away the world, the fear of a servant discovering them. She buried her fingers in the wavy thickness of his hair and returned the kiss, knowing it would have to last her for several days.

The kiss turned into several kisses. Evelyn felt her body begin to tingle with the unique heat and sensitivity that was always associated with the marquis. His hands gripped her hips, holding her tightly against him, increasing the forbidden passion a house full of people prevented them from fulfilling.

"I'll be back as soon as I can," he said harshly, then smiled. He released her with a visible reluctance, then stepped back. "You'd better run downstairs before I forget what's left of my good intentions. I'm hungry enough to take you right now, standing up if necessary."

Her expression said she'd never thought of making love in that position. Her eyes sparkled with just enough curiosity for Marshall to continue teasing her.

"Would you like it like that, Miss Dennsworth? Your

skirts billowing out around my legs while I'm deep inside you. I could lean you up against the wall. I've never taken a woman that way, but I'm willing to give it a try."

She blushed with embarrassment, but it didn't prevent her from saying, "Off with you, my lord, before you destroy what's left of my composure. I have duties to attend to that don't include wolfish marquises and dangerous desires," Evelyn said shakily. Could people actually make love standing up?

"Dangerous desires, is it?" Marshall laughed lightly. "I'll give you another, more thorough, demonstration when I return from Norwich. Until then, think about all the dangerously delicious things I'm going to do to your person one week from today."

With that, he gave her a gentlemanly bow and quit the library, leaving Evelyn's imagination running wild.

After several long, deep breaths, she made her way back downstairs. Entering the morning room, Evelyn sat down at the rosewood desk with its supply of fine-grained paper and envelopes. They would begin working on the menus today. Most of the guests would be staying at Bedford Hall. Maids and footmen were already busy in the guest wings, airing rooms that had been closed up since the death of the late marquis, freshening linens, polishing floors and everything that sat upon them. The whole household was busy, preparing for the festivities that would last a full week before the regatta set sail.

"If yer expecting her ladyship, she won't be coming downstairs today," Jemima March said, appearing in the doorway.

"Is she ill?" Evelyn asked.

"No," the lady's maid replied. "It's the day that has her feelin' poorly."

"I'm not sure I understand."

"Wouldn't expect you to," Jemima remarked sadly. "Today's an anniversary. Twenty years of marriage, if his lordship had lived long enough."

Twenty years. If only the summer could last that long.

"I shall go upstairs and see if Lady Waltham needs anything."

The maid shook her head, as if to say it would be a waste of time, but Evelyn ignored the gesture and made her way upstairs a second time, thinking this could very well be the day when she finally accomplished something. As expected, she found Lady Waltham sitting alone in her bedroom. The curtains were drawn against the brightness of the morning sunlight.

Marshall's stepmother was dressed in her formal widow's weeds, an unadorned dress of black barathea. Her face was pale and hollow eyed, her posture unfashionably stiff. She didn't look as if she'd been crying, but rather that she wanted to cry and had forgotten how to go about it. She had lost the man she loved and with him all aspirations for the future.

"I do not wish any company at the moment," Lady Waltham informed her. "And don't think to gainsay me this time, Miss Dennsworth. I will not be bullied or coerced by a member of the staff."

"I would be more than glad to comply with your wishes, your ladyship, if I thought they were sincere," Evelyn replied, "but I don't believe that you truly want to be alone."

The tightening at the corners of Lady Waltham's mouth betrayed her irritation. She wasn't used to people being disobedient or blatantly rude to one's betters. At the very minimum, she was accustomed to being pampered because her health was considered frail. When she spoke again there was a hint of desperation in her voice.

"Why are you doing this? Why do you insist on tormenting me under the guise of friendship? Isn't it enough that

I'm forced to tolerate your presence; what more do you wish to gain except the salary my stepson pays you?"

"To repay a kindness," Evelyn answered candidly.

"Then you seek to repay it with unkindness," Lady Waltham snapped.

Evelyn said a silent prayer, then sat down, folding her hands in her lap. "Tell me about your husband. Share your memories with me. Was he tall and handsome? Soft-spoken or boisterous? I know he liked to sail, that he loved the water."

Lady Waltham's shoulders slumped as her hands, covered with black lace to the knuckles, came up to cover her face. "I don't want to remember him. Don't you understand? It hurts too much."

Evelyn left her chair and moved across the room to sit down upon the ottoman at the foot of Lady Waltham's chair. She reached out and gently pried the woman's hands away from her face. "If you loved him, then the memories will be filled with love, as well. Let them give you the comfort you've denied yourself up to now."

For a long moment Lady Waltham looked as if she wanted to strike Evelyn, her eyes as cold as winter ice; then they blinked, and Evelyn saw the wet gleam of tears.

"Do you know what it's like to love someone so much it pains you to be away from them for even the space of an hour?" Lady Waltham asked viciously. "Do you?"

"Yes, I think so," Evelyn answered in a whisper. "Even when he's not with you, the knowledge that he will be there soon offers your heart comfort."

She knew the answer shocked Marshall's stepmother, but unless she named the man she loved, Lady Waltham would have no way of knowing it was the marquis.

The silence stretched into minutes, and Evelyn feared she'd pushed too hard, trespassing upon things that were none of her business, things too private for another heart to understand. Then she felt Lady Waltham's hands turn, to hold on to hers, gripping her fingers with surprising strength.

"George was handsome," she whispered softly. "Not in a rakish way. He was far too dignified for that. Marshall resembles him, the same dark hair, although his eye color comes from his mother. George's eyes were blue, darker than mine, and oh, so piercing. I remember the first time I saw him. He stole my breath, standing at the entrance to the ballroom, dressed in flawless black."

"Where did you meet?" She asked the question in a soft tone.

"At a masque ball held by the Earl of Leicester. It was my second Season. I had gained a proposal my first year out, but my father encouraged me to decline the man's suit." A weak smile came to her face. "He was right. George was the man I was supposed to marry."

"Was it a beautiful wedding? Large? Small?"

Another smile. This one stronger, more pleasing, came over Constance's face. "Small compared to most. But it was beautiful. We married . . . twenty years ago today." A tear slid down her face. "It sounds like a long time ago. But it wasn't. Not nearly long enough."

She wept then, openly, painfully, and Evelyn held her in her arms. Soon her own tears were joining those of Lady Waltham, tears she could shed without reproach or explanation.

Eventually Marshall's stepmother regained her composure. But once the words had started, they couldn't be stopped.

Evelyn rang for tea and listened as Lady Waltham recited the events of that first evening, the introduction that George William Bedford, the sixth Marquis of Waltham, had instigated. The story went on, how the marquis had taken to a shy young lady, how he'd patiently courted her, bringing her out of her shell until she woke each morning with a head full of thoughts that began and ended with him alone.

"He proposed before the end of the Season," Lady Waltham told her. "And I accepted, despite my misgivings."

"Misgivings?"

"Marshall," she admitted. "I didn't have the slightest notion how to go about being a mother, and it frightened me to think of it. Of course, George wouldn't hear of a long engagement. He wanted a wife, and he wasn't always a patient man."

A trait his son had inherited.

A faint smile came to Lady Waltham's tear-streaked face. "Of course, the moment I saw Marshall, I realized my fears had been wasted. He looked so much like his father that I loved him instantly. He was big for his age, tall and slender with the promise of nobility about him. We settled into a family with little effort after that."

Evelyn listened. It was easy to picture the couple, their love for each other, summers filled with boat races and lawn parties, little girls toddling after their father. As it was all too easy to imagine that same happiness in her own life, being married to Marshall, strolling the grounds of Bedford Hall with him at her side, standing on the beach with a mother's fear as he taught their children how to swim in the foamy surf, spending the rest of her life loving him and being loved.

It was a good hour before Lady Waltham drew in an exhausted breath and apologized for burdening Evelyn with her misery.

"There is no misery in hearing about someone's happiness, my lady. I envy you the time you had with your husband. So few women know that they have been truly loved."

Lady Waltham smiled. "You are an extraordinary young woman, Miss Dennsworth. And I regret my previous rudeness. Will you forgive me?"

"There is nothing to forgive. Now, why don't you rest. Lunch will be served soon, and if the day holds its sunshine, a walk along the beach might be to your liking. Catherine told me it was a habit you shared with her last summer."

"I've neglected my children," she said sadly. "Both of them. Winnifred is excited about the prospects of Lord Lansdowne proposing marriage, and I've yet to set eyes on the gentleman. Catherine is growing up faster than she should. Marshall has scolded me for not paying her more attention."

"No longer, I trust," Evelyn said, giving her ladyship's hands a firm squeeze. Their former coldness had dissipated, and she thanked God that Lady Waltham had finally accepted her friendship. "Each time you are tempted to stay in your room, think of a part of the house that holds a pleasant memory and visit it."

"Are you always this optimistic?"

"I try to be," Evelyn replied. "I've recently discovered that dwelling on things we have no control over can be a waste of time. It's best to enjoy each day and hope for the best."

What Evelyn didn't say was that she had begun to live on hope, the hope that Marshall's physical affection might miraculously turn into love. If not, she'd glean all the happiness she could from the summer, and pray that whatever providence had in store for their separate futures, the marquis would find a woman who loved him half as much as she did.

The prayer was a bittersweet wish, for she hated to think of him holding another woman in his arms, but it was foolish to think that he wouldn't marry one day. His title and an heir demanded that he eventually take a wife. In which case, Evelyn hoped she was like Lady Waltham, a woman with a heart capable of loving for a lifetime.

* * *

Lady Waltham's transformation was a gradual one, but by the end of the week, everyone at Bedford Hall was aware that the mistress of the house was slowly setting aside her mourning. She began rising early, requesting her morning tea on the terrace rather than in her room, then lingering to have breakfast with her daughters. A tour of the guest wings came next with instructions as to the placement of expected visitors, along with various other items that she had willingly allowed to regress into the hands of the staff.

There were more long conversations, private talks that allowed Lady Waltham to gradually rid herself of grief and take on the temperament of a woman who would miss her husband dearly, but one who also knew his memory was a comfort not a curse.

At Lady Waltham's insistence, Evelyn spoke of herself occasionally, relating stories of her childhood in Sussex, of being raised in a rectory, of her dream to one day open a dress shop. She was careful never to mention the marquis in any way that might arouse Lady Waltham's curiosity.

One such conversation happened on the beach the afternoon of the marquis's return to Bedford Hall. Lady Waltham was sitting in a wicker chair, carried down to the beach by a dutiful footman, while Evelyn sat by her side, knees folded on a plaid blanket. They had luncheon on the shore and were now relaxing, enjoying the brightness of the day. Catherine was walking along the beach, her pinafore hem wet from the waves she'd been told time and time again to avoid. Whenever she found a particularly nice shell, she'd come running up the beach to place it in a small wicker basket brought along for just that purpose.

"A dress shop of your own," Lady Waltham mused as a gale of wind threatened her black bonnet. She put up a hand to hold it in place until the breeze subsided, then turned to look at her companion. "A woman in business has more challenges to meet than the monthly rent," she said. "Are you sure you wouldn't rather marry? Your personality lends itself to being a wife and a mother."

"Perhaps someday," Evelyn said, wishing for all the world that it could be to the man she truly loved. "If the right man comes along."

"I thought he had," Constance said, her gaze turning inquisitive. "The manner in which we have spoken to each other of late leads me to believe that you have been in love. Are still in love."

Evelyn looked toward the ocean, knowing Lady Waltham would see the truth in her eyes if she tried to deny it. "There is a man, but I fear there will never be a marriage. Things . . . There are things in the way."

"Forgive me for prying. It is none of my business."

A short silence ensued, broken only by the rhythmic sound of waves rolling onto the shore and the chatter of seagulls. Evelyn hadn't lied when she'd told Lady Waltham that she wished to be her friend, but the relationship, developing at a fast pace, was still one-sided. She could listen to Constance—she'd received permission to address her ladyship by her given name whenever they were alone—but she didn't dare share her own secrets. It was a bit surprising to discover just how much of her life was now absorbed by the marquis. It left little to tell anyone, especially his stepmother.

"Marshall!" Catherine yelled, scampering toward the grass-covered dunes. "You're back!"

"So I am, kitten," he said, meeting her halfway, then scooping her up and swinging her around. "And your nose is pink from too much sun. Where's your bonnet?"

"Evelyn is watching over it for me," Catherine told him, then wiggled her nose. "Is it really pink?"

"Pink is a very pretty color," Marshall said, taking her

hand and leading her down the dune as elegantly as he might escort a young lady onto the dance floor.

Evelyn watched him approach, her heart beating wildly, then suddenly stopping the moment he was standing over her, his smile as provoking as it had been that day on Bond Street when he'd knelt to help her gather up the pins. She averted her gaze, not wanting to appear overenthusiastic because he had returned home.

"Am I to believe my eyes and ears?" Marshall said, leaning down to take his stepmother's hand. "The entire house is abuzz with the news. My stepmother has taken a likening to sunshine and fresh air."

"Stuff and nonsense!" Lady Waltham replied with a snap. "What good does it do to have a seaside estate and not enjoy it?"

"My sentiments exactly," Marshall laughed as he eased himself onto the blanket. He turned his eyes on Evelyn. "Whatever you did, I thank you, Miss Dennsworth."

The words were spoken with a heartfelt sincerity that threatened to bring tears to Evelyn's eyes, but she smiled instead, nodding slightly in acknowledgement.

"What she did was bully and coerce me," Constance said. "She has been nothing but rude and unflattering to a widow, and I consider her a true friend for her efforts."

"Then so shall I," Marshall replied.

He didn't touch her, but Evelyn saw the desire in his eyes. It was all she could do to keep from throwing herself into his arms. In that moment, seeing him smiling, his hair blown by the wind, his eyes bright with joy and excitement, Evelyn knew she would love him forever.

"How was Norwich?" his stepmother asked, as Catherine returned to the beach. This time with her bonnet.

"As Norwich always is," Marshall replied, digging into their luncheon basket to see if anything had been left over.

He found an apple. While he chewed he glanced at Evelyn, his eyes promising her a visit that very night. "Nothing unusual goes on there, or at least nothing that came to my ears. Ran into Granby. He'll be arriving a good week before the regatta."

"The man is a notorious rascal," Constance said, addressing Evelyn.

"And a good friend," Marshall said. "Not to worry, I'll keep him on a short leash."

"Make sure you do," his stepmother replied. "The last time he came to call, we nearly had a scandal on our hands."

Marshall laughed out loud. "You're exaggerating."

"Perhaps a little." Constance surprised them both by laughing. "Nevertheless, your sister is deep in the Season, and with Lord Lansdowne on the invitation list, I don't want anything unsavory going on."

"How is Winnifred?" Marshall asked.

"Your sister is fine," his stepmother replied. "A bit reserved, but then, she's no longer a child. One expects a young lady of her age to show some maturity. Have you given this Lord Lansdowne a thorough looking over. I shan't want Winnie to be mislead by his intentions."

"He comes with the Duke of Morland's personal recommendation," Marshall replied. Then turning to the side so only Evelyn could see his face, he gave her a wicked wink. "As for Winnie suddenly becoming reserved . . . Let's hope Lansdowne likes his ladies mature. I prefer them a tad more interesting."

"Don't be impertinent," Lady Waltham said, but without sharpness. "You'll give Miss Dennsworth the impression that you're as incorrigible as Granby."

"My apologies, Miss Dennsworth," he said, smiling all the while. "With that, I shall take myself back to the house." He stood, blocking the sun with his body. "Enjoy your afternoon, ladies."

Evelyn did her best not to stare as he waved goodbye to Catherine, then trekked up the dunes, his boots sinking ankle deep into the white sand.

"I fear it will be easier to marry off Winnie than it will be to find my stepson a suitable wife," Lady Waltham said. "He's determined to remain a bachelor as long as possible."

"He's still young," Evelyn said with as much composure as she could manage and without looking at Constance.

"Be that as it may, he still requires a wife. An heir."

"Of course," Evelyn agreed, hoping her voice sounded convincing.

"I've invited several prospective young ladies to the regatta festivities," Lady Waltham went on, unaware that every word pierced Evelyn's heart. "He will be polite, perhaps even flirt with one or two, though I doubt anything more will come of it. But then, one can always hope."

Fifteen

The wind was blustering from the north, bringing a driving rain that pelted the roof of the cottage. Beyond the door and closed shutters, the night was caught in the heavy grip of the storm. Evelyn had built a small fire, just enough to take the chill out of the air while she bathed. She put on a nightgown, one she'd bought before leaving London, and a dressing gown with blue embroidery and sat in front of the fire, brushing her hair.

Would the storm keep Marshall at the manor house?

Minute by minute the rain grew more irate, the rhythmic pelting turning into a furious downpour as sheet after sheet of water lashed the cottage. The sound of the sea was even louder, waves crashing onto the beach in wet slaps. The candles—there were no gaslights—flickered as the cottage proved to be as drafty as Marshall had predicted. But the fire was cozy, its light adding to the warmth, keeping the storm at bay.

Suddenly another sound joined the storm. Someone stomping their feet outside the door, ridding their boots of mud. Evelyn heaved a deep sigh of relief, then hurried to unbolt the latch. "You're soaked to the bone," she said.

"That I am," Marshall admitted, stepping inside, then leveling his weight against the door and a blast of wind until he had the latch secured. "I pity any packet boats on the Channel tonight."

As always, Evelyn felt no greater emotion than the moment when he was standing before her eyes. She was instantly enveloped by the present; past and future detached from her mind, the wrong and right of their love affair something to be worried about later.

"I was just going to brew some tea," she said, looking toward the fireplace and the kettle waiting to be hung over the low flames.

"I've something better in mind," he said, holding up a bottle. "Have you ever tasted cognac?"

Evelyn shook her head.

"It's the perfect drink for a night like this. Smooth and rich," he told her. "I had thought to celebrate with a bottle of champagne, but the storm made the decision for me."

She hung his slicker on the peg rack just inside the door while he removed his boots, placing them near the fire to dry. His hair was wet, clinging to his brow until he brushed it back with his hand. He had come to her despite the storm. Evelyn felt a twinge of womanly pride that he had left his dry, warm home and ventured out into the night, armed with a bottle of cognac and a need to be with her, even if the need was only physical.

"What are we celebrating?" She walked to the cupboard for glasses.

"My stepmother's resurrection, what else?" He raised his arms and pulled his shirt over his head, then tossed it onto the back of the small sofa that faced the fireplace. "I can't believe the difference. She was her old self this evening at dinner, chastising the girls, rambling on about the regatta party and all the matchmaking that will be done." He sat down and stretched out his legs, warming his feet. "However did you do it?"

"You were right. She needed to reminisce," Evelyn said, ignoring the reference to matchmaking. She didn't want to think about all the husband-hunting young ladies who were due to swoop down on the estate like a horde of well-mannered locusts.

"Reminisce?" Marshall mused, pulling the cork from the small, round-bottomed bottle. "I lost count of the times I tried to talk to her about Father. She always found a way to change the subject."

"You wanted to talk about your father; she needed to talk about her husband."

Marshall gave her a questioning glance as he stripped off his socks. It was easy to see that he was settling in for a long night.

Evelyn sat down, holding out the two glasses. Marshall tipped up the bottle, pouring a small amount of liquor into each one. After setting the bottle on the floor, he took one of the glasses, then using his free hand tugged Evelyn close to his side. She rested her head against his shoulder. He smelled like rain and wind and musky cologne.

"She needed another woman to talk to," Evelyn explained, knowing his male mind hadn't quite grasped the concept of her previous remark. She stared into the fire. "Lady Waltham loved your father very much. More than I think any of you realized. When you love someone as deeply as that, their death isn't just a loss, it's a loneliness that goes all the way to your soul. She didn't know how to express that loss, so she held it inside, clinging to it because she thought letting go of the grief meant letting go of your father's memory."

Marshall didn't comment because he wasn't sure what to say. Once again he was amazed by Evelyn's natural insight.

He knew that Constance and his father had had a good marriage, one based on mutual affection. He had never questioned his father's happiness; it had showed on his face. As for love . . . It wasn't a topic he'd ever discussed with a woman. He didn't feel comfortable discussing it with Evelyn, though God knew they'd talked about everything else in their lives. But discussing the love a man felt for a woman, or a woman for a man, was opening a door he'd rather keep closed for the time period.

He'd spent a great many hours thinking about Evelyn during his trip to Norwich. Thinking about her, missing her, wanting her. There was no exactness in his emotions, but rather a jumbled confusion that he credited to her decision to leave at summer's end. Evelyn enjoyed being his lover; her response was too open, too honest, for him to believe otherwise. Yet, she refused to speak of anything more than a summer affair.

Confident that he still had time to change her mind, Marshall reassumed the conversation about his stepmother. "I suppose it would be difficult for Constance to talk about the personal side of her marriage to anyone in the family," Marshall conceded. He took a sip of cognac before asking, "Just how personal have your conversations been?"

Evelyn laughed. "Not *that* personal."

He shrugged, then shifted his weight so she sank back into the crook of his arm. "How am I to know what women discuss when they're behind closed doors?"

"What do men discuss?" she prompted curiously.

"Now *you're* changing the subject." He kissed the top of her head. "Whatever was said, it seems to have had the desired effect. Constance is smiling again, and for that I thank you."

"You're welcome."

She lifted a hand and placed it over his bare chest. His skin was warm, his heart beating strongly under her open palm. As the storm continued to rage outside, Evelyn couldn't keep herself from snuggling closer to the reassuring warmth of Marshall's body. He hadn't kissed her yet, not the way she longed for him to kiss her, but resting in his arms was very nice. She sipped the cognac, liking its rich taste, the way it warmed her stomach while the fire warmed her bare feet.

She lifted her face to him, and for a moment they smiled at each other, silently recognizing and acknowledging their mutual desire. Marshall kissed her, drawing her fully against him.

"I missed you," he whispered, taking the glass of cognac from her hand and putting it aside.

"I missed you, too," she whispered, attempting a light smile that belied the depths of her feelings. It was so easy to imagine that they were like other couples, snuggling in front of a fire during a storm, content to hold each other while the rain swept up and down the coastline. But then, wasn't that what she had promised herself—a fairy-tale summer, months of imagining that the marquis actually loved her?

Putting her arms around his neck, Evelyn refused to let the future intrude on the present. She wasn't going to pretend that she didn't want Marshall, that she wasn't eager for the lovemaking that was soon to come. Outside the storm raged on, its wildness keeping the world away. Inside, there was the warmth of the fire and the man.

Marshall kissed her again, tasting the cognac on her lips and the sweet flavor that was uniquely Evelyn. He had missed her. More than he liked to admit, more than he was willing to admit. It still pricked his pride to think that she was going to leave him at the end of summer. Of course, he was still determined to change her mind. If it could be changed. There were still so many things about her that he didn't understand. Her unexpected decision to become his lover, the sympathetic way she had brought Constance out of a shell of grief, the unique pleasure he took from simply being in her company. She was unselfish in her giving, open and honest, vibrant and passionate.

He stared at her face for a moment. It was a dreamer's face, soft featured and still strangely innocent.

With a muffled sound of appreciation, he kissed her again. His hand found the ribbons at the front of her dressing gown, then the small buttons on the garment beneath it. He slid his hand inside, finding the soft weight of her breast, feeling its flushed heat as he ran his thumb across her nipple.

Evelyn gave herself freely to the pleasure, enjoying the touch of his hand as it moved over her breast, cupping and stroking, his fingertips pinching lightly. There was little warning. One moment she was being cradled in his arms; the next she was spread out on the rug in front of the hearth like a meal for feasting.

"Too many clothes," he said roughly. "I want the woman underneath them."

Evelyn's blood heated at the words. She said his name in a deep, heavy whisper.

Marshall looked at her, measuring the passion in her voice, the desire shining in her eyes, and knew that he'd never been wanted the way Evelyn wanted him at this very moment. No hesitation, no doubts, no flirtatious motives, just pure desire. He could see himself reflected in her eyes, see himself as she saw him—not a marquis, but a man. The knowledge forced the air from his lungs in a deep, satisfying breath.

The breath turned into a groan as Evelyn's hands moved slowly over his upper body. When she ran her hands over his chest, her nails raking his nipples, the tormenting pleasure made him shudder. He stirred hungrily, pressing her down onto the rug, covering her body with his larger one, claiming her mouth in a deep, hungry kiss.

The fire on the hearth burned on, but not as hot as the woman in his arms.

Her hands moved over him, their touch a silky caress. But it wasn't enough.

Marshall came to his knees, straddling her legs. He smiled. Then slowly, very slowly, he began to undress her, removing the cloth barriers that kept him from feeling her heat, from seeing the way her body was responding to his touch, his whispered words. Her nipples became tight, velvety peaks that begged for his mouth. Her stomach clenched when he ran his fingertips from the valley between her breasts to the indentation of her navel, then lower, brushing her private curls.

Evelyn closed her eyes as she felt Marshall's mouth on her breasts and his hands gently encouraging her legs to part. She was already on fire for him, her blood running sleek and hot, her body hungry. When his mouth moved from her lips to the taut peaks of her breasts, then slowly downward, she sucked in her breath and held it.

"No," she said, finding the strength to push him away. "I want . . . I want to . . ."

"What?" Marshall asked, his breath coming in a rush as he looked down at her. He wanted to part her legs even more, to move between them, to bury himself in her sultry heat. He wanted it so badly, he was aching.

"I want to touch you all the ways you touch me," Evelyn whispered. She sat up, curling her arms around his neck. Kissing him gently, then with all the desire she felt.

When Marshall stretched her out on the rug again, he was on the bottom. "Then touch me," he whispered feverishly. "Do whatever you want to me, sweetheart. But do it fast. I'm dying."

Evelyn laughed. "I don't know how."

Marshall's voice was deep, husky. "Follow your instincts."

Evelyn wasn't sure about her instincts, so she followed her fantasies instead.

Marshall's hands clenched as he felt Evelyn fulfilling those fantasies. Her warm mouth caressed his skin. He closed his eyes and felt her loving him, felt the hesitant way her lips and teeth and hands explored his body. When her hair skimmed over his blunt arousal, he made a tormented sound that brought a smile to her face.

"You're so strong," she said in a light whisper. "It's a shame you have to wear clothes. They hide just how much of a man you are."

"Are you saying you'll share me with the women of the world?" he asked, fighting the urge to finish what she was starting.

"Never, my lord." Her breath was a hot caress over his aroused flesh. "You belong to me for the summer, and I'm a very selfish woman."

"You couldn't be selfish if you wanted to," he replied, praying for control. It was slipping away, splintering with each touch of her mouth and hands. "Your heart is too big. Too generous."

Marshall gritted his teeth as she continued exploring his body, learning it as intimately as he had once learned hers. Her hands were fire, burning him wherever they touched. Her mouth was even more tormenting. He shivered and held back a groan as her mouth moved over him, tasting, learning, torturing him until he thought he might burst.

"No more!" he said, knowing his self-control had reached its limit. "You can tease me later. Right now, I want you too badly to be playful about it."

He dragged her up his body, burying his tongue in her mouth. He rolled, putting her beneath him again. Another shudder racked his body as he eased inside her moist, supple channel, into the very heat of her.

Evelyn felt her body unraveling, her senses whirling as Marshall pushed deep inside her. Pleasure ebbed and flowed as his hips rocked back and forth in hard, deep thrusts. He took her more deeply, more forcefully than he'd ever taken her before, and Evelyn reveled in the wonder of it, the pure, pulsating pleasure of belonging to him in the only way she could.

He slid his arms under her hips, raising her up, forcing her body to accept the pounding of his own, hard and deep, so deeply she could feel him touching her womb. Their bodies glistened with sweat, gleaming in the light of the fire, and still he drove into her, pushing her higher and higher, deeper and deeper into the passionate fire. The pleasure was so intense, so savage, Evelyn thought she would die. Then she did, a short, hot death that left her gasping for breath.

Marshall felt her release, felt the wet, hot pulse of her climax, and thrust even deeper, wanting the same thing for himself. When he found it, he groaned deep in his chest. The pleasure was like nothing he'd felt before. His body tightened, then exploded, as he willingly surrendered to his own passionate death.

Much later, after they retired to the comfort of the bed, he held her close while the storm moved down the coast and into the Atlantic. Rain still splattered against the windows, but it was a soft rain, a gentle remnant of nature's previous fury.

"Constance said you told her about wanting a dress shop of your own," Marshall said. In the dark, his expression changed, taking on a more pensive look. His gaze swept over Evelyn as she lay naked in his arms, her head resting against his shoulders, her hair a tangled array of golden brown curls. "She wanted to make sure your salary was adequate, that you'd have the money you need when the time comes. You made quite an impression on her. And on Catherine."

"But not Winnifred," Evelyn said. "It's too much to ask of her to forget what she saw that day. God knows, I'll never forget it."

"It's in the past. Over and done." He pulled her close, enjoying the feel of her naked skin against him. "Has Winnie been rude? If she has, I'll make sure she doesn't forget her manners again."

"It isn't a question of manners," she told him. "Your sister finds my presence puzzling, and reasonably so. Don't scold her for disliking me. It wouldn't be fair. I don't want to come between you and your family. I've made no greater impression on them than they have on me."

"Regardless, I won't have you treated disrespectfully."

"She hasn't been rude, not really," Evelyn insisted. "Please let it pass. The regatta guests will be arriving soon, and I'm sure she's anxious over Lord Lansdowne being one of them. Her future could be decided this summer. She's consumed with her own thoughts and worries."

Marshall disagreed, but before he could say anything, she distracted him with a kiss.

Evelyn didn't want to talk about the future because all it held now was a barren dream, years with nothing to fill the emptiness but the memories she could gather and hold on to after a brief summer in the arms of a marquis. But reality had to be faced, no matter how displeasing. "Winnifred is young and in love for the first time in her life. She needs your support, not your criticism. Catherine is a joy, and Lady Waltham is a good person. I can only imagine how much happiness she gave your father. He died knowing he was loved. God blessed him with three wonderful children, a life of material comfort, a title that brought respect and admiration from his peers, a wife that loved him beyond question. What more could a man want?"

She turned in his arms, folding her hands over his chest and resting her chin upon them. "As for my salary, it is overly generous, as well you know. By the time you return to London, I shall have more than enough to find a nice building and hang out a shingle."

"And where will you hang this shingle?" he asked, curious as to how she saw the summer ending. He'd worried about her for so long, protected her, cared for her, that it was hard to imagine she didn't need him to continue those things. It was also another thorn in his pride, a stinging reminder that she would still be on Bond Street, working toward her dream, if Lady Monfrey hadn't jumped to the wrong conclusion.

"I'm not sure," Evelyn replied. "England has hundreds of villages and towns. I'm sure I can find one that needs a good dressmaker."

It wasn't a lie. She had no idea where she would go when the time came to leave her kindhearted, passionate marquis behind. As far from London and Ipswich as possible, she thought, making sure her face didn't reflect her feelings.

"I don't suppose you'd consider—"

She pressed a finger to his mouth, knowing what he was going to say. She'd heard it before, his wish for her to return to the house on Lambeth Road, the passionate nights they'd share together if only she'd stop being stubborn. "Summer is a short season," she said. "Don't waste it. Love me again. Make me feel alive and beautiful and wanted."

"You are," he breathed heavily, pulling her beneath him again.

Their joining was another burst of flames, a passion that burned them all the way to their souls. It was gentle this time. Marshall wanted to possess her, to make her realize that she was running away from something grand and wonderful.

Evelyn arched against him, taking him inside, needing him in more ways than he could ever imagine. The lure of summer nights and memories still to be made filled her mind while Marshall filled her body. When the fire exploded this time, it left her feeling renewed and consumed, sated but sad.

Marshall's breathing was deep and steady as he slept.

Evelyn looked at the ceiling, her body exhausted from his lovemaking, her mind wide awake and filled with a hodge-podge of thoughts and feelings. She closed her eyes as a note of unhappiness came with the thoughts, the knowledge that the marquis wasn't interested in sharing his heart. Yet no matter how much she wanted to hang on to the hope that he might envision her as more than a mistress, the truth was impossible to ignore. The bridge of mutual desire forged the gap between them, but they were still from two different worlds.

Determinedly, Evelyn shook her black thoughts aside. The summer had only just begun. She had weeks to gather the memories she would take with her before her pride forced her to leave Bedford Hall.

Sixteen

The summer moved on. Evelyn's days were spent in the company of Lady Waltham, but her nights belonged to the lord of the manor. She stored every moment she and the marquis shared in her memory, the rainy evenings spent in front of a fire, the sultry nights that took them for long walks on a moonlit beach, early mornings filled with smiles and gentle lovemaking. Each day brought a new memory.

It was on one of those mornings that the guests for the regatta festivities began to arrive at Bedford Hall. The world was alight with sunshine, the breeze balmy as it swept over the Channel and onto the shore, bringing the scent of the sea with it. Evelyn was in the second-floor library, seeking a book that might lend itself to a leisurely afternoon spent reading, when she heard the sound of carriage wheels. She watched from the oriel windows that overlooked the circular drive fronting the manor house.

A gentleman stepped down from the carriage. Evelyn knew the visitor was the Earl of Granby. Marshall had told her that his closest friend would be the first guest to arrive. She studied the man for a moment, although there was little she could see from the library window. He was superbly dressed, his jacket cut from the best broadcloth, his vest from dark gray silk, his shirt undoubtedly purchased from Grieves. He moved with the same confident air that had first drawn her eyes to the marquis. She knew the two men had a lot in common; both were only sons, educated at Eton, then Cambridge. Like the marquis, the earl was in his early thirties, a wealthy, contented bachelor.

The sound of a footman rushing up the steps to inform the marquis of the earl's arrival forced Evelyn away from the window. She didn't want to be caught gawking at one of the guests, nor did she want to appear overly curious about the marquis's personal friends. Their acquaintance had nothing to do with her, nor did she covet an introduction when nothing could come of it but uplifted brows as to why the marquis would care to introduce a member of the staff to his honored guests. Discretion was a necessity. She might be ignorant of many of society's rules, but she knew enough to know that a gentleman didn't keep his lover this close to his family. The marquis had the rank to disregard opinion, if he chose to do so, but he also had two sisters and a stepmother. Any scandal attached to his name would soon adhere itself to them as well.

She selected a book, then exited the library in hopes of gaining the morning room before the marquis greeted his friend. Unfortunately, her timing was off by several seconds. The Earl of Granby reached the second-floor landing before she could disappear down the back stairs, a shortcut to the east wing that she used since becoming acquainted with the interior of the sprawling manor house.

They came face-to-face in the hallway. Up close, it was easy for Evelyn to see the rakish elegance of the man. The earl took no pains to hide his interest, his steely blue eyes surveying her from head to toe. Taking in the cut of her mint green day dress, his gaze lingered far too long on her breasts before moving slowly up to her face. He smiled, and she knew that Lady Waltham's assessment was an accurate one. The man was charmingly dangerous.

Unsure if she should acknowledge him by name—there was no reason she should know who he was—Evelyn hesitated, frantically searching for the appropriate greeting.

Blessedly, she was rescued from doing or saying the wrong thing.

Marshall came out of his study, two doors down the hall, strolling toward them with a smile on his face. "Granby," he said, holding out his hand. "Thought you'd be the first to arrive."

"I always am," the earl replied. "And the last to leave. I daresay, it's become a tradition of sorts."

"May I introduce Miss Dennsworth," Marshall said as smoothly as he would have introduced any lady of society. "My stepmother's companion for the summer."

"Miss Dennsworth," the earl said, immediately trapping her hand in a warm grasp, then bringing it to his mouth for a chaste kiss. "My pleasure."

The marquis cleared his throat as the earl's lips pressed lightly against her fingers.

Marshall's reaction told her that the Earl of Granby knew exactly who and what she was. It shouldn't have surprised her. The man was Marshall's closest friend. Realizing that Granby knew the circumstances of her relationship with the marquis, Evelyn found herself embarrassed and slightly angry that the earl was teasing her so easily. But then, gentlemen like the Earl of Granby made an occupation of teasing women. It was as pleasant a pastime to them as a weekend in the country, and just as meaningless. He was too well-bred to say anything out of turn, but he was also enough of a rascal to enjoy taunting his friend by paying her undue attention.

She withdrew her hand as politely as possible. "My lord," she acknowledged him, deciding to return to the cottage after delivering Lady Waltham's book. Now that the guests were beginning to arrive, her company wouldn't be needed until the festivities were over. Lady Waltham would soon have a house full of people demanding her time and attention. It was just as well. She didn't relish blending into the background while Marshall mixed and mingled with the peerage.

The earl caught her gaze and held it for a moment. Long enough for Evelyn to feel the intensity of his blue-gray eyes. He was indeed a handsome man, strong featured with a smile that could melt candle wax. She pitied any lady who found herself ensnared by that smile. It was inescapable, unless she were a woman whose heart had already been trapped.

"Please excuse me, my lords. Lady Waltham requires my attention."

"Of course," Marshall said, giving her a smile that spoke volumes to her heart.

She moved down the hallway, hearing two sets of footsteps fading away as the men entered the study. She was halfway to the morning room when she looked at the book in her hand and frowned. It was one Lady Waltham had read only last week. Frowning, Evelyn retraced her steps, realizing she'd taken the wrong volume from the shelf. She passed the study. The door was slightly ajar, and the sound of voices engaged in casual conversation drifted into the carpeted corridor. She would have kept walking, retrieved the proper book, and returned to the first floor had she not heard her name mentioned.

She paused just beyond the door, being careful not to be seen, as the Earl of Granby complimented his friend's taste in women.

"Miss Dennsworth is far more charming than you led me to believe," he said. "It's easy to understand why you enticed her to join you in the country."

"As long as I'm the only one doing the enticing," Marshall

replied. "Miss Dennsworth is not an option for practicing your charms. There will be ladies aplenty for that if I know Constance. She's no doubt invited every available female in the township."

The earl laughed, then said something that Evelyn couldn't quite make out. She felt a small wave of satisfaction that Marshall was warning other men away from her. It helped to ease some of her earlier embarrassment. Of course, there was no reason to warn anyone away. Though she could appreciate the earl's good looks, she had no interest in any man but the marquis.

Hearing a door open and close somewhere nearby, Evelyn hurried on to the library, found the right book, and made her way downstairs, using the main staircase this time. She deposited the book in the withdrawing room, to be read later by Lady Waltham. The large foyer clock, chiming the hour with its normal melodious accuracy, reminded Evelyn that she had promised to luncheon with Catherine and Miss Perry.

She and the governess had become acquainted, although Evelyn stopped short of referring to the middle-aged spinster as a friend. Charlotte Perry was a woman of extreme opinions, one who would quickly find fault with Evelyn if she knew of her involvement with the marquis. Miss Perry had small brown eyes that missed very little. She had been Winnifred's governess before taking on the daunting task of teaching Catherine. Like most governesses, she presided over the nursery and schoolroom with a will of iron and an insatiable guardianship of the two Bedford daughters. She kept to herself, as befitted a woman of her station, having little to do with the servants. Evelyn had first thought that her own status—a lady's companion being higher than that of a lady's maid—might nourish a friendship between herself and Charlotte Perry, but that had not been the result at all. If anything, Charlotte treated her with a cool reserve that often made Evelyn wonder if perhaps Winnifred had disobeyed her brother and told the governess of the event on Bond Street.

Evelyn had learned shortly after her arrival at Bedford Hall that the staff of a manor house had its own hierarchy. Carlow, the butler, and Mrs. Wyatt, the housekeeper, were both people with staunch convictions when it came to the management of the manor. During meals, Carlow sat at the head of the table, presiding over the meal. Mrs. Wyatt sat at the opposite end of the table, mimicking the place that Lady Waltham herself occupied in the large formal dining room. The seats between them were filled by footmen and maids. Conversation was limited to friendly trivialities. Occasionally Mr. Druggs would join them, adding a fresh voice to the discussion that usually centered around what was happening in the village. Anyone found gossiping about the family was immediately chastised by Carlow. Miss Perry never visited the kitchen table, preferring to take her supper in her quarters.

Seeking out the third floor, Evelyn wondered if she'd find Catherine studying Latin or French. Regardless of her opinion of Charlotte Perry, she was an excellent teacher, given to far more patience than most governesses or so Marshall had told her. But then, there were times that Catherine could try the patience of a saint. She was an extremely inquisitive ten-year-old, forever asking questions and blurting out assumptions that frequently earned her additional time in the classroom, conjugating verbs in an attempt to teach her forbearance.

"There you are," Catherine said, prancing down the hall to meet Evelyn. Blond curls bounced as she moved, her eyes the same sparkling blue as the ribbons in her hair. "I told Miss Perry you hadn't forgotten."

"I almost did," Evelyn admitted. "I apologize if I've kept you waiting."

"Come along, then," Catherine said, taking her hand and tugging her toward the schoolroom door. "Cook made gingerbread cakes."

The room was warm and full of light. There was the smell of ink and chalk and the beeswax that was used to keep everything polished to perfection. It was all vaguely pleasing to Evelyn's nose, perhaps because it was a different smell from the rest of the house, a more youthful one that suited Catherine and her mischievous smiles.

Miss Perry was sitting at her desk, wearing a brown dress and looking very much like a governess with her hair pinched back in a tight bun at the nape of her neck. Of late, Evelyn found herself looking at the woman and wondering if she might one day awake to find herself as stiff and lonely as Charlotte Perry. The dream of having her own dress shop, of maintaining herself as an independent woman, no longer seemed the grand adventure it had once been. It had taken on the form of necessity, a way to provide for herself, nothing more. As for thoughts of a family and husband, they had vanished completely, except in her dreams when the husband was a marquis and their children played on the green lawns and sandy beaches of an Ipswich estate.

Lunch was slices of cold mutton roast, bread and cheese, followed by gingerbread cakes.

They ate in a small room adjacent to the classroom. Catherine chatted away about the upcoming race and how she was absolutely certain her brother's sloop would be the first to circle the Thames's buoy.

"Have you ever been sailing?" Evelyn asked, hoping with silent but equal enthusiasm that the marquis would win the race.

"No. Marshall won't let me anywhere near his boat. He's says females and the Channel don't mix. I told him I could borrow a pair of breeches from one of the stable boys and tuck my hair under a red sailor's cap. No one would know that I'm a girl. I don't have breasts yet."

"Catherine!" Miss Perry gasped. "Mind your tongue. Young ladies do not put themselves about in such a brash manner."

"It's true," Catherine said, looking down at her flat lace bodice.

"That will be enough," the governess said, glaring along with the reprimand.

There was no further conversation until Miss Perry left the room to put the luncheon tray where one of the maids could find it and return it to the kitchen.

"I'm not sure I want breasts," Catherine whispered, leaning close to Evelyn so the remark remained one of their little secrets. "Winnie has them, and all she does is worry about finding a suitable husband."

Evelyn contained her laughter. "Whether you want them or not, I daresay you'll have them one day. And when you do, you'll be as worried about finding a suitable husband as your sister. It's the way of things."

"Do you worry about finding a husband?" Catherine asked innocently.

Evelyn stopped herself from telling the young girl an outright lie. "Sometimes," she replied. "I want a man who will love me the way your father loved your mother. When I find him, I'm sure I'll worry myself silly."

"You could marry Marshall," Catherine announced. "I know he likes you. I saw him watching you from his window this morning. You were walking across the lawn, and he was watching you and smiling the way Papa used to smile at Mama."

The unadorned comment made Evelyn want to smile in return, but she didn't dare. It wouldn't do to have Catherine repeating her observation to everyone in the household. "It was a beautiful morning. I'm sure his lordship was simply admiring the day, nothing more."

"Perhaps," Catherine said, shrugging her shoulders and sounding unconvinced.

Evelyn stayed until Miss Perry returned, then left Catherine to her lessons. As she walked across the lawn toward the cottage, she stopped and looked back at the manor house, wondering if Catherine was the only one inside who thought she would make the marquis a very nice wife.

It was the time just before dawn that Evelyn loved best. That quiet time of the morning when the sun inched its way above the horizon, and the translucent light of the moon began to fade quietly from the sky. She often sat outside to watch the celestial changing of the guard. It was her private time. Time to let her thoughts flow with no definite destination. A peaceful time that allowed her to reflect or plan as her mind saw fit.

This morning Evelyn's mind was consumed by thoughts of the past and the future. She'd always been strong-willed, determined to make her way in the world without settling for marriage simply because she needed a man to provide for her. But she'd let her experience at Clerkenwell cloud her judgment. It had been so easy to step into Marshall's open arms, to let him gradually take charge of her life and her heart. She couldn't blame him. He hadn't tricked her or made promises he had no intention of keeping. The decision to become his lover had been hers and hers alone.

She had followed her heart rather than the morays of her upbringing and society's restraints. She'd made the decision, and the consequences were hers alone to bear. Acknowledging that she had also accepted the hope that Marshall could come to love her. He was such a naturally loving man; his dedication to his family proved it, as well as his generosity in helping her overcome Lady Monfrey's accusation.

But like so many men, Marshall had come to the conclusion that marriage was an institute for the begetting of children and that to forfeit oneself to it too easily was a sign of weakness. He saw himself as a bachelor, a man committed to enjoying life to its fullest. She saw him as the head of his family, a man dedicated to his stepmother and sisters, a natural provider and protector. The summer was passing quickly, leaving her only a few short weeks in which to convince him that loving someone and being loved were two of life's greatest joys. He didn't acknowledge the need that Evelyn had recognized weeks ago. The Marquis of Waltham didn't need the gaiety of London; he needed a family of his own. Sons to sail the Channel with him and little girls to spoil and pamper. As the sun sent its first rays of light over the aquamarine water that separated England from the Continent, Evelyn sent up a prayer that she might be the mother of those children.

Several hours later, on her way to the manor house to join Lady Waltham for morning tea, a custom that had developed along with their friendship, Evelyn looked across the length of the grounds to see a phaeton approaching.

A footman came bustling down the steps of the main portico, the tails of his liveried coat flapping behind him. The first guest to step down from the open-air carriage was tall and elegantly dressed in a dark brown coat and matching trousers. He handed down a young lady wearing an olive green traveling suit with a sassy, feather and lace hat atop raven black hair. The second lady was a matronly female with an ample bosom draped in jet beads. Her hat sprouted a flamboyant gold feather and a cluster of red silk roses.

The marquis came strolling down the steps as the last gentleman stepped down from the phaeton. He was elderly, but his age didn't prevent him from standing tall with squared shoulders that said he had a lot more life left in him.

The Duke of Morland had arrived.

Having issued the invitations and recorded the requested responses in Lady Waltham's guest journal, Evelyn knew the younger gentleman was the Viscount Sterling, accompanied by his wife, Lady Rebecca. The older woman would be Lady Felicity Forbes-Hammond, a no-nonsense matron of society and Lady Rebecca's aunt.

The scene was repeated again and again over the course of the next three days as more phaetons, curricles, and carriages came rolling up the gravel drive to deposit guests at the front door of Bedford Hall. Evelyn watched from a respectable distance as the house began to fill with lords and ladies. She saw little of the marquis, his duties as host keeping him occupied late into the night. Carlow and Jemima supplied the names of the guests Evelyn couldn't readily identify. The Earl of Ackerman arrived two days after Viscount Sterling, followed by the Viscount Rathbone and Lord Kniveton.

It was Lord Kniveton who unexpectedly pulled Evelyn into the center of things. She was leaving the morning room after a brief visit with Lady Waltham when she met the distinguished gentleman in the hall. It was still early, and most of the guests were lingering in their rooms after a late supper followed by a night of music and dancing. It had been a warm night, and the music had flowed through the open windows of the manor's large ballroom, across the green lawns, reaching her cottage in drifting whispers of German and French waltzes.

Evelyn had tried not to think of the marquis dancing with the well-dressed, polished ladies his mother had invited to entice him into marriage, but she couldn't stop her mind from joining the music. She had never danced with Marshall. The ballroom was not something she could share with him, just as she wouldn't be able to share the upcoming luncheon on the lawn.

Pushing her thoughts aside because they served no purpose other than to reiterate the differences between herself and the man she loved, Evelyn dipped into a curtsey as she found herself face-to-face with Robert Hants, the Earl of Kniveton. "My lord."

"Miss Dennsworth," he said. "It's a pleasure."

She hadn't realized that any of the guests knew her name. The earl was a ruggedly handsome man. In his fifties with dark hair that had gone silver at the temple and striking amber eyes, he stood six feet tall. Nothing about his younger form had gone to fat. He was lean and trim, dressed in a charcoal coat and striped trousers. An emerald stickpin adorned the center of his white cravat.

Seeing her surprised expression, the earl smiled. "I asked Waltham about you. I must say his description was perfect. I recognized you immediately. Had you not fortuitously appeared, I had planned to seek you out."

"Is there something I can do for you, my lord?"

"It is I who should be offering a service, Miss Dennsworth. I am in your debt."

"My lord?"

"Lady Waltham," he said. "Her husband was my closest friend, yet I found myself unable to console her. Seeing her now is a balm to my heart. She is returning to her former self, smiling and laughing once again. For that, you have my gratitude."

"I've benefited from Lady Waltham's friendship as much as she has benefited from mine," Evelyn said. "No debt is necessary."

"I disagree," Kniveton said, placing her hand on his arm. "In fact, I insist that you cease your reclusiveness and join me for a stroll in the garden. It is a lovely morning, and I can think of no better way to spend it than in the company of a lovely lady."

Evelyn soon found herself in the south rose garden, strolling arm in arm with the Earl of Kniveton. He spoke of the former marquis, of a friendship that had begun in an Eton classroom and continued for over forty years. The earl enthralled her with the story of the first regatta he and the former marquis had sailed, of the fever of the race. She listened attentively.

"The wind was with us that day," the earl said. "Our clothes were soaked from the spray, our hands chapped from wet ropes, but our hearts were alive as only the hearts of young men can be. It's a day I shan't forget." The earl stopped walking for a moment. "I've bored you with an old man's tales," he said apologetically.

"No. I've enjoyed your stories," she replied. "Thank you for sharing them with me."

"Then may I invite you to share lunch with me?"

Evelyn looked toward the open lawn where footmen and maids alike were spreading white linen cloths over the tables they had carried outside. A small group of people was beginning to gather; others currently involved in archery competitions and croquet matches would soon join the crowd. Evelyn saw the marquis right away. He was dressed in riding clothes as were the other four gentlemen with whom he was conversing. They were standing away from the tables near a towering oak with long, sprawling branches that shaded the ground all around them. All of the men were young and handsome, but Evelyn saw only the marquis, his dark brown hat gleaming in the sunlight, his gaze shifting from the Earl of Ackerman to rest upon her as Kniveton escorted her across the lawn.

"Miss Dennsworth," he said, his expression friendly but reserved, belying the gleam in his dark eyes as she approached on the arm of a respected family friend.

"My lords," she said, holding on to Lord Kniveton's arm as she dipped into a graceful curtsey.

"So, this is the mysterious Miss Dennsworth," the youngest man in the group said. "No wonder you've kept her so well hidden, Waltham. She's enchanting."

"This young scoundrel is Viscount Rathbone," Lord Kniveton told her. "Beware of him, Miss Dennsworth. He's not to be trusted."

"You injure me," Rathbone said laughingly, before turning his charms on her. He looked at her conspicuously, openly admiring what he saw.

If Evelyn had thought Lord Granby's smile dangerous, it was only because she had yet to meet the handsome Viscount Rathbone. His hair was an angelic silver-blond, his eyes a blue-gray that gleamed with pure deviltry, and his smile—irresistible was the only word that came to mind.

"Enchanting," Rathbone repeated his previous compliment.

"Enough," Marshall said. "Miss Dennsworth is here to see to my stepmother's comforts, not yours."

His words hit hard. Evelyn removed her hand from Lord Kniveton's arm. She didn't need to be reminded that she had no place among the elite crowd gathering to luncheon on a selection of wild duck, curried rabbit, and baked turbot. As for the viscount, didn't Marshall know that no man could draw her attention away from him. His remark had been intended as a light reprimand for Rathbone, but she couldn't help but be hurt by it.

She was about to thank Lord Kniveton for his kind invitation, then take her leave, when Lady Waltham came strolling across the yard on the arm of the duke. Her gown swished delicately about her as she walked. The shade, a deep royal blue, flattered her hair and eyes. It was the first time since the death of her husband that she wasn't draped in black.

Lord Kniveton bowed at the waist as Lady Waltham stopped in front of them. He smiled at her, and Evelyn knew in that moment that Lord Kniveton was in love with

Marshall's stepmother. It was in his eyes and the way his voice softened when he said her name. Evelyn's heart went out to the man. How long had he loved Constance? How long had he had to endure the woman he loved being married to his best friend, a man whom she had loved in return, a man who had made her happy? And now he had to wait for her heart to heal enough to accept being loved again.

Evelyn knew she wasn't that strong. She would love Marshall for the rest of her life, but God willing she wouldn't be forced to stand by and watch as he married someone else. Loved someone else. The very thought made her heart go numb.

"Your Grace," the earl said, bringing her forward to meet the Duke of Morland. "May I present Miss Dennsworth."

Evelyn curtseyed, thankful that she'd taken time to practice. "Your Grace."

"I was just about to give Waltham my assurances that he need not worry about Miss Dennsworth being carried off by Rathbone." He turned from the duke to address Marshall directly. "Have no fear, she will be safe with me."

The duke looked at Evelyn, his eyes as astute as any she'd ever seen. "We are all in your debt, Miss Dennsworth. I have never seen Constance looking more beautiful."

Embarrassed by all the attention and unsure what to do about it, Evelyn looked away, toward the cast-top canopy that covered the main fountain of the garden.

"Don't be shy," Lady Waltham said. "I've been talking about you for days."

"Had you not been tucked away in your cottage, you would have encountered my thanks before now," the duke told her. "Are you enjoying Ipswich? It's a lovely estate."

The soft chime of the lunch bell saved Evelyn from having to reply to the duke's question. When Lord Kniveton offered his arm again, she accepted it, deciding lunch with an earl was better than conversation with a duke. Something about His Grace, the Duke of Morland, warned Evelyn that he wasn't a man easily fooled. In fact, she had the uncomfortable feeling that he knew she was more than a companion to Lady Waltham. It was an undecipherable feeling, but one she couldn't dispel as the group made its way toward the luncheon tables.

Lord Kniveton carried two plates to a small table shaded by a cluster of birch trees. Nearby, a sculptured dolphin spat water into the air. "I think we'll be comfortable here," the earl said, putting down the plates, then holding the back of a white wrought-iron chair until Evelyn was seated.

"Thank you," she said, wishing she could tell the earl that she was anything but comfortable. Everyone else might have missed Winnifred's censoring glance when she'd approached the table, but Evelyn had seen it, along with the lovely brunette who had sauntered up to the marquis and claimed him as a luncheon partner.

The young woman, dressed in yellow and white silk, was Sybil Radley, Lady Radley. Her father was one of the countless lords attending the regatta parties. Their estate was near Harwich, or so Jemima had told her. Sybil was one of the enticing young ladies whom Constance had invited in hopes of persuading her stepson to marry. The lady's maid had also informed Evelyn that Lady Radley had had her scheming, hazel eyes on the marquis ever since they were children.

"She's a sly one, she is," Jemima had said in the authoritative voice of an experienced lady's maid. "If his lordship isn't careful, he'll be married faster than an owl can blink."

Evelyn took a small bite of apricot tart and tried not to think of Marshall waltzing the beautiful Sybil around the ballroom the previous night. It was apparent that they were well acquainted, in the *proper* way a young lady should be acquainted with a gentleman. It was also apparent that Lady Radley was the kind of woman everyone expected Lord Waltham to eventually marry.

Looking down at her unadorned blouse and serviceable black skirt, Evelyn hoped she could escape as soon as the meal was finished. Like the statuesque dolphin, she was a fish out of water.

Seventeen

Evelyn did not see the marquis for two days. The fault was hers. After being forced to watch him smile and cater to Lady Radley and half a dozen other females at the lawn party, she had intentionally kept to herself. Since Lady Waltham had not summoned her, there had been no need to leave the cottage at all. She hadn't, except to walk along the beach in the early morning before any of the guests left their beds.

She was doing just that, strolling leisurely down the shoreline, stepping over dark, tangled clumps of seaweed left behind by the outgoing tide, when she heard horses galloping up behind her. She turned, moving to the base of the grassy sand dunes as three men came charging toward her, their mounts racing like thoroughbreds at Newmarket. The morning fog hadn't lifted completely. Realizing they didn't see her, Evelyn stepped back again, not wanting to be ridden over. Her feet slipped on a piece of wet seaweed, and she went tumbling down, landing in an unladylike lump on the damp sand.

Marshall reined in his horse, jumped out of the saddle, and hit the beach running.

"Are you all right?" he said, coming to kneel beside her.

"I'm fine," Evelyn muttered, wishing she could say the same thing about her posterior.

"Bloody hell!" Rathbone exclaimed, dismounting and tossing his reins to the Earl of Granby. "Didn't see you. My apologies, Miss Dennsworth."

Marshall helped Evelyn to her feet. Keeping his back to his friends, and his low voice, he asked, "What are you doing out on the beach this early?"

His voice had a sharpness to it that pricked Evelyn's temper. "Attempting to find a small piece of land that hasn't been invaded by the bloody aristocracy," she muttered.

Marshall wasn't in the mood for witty retorts. He was still shaking from the image of Evelyn being trampled under the hooves of three racing horses. "I'll take you back to the cottage."

"I can walk. It isn't that far."

"Is the lady all right?" Granby asked. He was sitting atop a strawberry roan gelding that was impatiently pawing the wet sand. The horse had been enjoying his morning run. The earl reached forward, quieting the large horse with a gentle stroke of his hand along the animal's strong neck.

"I'll take her back to the cottage," Marshall said. "Ride on ahead. I'll meet up with you later."

Evelyn didn't see the knowing smile on the earl's face; she was too busy brushing wet sand off her skirt. When she looked up, both the earl and the viscount tipped their hats before nudging their mounts forward. A challenge from Rathbone pitted the horses against each other within minutes.

"Are you sure you're all right?" Marshall asked, turning her around and giving her a thorough inspection just to make sure.

"Embarrassed, slightly bruised, but otherwise fully intact," Evelyn told him. "As for being out early, I could say the same thing of you, my lord."

"Do you want to ride Poseidon back to the cottage?"

Evelyn looked at the large stallion, a fierce-looking beast with a coat as sleek and black as a raven's wing. "I'd rather walk," she said, rubbing her bottom.

"Very well," Marshall said, smiling for the first time since he'd come galloping out of the fog.

They walked, saying nothing until they reached the cottage. He tied the stallion, then turned to find that she had already stepped inside, leaving the door ajar. He followed her, glad of any opportunity he could find to have her to himself, even if only for a few minutes. He'd tried several times to disengage himself from a house full of guests and make his way to the cottage, but it had proven to be an impossible task.

The morning stillness had yet to be disturbed by the sun, and the interior of the cottage was dim. She turned to face him, her hair billowing down her back, her face flushed, her lips parted. God, she was lovely. Not in the conventional sense, but lovely nonetheless. And he wanted her with a ferocity that made his blood run hot. He stepped toward her.

"Your friends will be expecting you," Evelyn said, unsure as to why she wasn't running into his arms. She'd thought of it often enough this last week, but seeing him in his true element, among the crème de la crème of society, was affecting the way she saw him now.

She kept telling herself that he wasn't like other high-born gentlemen, that his true nature had nothing to do with parties and ballrooms and the stuffy manners upon which society turned like a stylish wheel. The very reason they were together was his craving for a mistress.

"I can stay a few minutes," he replied, sensing her vulnerability, although he wasn't certain what had triggered it. He wanted to bolt the door against the world and spend the entire day making love to her. "I've missed you."

"How could you possibly have time to miss me, my lord?

You've been racing up and down the beach, waltzing the night away, playing billiards and cards and croquet."

"Does it help to know that whomever I'm waltzing with, I'm thinking of you."

"Don't patronize me," she said heatedly. "I'm not one of your witless lady friends."

"You're jealous!" He swung her up into his arms, then gently set her on the table, holding her in place when she would have wiggled away from him.

"I am not," she insisted, wishing she had managed her temper better. She could smell him, feel the heat of him, and it was wonderful. He would make love to her if she let him, but she didn't want him coupling with her, then hastily resuming the role of host to his hundred plus guests. She wanted the long, lingering hours when he held her in his arms, the time just before dawn when they lay in bed listening to the sound of the sea. She wanted his undivided attention, not a few snatched minutes between the day's scheduled activities.

"You sound jealous," he said, nudging her neck, then kissing it. "I'm flattered, Miss Dennsworth."

"Don't be." She tried to push him away, but he stood firm.

"If I wasn't worried about Granby or Rathbone charging to your rescue, I'd take the time to prove that you care far more than you're willing to admit," Marshall said teasingly. "Unfortunately, you are right. I am expected back for breakfast. That leaves me with just enough time for a kiss."

He caught her arms and drew her forward, looping them around his neck. Evelyn turned her head, thinking it would serve him right if she didn't kiss him for a week, but he caught her chin and forced her to look at him. His arm slid around her waist, his hand splaying wide at the base of her spine to gently urge her forward until her legs straddled his hips. Her lips parted as their bodies made contact, and his tongue swept inside, tasting her.

His tongue searched her mouth, probing gently, then retreating, building the pleasure until she was holding on to the lapels of his riding jacket to pull him closer. She could feel his heart beating as her hand found its way inside his shirt. His skin was hot and damp. She knotted her fingers in the crisp hair and pulled. His own hands were just as busy, freeing her blouse from the waistband of her skirt, finding his way inside it until there was nothing but her chemise separating his searching fingers from her breast. His thumb brushed across an erect nipple, and she flinched with pleasure.

"I want to taste you," he said, pulling away from her. "Your breasts are sweeter than any fruit. Bare them for me."

The heat of his body was warming away the chill of the fog-soaked beach. His gaze was focused on her with a sharpness that made her catch her breath. What she saw in their dark depths was intense, a fire that matched the one burning in her own blood. The feel of his body pressed intimately between her thighs brought back memories of all the times he'd touched her, kissed her, joined his body to hers until they had become one person.

It was frightening to realize that she couldn't refuse him.

She did as he asked, slowly unbuttoning her blouse, then lowering the straps of her chemise, until the soft material barely covered her aroused nipples. Looking into his eyes, holding his gaze, she untied the laces and spread it wide, baring herself.

Marshall looked down at her, at the creamy perfection of her breasts. He touched her, his fingers tracing the soft mounds with a reverence he'd never felt for any other woman. He could feel the heat building in her skin, that flushed warmth of arousal that told him the rest of her body was preparing itself to receive him.

Evelyn watched him as he bent his head and blew out a breath that brushed over her skin like a hot wind before he closed his mouth over one nipple, sucking it inside and creating a sensation that made her entire body quiver. He continued teasing and tasting, using his tongue and his teeth to build the need inside her, feasting on first one breast, then the other, until it was almost impossible to breathe. The more she fought the sensations he created, the higher they soared.

Then he was kissing her again, stealing her senses.

"I want more than a kiss," he whispered against her lips. "I need more."

Closing her eyes, Evelyn answered, "Yes."

"It will be fast and hard," he told her. "Do you want it that way? Fast and hard and deep?"

Before she could answer, he crushed his mouth to hers. She kissed him back, just as hungry, just as needy. He raised her skirt to find the drawstring at the top of her drawers. It came undone. He pulled her unwanted clothing out of the way. She clung to his shoulders, still kissing him, as his hands went to the front of his trousers.

Then he was inside her, pushing deep into her body. Again and again he drove into her: hard, fast, deep, then even deeper, so deep she thought she'd die from the pleasure. She moaned, but he didn't stop moving. It was as primitive as any coupling could be, fast and furious, fire burning out of control. She arched against him, the pleasure building, then suddenly exploding as the storm reached its zenith.

Marshall tensed as her climax brought him to completion. He squeezed his eyes shut as the pleasure took him, leaving him depleted and gasping for breath, but totally satisfied.

"That will have to last us until I can find a way to get away from the bloody peerage," he said, his voice soft and teasing. He groaned as she pressed herself tightly against him. "I'll have to walk Poseidon back to the stables. I'm too weak to ride."

HE SAID YES 277

"It serves you right," she mumbled lazily. "You were only supposed to kiss me."

He gave a wicked smile, then laughed. "The regatta starts tomorrow. One last kiss for luck."

"If you insist, my lord," she relented with a wicked smile of her own.

The next morning, Evelyn answered a knock at the cottage door. She found Druggs standing on the flagstone doorstep. The secretary was dressed in his customary brown suit and crisp white shirt. Looking past his shoulder, Evelyn saw a curricle waiting. It had rained during the night, but the morning was shining bright, the sky filled with wispy, white clouds. A brisk wind was blowing, promising a perfect day for sailing.

"Shall we be on our way?" Druggs offered her his arm. "The sooner we reach Harwich, the better our view of the harbor. People crowd the streets worse than market day."

Once he'd handed her into the curricle, Evelyn opened the parasol she'd made to go with her dress. She'd finished the elegant confection the previous week, having purchased the sea green fabric more impulsively than practically before leaving London. She'd designed it with something special in mind, and what could be more special than the opening ceremony of the Harwich Regatta. The skirt was cut to flow and spread out at the back, the front hanging straight and snug over a crinoline frame it had taken her days to adjust in order to present just the right silhouette. The hem was drawn up in small festoons that would allow for easy walking at the same time it displayed the proper amount of ivory petticoat. The pointed bodice fit snugly, emphasizing her narrow waist. It was a feminine design, one given to fashion and acceptability.

The trip to Harwich was thoroughly enjoyable. The day

was bright, the breeze balmy, the summer colors a treat to the eye. Harwich was a key port with links to seafarers that went back to the days of Drake and Raleigh. Ships had sailed from its harbor to defend England from the Spanish Armada. The port still served as a base for Her Majesty's Navy. The lighthouse, a lofty structure of honey brown brick, safeguarded the flow of packet boats and frigates that crisscrossed the Channel on a regular basis.

When the vehicle left the tree-shaded roadway, turning toward the village, the top of the lighthouse came into view. Long morning shadows stretched out like a lazing cat, adding a touch of elegance to the otherwise practical, flat-faced buildings that surrounded the docks. Ahead lay the harbor. Evelyn stared at the clustering masts of squared-rigged ships set against an archipelago of sun-bleached clouds. The water and sky seemed to take their color from each other, their individual boundaries merging in the bright morning light as seagulls cried and circled overhead.

A hundred types of hulls, so many they were moored in walloping rows, bobbed up and down on the waves. The graceful lines of sloops, large and small, lay alongside majestic clipper ships. The tall castle of unfurled sails and timber masts loomed over the flat decks of cutters and packet boats. The northern side of the harbor teemed with lean gunboats of the British Navy. Here and there the dark, stately lines of a warship lorded over the water with masterful menace, reminding everyone that Britannia now ruled the seas.

Druggs was forced to slow the curricle to a crawl. As he'd predicted the streets were filled with people. The crowd was assiduously gathered. Lords and ladies and acceptable local gentry mixed with villagers and men wearing seaman's gear: salt-bleached canvas breeches and striped jersey shirts. The air was a blend of salt and sea, opened kegs of ale, and woodsmoke from the sputtering fires of street vendors selling breaded sausages and plum duffs. A carnival atmosphere had taken over the town, and Evelyn looked at everything with wide eyes, absorbing the sights and sounds with childish wonder.

Oh, how she'd love to be strolling through the village on Marshall's arm. Not wanting to spoil her first excursion away from Bedford Hall, Evelyn pushed the disappointing thought aside. It was enough that he'd arranged for her to be here, to see him sail out of the harbor. He was sharing the day with her in the only way he knew how. It was a telling sign that Evelyn added to her stockpile of hope.

She looked around and smiled. At least she could be herself with Druggs. The secretary knew exactly who and what she was; she didn't have to guard her feelings or watch her words. She could enjoy the day and share in Marshall's enthusiasm, even if she was obliged to do it from afar.

As they neared the harbor, Evelyn saw Lady Waltham in the family's phaeton. Catherine was at her side, dressed in a pink silk dress with a matching parasol, and looking like a perfect little lady. Winnifred and Lord Lansdowne were standing nearby. The young lord was an attractive man in his late twenties with brown hair and eyes. Marshall had approved his suit of Winnifred, and Evelyn had to admit that they made an attractive couple.

She recognized more people as Druggs skillfully maneuvered them toward a hill that overlooked the harbor. The Viscount Sterling and his lovely wife were keeping company with Lady Felicity Forbes-Hammond and Lord Kniveton. Not seeing the duke or Marshall's other friends, Evelyn assumed the gentlemen were inside the Three Cups Hotel, the official clubhouse of the Harwich Yacht Club.

"Here we are," Druggs said, managing with his usual efficiency to find a shady place to stop the curricle. He handed her down. "There's his lordship's sloop," he pointed.

Evelyn strained her eyes, hoping to catch a glimpse of the marquis, but there was so much activity on board that she couldn't be sure whom she was seeing.

"He's standing at the wheel," Druggs said.

"I see him!" she said a second later, unable to contain her excitement. His dark hair was blowing in the wind, and she could see the smile on his face. He loved to sail. She waved, doubting that he could pick her out of the crowd, but wanting to wish him well regardless.

Suddenly the crowd went still as a curling trail of black smoke lifted up from a cannon on board one of the warships. The shattering boom was followed by a deafening cheer from everyone inhabiting Harwick's narrow streets. Evelyn watched as the sails were unfurled, their billowing canvas catching the wind to propel the ships across the water.

The race for the Thames had begun.

"When will we know if he's won?" Evelyn asked, turning to Druggs.

"They'll send a wire from the Royal Yacht Club in London," he told her. "If the wind holds, we'll know before nightfall."

"I hope he wins," she said. "He loves to sail."

"Yes, he does," the secretary agreed, his face brightening as a group of children ran across the street, shouting and teasing the way all youngsters do when their parents aren't close at hand. "Would you like to browse the shops?" he asked. "The marquis insisted that we make a day of it."

They did, inspecting the shops along the waterfront before finding a small eatery that specialized in spiced tea and pastries. Evelyn found Druggs to be an enjoyable companion. He spoke of his life, having been born in Yorkshire, and his family. She was surprised to discover that he was one of eight children.

"The joys of a large family can be overstated," he told her as they left the eatery and ventured into the center of the village to inspect more of the quaint shops that sold goods delivered by the ships that came and went out of the harbor on a daily basis. "Being the middle son, there were times that I dreamed of being an only child and not having to wear shoes that had been handed down from my older brothers."

"And I imagined having brothers, older ones to order me about and younger ones to tease me," Evelyn confessed. "But then, it's our nature to want what we don't have."

"At times," Druggs said. "But there's nothing wrong with a little ambition. One never knows what heights one may reach."

She met his gaze for a brief moment and found his expression solicitous, as if he were encouraging her to think beyond her current circumstances. They had never discussed her relationship with the marquis, to do so would be in the poorest of taste, and Druggs was a gentleman in his own right. But Evelyn couldn't help but wonder if Marshall had voiced some opinion of her, some hint of his feelings.

Not knowing how he truly felt caused her more distress than she was willing to admit. He was still the most generous, the most kindhearted man she had ever met, but no words of love had passed between them. She knew nothing of the workings of his inner mind or heart, nor did she suspect that she would unless she prompted the issue by expressing her own emotions.

She loved him desperately, and the memories of all they had shared in the short time they had known each other kept the hope in her heart alive. But she wanted more than memories. She wanted a future. A future filled with the happiness she knew only he could provide. Happiness and children and years of sharing. But before they could share a life, Marshall had to share his feelings. Did he love her? And if he did, would he reveal those feelings before summer's end?

With Druggs at her side, they entered a small shop. The interior was dim, smelled of incense, and was cluttered with all sorts of exotic paraphernalia: colored beads and painted paper fans, wooden carvings and ceramic figurines, seashells from the West Indies and the African coast. Evelyn held a creamy pink and white shell up to her ear, something Catherine had told her to do should she ever find one large enough, and was amazed that she could, indeed, hear a sound that resembled a soft roaring of the sea. She smiled as the shell echoed the memory of the night she and Marshall had made love on the beach with the moon and stars shining down on them.

"How much is this?" she asked the clerk, a pinched-face little man with a dark, weathered complexion and a gold tooth that gleamed whenever he opened his mouth.

"It doesn't matter," Druggs said, taking the shell from her hand. "If you like it, then you shall have it."

The clerk laughed. "Aye, that be the way, gent. Whatever it takes to please the lady."

"Isn't there anything else you would like? Some of the figurines are quite unusual."

Evelyn shook her head. "Just the shell, if you please."

She knew Marshall had told Druggs to spare no expense in making sure she enjoyed the day. The man had tried to purchase something in every shop they'd entered so far, but Evelyn had refused to give any particular item more than the briefest attention. The shell was different. It was a memento of the sea that she would always cherish.

The next shop on the crowded street was a millinery shop. Evelyn stopped to look at the hats, fans, and parasols displayed in the window.

"I've a thirst for a pint of ale," Druggs told her. "Go on inside. I'll wait for you across the street."

"If you insist," Evelyn replied, taking a second look at one of the bonnets in the window. She hadn't had a new bonnet in years. This one was very pretty with a blue ribbon around the brim and a small splash of colorful feathers that made it fashionable without being gaudy.

She entered the shop and began browsing through its wares. Its size, cramped but cozy, forced her to listen to bits of conversation and girlish laughter as young ladies from the village and neighboring estates tried on the most flamboyant creations the milliner had to offer. Three young women, two of whom Evelyn recognized, were gathered around a display of ribbons. One of them was Sybil Radley.

"He's spent the majority of the week with me," Sybil told her friends. "We walked in the garden last night after dinner. He spoke of the regatta, of course. But I'm convinced he's interested in more than sailing. We have waltzed together almost every night."

"I heard that Lord Lansdowne intends to announce for Winnifred. Lord Waltham will look to his own future once his sister is wed," one of the young ladies replied. "You've grown up together. My mother said gentlemen prefer young ladies who share a common background. I'm sure your families would applaud the match."

Evelyn's heart caught in her throat. They were talking about Marshall as if his future were already charted, predetermined. But then, that was the way of society. Courtships were plotted, marriages arranged, and wedding dates set based on social compatibility and the noble necessity of providing an heir. Love had little to do with the perpetuation of the peerage.

Evelyn stepped back, but not far enough to keep from hearing Sybil's reply.

"Although it isn't proper for a lady to flirt too openly, I intend to make the best of the summer," she assured her companions.

Forgetting the bonnet, Evelyn exited the shop. Once she was outside, she fought back the overwhelming urge to cry. Tears would serve no purpose except to draw her unneeded attention. With her insides trembling at the possibility that one day Marshall might very well marry the scheming Sybil or someone just like her, Evelyn opened her parasol and stepped away from the millinery shop.

Eighteen

Overhearing Lady Radley and her friends in the millinery shop had stripped the day of its gaiety, but Evelyn managed to appear lighthearted until Druggs deposited her in front of the cottage at day's end. With summer at its zenith, the evening light would linger, and she longed to take a walk on the beach, alone with her thoughts.

By the time night claimed the sky, wiping the heat from the air and sending cool, dark shadows over the land, Evelyn wasn't anywhere closer to knowing how Marshall felt about her than she'd been before traipsing down to the water and letting the waves spill over her bare feet.

She brewed a pot of tea, then sat quietly near the window, fighting off the mounting hopelessness that seemed determined to invade her mind. She shouldn't let gossip upset her, knowing full well it was based on speculation not fact, but the ensuing silence of the cottage, broken only by the soft sound of waves spilling onto the beach, brought nothing to convince her that she wasn't living in a fantasy world.

Was she foolishly mistaking Marshall's physical affection as love, or did he actually *feel* something for her? She told herself that he did, believed it when she looked into his eyes, but sitting alone in a cottage that she was occupying under false pretenses, it was difficult to imagine that he'd come charging back from London with a confession of love on his lips.

A knock on the door alerted Evelyn to a visitor. Thinking it was Druggs with news of the race, she made sure her dressing gown was buttoned, then opened the door. But instead of Marshall's efficient, strait-laced secretary, Evelyn found herself facing his sister.

"Good evening, Lady Winnifred," she said. "Does your mother have need of me?"

"No," Winnifred replied stiffly. "May I come in?"

"Of course." Evelyn swung the door wide and stepped back. "I was just about to have some tea. Would you care for a cup?"

"I am not here to socialize."

Evelyn did her best to be charming, despite the harshness of Winnifred's tone. "Have you heard results from London? Mr. Druggs told me that a telegram is usually sent."

"The Harwich Club took the trophy," Winnifred informed her impatiently. "My brother's sloop circled the buoy to claim the race."

"I'm glad. Please give his lordship my congratulations."

Winnifred said nothing. Instead, she began to walk around the main room of the cottage, as if she was looking for something. When she turned to face Evelyn, her expression was serious. "I've come to ask you to return the duke's pocket watch."

"What?"

"His Grace's pocket watch," Winnifred repeated. "He discovered it missing this morning. Mother has set the servants to searching, but I find myself doubting that it will be found in any of the likely places. The regatta prevented me from calling upon you before, but since the watch hasn't been found, I had little choice."

Evelyn was too shocked to do more than stare unbelievingly as Marshall's sister blatantly accused her of stealing the Duke of Morland's watch.

Not again! Please, God, not again!

"I know our servants too well to believe that any of them have taken it," Winnifred went on. "The duke checked the hour before retiring last night. I saw him handling the timepiece myself. It was a gift from his son, his only son, now deceased. I'm sure you can understand why it has a strong sentimental value to him. It is imperative that it be found and returned to him."

"And you think that *I* have it. That *I* can return it," Evelyn said, her temper rising in equal proportion to her fear.

Marshall was in London. If Winnifred went to her mother, told Lady Waltham what she'd seen and heard on Bond Street, what would happen? Would the local magistrate be summoned? Would she be hauled away from Bedford Hall in the same disgraceful manner? A jury would be unlikely to believe her a second time, especially if Winnifred testified that she'd been arrested once for the very same crime. There had been formal charges, a warrant issued. Regardless of the verdict, she'd been tarred by a black brush, and there was no removing the stain.

"My brother asked me to refrain from telling our mother of your previous experience with Lady Monfrey," Winnifred said. "However, I feel that I must. The duke is a guest in our home, a valued friend of our family. Were my brother in residence, I would allow him to handle the situation, but he is not. Therefore, I must ask you, Miss Dennsworth. Do you have the watch?"

"No."

Winnifred's expression was doubtful. "Would you consent to having one of the footmen search the cottage? I assure you, he will be discreet."

"As discreet as you in coming here to accuse me of theft without a smidgen of proof," Evelyn retorted angrily.

"I do not like this any better than you," Winnifred defended her assumption. "But, you were accused of theft in London, and despite the court's decision—"

"A verdict of *not guilty,*" Evelyn reminded her.

"Nevertheless, I would be remiss if I didn't inquire. Surely you can understand my reasons."

"I understand that you think me a thief."

Panic rose inside Evelyn as she realized that Winnifred felt duty bound to reveal the scandalous events that had taken place in London to Lady Waltham. Even if the duke's pocket watch was found, the damage would be done. The friendship Evelyn now shared with Marshall's stepmother would be shattered. No proper lady kept company with an accused thief.

"Did you sell it in the village?" Winnifred asked her. "Is there a shop where it can be purchased, retrieved before His Grace realizes it wasn't misplaced by his valet?"

"I did not take the duke's watch. I did not sell it in the village. I have no idea where it is, nor can I give you any guidance in finding it," Evelyn replied indignantly.

She wouldn't beg to be believed, or rant and rave and cry the way she had done on Bond Street. It had gained her nothing then, and she refused to be brought down by panic now. Whatever happened, she needed to have her wits about her.

"Very well, if you insist on being uncooperative, you leave me little choice," Winnifred told her. "If the watch is not found, or returned to the house by noon tomorrow, I will inform my mother of my suspicions and let her handle the matter."

Evelyn watched as Marshall's sister left the cottage. Fear choked her as she walked to the window and looked out at the night-darkened beach. The memories of that day on Bond Street came flooding back. The unbelieving faces as she'd cried out her innocence, Winnifred's among them, the awful stench of the jail wagon, the cold walls of the detention house, the feeling of utter helplessness. The only good thing had been the marquis. He had believed her, helped her, saved her.

But her knight in shining armor was in London.

Evelyn paced the floor of the cottage, doing her best to rationalize her decision to leave Bedford Hall as soon as possible. Stopping midway of the room, she studied the seashell on the mantel. She took it down and held it to her ear, but instead of the sea, Evelyn heard the fading sound of her dreams. Dreams she'd been foolish to believe could come true.

Turning on her heels, she went into the bedroom and began to pack. The mail wagon would be by early in the morning. She knew the driver, having made his acquaintance when she'd posted the invitations that had brought a swamp of guests to Marshall's family home. He was a friendly sort, and Evelyn was sure he'd give her a ride into the village. From there she could take a coach to . . . It didn't matter.

She should leave a note for Marshall, but she was afraid that whoever searched the cottage would find it. If she gave the letter to Druggs, she'd have to argue with the man about leaving, and she didn't want any more confrontations. He would try to convince her to stay until the marquis returned, but stay for what?

She'd be nothing but trouble for Marshall now. He'd be forced to explain why he'd brought her to Bedford Hall. Where in the world had he gotten the idea that a shop girl accused of stealing a brooch could help his stepmother? It was ludicrous. Unbelievable. So unbelievable that people would jump to the right conclusion, and then there'd be more trouble.

The best thing to do was to leave. To put Bedford Hall and everything behind her. The more Evelyn thought about it, the more she was convinced that she had little choice but to flee as quickly as possible. It slashed at her pride, cutting into the very fiber of her being. She wasn't a coward, but the thought of history repeating itself made her shiver with fear. If Lady Waltham had her arrested, there'd be no bribe to keep her safe. Even if Marshall could keep her out of jail, he couldn't erase the truth his sister was going to announce. No one could change the past.

No matter what happened, she'd never be able to gain Winnifred's friendship or respect. Marshall cared for his family. She couldn't stay and be the instrument that drove a wedge between him and people he did love.

As Evelyn tucked the seashell into her valise, she knew she should never have come to Bedford Hall. Her presence had been a deception from the very beginning. Lady Waltham would view her friendship as a mask, a disgusting disguise worn to cover up the sordid details of her affair with the marquis. God only knew what everyone else would think.

She would find a small village where she could open a shop. She would resurrect her old dream and, in time, make a new life for herself. The marquis would continue with his former one. It wasn't as if he loved her. She'd spent days and nights waiting for him to admit his feelings, yet he'd said nothing. He had held her in his arms, been inside her body, but no amount of intimacy had drawn the words from him.

Little by little the realization soaked in. Evelyn turned to stare into the mirror, and for the first time she realized that she had, indeed, been living a dream. Marshall didn't want a wife. His actions attested to the fact that he was content being a bachelor. She'd been a fool to allow the glint of love to blind her to the rightful reality of the situation, but she had hoped . . .

There was no reason to stay and prolong things. It was better to face the facts than forestall the inevitable. She had meant to leave at summer's end. Winnifred's accusation was simply speeding her departure.

* * *

It was just as well that Marshall had won the regatta, for the moment he returned to Bedford Hall his life became a shambles. Thinking of Evelyn and the private celebration he had planned for that very evening, he strolled into the house to find Druggs waiting.

"What the devil are you talking about? Gone!" Marshall shouted. "Gone where?"

They were in the study. Druggs had taken the precaution of shutting the door, anticipating his employer's reaction. "I can't say, my lord. She didn't come to breakfast two mornings past. When I went to the cottage to inquire if she might be feeling ill, I found it empty. All of her personal belongings are gone. I found no note, no explanation."

"There has to be a reason. She wouldn't vanish unless something was wrong," Marshall said, staggered by the fact that Evelyn had up and walked out of his life. He stared at Druggs, then walked to the liquor cabinet and poured himself a drink. He took a quick swig of brandy, then refilled the glass. "Something happened."

"I have searched my mind for a motive, my lord, but to no avail. We attended the opening of the regatta, as you requested. Miss Dennsworth seemed to enjoy herself. I daresay, she had a splendid time in the village, although I couldn't persuade her to buy more than a seashell. We returned to the estate, and I saw her safely to the cottage door."

"And she said nothing, did nothing, that made you think she was unhappy. That she was planning to vacate the premises the moment your back was turned."

"Nothing, my lord."

"What about my stepmother?"

"Lady Waltham is as curious as anyone," Druggs informed him. "She had me make inquiries, but so far I've been unable to discover anything that would offer an explanation of Miss Dennsworth's actions."

"How did she leave? Have you asked in the village? If she took a coach, someone is sure to remember. She isn't the kind of woman who fades into the background."

"People have been coming and going in mass numbers for the last week," Druggs said. "The regatta always fills the inns to overflowing. The coaches are packed to capacity, tickets bought and sold in a flourish of impatience."

"Damnation!"

The word didn't come close to describing how Marshall felt. He walked to the window of his study, keeping his back to Druggs, as he searched his mind for a plausible reason. Evelyn wasn't impulsive or spiteful. He closed his eyes for a moment, recalling the last time they had been together. He'd made love to her with a ferocity that had shocked even him. And she'd been willing, more than willing, to melt in his arms. He had sailed to London and back with her in his thoughts every inch of the way.

He turned to Druggs, thinking to issue an order for a Bow Street runner to be employed, but a knock interrupted him. "Who is it?"

"Winnifred," his sister replied.

Marshall glanced toward the door. He wasn't in the mood to be hugged and kissed and congratulated on his victory. Not now.

"Please, Marshall. I have to talk to you."

"We'll resume this conversation as soon as I've spoken to my sister," Marshall told Druggs, keeping his voice calm despite the panic that clutched at his chest. What if Evelyn hadn't taken a coach. What if she'd purchased a ticket on one of the packet boats and crossed the Channel? The odds of finding her weren't worth considering.

Marshall watched as his secretary held open the door so his sister and Lord Lansdowne could enter. The look on Winnie's face told him something was terribly wrong. Lansdowne looked just as serious.

"Marshall," Winnie said his name as she came to stand in front of him. "I'm so glad you're home."

He managed a smile, hugging her close as he looked to Lansdowne for an explanation. Something had his sister upset. Marshall hoped it wasn't second thoughts of the engagement he'd been asked to formally announce upon his return from London. He had his own love life to straighten out.

"I'm so very glad that you won the race," Winnie said, looking up at him with eyes that threatened to begin raining tears. "Mother is so very proud of you."

"You must tell him," Lansdowne said, taking a step forward.

"Tell me what?"

Winnie stepped from his arms and moved to stand beside Lansdowne. Marshall noticed that the earl took hold of her hand. He continued holding it while Winnie found the courage to speak.

"I'm afraid that I've made a terrible mistake," his sister began, her voice shaky from the stress of the confession. "I'm the reason Miss Dennsworth is no longer in residence."

"What did you do?" Marshall couldn't keep the anger from his voice.

Lansdowne released Winnie's hand so he could slide his arm around her waist and bring her closer. "Don't be angry with her for telling me, Waltham. I saw that she was distressed and insisted that she confide in me. We've been waiting for you to return."

"I'm here," Marshall said, controlling his temper but only by a thread. "Now, tell me what this is all about."

"The duke's watch," Winnie said.

Marshall held up his hand to stay her. "I need another drink."

He poured two, one for himself and one for his future brother-in-law. Handing off the second glass, Marshall walked to his desk and sat down. "Now, tell me what the duke's watch has to do with Miss Dennsworth's sudden departure. I will have a judicious explanation, Winnie."

"I accused her of stealing it."

Marshall came to his feet so fast his chair almost toppled over. "You what!"

Winnie burst into tears. "I'm sorry. I should have waited for you to come home. Carlow found the watch, but it was too late. She was already gone."

Marshall fought through his sister's sobbing words, trying to make sense of the bedlam that had broken loose the moment he'd arrived home. "My God," he said, sinking back into his chair. He thought of what Evelyn had gone through in London, the shame of being openly labeled a thief, the embarrassment of the trial. No wonder she'd gone missing. The thought of going to jail again must have terrified her. But this time, it had been his sister making the accusations. *His* sister!

Lansdowne comforted Winnie, giving her his handkerchief, before turning to Marshall. "Perhaps it would be better if I explained. Winnie can't talk about it without crying. She really is sorry that she jumped to the wrong conclusion."

Not as sorry as her brother.

"The duke's pocket watch came up missing the morning of the regatta. He mentioned it at breakfast, but you had already left for the village. Lady Waltham put the servants to searching, but nothing was found." Lansdowne paused to put a comforting hand on Winnifred's shoulder. "Having witnessed the unpleasant event in London, your sister naturally concluded that Miss Dennsworth might have had a hand in the disappearance. Granted, it wasn't the right conclusion, but one can hardly fault her for having reached it."

Marshall looked at his sister. "Winnie."

She wiped her eyes. "I'm so sorry, Marshall. I went to the cottage to apologize, to ask her to forgive my impetuous accusation, but she was already gone."

"Who else did you tell?" he asked, praying the entire household hadn't labeled Evelyn a thief.

"Only Nathan. I mean Lord Lansdowne."

"It's all right, Winnie," the earl said, giving her a soothing smile. "It's perfectly acceptable for engaged people to call each other by their given names. Don't worry, love. We shall locate Miss Dennsworth. Then you may offer your apology, either in person or by letter. Hopefully, she will be gracious enough to accept it, and both your minds can be eased."

"An apology *will* be given," Marshall said briskly. "Assuming Miss Dennsworth can be found, of course." He stared at his sister. "It's a good thing you have Lansdowne to champion you, Winnie. I'm sorely tempted to take a birch switch to your backside."

"That won't be necessary," Lansdowne told him. "I've already scolded her for not coming to me with her suspicions before confronting Miss Dennsworth. I gave her a stern lecture on the subject. She will listen to her brother until it is time to listen to her *husband*."

"I certainly hope so," Marshall replied, his mind bombarded with all the things he would have to set straight before he could return Evelyn to Bedford Hall.

"I think your sister could use a walk in the garden," Lansdowne said, helping Winnie to stand. "If I can be of any assistance in locating Miss Dennsworth, I am at your disposal."

"Thank you," Marshall said. "I will have Druggs make some inquiries. A wrong was done. It needs to be set right."

Winnie looked absolutely pitiful. "What shall we tell Mother? She's very upset that Miss Dennsworth left without saying anything. She fears that some harm has befallen her. I wanted to explain, to accept the blame, but I couldn't think of any way to make her understand without telling her the very thing you asked me not to."

"I'll think of something to placate Constance's worries,"

Marshall said, having no idea what at the moment. He was only just beginning to grasp the severity of the situation. Lansdowne was right. It hadn't been all that unnatural for Winnie to jump to the wrong conclusion. All she knew of Evelyn was what she had witnessed that day on Bond Street. And he'd added to his sister's confusion by insisting that she keep the information to herself. The blame was his. If he hadn't brought Evelyn to the country, none of this would have happened.

"Can you forgive me?" Winnie asked.

Marshall walked around the desk and opened his arms. Winnie stepped into them.

"You're forgiven," he said, hoping Evelyn would be as gracious when the time came for Winnie and himself to ask the same thing of her.

Winnie dabbed at her eyes with a lace hankie before meeting his gaze. "You like Miss Dennsworth, don't you?"

"Yes."

"Am I wrong to think that you hold an affection for her?"

Marshall took a moment to think about his answer. "No, Winnie, you aren't wrong. I like Miss Dennsworth very much."

"Then, I'm doubly sorry that I made such a disaster of things," his sister said. After a quick kiss on the cheek, she left the library on Lansdowne's arm.

Outside the cottage, the noise of the ongoing party to celebrate the regatta victory and Winnie's engagement was a muffled drum that joined the sounds of the sea and the wind. Marshall sat in a chair, facing the cold hearth, his elegant black jacket discarded, his cravat hanging loosely about his neck. He lifted a bottle of whiskey to his mouth and took a drink. He hadn't invited Granby to join him this time. There was no sharing tonight's misery. It was his and his alone.

In a few weeks the hunting season would begin; after that he would return to London and take up his seat in the House of Lords. His life would continue as it had before Evelyn had stepped into it, trapping him with her soft blue eyes.

An ache tightened his chest, so acute it was painful. He rubbed his hand over it, thinking all the while what Evelyn must be feeling at this very moment—betrayed, frightened, lonely. She was a sensitive, passionate woman. Whatever she felt, it was with her whole heart.

Something had happened to him when he'd met her. Something was happening to him now. Now that she was gone. He took another drink, telling himself that he couldn't blame her for running away. She'd been frightened. What woman wouldn't be. The prospect of jail was enough to frighten anyone. But why hadn't she left a note, or at least spoken to Druggs. The man was dedicated to her. Hell, everyone was dedicated to her. He'd had to fabricate a story to convince Constance that she hadn't abandoned their friendship, that as soon as her sick friend recovered, she'd call on the family again. There had been a note, but the wind had blown it under the table, and Druggs hadn't found it in time to prevent everyone from worrying. It had been an out-and-out lie, but Marshall didn't regret it. The falsehood had calmed Constance's worries, and bought him some time.

He would find Evelyn and bring her back. Winnie would apologize, and he would—

What? Confess that her leaving had taken the spark out of his life. That he'd come to the cottage tonight to get drunk, to bathe his memories in whiskey. What would he say when he found her? If he found her. There were thousands of dress shops in England, hundreds of villages where she could go, where she could call herself by any name and blend into the populace without raising an eyebrow.

"Granby said he saw you walking toward the beach."

Marshall turned around to find the Duke of Morland standing in the doorway.

"Is that whiskey?"

"Irish," Marshall said. "The best brew to drown one's sorrows."

Taking the bottle from Marshall's hand, the duke lifted it to his own mouth. After taking a drink, he sat down, keeping the bottle with him. "The Irish do have a way with spirits. If they ever put the same fire in their politics, we English will find ourselves in trouble."

Marshall said nothing. He wanted to be alone, but what good manners the whiskey hadn't washed away prevented him from insulting the duke.

"Care to tell me what has the celebrated winner of the Harwick Regatta drowning his sorrows?"

"No."

"Very well," the duke said, stretching out his legs and making himself comfortable. It wasn't a good sign.

The minutes stretched on. Marshall stared at the empty fireplace, his thoughts centered on the rag rug that covered the floor. He'd made love to Evelyn on that rug. The firelight had danced over her naked body as she'd looked at him, her arms open wide, her eyes alive with passion. He'd taken her, taken everything she had offered him, spilling his seed deep inside her before lying exhausted in her arms. Sated. Satisfied.

Is that why she had left? Was she carrying his child?

The thought sent a shiver of joy and fear through him, the two emotions so tightly bound together Marshall couldn't separate them.

"If I am with child, then you need not worry that I will become a burden."

"I will not turn my back on you or a child."

"I believe you. You're too compassionate, too honorable, to cast me aside. You would do your duty, I'm sure. A com-

*fortable cottage in the country, an allowance, perhaps you'd
even find time to visit the child once you grow bored with me
and retain a younger, more attentive woman to satisfy your
needs."*

The words that had been spoken months ago rang in
Marshall's mind until his head actually began to ache. What
had he done? How in the name of God had he convinced
himself that Evelyn would be happy being a mistress, a lover
to be hidden away?

He knew then, in a stark moment of despair, that he loved
her. Had loved her from almost the first. That was why he'd
persuaded her to come to Bedford Hall with him. He hadn't
wanted to give her up, because in doing so, he would have
been giving up her love. And she did love him. He knew her
feelings as well as he knew his own—now. A woman like
Evelyn didn't give herself to a man because of passion or
gratitude. Her character was too strong, her convictions too
deep. She lacked neither common sense nor courage. He admired that about her, along with so many other things.

She loved him. And yet she had left him.

He'd been stupid and selfish. But most of all, he'd been
blind to all that Evelyn had meant to him. He'd refused to acknowledge how much he cared, clinging to the idea that
marriage was to be avoided at all cost. He looked toward the
cottage windows. Evelyn had kept them open, weather per-
mitting. A shaft of moonlight found its way across the floor,
fading away before it reached the toes of his boots. He took
a deep breath, releasing it in a mournful sigh as he realized
what he'd lost.

"Your father used to come to this cottage to think," the
duke said, reminding Marshall that he wasn't alone. "The
night you were born, he sat staring at nothing, the same way
you're doing now." Morland chuckled. "If memory serves,
there was a bottle of whiskey that night, too."

When the duke took out his pocket watch to check the

time, Marshall felt his stomach knot so hard the whiskey threatened to come up the same way it had gone down.

"You look like you've just invited a ghost into the room," Morland said, his expression concerned. He tucked the watch back into his vest pocket. "What the devil has gotten into you tonight, lad?"

Marshall found himself blurting out the story, telling the duke everything that had happened since that fateful day on Bond Street. By the time he was finished, he was wiping the sting of tears from his eyes with his shirtsleeve.

"Well," the duke said once the story had been told. "I can't say what I would have done in your place. A man has to sort out his own mistakes. Sorry to hear that my pocket watch brought about such a calamity. But then, perhaps its for the best. I doubt you'd be soul searching so deeply if Miss Dennsworth hadn't left."

"I have to find her," Marshall said, his thoughts sobering now that he'd confessed his folly in wanting to turn a shop girl into a mistress. "There may be a child. I have to know, and she deserves to be told that she isn't wanted by the authorities. She shouldn't have that worry."

"No, she shouldn't," the duke agreed. "But I'm more concerned about what you intend to do once you've found her."

"Would you be shocked if I told you that I plan to marry her, if she'll have me?"

"Shocked. No," the duke said, coming to his feet. He put a wrinkled hand on Marshall's slumped shoulder. "But I will be disappointed if I'm not invited to the wedding."

Nineteen

The storm that had been lurking to the north finally reached London, sending down gray torrents of rain that kept all but the most stout of heart inside their homes. Summer was gone, the hunting season over, and Parliament had once again called its members to take up the business of the empire.

Marshall sat in his Mayfair library, the windows sheeted with rain. He had brought the family to London last week. There was shopping to be done for Winnifred's trousseau. She and Lord Lansdowne would wed after the new year. At least he was to be spared the opera and theater. Constance and Lord Kniveton would chaperone Winnifred. Things were settling down, life resuming the orderly pattern he had once thought preferable. But no longer. Evelyn's departure from Bedford Hall had forced him to confront his feelings.

He'd never imagined how it felt to be in love. To feel as if another person inhabited his body, to share every thought, every feeling. And yet, that was exactly how he'd felt whenever he'd been with Evelyn. She had become a part of him. She'd been his friend, and he missed her. His lover, and he was starved to hold her in his arms again. He loved her so much that at times his heart felt as if it would shrivel up inside his chest. Since the regatta, he had lived on memories, recalling the sound of her laughter, the way she smiled at him whenever she thought he was acting the aristocrat, the warmth of her body when they made love. There was no way he could get on with his life until he found her.

He hadn't given up looking for her. Druggs had discovered that she'd left Bedford Hall in the back of a mail cart. She'd taken a coach from Harwich to London, but the clues had stopped there.

Marshall walked to the window, brandy in hand. Was she in the city? If he called out his carriage and combed the streets, would he find her? God knew he'd tried everything else.

"Marshall, are you certain you won't join us this evening?" his stepmother asked from the doorway.

He turned to find Constance looking lovely in a dress of deep gold foulard trimmed in black lace. She was getting on with her life, thanks to Evelyn. "No, thank you," he replied, masking his thoughts. "I had planned to spend it at the club. It's Wednesday."

"Oh, I'd forgotten. Do give the duke my regards."

"I will," he replied before turning back to the window and letting the memories flood his mind once again.

Later, standing in front of his mirror, Marshall adjusted his cravat. His face showed the strain of the last few months. Catherine had commented on the gray that was beginning to show at his temples, and he had managed to make a joke of it. Frowning at the thought that he might grow old alone, Marshall turned away from the reflection and reached for his cloak.

It had stopped raining, leaving the streets gleaming under the light of the gas lamps that lined St. James Street. Marshall entered the club's main salon. When the footman told him the Duke of Morland was waiting in the subscription room, he made his way upstairs.

"Your Grace," Marshall said as he stopped in front of the large wing-backed chair where the duke was sitting.

"Waltham. Sit down. I've been waiting for you."

Marshall sat, waving off the footman who approached with a tray of drinks. He waited, knowing the duke hadn't sought him out just to pass the few minutes it would take to have their gaming room readied.

Morland reached into his pocket, withdrawing a slip of paper. He handed it to Marshall. "Fourteen Cross Street. Islington, near Chapel's Market. I understand she's taken to sewing for the theater. Several in that area, you know."

"You found her!"

"More like stumbled over her," the duke replied, his composure undisturbed by the shocked expression on Marshall's face. "I own the building. Don't manage the property, of course. Have a man for that. But I go over the ledgers occasionally. When I saw her name, I made a few inquiries. She's there. Safe and sound. Rooms on the second floor above a haberdashery."

Evelyn! She is in the city. Within reach.

"Well, off with you then," Morland chuckled. "Sterling will be joining us tonight. He'll take your chair. Unless, of course, you'd rather keep the lady waiting."

"Not bloody likely," Marshall said, tucking the paper away. His hand was shaking as he extended it to the duke. "Thank you."

He was down the stairs and out the door so quickly one of the club's footmen came dashing after him to deliver his hat and cloak.

Marshall tossed them into the carriage before fishing Evelyn's address out of his pocket and handing it to the driver.

The carriage moved east along The Strand, crossing onto Fleet Street before turning north on Farrington Road. Islington was up the hill from the city, a neighborhood of patchwork squares filled with houses, taverns, and eateries. The theaters weren't as well known as the ones in the West End, though Marshall had visited them on several occasions.

The trip took an excruciating hour, the city streets crowded with carriages and hansom cabs now that the rain had stopped. Marshall used the time to think. Why was Evelyn still in the city? Lack of funds was the obvious answer. She had left her salary behind, untouched according to Druggs. "Stubborn woman," he mumbled to himself, then smiled.

When he got his hands on her . . . The thought brought another smile to his face. God, he felt good. But not as good as he was going to feel.

The spire of St. Mary's Church loomed over the neighboring rooftops as the carriage came to a stop in front of No. 14 Cross Street. Marshall gave the haberdashery a brief glance, then walked toward the narrow alley that ran between the buildings. Rooms for lease normally had their own private entrance. When he found the door, he turned the ringer, setting a small bell to jingling on the second floor.

Evelyn opened the door a few minutes later. She was wearing a blue dressing gown. Her hair was down, falling about her shoulders in the mass of curls he remembered so well. Her eyes were wide, her face pale, shocked into pallid lifelessness by the sight of him.

"Miss Dennsworth," he said in his most formal voice. "I apologize for calling at such a late hour, but we have some unfinished business."

Evelyn stared at him, disbelieving her eyes and ears. She must be dreaming. She'd dozed off in the chair after finishing a hem on a crimson dress that would present itself on the stage of the King's Head Theater tomorrow evening. The marquis couldn't be real. He only existed in her dreams now.

"The air has a chill to it," Marshall said calmly, forcing the door open so he could step into the hallway where Evelyn stood staring at him. "Shall we go upstairs?"

She wasn't dreaming. Marshall was standing in front of her, looking devastatingly handsome. But how had he found her? "What are you doing here?"

"Reacquainting myself with a lost love."

He closed the door and locked it, pocketing the key instead of returning it to Evelyn. He'd found her. Things were finally under control, and he meant to keep them that way. He'd wavered between despair and anger for the last three months. Now all he felt was love. And relief. His heart felt renewed, replenished after months of being drained and empty.

"I . . . I don't know what to say," Evelyn said, almost sobbing. A surge of emotions tore through her. It was so powerful that for a moment she couldn't find her breath. "How did you find me?"

"First things first, my love," he said, pulling her into his arms.

His mouth came down on hers, hard and demanding. His tongue coaxed her lips to part, and then he was inside, tasting her. Evelyn clung to him like life itself, tears running down her face as he ravished her mouth. No matter how hard she had tried to forget him, she'd failed. His memory was too deeply engrained in her heart, too much a part of her to ever be forgotten. And she had remembered everything: how he felt, how he smelled, how he tasted. But, oh, reality was so much better.

When he finally released her from the kiss, Evelyn's knees buckled.

"None of that," Marshall said, lifting her into his arms.

"You will not faint. Unless there is an acceptable reason, of course."

"I thought I'd never see you again," she cried, burying her face against his chest as he made his way up the stairs. "The duke's watch. Winnifred came to the cottage and—"

"Hush, love, I know what happened. I threatened to take a birch switch to Winnie's bottom, but Lansdowne would have none of it. Nothing is amiss, sweetheart. You've no reason to be frightened. Trust me."

Trust him. She'd never stopped. Never once in all the weeks since she'd fled Bedford Hall had she stopped believing in him, wanting him, loving him. The times she had sat down to write him the letter she hadn't had the courage to write that night were countless. The words had flowed so easily from her heart, but she dared not post them for fear of what he might think of her now. He said nothing was amiss. Had the duke's pocket watch been found? Did Winnifred no longer think her a thief?

The door leading into Evelyn's set of rooms was open. Marshall stepped across the threshold and smiled. It was apparent that she'd become a theater enthusiast. The front room was cluttered with costumes. A black cape with a vibrant green lining was draped over the shoulders of a headless, wooden mannequin. There were velvet costumes and lacy gowns in bold, daring colors, hats with peacock feathers and long dangling ribbons. The small room was alive with color. It was easy to imagine actors strutting across the stage, their characterizations enhanced by the impressive costumes.

Marshall deposited Evelyn on a threadbare sofa, stretching her out as he bent down to place a quick, hard kiss on her mouth. His hands immediately began to relearn her body, spending an extra few minutes smoothing over her hips and belly. There was no plumpness, no warm rounding. She was more beautiful than he remembered. Her eyes were sparkling with tears, her lips red from his kisses. His body began to throb with heat. He wanted to strip her naked and take her on the sofa the same way he'd taken her the first time, but he held himself in check. There were things that needed to be said first, questions to be answered.

"Is there a child?"

"No," she said, her senses vibrating with so many emotions she was trembling. "Is that why you came?"

"The reason I'm here should be obvious," he said. "You *left* me!" His voice rose several octaves. "Bloody hell, woman, do you know what you put me through? I've damn well been going out of my mind these last few months. I ought to take a switch to *your* backside."

"I didn't know what else to do. I know it was the coward's way out. To run. But I couldn't stay." Her mind was slowly absorbing the chaotic facts that somehow Marshall had tracked her to Islington, that Winnifred's suspicions had been resolved. "I panicked," she confessed. "Winnifred was so sure that I'd taken the duke's watch. All I could think about was how it had been that day, the jail wagon and the constable, the prison. I—"

"Hush," he said, pulling her back into his arms. He held her tightly against him, partly because he wanted to reassure her and partly because he'd come so close to losing her he needed to reassure himself. "The watch was found, pushed under a piece of furniture by someone's foot because it had come away from its chain. Winnifred jumped to conclusions. She returned to the cottage to offer you an apology, to ask for your forgiveness, but you had already left."

Evelyn stared at him with wide, tearstained eyes. "Then she never told your mother?"

"No. She waited for me to return to Bedford Hall and confessed the whole unfortunate incident. I was furious. I still am. But there's nothing to be done about it. She will apologize. I hope you accept it. She is young and thought she was doing the right thing. Although she's done a good bit of growing up this summer, marriage will finish the process. Lansdowne is a good man." He cradled her face between his hands. "I'm sorry. I know how frightened you must have been. You should have waited for me or gone to Druggs. The poor man has been beside himself. He's quite taken with you, you know."

"He was always very nice to me," she said, wanting nothing more in that moment than for Marshall to keep talking to her. She had missed his voice. At times the loneliness was so unbearable, she'd walk through Chapel Market just to hear the conversation between the stall vendors and their customers.

Dreams of him had wrapped around her at night, his image keeping her warm. The days had been filled with as much work as she could manage, long hours spent hemming, altering, and creating costumes for the local theaters. Some of the actresses had commissioned her to make their street clothes, as well. If her references continued to grow, she'd soon have the money to open her own shop. Not the modiste she had once dreamed about, but a shop specializing in theatrical costumes. She'd discovered that she enjoyed working with the extravagant designs and colors the stage required.

Did he think to resume their affair? Since they were both now in London, did he imagine her giving up her work and moving into the house on Lambeth Road? As much as she loved him, and dear God, she loved him so much it hurt, she wouldn't be pulled back into an affair. Her body was throbbing even now, wanting him, wanting the completion only he could give it, but not without love.

Not this time.

As painful as their separation had been, she had come to realize that she could survive without him. It wasn't a happy existence. There would be no complete happiness without him, but she could find contentment in her work.

"Why didn't you write, at least send a note that would have relieved some of my anxieties?" he asked. "I had to fabricate a story about a sick friend to ease Constance's mind. She was sure some terrible mishap had befallen you. I returned to mayhem, Miss Dennsworth, pure mayhem."

"I'm sorry, but you of all people should know why I ran away," Evelyn told him.

"I understand," he said, gently touching her face. He glanced around the room. "Why Islington?"

"I met an actress on the way from Harwick. She ripped her gown getting out of the coach, and I mended it for her. She said the theater needed seamstresses and convinced me to apply for the position. It pays better than a couturiere. I should have enough money to open my own shop soon. And I've made some friends. Theatrical people are really very nice."

"So you've been here the whole time," Marshall said. "I set Druggs to searching the city last week. I was beginning to think I'd have to search the whole of England."

His words gave Evelyn hope, but they weren't the ones she needed to hear. "Our arrangement was for me to leave at the end of the summer."

"Did you really think that I'd let you walk out of my life so easily?"

"No," she said, keeping her voice calm despite the emotional storm that had arrived with the marquis. "I know what you had planned, my lord. You thought to convince me to return to London as your mistress."

"Yes," he admitted with a frustrated sigh. He was more nervous than he had expected. There was so much he wanted to say to her, and yet the words were suddenly beyond his grasp. Tipping up her chin, he kissed her slowly, his tongue probing into her mouth. Kissing her was easy, much easier than confessing that he'd been a fool for more months than his pride cared to count.

Marshall's kiss was everything Evelyn remembered it being. Warm and gentle, possessive and demanding. A slow heat stole into her senses, burning away the loneliness that had taken over her life since leaving Ipswich. She felt her resistance melting. If she didn't speak now, she wouldn't have the strength to deny him. Pushing her hands against his shoulders instead of locking them around his neck, Evelyn broke the kiss and took a deep, fortifying breath.

"I won't be your mistress or your lover, my lord. Not again. The summer is over. Our arrangement is over."

"Stubborn to the core," Marshall said laughingly. "God, how I've missed you. As for the summer, you left before the season ended. That means you owe me, Miss Dennsworth, and I intend to collect each and every day of the debt. In fact, I intend to keep you imprisoned for the rest of your natural life."

Evelyn swallowed hard. He couldn't be saying what she thought he was saying. But he was smiling at her, and the smile made her feel loved.

Marshall looked around until his gaze settled on a closed door. "Is that the bedroom?" He took her by the hand and pulled her after him. "A proper gentleman would wait for a proper wedding night, but I've never been all that proper."

Wedding night!

"You can't marry me," Evelyn argued, even though it was what she wanted. "What would people say? You'd be cut from society."

He didn't turn on the gas lamp; the light from the front room was sufficient for his purposes. The bed was small, but then, a man on top of a woman, or a woman on top of a man, didn't take up all that much room. As he began to undress her, Evelyn slapped at his hands and rambled on about not fitting into his world. A marquis required an acceptable wife, one born and bred into society. A lady like Sybil Radley. Besides, he didn't want a wife; he wanted a mistress.

"Whatever are you talking about? There's nothing unacceptable about you."

"Peers of the realm don't marry shop girls."

"Peers of the realm marry whomever they please," he said with authority. "Besides, I can't imagine being married to anyone else." His gaze turned possessive. "I'm sorry there isn't a babe. But then, it gives me an excuse to keep you in bed until there is."

He kissed her again, and the summer fire that had burned so bright flared anew. When he finally had her naked and stretched out on the bed, he kept kissing her until Evelyn thought she'd died and gone to heaven. Months of misery vanished under his expert touch.

"I missed you," he said softly, then licked at her ear. "The nights were hellish and the days endless. I went to the cottage every night and thought of you. I walked the beach in the morning and remembered you. I've never been so lonely. So lost."

His touch was as gentle as the words he whispered, light and caressing. The warmth of his fingers as he cupped her breasts brought tears to her eyes. She trembled in his arms, a shivery desire that grew and grew until she was lifting her hips, pressing against him, hungry to get closer. Her senses were on fire, spinning wildly out of control. It had been so long, so very, very long, and she needed him so badly.

He left her just long enough to shed his clothes. When he joined her on the bed, Evelyn went willingly into his arms. Every touch intensified the need. His fingers stroked and probed gently inside her, pushing her closer to the edge. She was empty and aching, and yet he refused to fill her. Instead, he made love to her with his hands and mouth, touching every inch of her, building the need until she was whimpering, shaking with desire.

"Easy, love," he said, knowing she was more than ready for him but wanting to prolong the pleasure. "This isn't goodbye, it's hello."

"I missed you so much," she said, running her hands over his body, relearning the muscular strength that she had thought lost forever.

"I wanted a mistress," he whispered, his voice adding to the seduction of his hands. "An uncomplicated woman who could please me in bed." He wedged his knee between her legs, opening them wider. "But what I found was a stubborn shop girl who turned my life upside down." He found her hands, and his fingers meshed with hers. "I found a woman who set my body on fire. A woman with a kind, caring heart, a woman who satisfies me all the way to my soul. I only thought I wanted a mistress. What I really wanted was a woman to share my life with, to give me children and years of happiness. You're that woman."

Another kiss, this one so tender it brought tears to Evelyn's eyes.

"And a thief. You stole my heart, Miss Dennsworth, and I'll gladly let you keep it if only you'll give me yours in return. I love you," he said, smiling down at her. "I love you."

Evelyn looked into his eyes, dark and gleaming with passion, and saw the truth. His gaze held the promise of a lifetime of happiness, of loving and being loved.

"And I love you," she confessed. Her legs raised to wrap around his hips, to hold him as deeply inside her as possible. "I've loved you . . . I'm not sure when it started. I woke up one morning and you were in my heart."

Marshall began to move, slow and deep. The urgency was gone. He'd found her, and he was going to keep her. "When did I start loving you?" he mused. "I'm not sure. I didn't realize it until you were gone." He moved again, filling her. "I knew the moment I walked into the cottage and found it empty that you'd taken my heart with you. The only way I could get it back was to find you."

There were no more words for a long time. He made love to her and she to him, the tenderness slowly giving way to fierce desire. The longing to have her, the need to possess her, quickly transformed itself into passion, and Marshall moved deep and hard. Evelyn's body opened to him, giving, craving. It was a passion born of need and desperation, of lost time and unspoken words, of hearts and minds. Their bodies met and parted only to meet again, to press and touch, to give and take, but most all of to love.

Marshall laughed with the joy of it. Evelyn cried, the wonder of being truly loved more glorious than she'd ever imagined. Much later, they lay limp in each other's arms. He rubbed her back as her head lay pressed against his arm, her leg over his thighs. It was the peaceful time that both of them had missed so much.

"How did Druggs find me?" she asked sleepily.

"He didn't," Marshall told her. "His efficiency has been lacking of late."

"Then, how?"

"Morland."

"The duke!"

Marshall brushed her hair back from her face. "He's your landlord. A strange twist of fate, but then, it doesn't surprise me. Fate has had its hand in our lives since the day I walked into Madame La Roschelle's."

"Then the duke knows about me? He must think me awful."

"His Grace thinks you're wonderful. Constance will welcome you into the family with open arms. Catherine adores you. Winnifred would like to be your friend, if you'll let her. Druggs has been as worried about you as I, if that's possi-

ble." He brought his finger to her lips to keep her from inter-
rupting him. "Morland wouldn't have told me where to find
you if he thought you unworthy. However, he did mention a
certain expectation."

"Expectation?"

"An invitation to our wedding." He kissed her again.
"There will be a wedding. Can't have our children born out
of wedlock. Think of the scandal."

"Marshall," she whispered breathlessly.

He laughed, then shifted their bodies, flipping her over
onto her back so he could look down at her. "Courtesy demands that I ask you properly, but a naked man on bended
knee is too laughable; so I shall ask you now, lying blissfully
naked on top of you." He joined their bodies, sliding deep
into her warm wetness. "Or rather, inside of you." There
were several more kisses before he finally got around to
proposing. "I love you, Miss Dennsworth. Will you marry
me?"

"Yes," she said joyfully.

It was the last word she spoke for a very long time.

The day dawned bright and cold, the sky a cloudless blue.
A thin layer of snow blanketed the city as a carriage stopped
in front of the west portico of St. Paul's Church. The Duke of
Morland stepped down. The majority of guests were already
inside the chapel, less than fifty at the insistence of the bride,
who had met only a small portion of them.

The Earl of Granby, suited in a gray jacket and trousers
that handsomely emphasized the color of his eyes, greeted
the duke near the south transept. "The bride is waiting there,
Your Grace." He pointed toward a small antechamber where
a liveried attendant guarded the door. "I will be attending the
groom."

"As Waltham attended Sterling only last year," the duke

remarked. He gave Granby a slow smile. "A bit of tradition forming, don't you agree?"

The earl grimaced at the prophetic remark. "Perhaps I should have Fitch do the honors."

"Busy yourself with Waltham," Morland chuckled. "I'll see that the bride gets to the altar."

Dressed in flowing white satin and seed pearls with a train trimmed in white feathers, a novel design that would be repeated several times the following Season, Evelyn was escorted across the tiled vestibule of the cathedral, past majestic Corinthian columns rising to a dome that displayed grisaille frescoes of the life of St. Paul and into the chapel where the Marquis of Waltham was waiting to make her his wife.

Gripping the duke's arm to steady her wobbling knees, Evelyn barely noticed the blur of faces as she made her way down the aisle toward the altar. When Marshall stepped forward to claim her, her heart was near to bursting. *Dreams can come true,* she thought, as they knelt before the altar. Hers certainly had.

When they were finally pronounced man and wife, Marshall lifted the veil that covered her face and kissed her so tenderly, Evelyn wept. When he whispered, "I love you," she smiled so brightly everyone in the church smiled with her.

The Mayfair reception was a boisterous affair with champagne and laughter and music. As the orchestra played, Marshall held her in his arms, their first waltz. They danced, looking into each other's eyes, forgetting the guests who watched them, losing themselves in heartfelt memories and the splendid future that was only just beginning. When the music stopped, Marshall kissed her to the applause of the crowd.

It was much later before the bride and groom climbed into a coach pulled by a pair of matched gray geldings. Snow was falling again, large white flakes floating down from a midnight sky. The fluffy snowflakes joined the roses adorning Evelyn's hair, adding a fairy-tale touch to a fairy-tale day.

"Finally," Marshall sighed, as the footman closed the door. "I was beginning to think I'd never get a wedding night."

"You're insatiable," Evelyn laughed, as his hands found their way underneath her ermine cloak. It had been a present from Constance, who had decreed that she couldn't be happier to finally have Marshall contently married to a woman she would always consider a dear friend.

"I won't deny it," Marshall said as his mouth settled on her earlobe. "But then, I've never denied wanting you."

"Where are we going?" Evelyn asked, arching her neck back so he could find more skin to kiss. "Not that it matters."

"I love you, Lady Waltham," her husband said as he pushed down some lace and began to nibble.

"Say it again."

"Lady Waltham."

"No, not that. The other," Evelyn whispered, blissfully content to be resting in his arms.

"I love you," he said between kisses. "As for where we'll be enjoying our wedding night, I'm surprised you haven't guessed. I recently purchased a small house on Lambeth Road. It's small, but cozy. I hope you find both it and your *husband* satisfactory."

"I can't imagine being more satisfied than I am at this moment," Evelyn said, with a captivating smile.

Marshall found the first of the two dozen buttons on the back of her dress. "You will be," he vowed, then set about keeping the promise.

About the Author

After years of enjoying life as a reader, Patricia Waddell decided to bring her dream alive by writing romance novels.

HE SAID YES is the first book in her new romance series, soon to be followed by HE SAID NO in February 2004.

Patricia enjoys hearing from her readers. You can e-mail her at *P.A.Waddell@att.net* or visit her author's home page at *www.patriciawaddell.com*.

Historical Romance from
Jo Ann Ferguson

Discover the Thrill of
Romance With
Kat Martin

__Hot Rain

   0-8217-6935-9   **$6.99**US/**$8.99**CAN

Allie Parker is in the wrong place—at the worst possible time . . . Her only ally is mysterious Jake Dawson, who warns her that she must play the role of his reluctant bedmate . . . if she wants to stay alive. Now, as Alice places her trust—and herself—in the hands of a total stranger, she wonders if this desperate gamble will be her last . . .

__The Secret

   0-8217-6798-4   **$6.99**US/**$8.99**CAN

Kat Rollins moved to Montana looking to change her life, not find another man like Chance McLain, with a sexy smile of empty heart. Chance can't ignore the desire he feels for her—or the suspicion that somebody wants her to leave Lost Peak . . .

__The Dream

   0-8217-6568-X   **$6.99**US/**$8.50**CAN

Genny Austin is convinced that her nightmares are visions of another life she lived long ago. Jack Brennan is having nightmares, too, but his are real. In the shadows of dreams lurks a terrible truth, and only by unlocking the past will Genny be free to love at last. . .

__Silent Rose

   0-8217-6281-8   **$6.99**US/**$8.50**CAN

When best-selling author Devon James checks into a bed-and-breakfast in Connecticut, she only hopes to put the spark back into her relationship with her fiancé. But what she experiences at the Stafford Inn changes her life forever . . .

Put a Little Romance in Your Life with
Georgina Gentry

__Cheyenne Song	0-8217-5844-6	$5.99US/$7.99CAN
__Comanche Cowboy	0-8217-6211-7	$5.99US/$7.99CAN
__Eternal Outlaw	0-8217-6212-5	$5.99US/$7.99CAN
__Apache Tears	0-8217-6435-7	$5.99US/$7.99CAN
__Warrior's Honor	0-8217-6726-7	$5.99US/$7.99CAN
__Warrior's Heart	0-8217-7076-4	$5.99US/$7.99CAN
__To Tame a Savage	0-8217-7077-2	$5.99US/$7.99CAN